The Fae Ingredient

Jason Bustard

Midnight Tide
PUBLISHING

ISBN: 978-1-958673-64-5

For Alex: amazing partner, dedicated mother, and kitchen wizard. The title of Chef belongs to her in our home. This story is dedicated to her, the love she has for everything culinary, and her love for the people she serves it to.

Other Books by Jason Bustard

Mira (2016, Adult Sci-Fi)

Available on Kindle Direct Publishing via Amazon

Other Books by Midnight Tide Publishing

Windsong

Stephanie E. Donohue

Life doesn't wait for tears to finish.

Eighteen-year-old Roxana Welhaven has lived her life by this motto. When her mother is diagnosed with terminal cancer, Roxana swallows her tears and vows to do whatever is necessary to save her.

Even if it means making a deal with a talking polar bear.

The bear offers to cure her mother, but only if Roxana lives with him for one year. When she agrees, the bear whisks Roxana through a portal to another world and gives her lavish accommodations in an enchanted castle. Although she's determined to serve her year and return home, the impatient and high-strung Roxana finds her heart drawn to the bear's tranquil nature. He's compassionate, clumsy and utterly adorable.

He's also a cursed man, trapped inside a bear's body.

True love won't be enough to break his enchantment. To save him, Roxana must embark on a treacherous quest to find his captor, a journey that will lead her east of the sun and west of the moon.

Secrets of Galathea, Vol 1

Elle Beaumont

Journey to the depths in this fast paced collection of four short stories, based in the same kingdom, spanning from centuries to weeks apart.

A merman and his brother are tasked with protecting what belongs to their people and failure is not an option. When two seventeen-year-olds witness their Prince threaten an infamous sea-witch, they have no idea how soon all of their lives will be intertwined, and what secrets lay in the depths. A prince must decide what is most important: the people or his relationship with his brother. And a soon-to-be-king must do what is right, even if it costs him everything.

Each story highlights a specific character and their current struggle in the kingdom of Selith, but one thing is always the same—the strength of the characters and the magic that lives within them

CONTENTS

ACKNOWLEDGMENTS

Thanks go out to my talented editors RoAnna Sylver and Melissa Eskue Ousley. Their patience and great advice helped to grow and refine this story in ways I never anticipated. Special thanks to beta readers C. Castille and L. Drane, whose insights enthusiasm (and mathematical expertise) made this possible, and to fellow author and culinarian, A. Parise, who was always available with a friendly word and did a marvelous copyedit pass. Finally, thank you to all of the friends who helped shape Beregoth through their imaginations, adventures and even defeats in this world. It wouldn't exist if not for all of you.

The amazing cover art was done by digital painter Natalie Bernard. If you love her work as much as I do, you can see more of it at
https://www.nataliebernard.com/

Last of all, thanks to Julia, Yan, Bobby and all the other cooks, real and imaginary, that inspired me to pick up my own chef's knife. Bon appetit!

Praise for *The Fae Ingredient*

"In a time where cozy fantasy is in, this novel is everything! A must read for those looking for low stakes."

-Elle Beaumont, Author of Seeds of Sorrow

"The Fae Ingredient is a fun, rollicking adventure – it brought me back to playing D&D around my family's kitchen table with friends on a snowed-in weekend."

-A. Parise, Author of The Fork

Kettles and Cauldrons

"The trick to cleaning an iron cauldron is to not burn anything in it to begin with. Apply a thin layer of seed oil with a clean cloth before using one for a boil and refrain from cooking things in them that are starchy or sticky. I find them to be excellent for soup stock."
- Seeker's Kitchen, Chapter 2, Tools of the Trade

RIVERDAY AT MANOR L'EAU was always busy. It was the one day the staff took in every tenday to halt other services while they cleaned and ordered the house. On Riverdays, all things once again found their places, floors were swept, and repairs were made.

Amandine knelt on her hands and knees inside a large cast-iron cauldron that had been turned on its side. She tried to steady the round base of the bowl with one hand while the other rasped a brush made of oak and stiff horsehair against the layer of char in front of her. There were several brushes, and they all had a use: horsehair and wire for iron. Knobbly birch for copper. Soft linen mops and mosswood scrapers for the glazed porcelain.

The brushes didn't belong to her, of course. Everything in Manor L'Eau belonged to Lord Estevan and his wife, Gia. They were good enough people as nobles went. The staff was treated well and Amandine had her own cot in the warm cellar near the pyrestone furnace that heated the enormous house. Her tenday stipend of two silver was twice what the scull working for the Potashe House earned to boot. So, the brushes weren't hers. But the job in the kitchens, scrubbing pots and cleaning plates and hauling garbage was hers. She did her best to do it well.

Grendel, the kitchen's fat, gray-striped cat, stuck his head into the cauldron next to hers. He blinked slowly and purred as he watched her brushes scrape at the blackened mess on the bottom of the cauldron. Amandine gently blew at him to make him move so she could reposition herself and get better leverage against the rounded surface.

She could hear the cooks, a Hill Folk woman named Sunflower and a human man named Kivel, gossiping while they prepared the kitchen for the following day.

"The barges are uppa' river this tenday, yah?" Sunflower said in the sing-song accent of her people. "Maytell the Chef'll be back in a tok with more'n them spices come round the bend from Irongate? Makes a nice kipper, yah?"

"He'd have to ride to Stoneman for those," Kivel opined. "He doesn't go that far until Starday. I think he'll be at the hamlet's market circle for meats. The smokehouse is low and Lord Estevan does enjoy his chicken."

"Funny, that," Sunflower said with a laugh. "Fancy lord nippin' a chicken like us plain folks."

"If my Gram made chicken like Chef does, I'd want it more often too," Kivel said with a laugh of his own. "Surly old bastard has Leonid's gift with a roast. I imagine he'll be back before sundown, though. That old horse of his can't see so well in the night, even with glowstone marking the road."

"Now, now, Juniper still has some life in 'im! You gathered all the ashes from the hearth and oven yet, Kivel?"

"Oh, leave the high oven Sun, there's coals banked in there, just in case."

"Oh! Righ' righ'!"

Amandine smiled at the banter. The cooks were nice to her,

mostly, and Chef Brutsche was a genius. Every noble family in the Gold Hills jumped at the chance to put their feet under Lord Estevan's table and sample the pinnacle of Serentian cuisine Chef laid out for his guests.

There was a soft rapping of knuckles against the outside of the cauldron. "Amandine, foal," Sunflower' voice called.

With a care not to roll the huge metal cauldron, Amandine backed out on her knees and looked up at Sunflower. She didn't have to look far. Like all Hill People, Sunflower was tiny. Amandine was taller than her when standing and she was only thirteen, accounting for three shivs. Sunflower was a grown woman twice her age, perfectly proportioned, if a bit plump, but like a human in miniature. Her sun-gold hair was braided back to keep it out of food and ash and her rosy cheeks beamed at Amandine.

"Them baggy clothes, tsk," she said, clucking her tongue. "We need to get ye a set that fits proper. Them belonged to the last scull and he were a lad twice yer size."

"They are comfortable enough, sah," Amandine said politely. The last scullery had departed to join the army in Irongate when he came of age. The trousers and shirt that she wore flapped about her small frame like a tent.

"Ye only say tha' 'cause you've ne'er had a set that weren't drapin' ye like a bedsheet. Or maybe a nice dress? Something green to match yer lovely eyes."

Amandine pursed her lips and made a face. She felt that dresses would leave you cold or get in the way. Shirts and pants were best, in her opinion. She wore her hair short, partly because she didn't own a hair brush, but also because it was easy to clean that way. Her skin was a shade darker than most of the House, as if she had a High Summer tan that never faded. Sunflower was obsessed with her eyes, however. They were green, perhaps greener than most, and the small woman often remarked on them, much to Amandine's embarrassment.

"All well, then," Sunflower said as she waved a hand and dropped the subject. "You've been here three seasons now. Just seems wrong that yer clothes still don' fit." Sunflower pointed to some hanging kettles above their heads. "Will you be a dear and fetch the larger tea ket'? That rascal, Hedgehog, made off with the co'orless steppin' stool again!"

Amandine looked about and noticed Kivel was not there, he must have stepped away, or Sunflower would not have bothered her with the task. She nodded and stood on her tiptoes to unhook the copper kettle and handed it to the cook.

"It's Riverday, sah," Amandine said. "I think Hedgehog took the stool this morning to dust the crystal. I can go see if he's done and fetch it?"

"No need, child," Sunflower said as she ladled water into the kettle and moved it to the low wood-fueled hearth to hang. "Chef told ya that he wants the cauldron scrubbed 'fore he rolls back from wherever he got off to. You best keep at it to avoid his ire, yeah? As for Hedgehog, I'll box his ears meself later. He should be askin', not grabbin'!"

"That isn't what I hear," someone said from the doorway. The voice was oil smooth, but with a whiff of something in it that hinted at its rancid nature. "Rumor is he grabs just about everything."

Sunflower turned red in embarrassment and her mouth twisted in a grimace, but she turned and gave a neat bobbing bow to the newcomer in the kitchen. Amandine quickly duplicated the gesture.

"Luminous morning, Taster," they chorused to the man in the doorway.

The tall, dark-haired, pale-skinned human with a thick mustache was Henri Nous, the house's Taster. He served the meals to the family, paid the staff, ordered the house, and was in charge of the kitchen when Chef was away. He held a silver tray of empty dishes from breakfast in his hands and thrust them out with a raised eyebrow.

Amandine hurried forward and took the tray from him. Dishes were her job. She bowed again and carried it to the large washtub in the back. She would have to wash them later. The cauldron was barely half-clean and Chef could be back any time.

As she unloaded the tray, Taster Nous turned his attention back to Sunflower. "Please clear out the high oven," he said with a sniff. "The kitchen smells like a charcoal pit."

"Taster, there be some coals banked in that oven. I think that Chef may—"

"Madam Sunflower," he interrupted. "Is Chef Brutsche here?"

"No, sah."

"Riverday is cold meals only, so we can clean, yes?"

"Yes, sah, but—"

"Cook Sunflower," Henri interrupted again, emphasizing her title. His eyes narrowed and his lip curled in distaste.

"Yes, Taster, I'll scoop the oven directly. Amandine, foal, I need ya to go fetch the steppin' stool after all, love," Sunflower said as she wrung her hands nervously.

The Taster nodded, turned smartly on his heel and departed. His feet had never once crossed over the frame into the kitchen itself. For someone who liked to order the kitchen's staff about, Amandine noted that he rarely deigned to set even a foot inside its boundaries.

"Did Kivel say what the coals were for?" Amandine asked. "Chef will be cross if there is a use for them."

"Nay, Kivel said they was just there in case. Taser Nous pays out the silver, and I don't want to give that old tusker any reason to short us again. Remember the day the co'orless pastries were cut wrong?" Sunflower said with a worried expression. "Just be quick, like a spearbill, so ye can get back ta that old cauldron."

Amandine nodded and hurried out of the kitchen and through the servants' pass to the Grand Hall. Grendel followed her, as he did most places in the Manor. She didn't stop, but did slow a bit as she passed the long window-mirror in the Grand Hall. Mirrors were outrageously expensive. Kivel had told her the glass was coated with an alloy of silver that only the dwarves knew how to make. Even though she was in a rush, the chance to look at herself in it was hard to pass by. Amandine had never owned a mirror and even the Lord's eldest daughter only had a small one on a handle, but this pane was huge. It stretched the length of the room and reflected the scene from the window on the opposite side of the chamber, creating an illusion of there being two windows when there was really just one.

The only thing that spoiled the effect was her reflection. Sunflower was right about the clothes, they really didn't fit her well at all. She had others, from her previous home in the city of Artemis to the East, but they had grown small on her since she had come here, so she didn't wear them anymore. Amandine made sure the cuffs were straight and she had no grime on her nose from the cauldron, and then picked up her pace again and hurried on her way.

She found Hedgehog, a stocky Hill Folk man only a bit taller than Sunflower, coming down off the rolling stool that she sought. A rack of sparkling crystal wine glasses sat behind him against the parlor wall. He mopped his brow with a cloth and adjusted his tousled dark hair as Amandine approached.

"Need the stool?" he asked in a voice that was surprisingly bass for his size. "I've just finished with the crystal. Sorry if I was a bother to Madam Sunflower. Tell her I will make it up to her later," he said with a wink.

Amandine folded the stool and tucked it under an arm. "You should tell her yourself, someplace other than the outer pantry. Nous knows what you're up to."

Hedgehog grimaced. "Puffed up busybody..." he grumbled as he turned to pick up a rolled carpet that needed beating. The roll was four times his size and likely weighed enough that even Kivel would struggle with it, but Hill Folk were uncannily strong for their small builds.

Amandine didn't understand why the two of them carried on as they did, playing at secrecy. The entire staff knew what was going on. "Is it against the rules for you to like Sunflower?"

Hedgehog cleared his throat and looked a bit flustered. "Erm, no, not exactly... she's a fine lady. And her fried eggs, Delinkhal have mercy on me... it's just there are proprieties..." His voice trailed off at the end. Grendel meowed and rubbed up against his legs. The cat was so large that he nearly bowled the small man over as he unbalanced his awkward load.

"Oh, hello, Grendel. Go catch a mouse would ye? Shoo, shoo." Hedgehog said as he tried unsuccessfully to direct the cat away from him with a foot.

"Like what? Neither of you is married," Amandine said.

"True, true. But since we also work together it's, well… never mind. Take the stool to her, lass. Thank you, Amandine." Hedgehog continued to grouse quietly to himself as he hauled the heavy carpet away.

Amandine shrugged. She didn't understand why it should be a problem, but Taster Nous was in charge of staff and controlled the coin, so Hedgehog probably avoided the topic for the same reason that Sunflower was going to clean the oven. If you wanted to be paid on time and in full, you always did what the Taster asked.

"What do you think of the Taster, Grendel?" she asked her shadow.

Grendel meowed, brushed past her ankles, and then flopped on his back to beg for a belly rub. Amandine rolled her eyes and stepped over him.

She helped Sunflower by holding the ashcan while she stood on the stool and used the oven rake to empty the smoldering pile from the top chamber. Then Amandine hauled the can out to the compost shed and added it to a larger pit filled with old ash and bits of char. Grendel trailed in her wake, but finally grew bored with the chore and wandered off into the garden to hunt. She used a ladle in a nearby trough to douse the remaining hot coals and then returned to the kitchen to clean the breakfast dishes... and that cauldron.

Chef Brutsche

"The title of 'Chef' has an interesting history. Unlike the more general title of 'Master' given to someone who has achieved mastery of a craft, the moniker popularized for the world's finest cooks implies a level of leadership skill as well as competency. Derived from an ancient Serent word for 'leader', the Chef is not only a master of their art, but of delegation, organization and presentation of their craft."

- The Art of The Meal, Foreword, Excerpt

AMANDINE WAS STILL struggling with the cauldron when Chef Brutsche returned in a cloud of wagon dust and pungent language. The squealing of the old wagon's misshapen back axle set Amandine's teeth on edge, and when the back door to the kitchens slammed she started so badly that she cracked the top of her head on the inside of the cauldron. Grendel, who also had his head in the cauldron, bristled and hissed and ran for cover under the washbasin.

"All you lazy milk sops, line up!" Chef bellowed. "Move your swine-bellied arses!"

Amandine rubbed her head as she stood and faced Chef. His hair was graying and he had dark, leather-like skin the color of hazelnuts. His shoulders sagged slightly as if he were tired, but his back was straight and his blue eyes watched everything around him like a hawk. Amandine had seen his gnarled hands juggle four different pans and stir a sauce all while barking over his shoulders at Kivel and Sunflower. His posture might seem slothful to someone who hadn't seen him in action, but Amandine and the rest of the staff knew better.

Sunflower and Kivel quickly stepped up next to Amandine and gave him their attention, although Kivel kept looking back over his shoulder at a pot he had abandoned to join the lineup.

"Listen up, periwinkles," Chef began, "I have a problem, which means you have a prob—Old Jack's shriveled balls, Kivel! What hook is stuck in yer craw?"

"Candied strawberry and treenuts, Chef," he replied quickly. "It's almost to simmer."

Kivel was a tall, rotund man with light brown hair and a bulbous nose. He stood half a head taller than Chef and was so wide as to make nearly two of the smaller man, but he kept his eyes locked on the wall behind Chef and twitched nervously as he glared at him.

Chef made a disgusted noise and waved a hand. "Drop in a tin-star leaf, two stirs then move it to the low coals and come back. It'll hold."

Kivel hurried away to do as instructed while Chef Brutsche watched him, his arms folded and his foot tapping impatiently. He sucked at his teeth while Kivel moved the pot. Amandine had noted the gesture before, especially when Chef was critically eyeing the performance of his cooks. She tried not to fidget. Grendel appeared from under the wash basin and wove around her shins.

When Kivel returned, Chef nodded at him. "Adequate," he grumbled, which was about as high a praise as anyone in his kitchen was likely to receive. Kivel stood up a bit straighter and Chef resumed his speech, but the initial fire had been quelled somewhat by watching Kivel work.

"As I were sayin', we have a problem. It would appear our patron is having a dinner reception this evening. None other than Lady Everdawn from Stoneman and her husband. Plus the usual entourage."

They all exchanged glances at that.

"The Magistrate for Irongate, Chef?" Sunflower asked. "The last time she called it was for Winter Night, and we had two tendays to prepare!"

Amandine remembered that dinner. It was her first experience with one of Chef's famous dinner parties. The memory of the dishes he had created for that night still made her mouth water. Especially the dessert.

"I really liked the egg puffs," she said without thinking, lost in the recollection. When Chef Brutsche turned his glare to her, however, she pressed her lips together and resolved not to make another peep. His gaze lingered on her as he continued to speak.

"Oh yes, ye all see the dilemma now, I hope? Riverday cold roast and bread ain't gonna cut it, fingerlings," Chef continued. "We are ta put on a proper dinner. Our best show."

"How da ye know for sure the High Lady is comin' 'ere, Chef?" Sunflower asked. "The Taster ain't said nothin' to us about—"

Just then, Taster Nous stepped into the doorframe he inhabited when delivering messages from the house, or when he simply wanted to boss them around. He pulled up short at the sight of Chef Brutsche and bowed respectfully.

"I didn't realize you had returned, Chef. I have instructions from Lord Estevan. We are entertaining Lady —"

"Yea, we know already, you stuffed pigeon," Chef growled at him over his shoulder. "Tell our patron the menu will be braised hen on a green nest, soft-peel fruits and hoar-root soup. Second course, spiced river clams in wine sauce, buttered striped squash on oats and pickled beets. Third, smoked boar thigh with candied strawberry and tree nuts and a boiled mash."

Amandine noted that he had included the candied strawberries Kivel had made. Surely he had no notion of them until he had walked in the door a moment ago. Had he just created that menu on the spot?

Taster Nous looked as startled by the litany as she felt. His moustaches twitched and his eyebrows rose with each addition to the list, but he recovered his composure towards the end. "Very good, Chef. I will choose wines for all of that to match and for dessert?"

"Sweet egg puffs," Chef said with a glance towards Amandine.

Amandine gasped and clapped her hands together, in spite of the stern look she got from Chef for doing so. The egg puffs! They were absolutely the best!

Sunflower winced. Chef didn't seem to notice, but Amandine did. She was pretty sure Nous noticed as well, but the Taster simply nodded and strode away, his posture stiff.

Chef glanced back at the empty doorway and grunted. "All right, then. Ye all heard the menu. Kivel, ye already made the glaze so do the thigh. Sunflower, visit the garden and gather the vegetables. Pot girl! Make sure we have clean ramekins for twelve and fetch the better soup pot. To the Pit with that old cauldron, scrub it tomorrow!"

Kivel was moving as soon as Chef turned away from him, and Amandine was about to do the same but saw Sunflower, bouncing on her toes, trying to get Chef's attention.

"Chef, sah, about them poofs…"

"Ah yea," Chef interjected without looking at her. "Visit the coops as well when ye are out back. Gather all the chicken eggs ye can, and bring the flat from the cold cellar too. Not all of 'em will be fit fer baking. Just chicken mind ya! The frelkin eggs make the batter the wrong color!"

"No, sah, I mean the high oven —"

"No need ta unbank the coals yet," Chef interrupted again as he gathered pots from hooks.

"There ain't no coals!" Sunflower said. "I…I raked the oven, Chef."

Amandine's heart sank. She was talking about the oven that Nous had ordered them to clean. This was going to be bad…

Chef Brutsche slowly turned to face the tiny woman. His face began to darken like a raincloud and Amandine felt a stab of pity for the cook. She looked absolutely ashamed as Chef sucked in a breath to begin his tirade. Grendel ran for cover again.

"I helped her!" Amandine blurted out loud. "Taster Nous told us to do it!"

He turned his gaze to her and Amandine braced herself for the shouting. It wouldn't bother her. She was used to shouting, and worse, but Chef, despite his snarly disposition, never used a switch, so compared to the Night Sisters from her old home in Artemis, this would be nothing. She could endure this for Sunflower. It wasn't her fault.

"Fools!" Chef Brutsche roared. "Blind mucking hagfish! The lot of ya! That dandy-arse whined about the smell didn't he? And ye listened to him! Now we have ta make fresh coals too! I should tie the three o' ye ta the mast as penance!"

"Sorry, Chef!" Sunflower said quickly, bobbing a bow.

Grendel popped his head out from under the washbasin and hissed at Chef Brutsche.

Amandine should have duplicated Sunflower's contrite gesture but a hard stone had settled in her gut and before she could control her mouth…

"No ship, no mast. Could I fetch ye a broomstick?"

Sunflower gasped and covered her mouth. Kivel studiously ignored the row and stirred his berries with great concentration.

Chef's angry face glowered at her a moment longer and then he rumbled in a flat, stern voice: "I would say ye are all kobolds in aprons, only kobolds are actually clever little shites."

The comment was addressed to the room at large, but his piercing blue eyes never left Amandine.

"Go and fetch my ramekins and my pot, girl. Then go an' get hardwood for new coals. Ye helped unmake it, so ye can help make it again."

Shortbreads

"Elven cuisine is difficult for humans to master. It is not a matter of the recipes being more complicated, or one of rare ingredients. Indeed, elven food is often the epitome of simplicity itself. The problem lies in the radically differing senses of taste, smell and cultural context that exist between the fae and mortals. While some things, especially sweet flavors, are mostly agreed upon, many others fall into varying categories of cultural bias. Cooking for fae requires not only skill, but empathy and insight into what flavors they find attractive and complimentary."

- Seeker's Kitchen, Chapter 7, Flavors of the Faewilds

"THOSE SET YET?"

Chef's voice echoed inside the high oven's burn chamber. Amandine pushed the last of the split hardwood logs into place and coughed. Even after the earlier sweep it was still incredibly sooty.

"Done," she called as she backed out of the deep chamber and slid down the brickwork sidewall. Her work shirt and trousers were stained black and she could feel the ash stuck in her short-cropped hair.

"Adequate," Chef mumbled as he peered inside to inspect her stacking. "We don't have the tide with us, though, so we'll need a bit of a push."

He pointed to a small cloth-covered dish on the block. "Wash yer paws and go sniff out Mister Green. Tell him I need a favor."

Amandine's jaw clenched. Mister Green made her especially uncomfortable.

"But he's a mage, sah, and he's fae. What if he magics me?" Amandine said in a near whisper.

"Bah. He's just an elf, one o' the better ones, and the tutor for the Lord and Lady's children. Least he don't be talkin' to the wind like Old Wizard Hemm in Stoneman. Get on with it now," Chef said as he slid the plate closer to her.

"What about the old stories..." Amandine began. It was all that she could do not to whimper. The idea of magic, of someone able to bend the very fabric of reality to their will, frightened her to her core.

Chef Brutsche seemed annoyed at her hesitation. "Don't be lookin' like a seal with a fish caught sideways. Mister Green has taken a shine to you, gods know why. And the best way to get a mage to do you a trick is to pay 'em in advance."

Amandine swallowed and nodded. "Yes, Chef."

He sucked at his teeth and frowned down at her. "He don't like me. He likes you. If I was afeared he were dangerous to ya, I would send Kivel, or even that useless ballast, Nous. He's nothin' scary now, fingerling. Go bribe the bastard for me."

She took the cloth-covered plate and traveled up the servants' stair to the second floor of the manor. Mister Green's study was on the north-facing side of the house with large, protruding windows that looked out over the rolling countryside that Lord Estevan oversaw. Grendel followed in her wake, as usual, meowing loudly as if she had a dish of fish scraps for him.

"This isn't for you. Shush, Gren," she whispered.

He ceased his begging but continued to trail her footsteps. His tail flicked in a questioning manner as he stared up at her.

"It's for Mister Green, so mind your manners!"

Grendel meowed once more and then remained silent as they crossed the upper halls. She passed Lily, one of the Hill Folk maids, as she was cleaning. Her dark hair was tucked up under a scarf and her lips pressed together in a look of disapproval as she eyed Amandine and Grendel.

"Morn', Amandine," she said in a sour tone. "I heard ya talkin' to that daft cat. Mister Green is teaching the younglings. End of the hall, now."

Amandine dipped into a small bow. "Thank you, sah."

"Surely. You should stop talkin' to the cat. Uppity critter will start thinkin' he's allowed at table," Lily said with a frown. "Allowing a cat to roam the halls. Honestly!"

As Amandine continued down the hallway, she saw the door at the end ajar, and a sonorous voice, Mister Green's, was speaking in a lecturing manner. A second voice, higher pitched, answered.

Amandine entertained the notion of turning back around. If Mister Green was giving lessons to the children, she should not interrupt. Just as she was about to commence her retreat, however, Mister Green called out through the open door.

"Please come inside, Amandine. You are expected."

Grendel immediately accepted the invitation and disappeared through the cracked door. She swallowed the lump in her throat and gently pushed the door fully open. The inside of the study was a riot of greenery. Hanging baskets of ferns and shrubbery dripped from the ceiling near the glass window panes. Shelves of books were interspersed with clay runnels filled with fragrant herbs and unusual flowers. The large windows that looked out over the countryside let in the warm, Low Summer sunlight and basked the room in a soft, golden glow.

Mister Green stood in the middle of the semi-circular room. He was as tall as a human man and wore clothes of a style and cut similar to what the nobles of Serentia wore, but tailored for his lithe frame. They were dyed in deep greens and earthy browns that contrasted sharply with his cream-like skin. His hair was pale silver, so fair it was almost colorless. His ears, long and pointed, extended like horns from the sides of his head, but it was his eyes that unnerved Amandine the most. Solid black and reflective like onyx, they were something not of this world—something fae and unfathomable.

The house's children, Marlette and Fiona, sat in small padded chairs before their teacher. Grendel lay in Fiona's lap, curled up like a fuzzy pillow as the girl stroked his striped fur. She had golden curls and freckles across her nose like her mother. Her mouth always seemed to be turned up into a bright, impish smile. She was, accounting for shivs, a year younger than Amandine and always pestering her about stupid things like what it was like to wear pants. She waved cheerfully at Amandine as she entered the room.

Marlette, the elder sister, had her hands neatly folded on her colorful linen dress. She was dark of hair and eye, like her father, and did her best to imitate his mannerisms and speech. She was two years, counting a shiv, older than Amandine and had begun accompanying her mother on social calls to other estates. She was kind enough, Amandine supposed, in the detached way her parents were. Her only acknowledgement of Amandine was a sideways glance before she dabbed at her nose with a handkerchief.

They did not speak, but Fiona's barely restrained mirth at Amandine's appearance reminded her that she had only just recently been halfway inside a dirty oven. Did she smell? It was likely that she did. Amandine sighed inwardly and tried to focus on her task. She resisted the urge to touch her hair and instead offered up her covered plate. It took all of her nerve to keep it from rattling.

"Chef Brutsche would like some assistance in the kitchens, Mister Green. I am sorry I interrupted your lesson," she said in a rush.

"Child," Mister Green said with a dismissive wave. "As I said, you were expected, so there was no interruption. We were discussing geography. You should join us."

Amandine gestured with the plate again and tried not to look at Mister Green's reflective eyes. "I am needed in the kitchens, sah. Please…"

Mister Green still did not take the plate. Instead he waved a hand to his books and to the map he and his students had been studying. "Children should be learning, not grubbing about in ovens. You can read, yes?"

"A little, sah, Olgothian trade script and some runes." Amandine said. She feigned interest in the books to avoid looking at the elf, but it was as if his gaze touched her somehow. She shivered slightly.

"In other words, as much as you need to read labels on bins and bottles in a kitchen. There is so much more out there, little one."

"It's what I know, sah. Please, Chef will be cross if I dally." Amandine gestured with the plate again for good measure. Silently, she prayed to Kayla for him to just take it and let her go.

"I imagine he's often cross for no other reason than it's his nature," the elf said with a smirk. "Marlette and Fiona, you would not mind sharing lessons with Miss Amandine, would you?"

"No, *soeje*," Fiona answered immediately. She used the elvish title for 'teacher' with a very convincing imitation of Mister Green's own accent.

"Father might grouse, but mother would agree," Marlette said. "However, she might make the cushions dirty," she added with a sniff.

Amandine mentally took back her positive appraisal of the girl. She was opening her mouth to retort when Mister Green spoke over her.

"Indeed," he agreed. He made a twirling gesture with three fingers and then softly exhaled.

Amandine gasped as a sensation like being dipped in cold water coursed across her skin. The air shimmered for the briefest of moments as if the entire world suddenly went out of focus. She looked at him then, into his eyes, as if it were an involuntary reflex. The void of them seemed to reach out and swallow her. She dropped the plate. Her heart raced. She was being spelled. Magic! She opened her mouth to scream—

And it stopped. Everything snapped back into focus and she managed just in time to contain her fright so that only a surprised sounding squeak escaped her lips. The entire experience had lasted the space of a heartbeat, and yet, with a thrill of horror she remembered that she had dropped the plate she was supposed to have given to—

It was floating, perfectly still in the air before her. Mister Green made a small beckoning gesture and the plate drifted lazily over to him. He plucked it from the air as if from the hands of an invisible servant.

"That's better, yes?" he asked the room at large.

Fiona laughed and clapped and Marlette nodded and smiled in approval. Grendel looked up when Fiona stopped petting him to see what had caused the interruption. Amandine looked down at herself.

She was clean. Not just the soot from the oven, she was completely clean. Her clothes felt lighter and smelled faintly of lavender. The grime under her nails from scrubbing that awful cauldron was gone. She touched her hair tentatively. The silky feel of it was so foreign to her that she didn't quite know if it was real. She did bathe, in the servant's bathhouse, twice a tenday, and laundered her own clothes, but she had never felt this completely *fresh* in her entire life. For the briefest of moments, she forgot her own pounding heart as the silky, individual hairs on her head slipped through her fingers.

"Now then, let's see what Chef Brutsche hoped to ply my services with," Mister Green said as he lifted away the cloth.

A plain white cake the size of a tea biscuit sat in the middle of the plate. It had the faintest swirls of something rose-colored in the thin glaze that topped it.

"*Yvustre,*" Mister Green said softly as he closed his eyes, held the plate closer to his face and inhaled deeply.

"What is it?" Fiona asked.

"Elven shortbread," Mister Green said in an almost reverent tone. "A rare thing indeed this far from my homeland. Do you know where your Chef procured these, Amandine?"

Amandine forced herself to stop playing with her hair. "Uh, I believe he made them, sah. I saw him take cakes like those from the high oven a fortnight ago, but then they were never served at tea. Sometimes if somethin' ain't right, Chef will chuck it and start again. That's what I figured."

"Not chucked, good child, cured. The oils in these delicacies require time to mellow after baking to achieve their full potential. A fortnight seems sufficient."

He gently plucked off a corner of the cake and popped it into his mouth. A look of sublime joy lit his face as he savored it.

"What does it taste like?" Marlette asked.

"I am loathe to share, but if young Amandine is certain that Chef can recreate this morsel, then I would be a poor teacher to deny my students a new experience. I must warn you that you may not enjoy the flavor as much as a member of my Court would."

He carefully portioned off small tastes for all of them, including Amandine. For a moment, Amandine thought of refusing the bite, but her curiosity was just barely overriding her fear of the elf mage. After all, the cake was one of Chef's creations.

"It is proper to hold it on your tongue as it dissolves, but if it does not agree with you, please do not suffer needlessly," he instructed before popping another bite into his own mouth.

Amandine thought about waiting to gauge the reactions of the others before trying it herself, but at a challenging glare from Marlette, put the bite in her mouth when she did.

She winced as something bitter, like pine needles, lashed at her taste buds. Fiona cried out and spit her bite into a handkerchief, causing Grendel to hiss and leap down from her lap. Amandine wanted to do the same, but saw Marlette watching her and held her mouth shut. The flavor shifted as the glaze melted in her mouth. The cake had a moist loamy texture, almost like dirt, but with a mildly nutty essence that took the place of the bitter. A moment later that was followed by an unusual mélange of tastes that reminded her of the way Lady Gia's favorite herbal bath mix smelled. Roses, clove, and something spicy she couldn't name.

Marlette made a retching sound. She shook her head and wiped her tongue in a most unladylike fashion on her own handkerchief. Mister Green was watching Amandine with a bemused expression. "What do you taste?" he asked.

As Amandine thought about the question, the last of the cake dissolved, leaving a faintly sweet aftertaste, like a trace of honey licked off a wooden spoon.

"It's like a forest," she said. "Pine and flowers and something sweet at the end."

"Life is sweet," Mister Green agreed, beaming at her. "Tell your Chef he shall have whatever he needs from me directly."

Gil

"The 'tenday', is the common method of tracking time since the change of the Calendar in 544. It has been standardized into the following days during the rule of Olgothia: Riverday, Starday, Thirdday, Fireday, Fifthday, Windday, Sunday, Ironday, Mistday, and Godhome. There are three tendays in a Cycle, and three Cycles in a Season. There are five Seasons in a Year, three during "shiv" Years, roughly corresponding to the angle of the sun and how much warmth it provides for farming."

- Lecture notes, Third Ironday, High Summer 1201

"EVERYONE PLEASE STAND back," Mister Green said.

Amandine found the remark a bit redundant. She was as far away as she could stand and still be in the kitchen, over by the door to the garden. Kivel had excused himself to said garden to harvest peas and Sunflower was by the pantry looking as nervous as Amandine felt. Grendel sat on the floor, right by Mister Green's feet and looked up at the mage, as if daring the elf to make him move. His tail swished like it did when he was hunting.

Chef Brutsche, however, stood behind and to the side of Mister Green near the high oven and was gesturing while he spoke.

"Three places along the bottom, if'n ya please. We need an even burn. Don't be turnin' it all to ash at once now!"

"Dear Chef," Mister Green said, shaking his head, "As I have told you before, I am not that kind of mage. I am a teacher, not a fighter, and using fire in such a manner is, frankly, unwise. That said, small fires are useful, so this will be a small fire."

Chef sniffed and took a step back. He folded his arms. "Right. Well, get on with it. Try'n not get magic all over the place."

Mister Green sighed and turned back to the oven. He extended a hand inside the opening to the burn chamber and began to speak. Amandine didn't know Elvish beyond the bare handful of words she had picked up listening to others, but she knew what it sounded like and this was not it. Soft, sibilant hisses and strong popping breaks between the words made the stream of vocalization sound almost like a fire itself. A sheet of rippling hot air escaped from the chamber as he withdrew his arm. Chef hurried over and shut the hatch.

Amandine breathed a sigh of relief. She hadn't known what to expect, but after the spell he had cast on her earlier, the simple incantation had been relatively innocuous.

"Right, well that'll put us back on track for tonight's guests. Luminous day to ya, Mister Green," Chef said.

"Luminous day, Chef Brutsche," Mister Green replied. "Might I indulge in another of those shortbreads?"

"Neya, ii fustillia neya cova. Kivet!" Chef said in Elvish.

"No need to be rude about it." Despite the retort he had a small smile on his lips. The expression combined with his eerie black eyes and sent a shiver up Amandine's spine. The shiver magnified when the eyes turned her direction. "Feel free to join lessons whenever you wish, Amandine," he said as he departed.

Grendel followed him out the door, his tail low as if he were stalking prey.

"I didn' know ya had Elven in ya," Sunflower said.

"I don't. Learnt to speak it when I was still pukin' over the side. Useful thing to know in the North Bends," Chef said as he resumed sorting eggs.

"In the lands of the Sea Kings, yah?"

"Aye."

"That where yer kin make croft?" Sunflower asked as she returned to the wood stove to stir the soup.

"Stop fishin' for grouper with sharkbait," Chef snapped as he finished his flat of eggs. "Pot girl, these 'uns are likely fouled. Any without cracked shells give to the pigs and chuck the rest in the pit. Bury 'em or they'll stink."

"Yes, Chef," Amandine said. She had been watching how he tested each egg between two fingers. It was a simple technique to find the ones that had compromised shells and had gone bad. She hoped he would start the puffs soon so that she could watch how he made them. To do that, though, she would need to hurry and dispose of the rotten eggs so that she didn't miss an important step.

Sunflower came down off a box she used as a stool and helped Amandine gather the eggs as Chef crossed the kitchen to take her place and check on his soup. With a grin, Sunflower leaned towards Amandine as she did when sharing gossip.

"I know ye don't like the magic, Amandine, and neither do I, I s'pose, but ye have to admit, Mister Green's got a fine look. 'Specially his eyes. They ain't the same shade as yer's ta be sure, but he cuts a striking figure, eh? I wonder if that's why the name..."

"Wait, what?" Amandine exclaimed, a bit louder than she should have. She was so surprised that she nearly dropped the half-flat of eggs she was holding. "His eyes ain't green!" she continued in a whisper after Kivel and Chef both turned to look at her.

"Well what co'or would you call them then, foal?" Sunflower asked with a confused expression.

"They're black. All black. Like night," Amandine hissed. "Are you making fun?"

Sunflower looked surprised and then hurt. Amandine instantly felt bad. The Hill Folk woman was never anything but kind to her, and she had no place to be snapping so.

"I'm sorry, Sunflower," Amandine said quickly as Sunflower finished putting the last few loose eggs from the discard bowl into the flat. "I shouldn't be sharp. They really don't seem green to me, though."

"That so," Sunflower said with a twist to her lips. "I do be wonderin' now who is making some fun, ya?"

Amandine was about to reply when the back door to the kitchens swung wide. The inside latch crashed against the wall and sunlight from the cart yard flooded the room.

Gil Crouste, the local hamlet's baker's apprentice and delivery boy, stood outlined by the frame, one boot still slightly extended where he had used it to kick the door. A look of utter surprise was on his face and a burlap-covered board that smelled of fresh baked bread was in his hands.

"Oi, easy on the door, Gil," Kivel scolded. "I just had it rehung today!"

"That's probably why it didn't stick like usual. Sorry, everyone." Gil said.

Gil was a large boy, in both girth and height. He was of an age with Marlette with sandy blonde hair and a riot of freckles across his nose. There was a smudge of flour on one of his temples where he must have carelessly wiped a hand while working.

"If you have a delivery, get it done and get out," Chef growled. "We have work ta be about and got no time fer kids tumbling about the kitchens!"

Gil stiffened, but ducked quickly inside and handed the board to Sunflower. The tiny cook had to extend her arms almost to their limits to grip it, but Hill Folk were strong for their size. She effortlessly hauled the load to a low shelf. Chef stepped away from his soup and grumbled while he fished in a belt pouch for Gil's payment. Amandine took the moment to slip by with the eggs and get on with her chore.

She made her way quickly across the yard to the sty. What Sunflower had said bothered her. Did she really see green eyes instead of black? Given thought, it didn't feel like the kind of jape Sunflower would make. She loved to gossip about who was with whom, and what all of the latest noble fashions were, but green eyes? It was just too odd. She tried to put it out of her mind and focus on her task.

Amandine fed the pigs and was hurrying to the ash pit with

the rest of the eggs when a voice called out to her.

"Amy! Wait up!"

Gil was crossing the yard. He waved enthusiastically.

"I'm busy, Gilly," Amandine said as she picked up her steps to the pit. "Can't stop to talk right now."

He fell in step beside her as if he hadn't heard.

"You are having the Magistrate for dinner tonight! That's exciting! I heard the Sheriff, Kimber Stolm, is going to be here with her wife. At least four other noble couples are coming as well. On a Riverday! It's so weird, right?"

Amandine tried to be patient with Gil, they had been friends ever since she had taken the job at Manor L'Eau. He was her only friend in this town, really. She didn't want to hurt his feelings, but Chef could start making egg puffs any moment and she wanted to be done with this chore as quickly as possible so that she could watch him.

"If you say so," Amandine muttered as she set aside the flat of remaining eggs and began digging a hole in the ash.

"I do! Nobles never travel or gather on Riverdays unless something is happening. Master Hawthorn says so. Have you heard anything about why they are coming all the way out here instead of meeting in Stoneman? I bet it's about the boglings! Someone in town said they stole piglets from Master Emmry!"

"Gilly, I like you, but if you keep me from getting back to the kitchens right now, I will break these over your head!" Amandine said, indicating the eggs.

Gil finally stopped talking and instead picked up a rake and helped Amandine cover the spoiled eggs. He didn't speak again until they were walking back to the kitchen.

"What's the rush?" he asked. "Are you in trouble with Chef Bugbear again?"

"Not really. Not any more than usual. But he is making egg puffs for the guests tonight and I want to watch! So either walk faster or go back to the bakery!"

He walked faster. "I don't get why you keep working for that goon. Master Hawthorne already said he'd hire you. As an apprentice like me even."

"Chef is a genius."

"Chef is a troll in an apron."

"Who is also a genius."

"That old bird has been here for years and has never taken an official apprentice, not even the cooks he works with. You're wasting your time."

"I don't need to be his apprentice. I watch him and I learn. I will be a chef too someday, you'll see!"

Gil smiled and shook his head. "Fine, have it your way. If you figure out how he does it, you'll make me one, right?"

"I. Need. To. Go."

"Alright, alright!. Hey, you going to Miss Jacinda's on Third?

"Of course."

"Oh, I almost forgot! Some old lady came into the bakery yesterday asking about you."

"About me?"

"Unless there's some other girl your age and description named Amandine running about the Gold Hills."

"Well, maybe there is."

Gil snorted in amusement and shook his head.

"It's probably nothing, Gil. Please, I really need to go!"

"See you later then!"

Gil waved and trotted off out the side gate and down the road as Amandine went the other direction.

She put the thought of Gil's strange old lady out of her mind. It had to be a coincidence. Everyone she knew who wasn't here lived in Artemis, hundreds of yarns and tendays of travel to the North. She grinned. Maybe she would make Gil an egg puff. But only if Chef Brutsche hadn't started them yet. Amandine ran the rest of the way to the kitchens.

A Slip of the Knife

"The Seasons of a Year follow this pattern: Low Winter, Low Summer, High Summer, Low Autumn, High Winter. Every three years, the sun takes a particularly high or low angle and the seasons of Low Summer, Low Autumn, and sometimes even Low Winter, drop off accordingly, leaving three or less. These years are called 'Shiv Years' and have special significance in both Human and Fae communities. In some nations, Low Summer is known by other names: 'New Tide' in Trenash lands for instance, and 'Greenest' in Bolath lands before the Calamity. Low Autumn is often called 'Fall' in Serentia. All former subject nations of Olgothia still follow the standardized naming when dealing with each other, however."

- Lecture notes, First Fireday, Low Winter 1201

AMANDINE WAS RELIEVED to see that Chef Brutsche hadn't started the preparations for the egg puffs. The flat of good eggs sat next to a bowl on the block, untouched. Chef stood over the shoulder of Kivel who was stuffing a shank of boar with minced onion and herbs. Amandine picked up a brass mixing bowl to polish and wandered closer to peer between them as they worked.

The thigh was cut in alternating strips along the bone and the flesh had been pulled out flat. Kivel was spreading the onion and herb mixture across the meat with his hands.

"Leave two fingers at the edges so the season stays inside when it's rolled, gah, make it three you skinny-fingered salt-lick…better.

Don't tear the folds! You ruin this leg an' I'll be spicing yours for the guests!"

Amandine wondered if he had actually ever cooked one of his assistants. It seemed to be a common threat.

Kivel was wearing a bandana around his hair to keep sweat and stray strands out of the food, but small beads forming on his bulbous nose and ruddy cheeks betrayed his nerves as he worked under Chef's critical eye. All he said was "Yes, Chef," after each correction as he focused on his task.

"Right. That's enough. Drill the bone then I'll roll it. You jus' hold the end," Chef said.

Kivel looked visibly relieved to be finished as he used a small hand drill to make holes in the thigh bone that would allow the marrow to flavor the meat. He set the drill aside and then held the end of the strip down. Chef nimbly rolled up the flattened meat using the bone as a spindle until it resembled a thigh again, with a spiral of onion and herbs tucked inside. He folded a flap of raw meat over the spiral to hide it and pinned the entire thing shut with long steel rods he had tucked next to the pouches on his belt. He gingerly peeked into one of those pouches and harrumphed.

His eyes darted to where Amandine was standing. She looked down at her perfectly clean bowl and began wiping it vigorously. Chef frowned at her and sucked at his teeth.

"I'll need to get some things from my pantry," he said over his shoulder to Kivel. "Wash yer paws! Good mind you! With the pumice! Then take our gawker and get to peelin' the turnips for the mash."

Amandine sighed, put the bowl away and then she and Kivel took turns washing out back. They came inside and sat opposite each other on small stools near the hearth and began peeling a sack of turnips. Kivel hummed to himself as he worked. She didn't recognize the tune, but it had the feeling of a love song, or perhaps a reel to dance to. The rotund man had a lovely singing voice, but rarely let it out unless he was drunk.

The large roots were difficult for her to peel, even with a smaller knife, but she did her best to help Kivel and not appear to be slacking off. As she worked, she occasionally stole glances over to Chef's pantry. It was a late addition to the kitchen, built specifically to his instructions. It was large enough to walk into, but the door and the walls were made of aged cedar and were windowless. A lock was inset to the door, a dwarf-crafted contraption with multiple mechanisms, to which Chef owned the only known key. She was positive that the contents of the pantry held the secret to Chef Brutsche's amazing food, and so she tried to peek inside every chance she could.

Her vantage from the hearth wasn't the best, but she could see the strips of dangling black cloth inside the door that were meant to keep bugs out when the pantry was open. She prayed to Kurloon for a breeze to ruffle them and give her a glance. She could faintly hear jars rattle and clink from within, but no wind arrived to rescue her curiosity.

"You want to know what he keeps in there?" Kivel asked.

"Very much," Amandine said as she craned her neck.

"So would I," Kivel chuckled. "I can tell you how he prepares a roast, trims the meat, styles it, how long he cooks it, but not how he gets the flavor. His spices are his secret, Amandine. Won't let a soul past that curtain. I tried to peek once and nearly lost my nose!"

"Did you ever try again?"

Kivel laughed. "I like my nose, large as it is. If you like yours, best take care where you stick it."

Chef passed through the cloth strips and she caught a tiny glimpse of something that looked like a clay pot on a shelf before the ribbons flapped back into place. He glanced up from the drawstrings of his belt pouches and their eyes met. She hurriedly looked back down at her turnip, but slipped and nicked a finger.

"Ow!" she yelped before sticking the wounded digit in her mouth.

Kivel looked up from his own bulb and smirked at her, then shook his head and resumed peeling.

Chef stomped over and glared at her for a moment and then pointed to the door. "Wash it and get a kip-leaf wrap from Nanny. Ye keep yer chum ou' of the mash now!"

"Yesh, Chef," Amandine said with a sigh around her finger.

"This is why I hate children in the kitchen," Chef grumbled under his breath as he turned his back on her to season the boar thigh.

Amandine made her way through the servant's hall, her thoughts drifted to what might be hidden behind the curtain in Chef's pantry. She was so deep into the fantasy about finding it unlocked that she nearly ran face-first into Taster Nous as he rounded a corner.

"Watch where you are going, urchin," he snapped. "Shouldn't you be in the kitchen?"

"Sorry, sah," Amandine said quickly. "I am going to see Nanny, sah. My knife slipped."

She held up her wounded finger and a small trickle of blood ran down one side. Nous recoiled and pulled a handkerchief from his sleeve to cover his nose.

"Colorless… ugh, go on then, and be quick about it. And since the creature only seems to listen to you, make sure that pestilential cat is outside before guests arrive!"

Amandine frowned, but bowed in acknowledgment as Nous sidled by her and continued on his way. None of the house staff liked Grendel. The maids complained that he mussed things they had straightened, and Sunflower often had to chase him away from food. Even Chef would sometimes run him out of the kitchen if he was being too much under foot. But Amandine liked him. He was a fantastic mouser and kept the pantries free of vermin. He was also quite cuddly… when he wanted to be. No one hated him more than the Taster, though. If Grendel tore into the kitchen as if his tail were on fire, a report of broken glassware or clawed furniture was soon to follow. Mistress Fiona's affection for the cat was probably the only reason Nous had not gotten permission to be rid of him.

"I hope you're staying out of trouble, Gren," Amandine muttered as she resumed her march to Nanny's room.

Nanny's abode was a small chamber on the ground floor, near the back of the manor. With a sigh, she gently rapped on the door with her uninjured hand. She heard a chair scraping from within and a moment later the door opened to reveal Nanny. She was an elderly human woman with long gray hair that she kept tied back in a large bun. Her dress was simple gray wool, and she wore no jewelery except for a pendant on a string in the shape of a rising sun, the symbol of the Lady of Light, Milintanth. Her skin was tanned and wrinkled with age, but her round cheeks and smiling eyes made her seem motherly in a way that Amandine found reassuring.

"Colorless night," she swore softly when Amandine held out her injured finger. "Come in, come in, Amandine. Let's get that seen to."

She shuffled away from the doorway and stepped creakily towards a chest of drawers on tall legs. It had numerous small bins that contained herbs, bandages and other things needed to tend minor injuries. Amandine followed her inside and moved around the old woman so as not to be in her way. Nanny's room was sparse, with simple furniture, but one corner of the space had been set up as a tiny shrine to the Divine Sisters: Milintanth, Ravenex, and Delinkhal.

Amandine crouched down next to it to examine the myriad of small devotions laid out for each of the goddesses. A sun carved from a seashell, a glossy raven's feather, a single straw of wheat from this year's crop, a bowl of sand, a smaller bowl of water, three tiny bones, probably from a mouse or rat, and many more.

"I'll bet some of that looks familiar now, doesn't it?" Nanny said as she slid open one bin and fished out a dried green leaf, and then a small roll of cloth from another.

"Yes, sah," Amandine said as she turned to look up at her. "I used to live with the Night Sisters in Artemis."

"I've heard," Nanny said with a smile. She used a small pair of shears to cut a strip from the roll of cloth. "The devotees of

Ravenex have long taken in those with no place else to go. Not many willingly seek out their goddess, after all."

"I found someplace else to go."

"Naturally. Let me see that finger, child."

Amandine held out her injured hand and Nanny wrapped the small wound with the leaf and then tied it close with the cloth. "Soak that in the bowl of water on the shrine there for a moment and then you'll be fine."

The water felt like ice as Amandine dipped her bandaged finger into it. She hissed. "Cold! Is this one of Milintanth's miracles?"

Nanny laughed and shook her head as she put away her things. "Oh my, no, no. I'm not the Lady, child. I am not even as skilled as the dedicated ones that practice medicine in her temples. It's just water. The herb causes a chill to the skin when you soak it."

"Will the goddess be upset that I am making the water dirty?"

"I doubt it. If it is used in the service of healing, I think no greater honor could be given to the Lady of Light. It's like what the Night Sisters do for those that have passed on, yes? All of the Divine Sisters have a place in our lives, but we get to choose which one is most important to us. But then, I think you've figured that out for yourself, haven't you?"

"I like Kayla, the Daughter of Joy," Amandine said as she watched the water seep up through the cloth on her finger.

"Milintanth's daughter? I think that suits you," Nanny said as she settled back into her padded chair. Amandine could hear her bones popping as she sat. "That should be enough. Off with you now. No more playing with knives!"

"I wasn't playing," Amandine said stiffly. Her fists clenched involuntarily at the warning and she felt the heat rising in her neck.

Nanny didn't reply, but the expression on her face made Amandine realize she was only teasing her. With a sheepish expression, she unclenched her hands, which made her wound throb.

"Thank you, sah," she mumbled as she stood up to leave.

"Surely," Nanny replied. "I am here for all the children of this House, not just the noble ones."

Amandine found Grendel waiting for her in the hallway outside Nanny's room.

"And where did you get off to? I hope you weren't into mischief. Lily will throw you out! Or Nous will!" Amandine scolded. She immediately felt bad for taking out her frustration with Nanny on Grendel. He was a good cat. For his part, Grendel seemed to care not a wit for Amandine's sharp words. He meowed in reply, rubbed up against her legs and heeled her as she made her way back to the kitchens. Near the parlors, Amandine passed Hedgehog, who was standing on a rolling stool to adjust a tapestry.

"You there! Roll me to the other corner, would ya?" he called.

Amandine carefully rolled the stool on the hard wooden floors until it was located under the opposite corner of the tapestry.

"Obliged," Hedgehog said. "And thanks for deflecting Chef's ire this morning. Sunflower mentioned what ya said and did."

"I, well…" Amandine stammered. "She was so upset. And I don't know why I said it, but…"

"Chit chat will not finish the drapes, Mister Hedgehog," Taster Nous drawled as he rounded the corner from the lower parlors. "And you, did I not ask that the cat be put outside?"

Amandine held up her bandaged finger. "I just arrived back from Nanny, sah. I'll make sure he's not a bother."

Grendel meowed as if in agreement.

"And she were helpin' me!" Hedgehog interjected. "Leave off, now!"

"Don't coddle her because she's a child," Nous sneered. "If Lady Gia hadn't vouched to put her on staff, she'd still be a vagrant in Stoneman. She has duties here that do not involve pushing your stool."

"Yes, well *I'm* the Butler, sah, so I will thank you not to be telling me how to manage *my* work. Know your place, Master Taster," Hedgehog snapped.

"I could say the same to you," Nous replied with a casual shrug. He sauntered away into the sun rooms, probably to gather the family's tea trays.

"That one's a great slithering egg-thief," Hedgehog muttered as he watched the Taster depart. "Mark me, Amandine, Chef is no celestial, he shouts and rails and says hateful things, but he don't hate no one for who they are, he jus' hates everyone equally. His is an honest bile. Don't ever trust one who says sweet things but acts like a bugbear when no one is lookin'."

"But we were looking, just now." Amandine said, confused.

"Ayup, but you see, to him, you and I *are* no one."

Eggs

"Eggs are an indispensable ingredient in any kitchen. Nothing else in all of Old Mother's creation has quite so many uses, in so many different dishes. They can rarely be substituted, and baked goods of nearly every stripe absolutely require them. All well-appointed kitchens should maintain a coop of well-tended hens or frelkin. Not only because of the importance of their eggs, but also because fresh poultry is always superior to salted, dried or smoked for most recipes."
- Seeker's Kitchen, Chapter 3, Essential Ingredients

AMANDINE RETURNED TO the kitchens and helped Kivel finish the turnips, then cleaned the block and swept up the vegetable scraps from Sunflower's task. A small pile of things, including the breakfast dishes, had accumulated in the wash tub so she fetched water from the well house and poured it over the dishes, then added salt and a dash of vinegar to the tub and began to scrub. Grendel rubbed against her shins as she worked, even when he got sprinkled with water from the tub.

Chef had still not started the egg puffs. Amandine watched him like a hawk from the wash station. If he did anything with the eggs or his mixing bowls, she'd be ready. She wondered why he made the puffs so infrequently. Was it because they used so many eggs? Possibly. The flat on the counter represented every chicken egg they had in the manor. Kivel would probably have to go to the hamlet's market circle in the morning if the hens didn't lay enough for breakfast. Amandine preferred frelkin eggs herself, despite their green yolks and foamy whites. The flavor was simply superior.

Still, she desperately wanted to see how Chef made the puffs happen. Savory and sweet at the same time, the fluffy caps of baked egg were just about the most incredible thing she had ever tasted. Even then, she had only eaten them once, last Fall, when Chef had made an extra and allowed Kivel, Sunflower and her to sample it.

"I hear it's going to be Lord Gaston and Lady Ophelia as well," Sunflower said to Kivel as they worked together, stuffing plucked and cleaned chickens for the first course. Kivel shrugged.

"This manse is central to all of 'em," he said. "Less travel for everyone to meet here if they have something important to discuss."

"Righ'," Sunflower agreed. "And it has Chef's chicken!"

"Which won't get done by you lot jawin'," Chef Brutsche growled as he inspected the high oven.

"Yes, Chef!" Sunflower and Kivel chorused.

Chef stepped away from the oven and reached for the flat of eggs. Amandine slowed her scrubbing and paid keen attention. He didn't begin, however. Instead he merely brushed the tops of the eggs as if caressing them, shook his head and turned his attention to the soup instead.

Amandine decided to chance a question. Normally she would only pester Kivel or Sunflower, and they would usually indulge her curiosity, but this was something that only Chef was likely to know. Still, she phrased her question carefully.

"Are the eggs no good, Chef? I can check the cold cellar or coops for more since the others are busy."

Chef Brutsche shook his head again as he sprinkled something in the soup and stirred the pot. "Naw, the eggs 're fine. They need ta be warm as the room yer workin' in before ye crack 'em. Ye just finish them dishes an' then set out the serving platters."

Amandine nodded and squirreled away that bit of information. A piece of the puzzle! The eggs needed to be warm.

Sunflower took the stuffed chickens and set them by the cooking hearth, then went outside to wash her hands. Kivel moved some cutting boards off his station and walked them over to Amandine's tub for scrubbing. "He won't show you," he whispered. "I have been trying to get him to teach me the puffs for years."

Amandine stuck her lip out at him in a pout. "I'll watch him then!" she whispered back.

Kivel just smiled at her and shook his head. "When you're done with the platters, come and help me finish the mash," he said in a louder voice.

The wood stove where the water for the mash was heating was close enough to Chef's favorite spot by the oven that she would have a good view while he worked. Amandine grinned and nodded thankfully to Kivel. Grendel meowed as if thanking him as well.

"Just don't get caught slacking off," Kivel said with a wink.

"Chef, sah," Sunflower called as she returned from the garden. "There ain't enough crinkled lettuce for the nests. The ca'erpillers been at it again."

"Aye, I thought that might be the case," Chef said as he lidded the soup pot. "Just use some o' the broadleaf as well. Space 'em out so it looks nice."

"But that's not the recipe—" Sunflower began.

"Fer one, it's my colorless recipe," Chef snapped. "Fer two, broadleaf is green. It's called 'on a green nest'. No one is goin' ta complain that we used different lettuce, ya worrywort."

"Sorry, Chef."

"Don' be sorry, lass," Chef said in a softer tone. "Jus' use yer head and solve the problem. It be good ta know that the fat caterpillars are fed. I'll have ta buy some crinkle from the market circle next Fireday. We jus' don' have time ta do it right now."

Amandine watched as Sunflower took a large head of broadleaf and began trimming. Then she placed the alternating leaves on the platters that would hold the chicken once it was cooked and carved. She finished each arrangement with a row of soft cheese balls that had been soaked in oil. The cheese was meant as a flavor compliment to the chicken, but they also looked like little eggs in the green nest.

"That's cute," Amandine said as she dried platters.

"It's a bit racked, if'n ya ask me," Sunflower said dryly. "Cookin' a mother bird and settin' 'er up with a bunch o' fake eggies."

Kivel chortled at the comment. Amandine cocked her head and thought about it. It *was* sort of macabre.

"That's the colorless point," Chef said as he stepped over to inspect Sunflower's work. "A noble patron once asked me ta make a dish that represented her house. Lady Iremelle, near the Maw. So I came up with this."

"Oh, an' how does this show her colors?" Sunflower asked.

"She bought an' sold labor contracts," Chef said.

Sunflower frowned at that. "Oh my…"

Kivel's chortling increased. "And she liked it, didn't she, Chef?"

"Aye," Chef said, shaking his head.

"Well, knowin' tha', who is this dish meant for in tonight's company?" Sunflower asked.

Chef Brutsche shrugged as he turned to the hearth. "Most of 'em."

Amandine was a bit baffled by the exchange. Chef had made a dish to insult someone? And she liked it?

"Did she not realize the jape?" Amandine asked.

"Nah, she got it," Chef said as he stoked the fire. "But some folk, when faced with their own ugly reflections, decide that they are lookin' at beauty instead."

A Menu Confirmation

"There are six recognized human tribes: The Trenash, Zulath, Bolath, Olgath, Serent and Kalebite. Although other splinter groups do exist, such as the Icewalkers of the North Seas, or the various jungle dwelling groups in Southern Serentia, these six comprise the bulk of humanity and trace their lineages all the way back to the Arrival."

> *- Lecture notes, Third Mistday, Low Summer 1201*

AMANDINE SLOWLY STIRRED the mash as she tried to watch Chef from the corner of her eye. He *still* hadn't started yet, but all of his prep for the egg puffs was complete. A mixing bowl and a set of clean ramekins awaited him at his station with small dishes of loose salt and crushed spiceweed. The eggs sat perched in their flat, like soldiers at attention, while Chef eyed the high oven and thoughtfully chewed his upper lip. Kivel leaned in to examine the mash and sprinkled some dried herbs into the mixture, along with a lump of warm butter.

"Make sure that gets melted in completely," Kivel instructed. "He won't start until the oven stops smoking," he added in a whisper meant only for Amandine.

With a sigh, Amandine looked away and focused on following Kivel's instructions. She wasn't often allowed to help actually cook the food, and so she didn't want to disappoint him. The dark yellow butter began to melt into a spiral as she stirred, making the mash look like a child's drawing of the sun.

Amandine loved to cook. Even simple things like this turnip mash gave her such pleasure to make that Amandine almost forgot about her obsession with the egg puffs.

"Ah! Hello!" a voice called from the back door of the kitchens.

Amandine and the others looked up and all eyes fell on the speaker. A young man, perhaps still within his teens, stood in the doorway. He was thin, and dressed in a sharply tailored coat and breeches that marked him as some sort of noble servant. In his arms was a wiggling dog. It was a small breed and, in Amandine's opinion, a bit silly looking. It had light fur and a dark, round face with a nose that seemed to be pushed flat against its skull. The young man's dark hair was slicked back from his forehead and tied in a tail that fell past his shoulders. Similarly dark eyes scanned the kitchen's inhabitants and settled finally on Chef Brutsche.

"You must be the head cook," he said brightly. "I was just—"

"Leavin'," Chef interrupted. "And get that drooling mongrel out of my kitchen!"

"Oh, I will leave presently," the young man continued. He set the dog down and it proceeded to walk over and sniff at the dish-washing station. Grendel poked his head out from under the tub and sniffed back, curiously. "But first, I have come to confirm the menu for—"

A knife sailed through the air and stuck fast in the side of the wash basin. The dog yelped and scurried back to its master, its small claws skittering on the packed clay floors. Grendel hissed and retreated under the tub. Chef casually unsheathed another paring knife from his belt and bounced it in his hand.

"Get. Out." he said.

"You are very rude!" the young man complained.

"Says the fop who walks into *my* kitchen, with a dog no less, and has yet ta even offer his name! Yer noble patrons will either eat what I serve them, or not eat at all. There's yer confirmation!"

"I'm Fredderick," the young man said with a frown as he gathered up the quivering dog. "I will relay your message."

"Ye do that, Fred," Chef grumbled.

"Your knife," Fredderick said. He waved a hand and the blade stuck in the side of the wash basin unstuck itself and glided gently through the air to where Chef stood and clattered onto the table.

Amandine's breath caught. He was a magician! Besides Old Wizard Hemm and Mister Green, she had never seen or met another. And he was so young! In her mind, mages were either always old gnarled folks with fancy robes, or dark, fae creatures.

Chef Brutsche seemed completely unimpressed by the display and simply stared at the interloper until finally, without another word, Fredderick turned and left, gently closing the door behind him as he did.

"Well, that was excitin'!" Sunflower said with forced cheer. "Who do ya think he was askin' for?"

Chef examined his knives and returned them to his belt. "Don't matter. Prim and picky nobles will spite a fish fer the bones. I won't have none of it!"

He reached out and touched the eggs in their flat. With a nod, Chef pulled his bowl closer and began to roll up his sleeves. Amandine craned her neck so that she might see around his arms and observe what he did next. Grendel also emerged from under the washtub and sniffed the air as if anticipating Chef's next move.

Taster Nous appeared in his doorway. He sniffed as if he had caught a bad odor. "Chef Brutsche! I have a need for assistance in the parlors."

Chef rolled his eyes at the new interruption. "Ya can't have my cooks before the roast is done! Go get Hedgehog ta help ya."

"He is already assisting me and there are more guests than expected. I need a runner."

"My cooks are busy, go run faster."

"She looks freshly bathed, and she is not a cook, yes?" Nous said, pointing to Amandine.

"No!" Amandine blurted out before she could control her mouth. Everyone in the kitchen turned to look at her. "Uh, I mean. I don't, um…"

"Go get yer livery on, fingerling," Chef Brutsche said with a harumph. "Make sure the pretty nobles have their nibbles and sips."

Amandine stepped away from the wood stove and bowed politely. Kivel gave her an understanding pat on the shoulder.

"Yes, Chef. I'll be in the parlors presently, Taster Nous."

Nous sniffed again, turned on his heel, and vanished from the doorframe. Chef shook his head and returned to watching the high oven.

Amandine made her way to the stairs that led down to the warm cellar and her cot. Her livery was hung on a peg next to where she slept. Not much else was in the warm cellar. Most of the space was taken up by the enormous pyrestone furnace that heated the manor when it was chill. Its bulbous, black iron body constantly radiated warmth, and a soft orange light escaped the slats on the front panel. Sacks of drying wool, used to stuff mattresses and quilts, were stacked against one wall. Amandine's cot was against the opposite wall, surrounded by crates of foodstuffs that needed to be kept dry and warm.

She shuffled dejectedly across the packed earth floor. Grendel followed her and meowed plaintively.

"I know, Gren, it's not fair. Maybe Kivel will…"

With a sigh, Amandine left the thought unspoken. She pulled the livery off of its peg over her cot. It consisted of a knee-length tunic with a high, buttoned neck that was dyed in stripes of House L'Eau's colors: white and blue. It fit over her work clothes, but the cuffs and neck were very tight and it took Amandine a moment to properly fasten the buttons that held them closed. Grendel sat on the bed and watched her with lazy blinking eyes as she fought with the buttons.

"You probably think this is really funny, don't you?" Amandine groused at the cat. He didn't answer, of course, but it seemed to her that his tail swished in a very smug fashion as she pulled the tight buttons into place.

The garment was stifling, and since it was worn over clothes, it was also hot, especially in close proximity to the pyrestone furnace.

"Come on then, Grendel. Let's get out of here before I roast like that boar shank."

Meow.

"I'm so glad you approve," Amandine muttered as she trudged back up the stairs.

As she approached the top, she heard voices in the kitchen. One was Chef, and the other one...

"We're busy in here righ' now, who in the hells are you?"

"A traveling woman of faith, and I can *see* that you are very busy, so I shall be brief."

Amandine's breath caught in her chest. She *knew* that voice. She had been lectured by it so often that she would recognize its quiet, firm cadence anywhere.

"Sister Corbin," she hissed to Grendel. "What is *she* doing here? How did she find me?"

Very slowly, Amandine peered up from the stairwell into the kitchen through the gap made where the door to the warm cellar hung on its hinges.

Chef was standing with his arms folded over his chest and looking extra surly. In front of him stood a small human woman in dark gray robes with a hood. The hood had been pulled back to reveal a weathered face with a small round nose, fair skin, gaunt cheek lines and a deep furrowed brow. Sister Corbin's hair was dark brown with a stark white stripe that ran from her left temple all through the rest. It created a swirl of white and brown in the bun that sat on the back of her head like a stale cross-loaf.

When Chef simply continued to glare at her, Sister Corbin cleared her throat and continued. "I am looking for a runaway from the Convent at Artemis. A girl named Amandine. I was told she is a servant of this house. This is the servant's entrance, yes?"

"That depends on who ya serve," Chef said as he continued to stare down the small woman.

"I serve only the will of the Goddess," Sister Corbin said with a frown. She indicated the clay pin holding her cloak, the shadow bonnet symbol of Ravenex, the Goddess of Night.

"Well, ain't no one dead here by the name of Amandine."

"The girl I am looking for is not dead, I hope."

"Well that's odd. It was my understandin' that your order mainly dealt with dead folk."

"She was a ward of the Convent. I was dispatched to find her."

"Long trip for a runaway orphan. Why are you really here?"

Amandine held her breath. The way Chef was talking to Sister Corbin was incredibly disrespectful. No one talked to godsworn like that. Was he covering for her? Why? She hadn't told him a thing about the Sisters, only that she had traveled from Artemis. Sister Corbin was a fierce woman despite her soft spoken ways. Who would win this battle of wills, she wondered.

Sister Corbin sighed and also folded her arms. "I am here exactly for the reasons I stated. You are the cook that hired her then?"

Chef rolled his eyes at the ceiling and placed his hands on his hips. "You are the second strange face to enter my kitchen today and call me a cook!" he boomed. "Cooks follow recipes, Chef's create 'em. I am the Chef here, sah, and I do not have the time to help ya sniff out runaways while I am workin'. Kindly see yerself out!"

"If Amandine is here—"

"If," Chef snarled, interrupting her, "the Amandine that works here is even the one ye are lookin' for. Lots of folk with that name after all. Have a surname by chance?"

"She's an orphan, so no."

"Then I'm afeared I can't help ye. Safe night to ya, Sister."

Sister Corbin faced Chef a moment longer, bowed politely with a twist to her lips and departed through the door to the wagon yard. Amandine could hear the latch click, the kitchen had grown so silent.

"What was that all about?" Kivel asked. "Did you really just throw a godsworn out of the kitchen? That's bad luck, Chef!"

"Bah. Superstitious eel bait," Chef snapped. "Anyone could put a pin on their cloak and say they're holy. We have a job ta do, back to it!"

"Yes, Chef," Sunflower and Kivel said.

Amandine cautiously stepped out of the stairwell and into the kitchen. She expected that Chef would have questions like: Did she really know Sister Corbin? Was she a runaway? What made her leave Artemis?

When he saw her, what he said instead was: "What took ye so long? I don' want that lamprey, Nous, darkenin' my door again, so hurry along and keep him out of our nets!"

"Yes, Chef!" Amandine squeaked as she moved quickly past him and out through the door that led to the house. Grendel chased behind her and meowed in a plaintive fashion.

"I don't know how she found me, Grendel, but I'm not going back. I'm not!"

Grendel purred as he followed her to the parlors.

Dark Rumors

"Despite Serentia's leading role in the downfall of the Olgothian Empire, the political structure adopted after the revolution bears many similarities to the system it replaced. Slave labor, of course, is a thing of the past outside of Olgothia, but political power is largely concentrated in the aristocratic class that owns and oversees the sprawling farmlands, forests and mines of the Free Lands. Towns of a certain size may petition for a mayorship and elect their own leader, but such petitions are rarely successful. As for the ones that are granted, such elected mayorships are one of the few gateways into the aristocracy that are available to the common folk and many a commune has found itself as yet another noble holdfast within a scant few generations."

- Lecture notes, Second Mistday, Low Summer 1201

WITH A SIGH, Amandine tugged at the tight collar of her livery and tried not to grind her teeth. Grendel sat behind her against the wall, cleaning his paws in a bored fashion.

The lower parlor was actually twice as wide as the Upper Parlor since it combined with the East Sunroom. Lord Estevan and Lady Gia enjoyed the morning sunshine and so an extended picture window had been installed that ran nearly the length of the outer wall. The rugs were covered with comfortable chairs, three different stuffed sofas, and many smaller stools and padded benches. Large clay pots filled with earth sat in each corner of the room and contained flowering shrubs that Mister Green had coaxed into growing indoors.

The entire house staff stood at the fringes, or moved between the chatting noble guests to offer trays of dried fruit, nuts, and sundries. Amandine's job was to stay in her corner, remain silent, and if Taster Nous or one of the maids gave a signal, hurry and fetch whatever it was they needed: food from the dry pantry, wine bottles from the cellar, or any other small thing that was requested. It bored her to tears. She had been so close! The secret to the egg puffs was going to be hers and that awful, hateful, mean old—

"Amandine!" Taster Nous hissed as he passed her. "Wake up, child. Lily is signalling for you. Hop to! When you are done, take that mangy animal and put it outside!"

Startled, Amandine bobbed a bow to the Taster and walked quickly across the room to where Lily, one of the house's maids, was waiting. Grendel arched his back at the Taster who kicked a foot at the cat. He made a dash after Amandine to escape.

"Don't antagonize him!" Amandine said softly to Grendel. "You know he hates you!"

Grendel meowed in a way that Amandine thought sounded rather sulky.

Lily made an impatient gesture as Amandine approached. The dark-haired Hill Folk woman was plump, with a pinched face that rarely held any mirth.

"There ya is, child," she softly hissed. "Scurry now and fetch a fresh bottle for Lord Estevan and his friend. Get one o' the LeRue Estate tags on the oakenwood rack. And for Delinkhal's green, put the cat out!"

Amandine sighed and nodded. Lily was standing just behind and to the side of Lord Estevan. He was tall, with white wings in his close cut hair and a generous smile. That smile was muted as he spoke with another noble, a woman named Lady Jadet Urel. She was severe, older than Lord Estevan by a stretch, with her blonde hair pulled back so tight that Amandine thought it a wonder that she didn't look cross-eyed.

Lord Estevan paused what he had been about to say to Lady Jadet and looked down. "Ah, Amandine is it? Helping the Taster this evening? Good lass."

"Yes, Lord Estevan," Amandine said with a bow. "I am fetching a bottle for Maid Lily."

"Not that awful LeRue swill," Lady Jadet interjected. "Anything else, please."

"Miss Amandine is our Scullery," Estevan said to Jadet, "and my youngest has taken quite a shine to her. I hear Mister Green has offered you lessons. I think it would be wise to accept such an offer."

Lord Estevan finished the remark with a flat stare at Amandine which made her blush. She tried very hard not to gain the attention of the Lord and Lady. A good servant was an invisible one, or so the Taster would say. In any case, Amandine preferred the noisy kitchen to the quiet halls of Manor L'Eau.

"I will seek him out when my duties permit, sah," Amandine said.

Lady Jadet snorted derisively. It was obvious what she thought of servants taking lessons with the Lord's children. Mercifully, Lord Estevan nodded and returned his attention to Lady Jadet. Amandine contained a sigh of relief and turned to leave, but Lily caught her sleeve. The maid's pursed lips told her what *she* thought of the exchange as well.

"Nay th' LaRue," Lily whispered. "Grab a bottle o' the Clement from the ashwood rack instead."

Amandine picked up Grendel, who meowed at her in protest, and dropped him outside the back door to the gardens before she hurried to the cold cellar and began locating the wine Lily had asked for.

She carefully sounded out the Olgothian script that underlaid the ancient Serent text on the tags that hung from the necks of the bottles. The upper text was undecipherable to her, she couldn't read any Serent. Most people outside the nobility couldn't. Everyone used Olgothian because they had once ruled everything and made their language the common one for the entire land. Or that's what she had been told anyway. They didn't rule anyone but themselves anymore, but everyone still used Olgothian to write books and label things. It's what most humans and Hill Folk spoke too. Languages like Serent and Bolath hadn't been spoken aloud by the common people in hundreds of years.

"Cle-mu-e-ant" Amandine said aloud slowly as she found the correct bottle. She pulled it, used a nearby rag to dust it off, and hurried back upstairs.

When she returned, the circle of nobles speaking to Lord Estevan had grown. Lady Jadet had been joined by her aged husband, a wrinkled prune of a man who smiled at everyone and walked with a cane and the assistance of one of his grandsons. Also present was Lady Ophelia, a prim, dark haired beauty who was also one of the larger land holders to the North of Stoneman. Next to her was fat, jolly, Lord Miller, who, as one might infer from his name, ran the largest grain mill in the region.

Then there was Kimber Stolm, the Sheriff. She wasn't noble, technically, but as an agent of Lady Everdawn and the primary collector of taxes and enforcer of the Council's laws, she held a great deal of authority. Amandine had always been a little in awe of her. With short, graying hair, pale skin and muscular physique, she was the exact opposite of every other woman in the room; hard instead of soft, straight instead of curved. She had cold, blue eyes and a clipped, no-nonsense tone that tended to cut con-versations short rather than engender them. The Sheriff was also the only person armed. A long knife, practically a small sword, was clipped to her belt. Its pommel was carved in the shape of a raven, the symbol of her office.

Her wife, Sheeria, stood at her left side. She was an Olgothian woman with dark ebony skin and long, carefully bundled hair that was red-brown like autumn leaves. It hung in waves all the way to her waist. Her dress was wool instead of linen, but Amandine could only tell the difference as she passed close by, the weave was so fine. It was the color of a sunset, drifting from dark red and orange to yellow near the hem. The dyes alone probably cost a fortune.

"With respect, Lady, that notion is pure wishfulness. The Council will not send soldiers for such a small matter," the Sheriff said to Lady Ophelia.

Amandine handed the bottle to Lily and started to leave, but the tiny woman motioned for her to stay. "Help me pour," she whispered.

So Amandine held the tray of glasses while Lily poured and handed them out to the guests. Lady Ophelia took her offered glass, sipped it and then frowned at Sheriff Stolm.

"Small matter?" she said with disgust. "It's costing me a fortune in lost livestock!"

"And grain bags are missing from my warehouse!" Lord Miller added angrily. "This isn't a *small* matter."

"It seems unlikely that boglings would steal sacks from a warehouse," Lord Estevan said. "That sounds more like common thievery to me."

"On that account, the Captain of the Guard in Stoneman, my own brother, Rivaldo Stolm, will be investigating," Sheriff Stolm said. "Rest assured, he will discover who has been pillaging your warehouses, sah."

Lord Miller sputtered indignantly. "My foreman has already followed the trails of torn bags and spilled grain. They lead directly into the fens! It's the colorless goblins, I tell you! Irongate needs to assist us!"

"Oh my, you young folk really don't get it, do you?" Lady Jadet said with a smirk. "I'm afraid the Sheriff is correct. High Chancellor Martovin will never send troops to a backwater like this, just to deal with a few boglings. "

"Quite strange for boggers to kill cattle," her husband added wheezily. "Rather large beasts for such small creatures."

"Vicious little monsters!" Lady Ophelia hissed. "Why they are abided in civilized lands is beyond me!"

"Surely Lady Everdawn will petition the council for us?" Lord Miller asked.

Lord Estevan raised a hand and spoke. "Calm yourselves, please. Lady Everdawn has always listened to our concerns and petitioned on our behalf in the past, why should this time be any different?"

"And you are not the only ones suffering losses," Sheriff Stolm added. "My wife's yearlings have also been attacked when sharing the Western pastures with Lady Ophelia's cattle."

"Yearling goats and sheep not old enough to milk are *not* the same as full grown stock beef," Lady Ophelia quipped. "If it's such a loss to you and yours, perhaps your brother and his people should go and handle it?"

The Sheriff's lips pressed into a line. "The Stoneman militia is not an outrider force. Captain Rivaldo and his sergeant are the only two that have any real experience in the field, and that is against human foes, bandits and slavers, not fae. Do not underestimate goblins because they are small."

Amandine noted that Sheeria remained silent during the exchange. She still smiled pleasantly at the nobles across from her, but Amandine thought she detected a certain strain around her eyes. Especially at the mention of the boglings. Come to think of it, Gil had also mentioned boglings earlier, after he had made his delivery. Perhaps he had been right about what the nobles were in a fret over.

A hand waved in front of Amandine's face. She hadn't realized how intently she had been listening to the conversation. Lily withdrew her hand, took the empty tray from her and made a shooing motion.

Reluctantly, Amandine retreated back to her corner. This had to be why all the nobles were gathering on a Riverday. Dark fae attacking livestock was far more interesting than the usual dry noble banter. She wished the guests were closer to her so that she could maybe hear more.

"You look bored."

Amandine glanced over to her side. A chair that she could have sworn was empty a moment before now contained the young man and funny looking dog from earlier in the afternoon. The dog wiggled happily and yipped at her, but otherwise sat contently in the young man's lap.

"I'm working, sah," she replied.

"Easiest work I have ever seen," he commented as he stroked the dog's head. "I thought I saw you in the kitchens earlier?"

"I'm the house scull, sah. I'm just helping with all the guests tonight… who I am not really allowed to talk to."

"Oh, not to worry. I don't think I technically count as a guest," he said jovially. The dog barked. When Amandine didn't answer he continued. "That's alright then. You stand there and work, and I'll talk. My name is Fredderick."

"I know."

"Yes, well, Dumpling and I are great admirers of fine cooking, and your Chef Brutsche has quite the reputation," he continued while making lazy swirling motions in the air with his free hand. "You must have learned a lot under his tutelage."

"He doesn't teach—wait. Your dog's name is 'Dumpling'?"

"Well, yes. He sort of looks like one, right?"

Dumpling barked again and Amandine couldn't help herself. She smiled and stifled a laugh. "Yes, very much so," she conceded.

"You said that the Chef doesn't instruct you, but I saw you stirring a pot today."

"Oh, I sometimes help his assistants, but mainly, I clean up and fetch things. He doesn't teach me. I watch, though."

"So you have learned some things then. Do you like to cook, Miss Amandine?"

"Very much! Sometimes I help out at the soup kitchen, on Thirdday in Stoneman. Miss Jacinda—"

"Amandine!"

Taster Nous had appeared while she was distracted. She managed to avoid jumping when he startled her, and quickly turned to him and stood up straight.

"Yes, Taster?"

"Pay attention, child! Who are you talking to?" he demanded.

Amandine opened her mouth and looked to Fredderick to explain but the seat he had been occupying was now empty.

As she stared in disbelief at the empty chair, Nous cleared his throat to call her attention back. "Indulge in fanciful conversations later," he grumbled. "I need you to run to the kitchen for sundries and request a time for dinner, so that I can see the guests are seated appropriately and not kept waiting." He stressed the last three words in a way that Amandine understood to mean she should not dawdle.

"Yes, Taster," she said quickly. "On my way, Taster!"

She hurried from the foyer and through the service hall to the kitchens. When she arrived she found Kivel and Sunflower preparing plates and Chef Brutsche inspecting the roasting chickens.

"Taster Nous sent me for sundries and to ask—" she began.

"Get out!" Chef Brutsche roared without looking up from his task.

Amandine turned on her heel to leave, but Sunflower caught her arm.

"I made up a tea tray of nibbles, foal. Right there by the door. Don' ya mind Chef. He's proper cross eyed that twice the guests shown up this 'eve. Might'n be enough chicken and roast to go about."

Amandine smiled gratefully and picked up the tray. "I overheard some of the guests talking about dark fae. Boggers have been killing livestock in the East Pastures."

"Oh my," Sunflower exclaimed. "That would explain why they are all in a tizzy now, wouldn't it."

"Rubbish," Chef said, turning from the chickens. "Goblins eat bugs and fish and frogs. Nuts and mushrooms and other things that grow in the fens. They don't eat cattle. Stop listenin' to noble nonsense and get that tray ta Nous. Then, tell him ta piss off, from me."

Amandine took the tray and hurried out of the kitchen. On her way to the parlors, she examined what Sunflower had created. The tray was covered in small toasted rounds of a thin loaf of bread, meticulously sliced, each with an artful swirl of chicken liver pate and topped with seasonal berries. She imagined they would be both savory and sweet, with just a bit of tart from the berries. Sunflower excelled at creating intricate small nibbles like this. She wanted to try one, but didn't dare. Removing one from the pattern they had been laid out in would make it painfully obvious that she had taken it. Maybe if she rearranged them just a little...

Nous rounded the corner before she could, however. His moustaches were practically bristling as he spied her with the tray. She quickly held it out to him and he snatched it from her hands, unsettling the flower-like pattern of snacks and nearly spilling them.

"What took so long?" he demanded. "Did you get lost on the way to the kitchens?"

"No, sah. Chef Brutsche asked me to tell you that dinner will be ready soon and to please not disturb him while he is working."

The Taster frowned at her for a moment. "Those were his exact words?"

"They were the words he meant, sah."

"I see. At least *you* pretend to have manners. Uncouth barbarian, Chef indeed!"

Nous walked away, muttering, and Amandine returned to her corner in the parlor. She was slightly disappointed not to find Fredderick in the chair when she arrived. He was odd, she decided, but not nearly as frightening as Mister Green. She liked Dumpling.

She continued to run errands for the maids and Nous a while longer, but heard nothing else new about the goblins. Kivel appeared in the entry to the Foyer dressed in his livery and rang a small chime to announce that dinner would be served. The nobles filed out and the maids began to clean up glasses and plates. Amandine moved for the kitchens, but Kivel held out a hand to stop her.

"Chef wants you to help me serve, since you are clean and already dressed," he said.

Amandine could barely hide her disappointment. "But—" she began.

Kivel shook his head and shushed her. "Chef knows you are snooping little one, he's not stupid. Crass, a bit mean, and often foul mouthed, but never stupid. I told you he wouldn't teach you. You'll get another chance if you keep your head down and follow instructions."

She sighed and looked down at the floor. Kivel patted her head in a way that felt rather patronizing, but she knew he meant it to be affectionate. He and Sunflower *did* teach her when they could, and Chef trusted them more. Maybe he or Sunflower would learn the recipe and technique soon and she could learn it from them.

The thought brightened her a bit as she followed Kivel back to the kitchens to fetch plates of food for the guests. They served the meal in an order indicated by Taster Nous that Amandine imagined had something to do with how important each person at the table was in comparison to the others. She found it interesting that Sheriff Stolm and her wife were served before many of the nobles present.

Magistrate Everdawn had joined the party and was seated at the opposite end of the great table from Lord Estevan and Lady Gia. She was a round-faced, gray-haired woman with a warm smile and a casual air to her manners that Amandine found a touch different from the others present. She seemed to Amandine a bit like Nanny and less like her peers. Everyone deferred to her, however, in the most respectful way. If there was anyone truly in charge of the Gold Hills of Serentia, it was Lady Mariana Everdawn.

"Well then," Lady Everdawn said as the last plate was placed. "I do not want to deny anyone the pleasure of their first bites of Master Brutsche's cuisine, but we should probably get on with the business of discussing remedies for the problems in the Eastern Pastures before heads become clouded with wine and food. Lady Ophelia, would you be so kind as to detail your complaints fully to the rest of the party, in case anyone here has not heard your perspective yet?"

Amandine didn't hear all of what Lady Ophelia said as she returned to the kitchens to await the signal for the next course, but she already knew the gist of it. Chef Brutsche was rooting about in his private pantry and Sunflower was standing by the door to the garden, fanning herself with a small plate. Grendel dashed past her feet and into the kitchen to go hide under the washtub. She frowned at the cat, but didn't try to stop him.

"Sure," Sunflower grumped as they walked in and pulled up stools. "You lot get all fancy and carry plates while I were put to lug about that great co'orless thigh. Like'n ant with an apple, I was!"

"They were heavy plates," Kivel said, flapping his arms. Sunflower kicked him in the shins. "Ow," Kivel complained in mock pain.

"Yer lucky I canna kick high'r!" Sunflower declared.

The kitchen smelled like egg puffs. Amandine's mouth watered at the thought of them as she eyed the high oven. "How long until they're done?" she asked.

"When they're done, girl," Chef said as he emerged from his pantry. "Ye can't rush 'em or they fall flat. Are all the fancy lads and ladies eating their supper?"

"Yes, Chef," the three of them chorused.

"Then you swabs can have a tot wit me," Chef said, holding up a bottle. Amandine brightened. She had never gotten to try one of the Chef's cordials. "Except you, fingerling," Chef amended. "I have some berry nectar for you." Amandine wilted a little. The nectar was the base of his sweet liquor, and she liked it quite a bit if she was being honest, but she really wanted to try the finished product.

Chef handed out small crystal glasses to each of them and raised his own. "Good work, crew. In yer eye."

"In yer eye," they echoed back at him, and drank.

The Shepherd

"Olgothian cuisine is a complex and varied experience. The numerous layers of Ologthian society have many culinary traditions, often quite different from one another. When preparing a meal for Olgothian guests, a knowledge of their social backgrounds (assumed or actual) is useful in preparing dishes that will excite and satisfy. As a nexus of trade between the nations, Olgothian food of all castes often employs unique fusions with the cuisine of other peoples, many of which I find to be better than the dishes in their originating countries. When preparing such a meal for myself, however, I find that I prefer the heavily spiced stews and fish enjoyed by the lower castes as opposed to the minimalist and pure presentations preferred by the nobility."
  - Seeker's Kitchen, Chapter 6, The Many Flavors of Olgothia

AMANDINE WATCHED FROM the corner near the washtub as each puff exited the oven. Kivel stood by the hatch with a tray as Chef reached inside and used a pair of long-handled tongs to remove the ramekins. He placed the last one on the tray and gently poked at the steaming golden cap of baked egg with a gnarled finger. The entire kitchen smelled like them. Amandine breathed in deeply and let the rich smell suffuse her.

"Ayup, they're done. Take 'em to the block," Chef said. Kivel nodded and carefully moved the tray to the enormous flat butcher block.

"If ye were a hound, yer nose would be pointin'," Sunflower said to Amandine softly from her station nearby. She smirked and touched her own nose.

"They smell so good!" Amandine said, keeping her voice down. "I hope we can try one again."

"There won't be no samples tonight, crew," Chef said as he latched the oven. "Too many extra guests, some 'll have ta share as it is."

With careful steps, Kivel reached the block and set the tray down. Chef produced a small tin that Amandine knew was filled with a sweet white powder. He sprinkled some on the top of each puff and then tossed a small pinch over his shoulder.

"Let 'em cool fer three or four slow counts of fifty, then serve 'em. Add the pastry knives to the service, Sunflower. Seein' as sharin' will be needed."

Sunflower nodded and pushed her box over to the cabinet that held the bits of silver that were not kept in the dining room. Amandine moved to watch Kivel as he used a thin strip of hammered steel to separate each puff from the sides of its ramekin.

"What's that for?" she asked.

"Makes it easier to lift out if they want to split it," Kivel explained. "It's delicate, please don't distract me."

"Aye, leave the man be," Chef grumbled. "I'll have a task fer you in a mo'."

Taster Nous appeared in his doorframe, his gloved hands locked behind his back. "Chef. I require the scullery again."

"She has tasks in here. Dishes'll be comin' soon," Chef said without looking at him as he watched Kivel work.

"This relates. There is a large amount of straightening to be done in the parlors, but Maids Lily and Sundrop are still serving wine. The Magistrate requested more to drink while they deliberate. If they decide to retire to the parlors, then the rooms need to be tidy."

Chef finally turned to glare at Nous as he finished his explanation. "Amandine," he barked while his eyes locked with

Nous'. "Go help the Taster tidy his hold, since it seems his dainty hands be too broken ta lift empty wine glasses."

Nous sputtered indignantly, but Chef returned his attention to Kivel and the egg puffs. With a snarl, Nous gestured sharply for Amandine to follow and vanished from the entry. With a sigh, Amandine buttoned the neck of her livery and followed him.

His moustaches quivered as he muttered unkind things about Chef Brutsche all the way to the parlors. He paused his litany only as they passed through the dining room, where the nobles were still deep in conversation. Hushed voices and worried expressions were being passed around the table. Amandine strained to hear more about what they were saying, but only caught snippets about "boglings" and "trade impacts." She noted that the Sheriff and her wife were not seated. Perhaps they had retired early.

When they arrived at the parlors, Nous merely pointed to Hedgehog, who was clearing crystal glasses onto a small cart, and stalked away.

"Ah, Amandine, come to help gather the ones that need polishing? A tip of my hat to ya," he rumbled in his deep bass voice. "I'll keep clearing tables and look under the chairs and such if you'll reach down the ones on shelves. Check the plants too. For some reason, folk think the shrubs are there to hold empty glasses for 'em."

Amandine nodded and began scouring the room for misplaced crystal, rumpled napkins and small clay plates that still had crumbs of food. She found one of the latter being dutifully cleaned by Grendel in a corner.

"Gren, if Lily caught you doing that, she'd give you a swat!" she scolded. Grendel meowed in protest as she took the plate. With a glance over her shoulder, to be sure no one was watching, Amandine dumped the rest of the cold roast and pâté onto the floor at Grendel's feet, but kept the plate.

"Make sure you get it all, and don't say I never helped you out!" she whispered softly to the cat.

Hedgehog had been right about the shrubs. Amandine found three glasses in their branches, one still half full of wine. As she gathered them up, two people entered the parlor, talking softly to one another.

The first was Sheriff Stolm's wife, Sheeria. The other was Mister Green. Amandine almost didn't recognize him at first. His clothes were dyed in a mixture of greens and earthy reds. The strange tailoring bared his midriff and the sleeves of his shirt flared at the cuffs with long tapers that draped past the backs of his hands. The pants were loose-fitting and flared at the bottom as well, but the hems stopped well short of his ankles. He was wearing no shoes.

Amandine tried not to stare, but the outfit was so bizarre compared to his usual, finely tailored, clothing that she couldn't help herself. As she returned to the rolling cart and dropped off her dishes, Mister Green spied her looking and smiled. His not-green eyes seemed to swirl darkly as they locked onto her. He bowed slightly to Sheeria and approached.

"Miss Amandine," he said. "I see you are helping the house staff tonight. I was wondering if you had given any more thought to my offer of lessons?"

"I didn't see you with the guests tonight, sah," Amandine said, deflecting the question. She looked away at the cart of dishes to avoid his eyes.

"I was with Nanny and the children. The Taster worried that my decision to wear my people's garments would scandalize the guests. I encountered Lady Stolm walking the gardens and we have been having an interesting conversation."

Sheeria spoke. Amandine hadn't noticed her approach, she stepped so lightly. "Ugh, please, no 'Lady' nonsense. The airs Kimber and I affect living adjacent to nobility are tiring enough as it is. I am a shepherd, sah, not an aristocrat." She looked down at her feet. "Oh! Hello!"

Grendel had crossed the room and was rubbing against Sheeria's shins. His tail flicked happily.

"Pleased to meet you, La—Madam Sheeria," Amandine said with a small bow. She turned towards her so as not to seem impolite, but Mister Green's gaze still made her skin crawl.

"Just Sheeria is fine," she said as she watched Grendel weave about the hem of her dress. Her bright smile widened at the correction, and the mirth in her eyes made Amandine relax a little bit.

"Sorry," Amandine said. "I just... I don't often talk to folk... like... like you, Sheeria."

Sheeria looked back up at Amandine. "Folk pretending to be nobles or Olgothians?" she asked.

"Both, actually," Amandine said with a blush.

"Don't be embarrassed, child. It's true, there is no love lost between my homeland and Serentia, and for good reasons, on the whole. *Soeje* Arentilinanthian will teach you all about it, I'm sure, if you accept his lessons."

Amandine stood gaping for a moment and tried to mouth the multisyllabic jumble that Sheeria had delivered so effortlessly.

"Ah, the people of this house know me simply as Mister Green," he explained to her. "Elvish names are difficult for many humans. I must commend you on your pronunciation. You even included the correct inflections."

Sheeria dipped her head, "*So iya velna, mithanth.*"

"*Mithanth, cova si,*" Mister Green replied.

Amandine tried not to fidget. "I should continue helping the Butler," she said. "Please don't allow me to interrupt you."

"It was I that interrupted you, so I should apologize," Mister Green said. "But I believe that Master Hedgehog has completed his task."

Amandine looked around. The cart was gone and Hedgehog was nowhere to be seen. Her heart sank. Sheeria seemed very nice, but she wanted to be anywhere but in the same room as the elf.

"If it's not too personal to ask," Sheeria added, "I am curious about something. Where are you from, Miss Amandine? Does your family hail from Bolathvia?"

Feeling incredibly self-conscious at the attention, Amandine decided that not answering might insult Sheeria, and she didn't want to upset the Sheriff. "No, sah. I never knew my parents. I was raised in Artemis by the Night Sisters."

"Ah, yes. The adherents of Ravenex. Green eyes are not really a Bolath trait, are they? I thought perhaps you were former *indentoorad*. Many refugees from Bolath lands became ensnared by debt-holders in Olgothia, but our stories are a bit different after all," Sheeria said.

"I don't understand," Amandine said. "What does that word mean?"

"Ancient Olgath, or a very near dialect," Mister Green interjected in his lecturer's tone. "As I recall, it means 'One who is indebted', or something close to that."

"Just so," Sheeria said with a nod. "Many former *indentoorad* come to Serentia to live lives free of their old debts. I thought that... well, no matter." Sheeria's expression became distracted as if she was remembering something. Her smile never faded though, so it must have been something pleasant, Amandine decided.

Amandine sometimes wondered about her parents: who they had been, what had become of them. Perhaps they had also escaped Olgothia at some point. "If it's not too much trouble, why do you ask, sah?" she asked Sheeria.

"Oh, forgive me, child. I wasn't trying to pry. Well, perhaps a little," Sheeria replied as her attention returned to the present. "If you were *indentoorad*, I would have liked to know how you came here, or if others had been freed with you. Not many make it East of Olgath's Maw." Her smile slipped a little. "You see, I was *indentoorad*. Serentians use the word 'slave' but," she paused as if considering her words. "It's a bit different, but not by much. Kimber and her comrades freed me long ago when we were both still shy of twenty years."

"You were a slave?" Amandine asked. "But I was told that, um," she pointed to her own arm in an attempt to explain. She desperately hoped she wasn't being rude.

"That all dark skinned Olgothians are nobles? Didn't I tell you I am just a shepherd? It's all I've ever been, Akradath as my witness. Olgothia is a complicated place, Miss Amandine. The station you are born to is far more important than the color of your skin. My mother was very low caste and we were forced into *indentia* in order to survive. She simply could not afford to feed me and my brother. Worse, debt holders often abuse their control of those they hold account on and our situation was... not so luminous. Let us just say, when Kimber and her friends released my family it was the second happiest day of my life."

"What was the first?" Amandine asked.

"The day I married Kimber, of course," Sheeria said with another wide, bright smile.

As if she had been summoned, Sheriff Stolm strode into the room from the neighboring parlor. She had a weary expression on her face. "Well that situation has been handled. Thank you for bringing it to my attention, Mister Green. Now to deal with the other brats in the dining room."

Mister Green bowed from the neck, politely. "I hope you were not too harsh in judgment. He requires discipline, but also instruction."

"Only as needed. He's impossible sometimes," the Sheriff said.

"Indeed," Mister Green agreed.

When Kimber passed Sheeria, she held out her hand and Sheeria extended hers, their fingers brushed and a smile flickered across Kimber's face before her usual stern expression returned. She exited in the direction of the dining room.

"She works too hard," Sheeria said, almost to herself. "Nobles will never be pleased with what they have, no matter the nation."

"Very true, unfortunately," Mister Green said with a nod. His solid black eyes narrowed and he glanced in the direction of the dining room. "I do not care for the path their talk has taken in regards to the boglings. I can hear bits of it from here. Very troubling."

"I overheard them speaking earlier," Amandine admitted. "They say boglings have been killing your sheep, sah, so what should they do?"

"I am not sure, Miss Amandine," Sheeria said with a glance aside at Mister Green. "But whatever Kimber decides, she will have to balance her decision between what the nobles want, her duty to the Magistrate, what she can reasonably accomplish, and what is best for everyone. Kimber is always trying to please everyone, and it's simply not possible."

Mister Green frowned. "If memory serves, her path will be quite clear."

"Deep wounds heal slowest," Sheeria said, as if she were agreeing with him.

Amandine didn't really understand what they both meant, but the mood had noticeably changed, and so she held her questions.

Mister Green's head suddenly snapped away from the dining room and back to Amandine. "I also wanted to ask… I ran into a Night Sister wandering the gardens as well. I'm afraid I made her quite uncomfortable, but she did venture to ask me about you, Amandine."

"About me?" Amandine asked warily.

"You were a ward of her convent in Artemis, yes?"

"I did come from Artemis, sah."

"So do you know this Sister Corbin?"

Amandine pressed her lips together. Fiona often told her that Mister Green was adept at discerning lies. Even harmless, stupid ones. Amandine wasn't sure what she should say. How much did Mister Green know about her past?

"I see," Mister Green said after a moment of silence. "Well, I told her I had no students by that name, but I do hope that changes."

"It's a wonderful opportunity," Sheeria agreed with a nod. "I had an elven tutor as well. A lovely woman from the Court of Breaking Dawn. You cannot ask for a better teacher."

Mister Green nodded back to her politely in acknowledgment of the compliment.

"Since the task here is finished, I need to return to my duties in the kitchen, sah," Amandine said with a quick bow to both Sheeria and Mister Green. "It was very nice to meet you, Sheeria."

"And you, Miss Amandine. Please tell your Chef that I enjoyed his chicken immensely," Sheeria said.

"Next Starday, lessons will be in the garden. You are welcome to attend," Mister Green added as Amandine walked quickly away.

"Thank you, sah," Amandine called over her shoulder as she exited the room. Once she was out of sight, she let out the breath she had been holding. Talking to Sheeria had been pleasant, but Mister Green made her feel like bugs were crawling across her skin. Did Sheeria see green eyes like Sunflower? She shuddered and hurried her steps.

It appeared that Sister Corbin was still lurking as well. Amandine wasn't sure what to do about her. The canny old woman didn't miss much and obviously knew that Amandine was here, despite the things Chef and Mister Green had said. She would have to be cautious when leaving the manor.

The nobles were still talking as she passed the dining room. Sheriff Stolm stood behind Lady Everdawn's chair looking grim. Amandine gazed forlornly at the small plates and ramekins that were covered in the remains of the egg puffs.

When she entered the kitchen, she found Sunflower and Kivel sitting on stools around one of the prep tables. Chef's pantry was open and she could hear him rattling about inside. She craned her neck to try and peek, but Kivel patted a seat next to him and she sat down.

Her eyes grew wide as Sunflower slid a small plate over to her. The plain white dish held a corner of an egg puff, complete with the sweet white powder.

"Lady Ophelia sent half o' hers back because she claims sweet things do na agree with her," Sunflower said while rolling her eyes. "Better eat it up quick, foal. I had ta wrestle it from Kivel's greedy face!"

"I only had a nibble!" Kivel protested. "I intended to share!"

"Ri', sure ya was," Sunflower said with a grin.

Amandine didn't need to be asked twice. She picked up a fork and took a bite. The mix of savory and sweet danced across her tongue as she slowly ate the morsel.

"Oh gods," she said. "How does he do it?"

Mashed Potatoes and Parsnips

"The humble potato. Often derided as bland compared to its more piquant cousins, its lowly stature is due in large part to Serentian prejudices. The simple tubers grow exceedingly well in the loamy, dark soil of the Wolfshenta basin and have been a staple food to both Humans and Fae for centuries. In lands where they do not grow as well, such as Olgothia, they are considered quite the delicacy. Simple baked potatoes of the large brown-skinned variety are a feature in many noble dinners in the Maw and beyond, and at least one, rather long winded, Zulathan poem has been penned in their honor. Love them or loathe them, potatoes are a must for any well-stocked kitchen."
*   - Seeker's Kitchen, Chapter 3, Essential Ingredients*

AMANDINE ENJOYED WORKING for Miss Jacinda in the soup kitchen. Everyone liked her, common or noble, and even Chef Brutsche seemed to have a grudging respect for the cheesemaker. She was married to the innkeeper, Bertrand Kale, and Amandine had first met her when she had been staying with the couple upon arriving in Stoneman.

Miss Jacinda was ephemeral and beautiful. She had the dark ebon-wood skin of her Olgothian father, mixed with the long-limbed grace, flowing hair, and slightly pointed ears of her fae, elven mother. Most folk behaved as though she were the unofficial queen of Stoneman. It was rumored that even Lady Everdawn sometimes sought her council on civil matters. Not that Amandine paid much attention to politics. To her it seemed mostly like old boring people trying to impress other old boring people with how much money they had.

With her hands clasped behind her back to stop from fidgeting, Amandine waited while Miss Jacinda sniffed at the bowl of mashed potatoes and parsnips that she had prepared.

"Oh my, that's delicious, Amandine!" Miss Jacinda exclaimed after trying a spoonful. "Well done!"

"Thank you!" Amandine said, her cheeks flushed, both with the heat of the tiny kitchen and pride at the compliment.

"Ish rewy gud!" Gil added, his mouth full of mash. Amandine swatted his hand with a stirring spoon. He yelped.

"You are supposed to be helping, not eating!" she scolded him.

"Sawy," he said around another spoonful.

Miss Jacinda laughed. "It's all cream, loves. We have plenty of the roots to cook, so eat as much as you like. If you are done with this pot, Amandine, go ahead and start a second and I'll begin serving."

"I will!" Amandine chirped happily as Jacinda took the pot with her to the dining room. She narrowed her eyes at Gil and his bowl. "Be helpful!"

"I am helping!" Gil protested. "I am making sure it tastes right."

Amandine slapped his hand with the spoon again.

"Ow, ok! I'll strip the herbs for the next pot!"

Amandine nodded in satisfaction and began pulling potatoes out of a nearby sack and slicing them for boiling. She liked working with the knives in Miss Jacinda's kitchen. Other than peeling vegetables, she wasn't really allowed to do knife work at Manor L'Eau, but Sunflower had taught her a few things and she watched Chef Brutsche very carefully. She wasn't as fast as either of them, but she worked methodically to make sure all her cuts were even.

"Why are you being so careful?" Gil asked as he stripped sweetbrush leaves from their stems and put them in a bowl. "Can't you just cook 'em whole?"

"Sure," Amandine replied. "But they are all different sizes. If you cut them closer to the same size, then they cook more evenly and it makes the mash less lumpy."

"Ah. Chef Bugbear teach you that?"

"Cook Kivel did."

"I like him."

"Me too."

"He's a decent sort, for sure," a third voice said.

Amandine and Gil both jumped and looked up. Fredderick was leaning against the wall of the tiny kitchen, holding Gil's bowl of mash. He tasted a spoonful and made an approving noise. "This is really good."

"What are *you* doing here?" Amandine demanded at the same time Gil asked, "Who in the Pit are you?"

"He works for one of the noble families," Amandine said quickly over her shoulder. She turned back to Fredderick. "Where is Dumpling?"

"Playing with the children in the dining hall," Fredderick said before taking another bite.

"Dumpling?" Gil asked.

"His dog," Amandine said. "Stop interrupting!"

"But how did he even get in here?" Gil asked in an exasperated tone. "The curtain never moved!"

Amandine paused. His odd comings and goings might be magic, she supposed. But Gil didn't know that and she wasn't sure she should say anything. Fredderick saved her the trouble. With a twirl of his spoon, his entire body and the clothing he wore took on the appearance of the wall behind him, then a second later even the outline of him vanished. Only the bowl, still suspended in mid-air, revealed his location.

"By the gods!" Gil exclaimed. "How did he—"

Amandine turned and slapped a hand over his mouth and shushed him. A moment later Miss Jacinda poked her head through the curtain, looking concerned. "Is everything alright?" she asked.

"We're fine, sah. Gilly just spilled some herbs," Amandine said quickly. Jacinda pursed her lips and shook her head and ducked back out again.

Amandine waited for her footsteps to be absorbed by the sound of people talking in the dining room before she removed her hand from Gil's mouth and turned back to the floating bowl.

"As I was saying, what are you doing here, Fredderick?"

He reappeared in a ripple of light and Gil gasped again. Amandine shot him a look and he clamped his jaw shut.

"You told me you came here on Third," Fredderick said with a shrug. "I wanted to continue our conversation about your employer."

"Chef Brutsche? What about him?"

"You had mentioned that you watch him work. I am really interested in his technique. This is one of his recipes, right?" Fredderick asked as he took another bite of mash. "Gods, this really is good."

"Sort of. Cook Kivel taught me, and I had to modify it to use the parsnips that Miss Jacinda acquired for the soup kitchen, but the herbs are mostly the same."

Fredderick looked slightly surprised. "You... modified it?"

"Yes. Parsnips have a sharper flavor than turnips, so I had to add more sweetbrush and goldleaf. I also added some of Miss Jacinda's sweet cream." Amandine began chopping potatoes again as she spoke, but kept an eye on Fredderick in case he disappeared again.

"I'm impressed," Fredderick said as he looked down at the bowl of mash. "You have a talent of your own I think."

"Thanks," Amandine said. She smiled in spite of the heat in her cheeks at the unexpected compliment. "But I still have a lot to learn."

"Like how he makes the egg puffs," Gil interjected. "Amandine can cook anything she's seen made at least once, but he won't show anyone how to do it."

"Ah yes, Chef Brutsche's signature dish. I understand that it's something of a rave around here, and I never quite understood why," Fredderick said.

"Oh, why is that?" Amandine asked. "They are amazing!"

"That's just it. Perhaps here they are novel, but in bigger cities like Artemis and Irongate the technique for making them is well known. I have had them on many occasions. Sweet, savory, spicy, even."

Gil's eyes were wide. "You've been to Irongate? And Artemis?"

"Hey, I was born in Artemis," Amandine said. "It's not as special as it sounds."

"Yes, well," Fredderick said, returning to his point, "I finally had a chance to sample one of his puffs last night and it was incomparable. It's not just a good example of the craft, it is possibly the best example of it I have ever tasted, and I would really like to know why."

"Because he's a genius," Amandine said stoutly. "Everyone says he's a mean old grumpus, and sometimes he acts that way, but I think that's because they don't understand him."

"And you do?" Fredderick asked.

"I... think I do," Amandine said, suddenly feeling self-conscious. "He loves what he does more than anything in the world, and when you love doing something that much, you protect it, right? So when people judge or act haughty, you snap at them. I think he's just gotten in the habit of snapping at everyone, just to be safe."

"Like those horned turtles we catch in the shallows," Gil said with a laugh. "Snap! Snap!" He mimed a turtle beak with his hands.

Amandine rolled her eyes at him, but didn't correct him. He would be mortified if she revealed that the turtles she had caught had been made into soup.

"I see," Fredderick said. He rubbed the side of his cheek with the spoon, deep in thought. "That might also explain his fortress of a pantry, yes? A great Chef must have special ingredients to be held close and kept secret."

"Oh, yes! Exactly! I *really* want to know what he keeps in there, but the lock is dwarf-made and he never lets anyone in, not even Kivel and Sunflower!"

Fredderick took on a smug expression and leaned forward slightly. "I had a peek. Last evening."

"How did—" Gil began and then it dawned on him. "Oh, right! That thing you can do. How do—"

Amandine cut him off. "What was inside?" she asked eagerly.

"Lots of tins and jars without labels. I didn't recognize any of it, but there were also these," Fredderick said. He put the spoon in his mouth and fished around in a pocket of his coat. He removed something and set it on the edge of the block where Amandine was chopping. It was black and lumpy, only a few inches across.

Gil wrinkled his nose. "Ew, it looks like a turd."

Amandine tentatively reached out to touch it. It didn't smell. The outside was dry and slightly soft. "What is it?"

"I am not really sure," Fredderick admitted. "It's a plant or maybe a mushroom... I think. He had several of them tucked into a tray of salt under a cheesecloth."

Fascinated, Amandine picked up the lump and sniffed it. It had a dry earthy smell, but wasn't as stinky or terrible as it looked. She tentatively touched the tip of her tongue to it.

"Oh gross!" Gil said with a grimace. "You don't even know what it is!"

"If he cooks with them they shouldn't be poisonous," Amandine said defensively.

"I wouldn't be so sure," Fredderick said. "I have heard of things that are poison until cooked properly, like pufferfish."

"What's a pufferfish?" Amandine asked.

"Oh, I know! Wizzlecog had one!" Gil said, "It was stuffed and mounted. It looked like a ball with spines and fish fins."

"Who is Wizzlecog?" Fredderick asked.

"The Stone Folk proprietor of the general store near the Stomping Golem Inn," Gil said. "He's odd, but his shop has lots of interesting things inside."

Amandine shook her head. "Pufferfish sound weird. Anyway, I'm not dead, but it doesn't taste like much either. He must do something to them when he cooks."

"Without a doubt," Fredderick agreed. "Wouldn't you like to know more?"

"So why exactly do you care?" Gil asked Fredderick with narrowed eyes.

"I like good food," Fredderick said as he took another bite of the mash.

"But snooping around Manor L'Eau doesn't seem right!" Gil protested.

The boys began to argue, but Amandine barely heard them. She peered closely at the strange lump and thought furiously. Maybe someone else in Stoneman knew what it was? Chef had to procure them from somewhere, but it didn't look like anything she had ever seen in the market square. She set it on her cutting board and tried slicing it. It was firm, but cut cleanly in half without any sawing. The inside was slightly spongy and filled with vein-like patterns of a lighter color than the more dense outside skin. She smelled it again and an aroma like toasted nuts and garlic and musty earth filled her nose. There was something else there too, something familiar…

"Amandine, have you begun the next pot of mash, dear? This one is running out," Miss Jacinda called from the dining area.

She scooped up the halves of the lump and stuffed them in her coat pocket. "Oh stop it, you two," she said to Gil and Fredderick, who were still arguing. "Gil, we have work to do. Fredderick, thank you for the information, but I agree with Gil. Stealing from Chef is wrong. Please don't do it again."

Fredderick shrugged. "Suit yourself, but it's a keen mystery, is it not?"

"I like my job at Manor L'Eau, and I owe it to Chef Brutsche. Sure I want to know more, but I will find out myself."

"He obviously isn't going to tell you anything. He's the only Chef I have ever seen without at least one apprentice. How many years will you wait? Until you are as old as Kivel and that halfling woman and still don't know anything?"

"Hill Folk!" Gil said. "Only witless trolls call them halflings! Get out!"

Fredderick raised an eyebrow but said no more. He set the empty bowl on the table and promptly vanished.

Amandine gently patted Gil on the shoulder. He was still fuming at the "halfling" remark. Master Hawthorne, the baker, was nearly family to him. He was also Hill Folk, like Sunflower and Hedgehog and others that Amandine worked with, so she understood.

She also understood that people were sometimes mean without intending to be. Fredderick didn't strike her as malicious. A thief certainly, but Amandine had known those who needed to steal to survive, back in Artemis. While she disliked stealing on principle, she didn't want to judge. She wondered which noble family he was bound to. He never had fully explained who he worked for the other day.

"You know what the worst part is, Amy?" Gil asked.

"What's that, Gilly?"

"The bastard ate my mash."

Half a Horse

"Dwarves are fascinating people. They are sometimes mistaken for fae, but are not actually related to the Fae Courts or any other branch of that lineage. Their clans and family lines stretch back to the age of the First Peoples of Beregoth, the Giants, whom they served, and which warrants a series of lectures all their own. They are carnivorous and subterranean, but after the Arrival developed a taste for beer and spirits distilled from grain, and have mastered those crafts. Their unusual eyes allow them to see, after a fashion, even in the complete absence of light. They have short, sturdy builds and copious hair that aid them in surviving in the cold depths beneath the earth, where they have constructed grand cities carved from living stone. The Seven Hammers clan is allied with Serentia, and their capital, Anvilroot, lies at the headwaters of the mighty Wolfshenta river, which flows through that nation."

- Lecture notes, First Starday, Low Autumn 1201

AMANDINE AND GIL were crossing the market circle in Stoneman. It was the shortest route from Miss Jacinda's soup kitchen to the North Gate and the road that led to Manor L'Eau. The concentric circles of stalls were one of the busiest parts of Stoneman and Amandine liked to watch the merchants and their customers. The energy of the market was subdued today, however. The usual locals had their stalls open, but the bazaar-like atmosphere that ruled when the ships were in was absent. Customers flitted from stand to stand like bees in a field, their baskets full of Low Summer vegetables, fresh baked bread, and other items produced in and around the Gold Hills and Fording Towns.

"On Riverday, Sunflower said that the barges were upriver this tenday," Amandine said.

"Yeah, all the goods up from Irongate. Stuff the coast-runners bring from The Dutchy and 'round South from Tren," Gil said as he munched on an apple.

"So the barges will come downriver next? From Anvilroot?"

"Yeah. With a tenday in between, more or less. I think Master Hawthorne is expecting something from that direction, actually. He's been asking me to check with the dockmen on Stardays. To see when the next barges are expected."

"Oh, what is it he's expecting?"

"Beer and goldmash probably."

"Master Hawthorne drinks a lot?"

"Naw, he keeps a small flask of 'mash around and his wife, Madam Sparrow, you know, the weaver? She really likes honey wine, but Old Gert makes that near the Hamlet. The beer is used in some of his breads. The really dense ones that he bakes for High Summer Pinnacle and Winter Night. Dwarves make the best beer, it's said."

"Aha," Amandine said as she nodded. The thick, rectangular loaves were wonderful for soaking up gravy and stew. Chef bought them for feast days as well.

"That old lady was back in the hamlet again this morning. Talking to Old Gert, and to Madam Sparrow. I'm pretty sure she really is looking for you, Amy. Who is she?" Gil asked around a mouthful of apple.

"She's Sister Corbin, from the convent in I lived in before I came here," Amandine said. "I don't know how she found me so far away from Artemis, but I need to avoid her, Gil. I do *not* want to go back with her!"

"Was it really that bad there?"

"Yes. Promise me, Gilly. Promise you will not help her!"

Gil frowned. "Hells, Amy, I wouldn't help that old bat even without swearing. I don't want you to leave!"

"Thanks, Gil. And I'm sorry. I trust you, but I feel like I have been looking over my shoulder all day. Imagining running into her here in Stoneman. I hate it."

Ahead, near the raised stage sometimes used for announcements and auctions, a crowd had gathered. The mood of the gathering seemed off to Amandine. Voices were low and tense. Worried expressions were shared between the members of the throng as the semi-circle of townsfolk hovered around whatever had drawn them there to begin with.

Gil had noticed too. "I wonder what all that's about," he wondered aloud.

Had she still been in Artemis, Amandine's instinct would have been to avoid such a gathering. They rarely meant anything good, and for a small person on the streets of a big city, avoiding trouble was paramount. But here, in Stoneman, it was unusual. More than unusual. She decided that she really wanted to know what they were looking at.

"Let's look," Amandine said as she veered to join the crowd.

Gil nodded and stuck the apple in his mouth as he joined Amandine in ducking between the humans and Hill Folk to get a better vantage.

When they reached the center, Gil made a choking noise, hurriedly removed the apple from his mouth, and looked away.

The carcass of a horse, partly covered by a sheet of burlap, lay atop a small grain cart; the flat kind with no sides. The tiny cart would not have held a full-sized horse, but the remains all fit because, by Amandine's estimation, most of this horse was absent.

The head, which peeked out from the cloth with a horrible death-rictus frozen on its face, was still attached to part of one shoulder and leg. The middle of the animal was completely missing and only part of a back leg, which included a hoof, remained of its hindquarters.

"Old Jack's Luck," Gil swore. His face was a mixture of shock and horror. "What happened to the poor thing?"

Amandine shrugged and crouched down to have a closer look.

"Something ate part of it," she said.

Gil opened his mouth to reply, then shut it again and looked green. He eyed Amandine sideways as she considered the dead animal thoughtfully.

"It really doesn't bother you? Seeing the poor beast like this?" he asked.

Amandine shook her head. "I'm more curious than bothered. I used to help the Night Sisters with dead people all the time. Sometimes folk who had been done for by violence. I feel sorry for the horse, sure, but it's only a body, Gilly."

Gil liked horses, and Amandine felt for him. He remained silent as she continued to examine the carcass. Something about the remains was odd, but she couldn't put her finger on it.

A human man near the cart, the beast's owner perhaps, was gesturing wildly with his hands to a town guard as he spoke in a high-pitched, strained voice.

"I was riding from the Le'Grange jus' after dawn and stopped to let my horse graze. It weren't night I tell ye! I went down the crick a bit to drop a string for a fish and found my ol' girl in this state when I returned! Ground was all churned up like there'd been a fight. I ran for the nearest 'stead and borrowed a cart. The farmers there say their milk cow were also taken like this! The guards got to do somethin'!"

"I hear you, sah, but why are you hauling this mess through the market? How did you even get it past the North Gate? Akradath's light, you can't drag this through town!" the guard said. Amandine got the impression that he was repeating himself by this point, but the man with the dead horse was not coop-erating.

"It were the dark fae!" a voice from the crowd shouted. "The roads near the fens ain't safe!"

"The Halifax trains have no' been set 'pon. The dark will away with the careless!"

"Boglings did it!"

"Mayhap it's a Grim!"

"Send the town guard into the swamp!"

"Goblins stole my socks! Right off the line!"

"Pull the other one!"

The guard raised his arms and tried to quell the crowd, but the scene was starting to become rowdy.

Amandine hardly noticed as she examined the gruesome head. There was a pungent smell, but not like rot. It reminded her of the embalming oils the Night Sisters would use to stop rot, in fact.

"There are no flies," she said quietly.

Gil swallowed and took a closer look. "Yeah, that's weird," he agreed.

"Make way!" a commanding voice bellowed from behind the crowd. "Come now, sahs, let's have some order if you please!"

The group parted and made room for three newcomers. Amandine recognized all of them. The first was Rivaldo Stolm, the captain of the town militia. He shared many similarities with his elder sister, the Sheriff, in hair, skin, eye, and profile, but his manner always seemed more relaxed to Amandine, as if nothing was ever quite as serious as it should be. He wore a dark blue cape over his brightly polished chainmail and held his helmet under one arm. His eyes fell on the dead horse and his expression became slightly less cavalier as he ran a hand through his wind-blown hair.

To his left was Xia Xian, his Sergent-at-Arms. She was human, but short, even for a woman, with the tightly curled hair, dark eyes, and yellow-brown complexion common to Zulathians. She kept her hair cut close, like Amandine's, and wore her chainmail armor with no sleeves and no skirt, just leather leggings with boiled plates sewn on. Her eyes barely registered the dead animal and instead tracked the crowd milling about as the fingers of her left hand drummed the hilt of her curved sword.

The third newcomer was the only full-time dwarf resident of Stoneman, Boomer McKragen, the town's stonemason and engine-eer. He had a wild mane of red-brown hair that seemed to meld with a full, braided beard that dropped nearly to his knees. He was only a bit taller than Amandine, however, which made the facial hair seem extravagant. He was dressed in his smock and heavy leather gloves, as if he had come directly from his workshop, and a pair of dark, green-tinted goggles covered his eyes. Dwarven eyes were very sensitive to sunlight.

"Well that's a mess," Boomer observed. His accent was thick and his voice gravelly. "Can na' well ride it without the middle part."

Rivaldo frowned at the jape, but said nothing and stepped aside to speak quietly with the distraught owner of the horse.

Xia continued to scan the crowd, who eyed her warily and likewise became more subdued.

Boomer grunted and knelt closer to the head of the dead horse and flicked the green lenses up on hinges to look at it with his gaze unimpeded.

His eyes were bizarre to Amandine. The iris of each was elongated and sideways, almost like a goat's, but as a pair of ovals, with the smaller ones being closer to his wide, bumpy nose. The sunlight made him squint, and his brow furrowed as he studied the carcass. He noticed Amandine crouched across from him, and nodded at her.

"Auch, I know ye. Yer the whelp that Old Brute hired as his scop, ri'?" he asked. When he spoke, two rows of shark-like teeth were revealed, pearly white and serrated.

"Yes, sah. Amandine, sah." she replied, while trying not to stare at the dwarf's strange eyes and teeth.

"Solid stone, Brute. Fer a human."

"I think so too, sah."

"Then yer in the smaller fragment, fer sure."

"Do you think boglings killed the horse, Master McKragen?" Amandine asked. "I heard at the manor that they have been killing cattle in the East Pastures too. And stealing grain."

Boomer squinted at her. "Beetle on the ceiling during noble talk, eh? I imagine you hear all sorts o' stuff from them with the floppy hats."

He looked back down at the horse and poked it with a finger. "Ye think if boglin's had a hankerin' for horsemeat, they'd take the whole blasted thing, ri'? Never heard of them baking bread either. But who's to say? Strange, muck-covered wumpuses those boglings are. Never did like 'em."

Rivaldo turned from the man he was interrogating and addressed the crowd at large.

"Please move along. No crime has been committed here except poor judgment. I'm sure the Magistrate and the Sheriff will consider this incident as they decide what to do about whatever has been killing livestock. Do not travel alone in the dark. Do not leave animals unattended. That is all."

The crowd began to disperse, but Amandine could still hear the muttering. The mutilated horse had shaken many of them. She stood to leave as well, but Boomer reached out and poked her arm. His hand, even gloved, was rigid and strong. It was like being prodded with a stick.

"If you wan' to learn about the fae, you should probably jus' ask that elf you got livin' in Lord Estevan's big house. The Starlight Court *gyre* that likes to wear human clothes."

"Mr. Green?" Amandine asked.

"Yea, that's the leaf-lover. Like a book with legs. Ask him."

Amandine swallowed. She had managed to mostly avoid Mr. Green since the dinner party, but it felt rude to say so out loud.

"I will, thank you, sah," she said instead.

Boomer stood and ambled away in the wake of Captain Rivaldo and Xia while muttering to himself. "Bloody waste of good horsemeat. Daft boglings…"

Gil looked at his apple, grimaced and tossed it in a gutter. "Let's go get my horse from the Stomping Golem, Amy. I want to get home before dark."

"I'm sure Crust is fine, Gilly. Nothing has been attacked inside the walls, right?"

A guardsman walked by them and took up the hand cart. He lifted the handles and the leg with the hoof slid off the back and tumbled into the street.

"But yes, let's get home before dark," Amandine agreed.

Butterflies

"Sundrop for light, stardrop for mercy, placed atop the altar firstly.
Next is grain for harvest 'morrow and then a darkbloom, full of sorrow.
Scatter knots and golden feet, a laurel green for life so sweet.
Ginnyweld to calm the seas, and glorydram for war to cease.
Leave Ol' Jack not twig nor leaf, or luck will pull you underneath."
*   - Children's Godhome Rhyme, Author Unknown*

AMANDINE WAS ONCE again crouched inside the large iron cauldron. Chef's forbearance on the task had reached an end, and she was struggling to catch up. She scrubbed at the char on the bottom of the bowl with a will. The decrepit hunk of iron was like an old adversary, and she was not going to let it win this time.

Grendel sat nearby cleaning his paws as the cauldron rocked. The kitchen was otherwise unoccupied. It would be bells yet until dinner prep began, and the Lord and Lady had opted for a cold luncheon, so Chef had taken his horse and cart to the Hamlet. Sunflower was tending the vegetable garden, and Kivel, well, Amandine wasn't exactly sure where he was, but she imagined it involved hiding from Nous and taking a nap.

She tried not to think about the strange mushroom-thing that Fredderick had given her. Upon returning back to Manor L'Eau, her first instinct had been to ask Sunflower or Kivel about it, but then she didn't want them to think she had taken it. Amandine desperately wanted to know what it was, but she wasn't going to get answers in the manor, so she scrubbed the cauldron to keep her hands and mind busy and off other subjects.

"Colorless old scrap!" Amandine swore as her brush slipped and she jarred her elbow. A numb, tingly sensation shot up her arm. She didn't often swear. A fierce mouth, in her experience, was often more trouble than it was worth. Sometimes, though, a thing just had to be said. She retreated from the cauldron and rubbed her elbow.

"Dark take you! You battered, stupid…"

"Milintanth's heart, do you often inflict such language on the cookware?"

Amandine cringed as she turned to face Nanny, who was standing in Taster Nous' doorway.

"Luminous day, sah," she said with a small bow. Her cheeks burned like fire from embarrassment. "Chef isn't in, sah."

"It's well, then, that I ain't lookin' for him," Nanny said as she crossed the boundary into the kitchen. "I were seekin' you out, actually."

"Me, sah? What do you need me for?"

"I would like some young hands to help me in the walkin' gardens. I was goin' to cut some fresh flowers and herbs for the shrine, but these old fingers don't work the shears as smooth as they used to. Will you help me, Amandine?"

Nanny's wizened face smiled warmly at her. If she was being honest with herself, an excuse to shirk the cauldron sounded wonderful.

"I'll help!" Amandine said quickly. "Come on, Grendel!"

She and Grendel trailed Nanny through the manor to the doors that led to the garden terrace.

"What are you going to cut, sah?" Amandine asked.

"A few and a few," Nanny said as she undid the latches. "White stardrop for Milintanth, sundrop for her husband, Akradath. A fresh sheaf o' wheat grass for Delinkhal after that, and a shadow bonnet for Ravenex. Then perhaps we'll see if the lover's knots have bloomed for Kayla, yes? Or a dancer's foot for Leonid?"

"I would like that," Amandine said. She didn't often visit the manor's shrine, she preferred the Shrine of the Revered in Stoneman. Using the family's private altar felt intrusive. Still, helping Nanny sounded far more interesting than her continued struggle with the old cauldron.

They slowly toured the gardens, walking between the high hedges and along stone footpaths through the flowers. It was laid out in rings, with the outermost bands planted with shady trees, and the inner rings carved into broken circles of flowerbeds and tall shrubbery. Amandine had explored it before, but on her own or with Grendel. When she first arrived here, in the Low Autumn of the previous year, the flowers had not been in bloom. Now, the pathways were a riot of colors, every hue a person could imagine, and then some.

Nanny would stop when she spied a flower or herb she wanted and Amandine would use a small pair of steel shears to snip off a bud or a leaf. She learned the names of every flower and bush they passed. Many of the plants were the same as those she had seen in and around Artemis, but what people called them here was different. The fragrant weed Nanny called spriteleaf was known as elf-mint, for instance.

Amandine stroked the bright green leaves of the plant. "The Night Sisters use this. To cover up the smell of dead bodies."

Grendel sniffed at the herb that she was touching. He sneezed and shook his head in irritation.

"Oh? I imagine that works well," Nanny said thoughtfully as she indicated that Amandine should snip some for the basket. "It's also good for tea."

"Oh, gross!" Amandine said in disgust. The idea of drinking it made her tongue curl up. Grendel meowed as if in agreement.

Nanny smiled and shook her head at the outburst, but said nothing as she tucked the herbs away.

They turned a corner and Amandine's breath caught. Standing in the middle of the path was Sister Corbin. She was still in the same gray robes and cloak Amandine had seen her in when she spoke to Chef, but her hair was done differently; gathered into a high tail that draped over her shoulder. The white stripe reminded Amandine of a badger.

She smiled broadly and Amandine frantically cast about for someplace to hide but ultimately settled for stepping backwards behind Nanny.

"Amandine! I have been looking all over for you. Quite literally," Sister Corbin said. "I missed your little outing to Stoneman, I'm afraid, but I am pleased to see you are actually here."

"Luminous day to you, Sister," Nanny said with a warm smile. "I take it you know Amandine, then?"

"Sister," Corbin replied coolly by way of acknowledgement. She immediately turned her gaze back to Amandine without answering Nanny's question. "Gather your things, child. We have a long trip back to Artemis."

"I'm not going!" Amandine said, her temper flaring. "You can't make me!"

Sister Corbin took a step forward, Amandine took a step backwards. Grendel hissed and arched his back, and then, to Amandine's surprise, Nanny stepped between them.

"She is a ward of the house, sah," Nanny said, still smiling. "Surely it is the cause of those who oversee the Convents to ensure their wards are sent to families that will care for them?"

Sister Corbin paused, as if evaluating the elderly woman across from her. "Families," she said in an all too familiar corrective monotone. "Families that lack for children or have the means to care for more. Here she is a servant. Who is seeing to her care? Her education? That tree stump in an apron? The cursed fae wizard? You?" She spoke the last word with a level of scorn that stung Amandine even though the jibe hadn't been directed at her.

Nanny continued to smile as if it had not been an insult. "All of us, I think, and some others for measure. She is cared for, Sister."

"A ward of the house then, is it?" Sister Corbin said through pursed lips. "I had hoped to speak with the Lord and Lady here on that matter, but the Lord is away, and the Lady will not discuss it with me unless both of them are present. It seems for now, I must abide. But she will be coming home to Artemis. This entire adventure of hers has been nonsense."

"It's not nonsense!" Amandine blurted. "I have friends here! I'm learning to cook! I am going to be a chef! I don't want to be a Night Sister!"

"A chef," Sister Corbin said as if the words amused her. "You are so much better than that, Amandine."

"I'd say we have a rather unconventional Chef, Sister. You should sample his fare." Nanny said.

"And is he teaching her then? Has she been made an apprentice?" Sister Corbin shot back.

Neither Amandine or Nanny answered. She wasn't his apprentice, he wasn't teaching her. Nanny had stopped smiling.

"I see. Well, she was already apprenticed to me as a Bone Guardian. An honorable profession dedicated to the gods. Instead she has run halfway across Serentia to play at being a cook. Unacceptable. She has sworn obligations to our order."

Amandine was so angry that her teeth hurt from clenching them. Her hands were balled into fists. She didn't dare say anything, lest her mouth land her into even more trouble than she already was.

"Well, until you have spoken with the Lord and Lady, I will vouch for her. Or will you also deny me even that courtesy, Sister?" Nanny said with an uncharacteristic edge to her voice.

Sister Corbin grimaced and looked away. Amandine thought for a moment that the reaction might be a sign of shame, but her face quickly schooled itself back into its usual scowl.

"Very well, healer. As the goddess dictates. But I will have my say before the Lord and Lady. We will speak again, Amandine."

Sister Corbin turned and strode away. Amandine let out a breath. She looked up and saw that Nanny was still watching Sister Corbin's retreating back, thoughtfully.

She looked down at Amandine and blinked. "Unpleasant woman," she grumbled. "I'll bet she was a strict teacher, eh?"

Amandine nodded.

"Well that means you probably learned something, in spite of her character flaws," Nanny said with a grin. "Come along now, there are still herbs and flowers to gather."

As they approached the middle of the concentric hedges, Amandine heard people talking, hidden behind the foliage. She recognized Marlette's voice and then Fiona's.

"The children are in the garden today, sah. I don't want to trouble them," she said.

"We won't be troublin' nobody," Nanny said with a chuckle. "Come 'long, now."

Grendel ran ahead of them at the sound of Fiona's laughter and disappeared around the edge of a particularly large heartleaf shrub.

Amandine turned the corner after him and froze in her tracks. In the center of the circle of hedges, seated on a stone bench, were Lady Gia and her daughters. Lady Gia was a tall, thin, pale woman with freckles across her nose. Her long brown hair was of a shade that reminded Amandine of the color of tea with milk in it. She was wearing a white dress with blue frills that left her arms and freckled shoulders bare. Marlette and Fiona were sitting to either side of her, in similar dresses dyed yellow and sky blue, respectively. Grendel had found Fiona's lap and was curled up contentedly. All of them were watching Mister Green.

His sleeves were rolled up and his arms were outstretched. A gentle breeze swirled his pale silver hair. His hands rotated slowly at the wrists, and surrounding each of them, like a tiny storm of flower petals, were dozens of colorful butterflies.

"It's Starday," Amandine whispered. First Corbin and now this? It was like the gods were out to get her.

"So it is," Nanny agreed. "Why are you whispering?"

Mister Green turned his head and smiled. The expression never seemed to fully reach his swirling eyes.

"Just in time for the nature lesson, Miss Amandine. I'm pleased you decided to join us."

"I didn't, I was—" Amandine began.

Nanny deftly plucked the shears from her hand and reached up to snip a lover's knot from the heartleaf shrub. She tucked it into Amandine's hair above her ear and then gently nudged her towards the group. With a nod and a wink, Nanny turned and left, with more than a little spring in her step.

"Sneaky old badger," Amandine muttered with a scowl. This had probably been Nanny's plan even before they stumbled into Sister Corbin.

"Come closer, Amandine," Mister Green said as he beckoned with one of the hands that swirled with butterflies.

Amandine hesitated. Why were the butterflies doing that? It had to be magic. "I—"

"Oh, please!" Fiona exclaimed. "Come and see! It's beautiful!"

Lady Gia raised an eyebrow at her, but smiled and nodded. She made several gestures with her hands towards Amandine. The hand motions had meaning. Lady Gia was deaf and mute and used them to speak, but Amandine didn't understand any of it.

Marlette rescued her a moment later: "Mother says you should come and enjoy the sun with us."

Amandine felt trapped. She absolutely couldn't refuse a request from Lady Gia without offering insult to House L'Eau, and she didn't want to risk running into Sister Corbin alone, so she swallowed her nerves and stepped forward.

She took a seat on the smooth marble next to Fiona. Grendel stretched, hopped over to Amandine's lap and curled up again.

Fiona giggled. "He likes you!"

Amandine scratched Grendel behind the ears. "Yes, I suppose he does."

"So, as I was saying," Mister Green intoned in the voice he used while lecturing. "These tiny, colorful creatures are key to the proliferation of many plants. Any plant that flowers, from lowly weeds to towering *kusevra* trees, like those that my kin to the North build their dwellings upon, benefits from their attention. Each variety has a preference, in fact."

Mister Green turned a wrist and a small yellow butterfly arced away from the pack and landed on the hem of Marlette's yellow dress.

"This one feeds almost exclusively on itch thistle," he said with a graceful gesture.

Another butterfly, white with brown spots, tumbled away and lit upon Lady Gia's forehead like a diadem.

"And that one subsists on the nectar from stardrops and funnel-weed," Mister Green continued. Lady Gia gasped and clasped her hands together as she tried to look up at the butterfly.

A third with emerald green and black wings flew away next and landed on Fiona's neckline.

"In my homeland this one does not exist. It's far too cold. The Court of Breaking Dawn calls them *orestra*, and they feed upon the sap of the great pines. I imagine this one is from the small stand that is East of the manor."

"It's gorgeous," Fiona breathed.

"It's a sacred animal in that Court. It's said that—where are you going?" Mister Green interrupted himself as a small black-winged butterfly broke away and flew to Amandine and then settled atop the flower in her hair.

"Ah, yes," Mister Green said. "That one enjoys the nectar of lover's knots. It seems you brought her favorite meal with you, Miss Amandine. Most considerate."

"Do you use magic to control them?" Amandine asked as she tentatively reached for her hair.

Mister Green's reflective black eyes narrowed slightly. "Just a bare touch, like a breeze that makes a candle flame dance. But not that one. She flew to you of her own volition. It's unkind to hold them here any longer when they should be doing what butterflies normally do. Off with you all now!"

He made a gentle shooing motion with his hands and the small flurry of butterflies dissipated back into the garden, including those that had landed on Lady Gia and her children. The small dark one on Amandine remained, however.

"Interesting," Mister Green murmured while regarding her. Before Amandine could ask what he meant, he launched into another topic.

"I'm glad you're here," Fiona whispered to her. "Marlette is always shushing me."

"But that's because we should be listening to your teacher, right?" Amandine whispered back.

"I do listen!" Fiona protested. "I do, but sometimes, I just want to—"

"Shhhh!" Marlette hissed.

Fiona rolled her eyes and looked at Amandine as if to say "See?", and then returned her attention to Mister Green's lecture on trees.

No more magic was employed, for which Amandine was grateful, and the subject was actually rather interesting. Amandine had never given much thought to trees, one was mostly like any other. Mister Green's explanations of what different leaf shapes meant, and how their roots worked were equally fascinating. There was one fact in particular, however, that made Amandine sit up and take notice.

"Cinnamon is tree bark?" Amandine asked, incredulously.

"Indeed," Mister Green said with a nod. "It is not native to Beregoth either, but rather it's believed that it came across the seas with the Ancient Humans during the Arrival. It grows quite well in the jungles and forested areas of the West, in Trenash and Zulath lands, although I do believe some are cultivated by my kin to the North."

"I really like cinnamon on toast," Fiona said.

"It is, I'll admit, one of the better things that humans brought to this land," Mister Green agreed.

Lady Gia made a series of rapid hand motions and Mister Green nodded to her. "Indeed, Lady, I will cover the Arrival, to the best of my knowledge in later lessons. Although my expertise is not really in that part of history, I do know some."

"Excuse me? Lady Gia?"

Everyone turned to look at the newcomer in the garden circle. Hedgehog was panting and puffing as if he had jogged from the house. He wiped his forehead with a handkerchief and gestured to the human towering behind him. The man was dressed in chain mail and leather, with the blue half cloak worn by the Stoneman guardsmen when they were on official business outside the walls.

"Sahs," the guard rumbled in a rough voice. "Forgive the intrusion. I was sent by Captain Rivaldo and the Sheriff to inform you that there has been another goblin attack. Last evening."

Lady Gia made several sharp motions with her hands and seemed concerned. Her posture had become stiff and her previous air of relaxation vanished.

"Mother asks why this involves us?" Marlette asked aloud, translating for her.

The guard looked from Lady Gia to Marlette as if realizing something and then said slowly: "Forgiveness. Can you please tell her that—"

"She watches your lips, sah," Marlette interrupted sharply. "Look at her and speak clearly and she will understand you."

The guard bowed deeply. "I meant no offense, Lady."

Lady Gia sighed and nodded and made a hand motion for him to get on with it.

"Lord Estevan was in council with Lord Miller when the news arrived. He is riding to Lady Opehlia's manor in Jacob's Fording Town to discuss the matter. A cattle train going to the Stoneman stockyard was hit, just before sundown yesterday. More than cattle were lost this time, Lady Gia. Your husband would like you to ride and join him tomorrow and I will escort you, but he asks that you please do not try to travel the roads that far North this evening."

Amandine frowned thoughtfully. Jacob's Fording Town was half a day North of Stoneman near a bend in the river. Being caught out after dark fell, especially with the attacks, sounded risky.

Marlette and Fiona also exchanged worried looks. Lady Gia tapped a finger against her lips, thinking. A moment later she stood as if a decision had been made. Her hands flashed a few simple hand motions to Mister Green, who bowed.

"Naturally, Lady," he said.

Marlette stood and performed hand signs of her own, the expression on her face made it seem that she was pleading with her mother.

Lady Gia flicked a sharp slicing motion with one hand, cutting the silent argument short and then strode away. Hedgehog and the guardsman trailed in her wake.

"But I can do it!" Marlette said aloud, her frustration evident. "I can be her voice. I know *livete* better than anyone!"

Mister Green made a pacifying gesture towards the young woman. "Yes, but you see, It's my belief that your mother wishes for you to have your own voice as you come of age, not just be seen as hers. Maid Sundrop knows more than enough of the signs to translate for Lady Gia."

"She's going to ride to the fording towns tonight despite what Lord Estevan suggested, isn't she?" Amandine asked.

"Quite likely," Mister Green said with a frown. "Another reason she may not want you along, Marlette. Come, lessons are done for now. We shall seek out Nanny and find some amusement until dinner. Perhaps stones?"

"To the Pit with stones!" Marlette snarled. She spun and stalked away from them into the maze of hedgerows.

"Big Sister! Wait!" Fiona cried. "I'll go get her, *soeje*! I can usually cheer her up!"

Fiona bobbed a quick bow to Mister Green and dashed off after her sister into the hedges.

Amandine was alone in the garden with Mister Green. Slowly, she slid off the bench, displacing Grendel, and began to creep away.

Grendel let out a disgruntled meow at being tossed from his napping spot. Mister Green looked away from the direction Marlette had fled and seemed to snap out of trance, as if he had been momentarily deep in thought.

"Still here, Miss Amandine? That's good. I wish to ask you a question," he said. His voice had a serious neutral tone that put Amandine on edge. It was the same sort of tone Sister Corbin would take when she was about to upbraid her for something.

"Y—yes, sah?" she asked, frozen to the spot.

"I won't ask *if* you are afraid of me. That is obvious. I will ask instead, *why*?"

He steepled his fingers together and pressed the tips to his chin as he studied Amandine intently. "Be honest," he added.

Amandine's mouth felt like there was sand in it. Was he going to magic her again if she gave the wrong answer? Surely he wouldn't, but then she decided a safe answer was best.

"Sah, I—" she began.

"Honest," Mister Green repeated, interrupting her.

With her tongue stuck thickly to the top of her mouth, Amandine suppressed a whimper. He knew she was going to fib to him. Instantly. Fiona had been right. He hadn't even made a move. His hands were still against his chin, his eyes never left hers. Chef would be ashamed of her right now, she thought. He had told Mister Green off, in Elvish no less; not to mention Sister Corbin. She could do better!

"Magic, sah. It's the magic I'm afraid of, not you," she said softly. It wasn't totally honest, but wasn't untrue either.

"I see. Not completely irrational then, but if I may ask, what conjure or warping have I created that has distressed you?" he asked.

Mister Green's hands dropped away to be folded behind his back, out of sight. Like a soldier sheathing a blade, Amandine thought.

She considered his question. He had cleaned her, which had been distressing, but also sort of nice. He had helped Chef Brutsche with the fire in the high oven. He had beckoned butterflies and made them do tricks. Was any of it really that bad?

"Those who twist reality do the work of Chaos and are against Natural Order. Only the gods should have such dominion,"

Amandine recited. The words were from part of the creed of the Night Sisters; doctrine that they had drilled into her almost daily.

Mister Green closed his eyes and nodded. "Ah yes, the Ancient Order of Night. Ravenex's followers have always taken a harder line on practitioners than other religious sects. You say these words, and yet you wear a favor of Kayla in your hair, miss. What is it that *you* believe?"

"I believe that magic destroyed half of the world, sah. The Great Wastes and the Sea of Glass and that thing they call the Conflux in Bolath lands. It's been a scourge, sah!" Amandine said. She barely managed to keep the quaver out of her voice.

"All of those things were created, partly, with magic. Terrible magic," Mister Green said with a sigh. "But let me ask you. Have you ever seen them, Miss Amandine? The spiderweb cracks made by hoofprints in the sheet glass of the Sea? The swirling mists and terrible creatures of the Conflux?"

"No, sah."

"I have. I have seen it all, and other things just as terrible of which you know nothing. Do you know how?"

"You've studied them, sah? Visited with caravans?"

"Miss Amandine, I am, by human calendars, four hundred and ninety-seven years old. Yes, I have read about them in books, because I wrote many of those books. I know them in detail, because in at least a few cases, I helped create them. I was *there.*"

Amandine's breath caught and she took an involuntary step backwards.

Mister green paused at her reaction and cocked his head. "You say you do not fear me, and yet…"

With a swallow Amandine averted her eyes from his. "Forgive me, sah, I didn't mean to offend."

"I am not offended," Mister Green said slowly as if considering his words. "You always look away. What do you see when you look into my eyes, Miss Amandine?"

Amandine swallowed again and shook her head. She wanted to run, but her feet felt frozen to the ground.

"Answer me, please," Mister Green insisted. His hands dropped to his sides again.

"Nothing!" Amandine blurted. "I see darkness, sah, and… and it scares me. Please, let me go!"

"I am not holding you here," Mister Green said softly. "By magic or even force of will. Your inaction is your own. What you are seeing is not false. No, it is a truth you see, and such insight is rare. There are few who can see through fae glamours. It's an ability that not even many practitioners can avail themselves of."

"I can…see through magic?" Amandine asked as she eyed Mister Green sideways without turning her head.

"Glamours are not magic, child, but something different, something ancient. Part of who fae are, like skin and hair and bone. Look at me."

Amandine shook her head again.

"My point is not to frighten you further, dear child. I am trying to offer you perspective," Mister Green said as he stepped closer to her. "Many of those things you spoke of were tragic, and terrible. Often, mistakes were made, for we are all mortal, and fallible. My eyes, as you see them, are a mark of my failure. A heretical brand. Still, it took the efforts of many mages. Many, many, *powerful* mages, to have such effects upon the world. I alone could never do anything so catastrophic, even if I had the mad desire to try. Do you know what the greatest weapon against fear is, Miss Amandine?"

"No, sah."

"Knowledge. Understanding a thing gives you power over it. If you allow me to instruct you, no terror this world can offer will give you pause, for you will have the knowledge to overcome, avoid, or defeat it."

Amandine looked up at Mister Green. His shadowed eyes seemed to swirl. Looking at them made her feel slightly dizzy, but now she knew what they meant, and knowing made her feel… different.

"I want to learn to cook, sah."

"And when you travel, in pursuit of your goal to be like Chef Brutsche, with what will you arm yourself?" Mister Green asked.

He smiled. It was just as eerie as usual, but Amandine felt as if something was different this time. Like an acknowledgement, unseen and unspoken, had transpired. She could see past the black eyes and silver hair of the ancient fae for the first time.

Amandine considered his question. Her entire time at Manor L'Eau had been in pursuit of the knowledge she wanted from Chef, but perhaps there was something she could learn from Mister Green as well. Sister Corbin's complaints, as much as they hurt, were not without merit. She decided. With a deep breath, Amandine lifted her chin and spoke. "When is the next lesson?"

"This Fireday," Mister Green replied.

"I'll be there, soojee," Amandine said, mangling the pronunciation of Mister Green's elven title.

"Close enough," Mister Green said.

Shivs

"Shiv years were initially brutal for humans living in Beregoth. The rapid changes in weather during these shorter years ruined human crops. Driving rain and, in the northern climes, hail, devastated entire settlements. It was through the intervention of elven and dwarven allies that humans survived those early years after the Arrival, but the sole records of those times are ancient, and from the perspective of those Elves and Dwarves. Very little history written by humans during that period has survived to this day. That said, the traditions around the end of a shiv, Shiv's End, stem from these very ancient times, and the celebration of life persevering through hardship is central to the human perspective on these events."
    - Lecture notes, Fifth Sunday, Low Winter, 1201

"I THINK THAT'S the last of them for today, Amandine," Miss Jacinda said as she wiped her hands on a small towel. She folded and flipped the cloth over her shoulder in one motion before she swept up a stack of freshly cleaned wooden bowls into her arms.

"I'm almost done, sah," Amandine said.

Her voice echoed from inside the large soup pot she had been scrubbing. It was an extravagant thing made of shaped copper, like Chef's "better" soup pot at Manor L'Eau, but three times the size. Amandine preferred it to the old iron cauldron in Chef's kitchen. Very little stuck to the smooth sides and it was satisfying to see it gleam when she had finished cleaning it. Lord Estevan and Lady Gia had been away from the manor for nearly a tenday, which meant no further encounters with Sister Corbin. It also meant that kitchen duties had been light, and Amandine had been practicing cooking on her own. The soup she had made today for the shanty folk had been one of her best so far, but still not quite as good as her mash had been.

"Herbert is closing the front. Thank you for helping, as always, Amandine. You did extra work this tenday with Gil absent," Miss Jacinda said as she stowed the bowls in their chest and discarded her towel.

Amandine emerged from the enormous pot and stood it up on the floor to inspect her work.

"It wasn't Gil's fault, Miss Jacinda. Master Hawthorne's shipment arrived from Anvilroot and they have been making his specialty beer loaves for three days. I tried to go visit and Madam Hawthorne gave me a sweet roll and chased me away. She said he can't be distracted right now."

She took a clean rag from the table nearby and polished the rim of the pot. Miss Jacinda smirked at her and put a hand on her hip. "And are you in the habit of distracting Mister Crouste?"

"No, sah. It's very rude to disturb someone while they are working."

Miss Jacinda laughed, which made Amandine stop what she was doing and look over at her. "What's funny?"

"Not a thing, love," Miss Jacinda said. "You did the work of two people today, *and* I now know to get a jump on my bread order for the Golem. Those loaves will be gone instantly once Master Hawthorne decides they are done!"

Amandine didn't think that her explanation had accounted for the laughter, but decided to let it be. Miss Jacinda often found things amusing for odd reasons. She shrugged and returned to polishing the copper.

"You can leave that," Miss Jacinda said. "The sun is dipping and you have a long walk back to the manor. It's already cleaner than when you started."

"It's fine, sah. I think I want to do some shopping in town tomorrow," Amandine said. "And I have an errand for Chef."

The truth was, she wanted to investigate the strange—thing—Fredderick had taken from Chef's pantry, and having a day in town without Gil was the perfect opportunity. She had gotten permission from Chef to take the extra day off on the condition that she also purchase some sea-water salt from the market circle. Sunflower had also suggested that she buy a dress. She was not going to do that.

Miss Jacinda frowned and raised an eyebrow at her. She lifted her apron off and hung it nearby and then took a moment to smooth her red linen dress and adjust her hair. Amandine found her silence a bit disconcerting.

"Where will you be staying overnight then?" she finally asked.

"There is a flophouse in the shanties. Two copper for a cot and a curtain. I've stayed there before when it was raining and—"

"Colorless night, absolutely not," Miss Jacinda said, cutting her short. "Herbert! Herbert, come in here, please!"

Herbert was Miss Jacinda's aged human assistant. He normally minded the creamery on soup kitchen days, but had been helping out since they were short. He poked his wizened, white-tufted head through the door and smiled at Miss Jacinda. His lack of teeth made the expression seem rather ghastly in Amandine's opinion.

"Yes, Miss?" he asked in a wheezy voice.

"Please go to the inn and find my husband. Tell him to reserve an upstairs room, one of the singles. We should have a few yet. If by some strange chance they are all taken, have him hold one of the doubles."

Herbert nodded. "And who shall be taking the reservation, Miss?"

"Miss Amandine."

"Oh, no, sah!" Amandine said. "I couldn't! The rooms are very expensive, and I—"

"Nonsense. The shanties are no place for a young lady," Miss Jacinda said, interrupting her again. "And if you are thinking of the coin, it's no worry, honestly. Vacancy is up this tenday, thanks to the nonsense with the dark fae, and I'll not have my favorite assistant robbed or worse just to spare a few silver."

Jacinda was practically glaring at Amandine now, as if daring her to come up with another excuse. Amandine relented.

"Thank you, sah," she said.

The old man flashed his huge, gum-filled smile at Amandine, bowed to Miss Jacinda and tottered off. A moment later Amandine heard the door to the dining room shut.

They stood there a moment more looking at each other. Amandine wasn't sure if she had made Miss Jacinda upset, or if she was being rewarded. It felt like both. She looked down at her feet.

Jacinda turned her head to the ceiling and sighed. When she looked back at Amandine her lips were twisted into an expression somewhere between annoyance and... frustration? Sadness? Amandine didn't like it one bit.

"You are a wonderful person, Amandine, and more street smart than many young women I have known. I am not your mother, wherever her luminous soul may be, and I am not trying to be. But let's face some facts: firstly, the grubby street urchin Berty and I took in last year might have passed through a shanty-town flophouse unnoticed, but the budding lady standing before me absolutely would not, even in terrible baggy clothes. I want you to be safe."

"I understand, sah," Amandine said, still looking at the ground.

"I know you do," Miss Jacinda said. "I have been to Artemis. It's not all marble columns and hanging gardens, is it?"

Amandine looked up. "No sah, it's really not."

Miss Jacinda nodded as if that settled the matter. "Come along then. Honestly, leave the colorless pot, you can already see your face in it."

After one final lick of her rag, Amandine rolled the pot into its cupboard and followed Miss Jacinda out of the soup kitchen.

It was a small building, midway between the shanties and the market, tucked back on a side street that mainly held townie houses. They stood one and two stories in uneven rows. Each had multiple doors. One house could hold sometimes as many as four or five families, each with their own one or two rooms. It was late in the afternoon and the shadows were long. Smoke rose from the many flues extending from the tops of the houses as the residents of Stoneman prepared meals over simple wood stoves. The smells of a hundred different stews, roasts, and baking fish filled the air. Amandine breathed it in as they strolled the lane, riverward, towards the markets and the square that held the inn.

"Can I ask you a question, sah?" Amandine asked after the uncomfortable silence had stretched long enough.

"Certainly," Miss Jacinda said with a smile.

"Why does everyone call you 'Miss'? You're married to Master Kale, right?"

Jacinda's face scrunched up and she barked a short laugh. "Because I prefer it, and have made my wishes known. 'Madam' sounds pretentious and stuffy. The old hamlet biddies can keep it."

"I didn't mean to be rude," Amandine said.

"No, it's an honest question. I am *not* offended," Miss Jacinda said with another indulgent smile for Amandine. "Never stop asking questions that come from a place of honest curiosity, Amandine."

"Do people still sometimes use the other title?"

"Out of town folks. Constantly. The ones that don't mistake me for Bertrand's daughter anyhow."

Amandine had never really considered it, but looking up at Miss Jacinda, it struck her that she really did seem a great deal younger than Bertrand Kale. Not that it was completely unheard of, but…

"The real burr in my hair is that I'm his elder by over five years and a shiv," Jacinda said.

Amandine blinked. "Wait, you are older than Master Bertrand?"

Miss Jacinda pointed to one of her delicately pointed ears and grinned. "Mama was from the Court of Breaking Dawn. She still lives there. North of Artemis."

"Oh! Yes of course, I... forgot," Amandine admitted.

"Miss Jacinda, a word, if you please."

The voice came from a deep shadow between two buildings. Amandine tensed and was ready to run if it was a thief, but Jacinda steadied her with a hand.

"Don't lurk, Mando, you're frightening enough. What is it you want?" she said.

A short, muscular human man wearing an open dockman's shirt stepped out of the shadows. He had dark brown skin and was bald, but his entire scalp was tattooed with lurid red and orange flames, like a crown of fire.

He eyed Amandine and then looked up at Jacinda with a raised eyebrow.

"Keep it brief, sah, you know it's a soup day," Miss Jacinda said in an exasperated tone.

"Trouble with Halifax. Demanding unload fees at the Southwest dock again. Your kin sorted them, but I thought you should know since it will affect your business."

"Yes, it would. The creamery is not entirely self-sufficient. Thank you, sah."

Mando nodded and after another look at Amandine, turned and disappeared back between the buildings into the shadows.

"Who was that?" Amandine asked.

"Mando Fame. He runs the dockman's union here in Stoneman. You would do well to avoid him, Amandine."

"What was he talking about?" Amandine asked as they resumed walking.

"Halifax is squeezing folk looking to move goods through the barges rather than the trains. It's an old game. A constant push and pull between the trade consortiums. It's nothing you need to be worried over."

Amandine considered this as they walked. She didn't know much about the Halifax, other than they moved goods around

Serentia, and even between nations. They were one of the largest merchant coalitions in the world.

"It seems to me that if they are being unfair, then folk should just use other trains, why let them behave like that?" she mused out loud.

"Capacity," Jacinda said simply. "No one else is as large and well equipped. Before the trade consortiums began during the reign of Olgothia, things were hard, Amandine. My great grandmother was alive for some of it, and well, shiv years killed a lot of people. Humans especially. The rapid swing from the winters to High Summer and back kills crops. Unless there is food carefully stored, people starve. That's why we call them that, Amandine. Shiv years. Hunger is like a knife in the ribs."

"I see," Amandine said. "So Halifax helps prevent this by moving food around, making sure everyone has a share?"

"And get paid well for doing it, yes," Jacinda said with a nod. "They sometimes try to take more than they should, but the truth is the world needs groups like Halifax and the Olgath Cartels to function. Innovations by the Dwarves and the Stone Folk have helped somewhat too. My basement aged cheeses last three times as long as they would have even four generations ago. Saving up for shivs is not as worrisome as it once was."

"I hate shivs," Amandine said with a grimace. "We always had pickles at every meal during shivs, back in Artemis. With the Night Sisters, I mean. After Shiv's End, we were given tree-sugar cakes as a treat. The Sisters never let us have those any other time."

"You haven't been here long enough to see one of our Shiv's End feasts. I think you'll really enjoy it."

Chef Brutsche would pull out all of the things in his pantry for such an event, Amandine had no doubt. She could scarcely imagine the delicacies and rich dishes he might create for such a celebration, especially for a noble house. Her mind ran wild with the possibilities.

Amandine smiled. "It feels strange to say, but I am looking forward to it."

Oats and Signposts

"Inns are a Seeker's home away from home. Some smaller ones will have an open hearth where you can cook for yourself, while other, more established places will often be equipped with a full kitchen and staff to do the cooking. Always bring your own mug to save on fees when using the taps, and because it's probably cleaner than anything the house owns. Inn kitchens and common rooms are amazing places to learn new recipes and try new flavors, or even just to get the local gossip. If the house seems friendly, make acquaintance with the proprietor, tip well, and never bring your work inside with you. Do all of this, and you will never lack for a good meal, a warm drink, or a comfortable bed to sleep in, no matter where your feet take you."

*   - Seeker's Kitchen, Chapter 12, On The Road*

AMANDINE YAWNED AS she ambled down the stairs of the Stomping Golem. She had never stayed in such a comfortable room before. The heavy quilts and wool-stuffed mattress had felt like sleeping in a fluffy cloud. Sunlight poured through the round portals that illuminated the stairway and made tiny motes stand out in the beams like sunlit fog. She almost felt as if she were still dreaming.

The smell of bacon frying hit her nose and Amandine's mouth began to water. Her body felt curious after sleeping in such a comfortable bed instead of her pallet. Parts of her were sore and stiff, but they were a different set from the ones that normally hurt when she woke up. She hobbled a bit as she reached the bottom of the stairs and moved in the direction of the common room's dining tables.

The walls of the Stomping Golem were solidly built from split timber, mortared brick and plaster, similar to how Manor L'Eau was constructed. It was an expensive way to build a structure, but sturdy, which was how one might describe nearly everything about it. The inn was the tallest building inside the walls of Stoneman at three stories, with multiple chimneys, made even larger by the attached creamery run by Miss Jacinda. The bench Amandine took a seat on was polished oak, put together with joinery instead of nails, and lacquered so that the smooth sanded surfaces of both the seats and the long table could be easily cleaned with a damp rag.

There weren't many people in the common room, but that was typical when the barges were not in. The giant table dominated the room, but only a few half asleep customers sat along its benches.

Around some smaller tables stood tall screens made from reeds and finely dyed linens that afforded wealthier customers some privacy while they dined. Over against the wall by the service counter was a stack of nine large casks filled with a variety of beers and ales. The house would provide mugs for a fee, but many folk brought their own, and simply tossed their coins down for refills.

Food was delivered by a young human woman, who looked at least part Zulathan, with tight, curly black hair, bright gray eyes and skin of a warm, yellow-brown color common to people from that land. She called herself Tilly, but other than her name, Amandine knew nothing about her. She stopped by where Amandine was sitting and slung her cleaning rag over her shoulder.

"Have a bite? Berty has rashers, soaked oats, apples and pears, and some stew from las' nigh'," she said in a thick townie accent.

Amandine knew she should eat something, but the meat and fruit were probably more than she could afford. "Just oats, please. And a slice of toasted bread?"

"Sounds lumi. Gil Crouste not with you today?" Tilly asked.

"No, I think he's working this morning. Why?"

Tilly blushed and left without another word. Did Gil have an admirer? Amandine grinned at the prospect of teasing Gil and then double checked her coin to make sure she had enough copper for the meal. Most of her money was spent on ingredients for her own cooking experiments, and paper for her tiny notebook. Dear gods, paper was expensive here. Still, she had managed to save nearly a gold crown and a half since she had come to Stoneman, but most of that was still tucked with her other valuables beneath her cot in the manor's warm cellar.

Her real reason for staying in town was not to shop, not really. She checked that the halves of the strange mushroom were secure in her money pouch, removed the two copper coins the bowl of food would cost, and cinched the ties again.

Once she had eaten, her goal today was to find someone, anyone, in Stoneman who knew what the odd thing was. She would start with the traveling merchants, and then maybe work her way through the docks. Talking to people Chef might know, locals in other words, was out of the question. If he found her in possession of something from his pantry...

Amandine shuddered involuntarily. "I should just get rid of it," she hissed softly to herself. "Chef would be so mad!"

"Oi, don't be looking so grumpus, girl!" a deep bass voice boomed from behind her.

Amandine jumped in her seat a little, but a strong hand settled gently on her shoulder. She looked up to see Bertrand Kale, the owner of the inn beaming down at her.

He was a mountain of a man, still tall and strong despite his gray hair and beard. His left leg limped from an old wound, but he never failed to greet any traveler with a warm smile and jolly laughter.

"Jacinda told me you was stayin', but you didn't come to have a chat. Jus' took to your bed like a bird to nest," he rumbled.

"Sorry, Master Kale. I was really tired," Amandine said.

She had been sleeping in the inn's barn and helping at the soup kitchen when Chef had approached her about the job at Manor L'Eau, and Bertrand seemed to always have one of her favorite sweets or fruits on hand if she stopped in to visit. This time, though, she didn't want to be caught with what she had, or have to explain with lies what she was really doing in town. So she had avoided him when she retired.

"If you spend all your time helping my wife, but don't come to see old Bert, then you might bring a tear to my eye, lass," Bertrand said. Despite the words, he had a gleam in his eye that wasn't a tear. He was having a bit of fun at her expense.

Amandine pouted at him and his veneer broke. "Dear gods, you're precious," he chortled. "Here, have some breakfast. And put those colorless coins away. Repay me with a conversation later, girl."

He set a large wooden bowl of steamed oats in front of her. More than that, a heavy pat of Jacinda's sweet yellow butter was slowly melting in the middle. A pair of large stickle-berries made for eyes, and two "ears" of thick cut bacon stood up out of the bowl at angles. The porridge bunny gazed up at her as Bertrand produced a polished wooden spoon from an apron pocket and, with a flourish, set it next to the bowl.

"Oh, thank you!" Amandine exclaimed.

She sometimes hated how Bertrand would treat her like she was a child half her age, but the funny bowl of rabbit-faced porridge was identical to the first meal she had ever been served in Stoneman, the rainy night Bertrand and Jacinda had taken her in.

"How do you like workin' for old Brutsche? Is he keepin' his bile in check?" Bertrand asked.

"Not at all, sah," Amandine said as she stirred the butter into the oats. "But I don't mind. I am learning a lot!"

Bertrand's eyebrows climbed his forehead. He seemed surprised. "He teachin' you?"

"No," Amandine said around a mouthful of oats and a stickle-berry. "Kivel and Sunflower do, though, and I watch."

Bertrand nodded. "Can learn a lot by watchin', more by doin', but havin' a teacher helps."

Amandine shrugged and stuffed another large spoonful of oats into her mouth. She hadn't realized how hungry she was. She might have forgotten to make a bowl for herself after the service last night at the soup kitchen, preoccupied as she was.

"It's not goin' to run from you," Bertrand said with a laugh.

"It's so good," Amandine said softly.

"Just about the hardest thing in the world to make badly, but I'm glad you like 'em."

"It's not just about the taste. I like the way it makes me feel. Thank you, Berty!"

Bertrand ruffled her hair and then limped away to the kitchens.

Amandine finished her breakfast and departed the inn to begin her search. The square the Stomping Golem sat in was shared with two other large buildings situated around a circular fountain.

The fountain was one of Amandine's favorite things in town. On warm days it would spray water ten feet into the air, which provided a cooling mist for folk traveling between its neighboring businesses, but even more, it was built and plated in sheets of gleaming orange metal and patina-covered copper. Numerous brass animals and monsters shuffled and spun with the flow of water and even spat smaller streams from their mouths into the basin below. A clock was embedded in the center and always told the perfect time of day, rain or shine. The enormous clockwork was maintained by the proprietor of the general goods store, Brinkenbrak Wizzlecog.

Wizzlecog's Emporium itself was a ramshackle-looking two-story building that seemed to be made up of parts borrowed from seventeen other buildings. Stone columns connected to cedar awnings that held up walls made alternately of brick, pine boards, clay daub and stone. The prow of a small boat jutted out of one side of the second floor that Wizzlecog used as a porch. Where the boat connected to the main building, its mast acted as one of the supports. At the top of the pole, a pair of flags, for Serentia and

Anvilroot, flapped in the breeze. Glass doors, like the kind found on a lord's parlor, led into the second story from the deck. A large brass device sat near them that Wizzlecog sometimes moved out to the edge and peered through, into the evening sky. The chimney was a bronze and brass-fitted thing with multiple pipes that often spewed interesting colors of smoke.

The other building was Telvor's Apothecary and Herbary. It was a large, one story, square building most notable for its slanted glass roof. Telvor claimed it allowed him to grow herbs and fungi that normally would not sprout during the winter cycles or that were native to warmer climes to the South and West.

Amandine paused for a moment and thought. It was likely that Telvor would also know what that mushroom was, but the Apothecary made her nervous. He was a dark-eyed Zulathan man with many strange tattoos. His medicinal skills were exemplary, and he never charged a single copper to treat the town's children, but his remedies often tasted vile. He was also known to dose those who acted foolishly, in addition to those who were sick. If she wasted his time, she would probably end up chewing some bitter herb as penance. More importantly, he sometimes did business with Chef Brutsche, so she gladly scratched him from her mental list.

Wizzlecog was another possibility, however. "Wizzlecog has seen just about every odd thing that has ever passed through this town," she said to herself. "I bet he'll know what this is!"

As Amandine approached the door to the Emporium however, it suddenly opened, barely missing her nose. There was a large amount of barking and shuffling feet as Dumpling dashed by her legs into the square, followed immediately by Fredderick.

"And stay out!" an angry high-pitched voice cried from within. The door swung shut and slammed so hard that the wall shuddered slightly and shed a bit of plaster. The shingle above the doorway rocked back and forth with the impact.

Fredderick looked annoyed at first, but when he spied Amandine, a smile lit up his face. "Aha! Hello there, Miss Amandine! On an errand for the Manor?"

"No, I am here for myself, sah," she replied warily. "Master Wizzlecog sounded angry. Did you try to steal something?"

"I would nev—" Fredderick began, but when he saw Amandine's expression he quickly retracted. "Not this time, no."

Dumpling yipped and trotted over to sniff at Amandine's shoes. She reached down to scratch his head. "I was going to ask him about that thing you found, but perhaps I should try elsewhere."

Fredderick looked back over his shoulder at the closed door. Another small flake of plaster drifted down from the wall. "Yes, that might be wise."

Amandine sighed and started to walk away. Fredderick trailed behind her with Dumpling at his heel. "So where are you going instead?"

"I think I will ask the traveling merchants currently in town. Then perhaps those that work the river."

"You won't find many. On account of the boglings, most are staying in the fording towns, or across the river in Waterbeetle. You heard what happened, right?"

Amandine glanced back at him, but kept walking. "I know Lady Gia was called away to the fording towns by her husband, days ago. She hasn't been back yet. Boglings attacked cattle coming to market, they say."

"When the sun was still up no less!" Fredderick added. "Everyone is scared, but Kimber won't commit the guards, and merchants traveling by road are rerouting around Stoneman, even if it takes them yarns and yarns out of their way."

Her eyebrows rose at his familiar use of the Sheriff's name, but Amandine decided to say nothing. Fredderick struck her as the type that didn't really care for social niceties.

"Well, I'm going to try anyway," she said.

"Can I help?" Fredderick asked.

"You took it, so I suppose… but please don't steal anything."

"I'm not a mimic-bird," Fredderick said with a laugh. "I can refrain when it's not to my advantage."

"Then I'm glad we've established that you are smarter than a bird."

Fredderick pressed his lips together and glared.

Amandine nodded, satisfied that she had made her point and continued down the street towards the markets. Fredderick followed silently, Dumpling trailed in his wake.

Ahead, Amandine caught a glimpse of a familiar cloak and white striped hair. "Oh hells!" she cursed.

"Such language," Fredderick said with a grin. "Forget something?"

"No, we need to go another way," Amandine said as she turned around.

"Why?"

"I don't want that old woman to see me, come on!"

"The Ravenex Sister with the stripe?" Fredderick asked.

"Yes! Come on, quickly, she's coming this way!"

"No time," Fredderick said. He reached out and embraced Amandine from behind, placing his chin on her shoulder.

"Fredderick! What are you doing! Let go!" Amandine protested.

"Sorry! We need to be touching for the magic to work. Hold still!" Fredderick whispered in her ear.

Magic! Amandine was torn between fear and embarrassment, but bit her tongue as a ripple crossed her skin like cold water. She could feel Fredderick breathing against her neck. She stiffened as Sister Corbin strode by them. The Sister glanced at them, shook her head and continued on.

"Disgraceful," she muttered in disapproval, but did not stop.

Once she was out of sight, Amandine's skin rippled again and Fredderick let her go. She rounded on him and pushed him hard with both hands causing him to stumble backwards.

"Of all the rude, disrespectful..." she growled. "What did you do? Make us invisible?"

Fredderick rubbed his chest and looked sheepish. "No, that only works on me and anything I can hold in two hands. You are a bit large for that. I created an illusion."

"Of what?"

"A young couple being, uh… friendly."

"You made an illusion of kissing me?"

"No, we looked like totally different people! It was the first thing that came to mind. Sorry."

Amandine threw her hands in the air. That explained Sister Corbin's reaction to them in any case.

"Sorry!" Fredderick repeated, his face turning red.

The embarrassment seemed genuine, which was striking to Amandine given Fredderick's seeming nonchalance about anything proprietary.

"Fine," she conceded. "It did work. Thanks for that, but never again without my permission. At least pick a different illusion!"

Fredderick nodded emphatically. Dumpling yipped as if in agreement.

Amandine gestured for Fredderick to follow. "Let's hurry on. She is probably going to pester people I know about me. I want to be done and back to the manor before I bump into her again."

"Right, to the markets then," Fredderick said, clearing his throat. The blush hadn't completely subsided, but he seemed to be regaining his composure.

His prediction on the number of merchants in town proved true, however. Amandine had never seen the market so empty. Many of the local farmers and merchants were also not present. The only one Amandine could find that might have an idea about the mushroom was a grain merchant from Greenest, and he quickly chased them off when presented with the odd mushroom halves.

"I suppose it does sort of look like scat," Fredderick said as they made their way to the Western gate. "He didn't need to threaten you, though."

Amandine waved a hand around towards the smattering of people in the market. "Everyone is on edge. Do you see their faces? You'd think the boglings were taking people and not cattle."

Fredderick paused. Amandine turned and looked at him.

"What?" she asked.

He reached down and picked up Dumpling who was whining about not being carried.

"I thought you knew. Seeing as you were with Lady Gia. The cattle train that was hit, the drivers were lost too. Three hamlet folk and the train's master, Lady Ophelia's younger brother."

Amandine's eyes widened as she recalled what the guardsman had told Lady Gia: "More than cattle were lost…" she murmured.

"Well yes, that's what I just said," Fredderick muttered as Dumpling began licking his face.

"I was just recalling what the guardsman told Lady Gia. No wonder she was so upset," Amandine said.

"Some braver folk have tried searching the fens and the woods during daylight, but good luck finding dark fae when the sun is out. No one has been fool enough to try it after sundown."

"And they are sure it's boglings?" Amandine asked. "Chef seems to think otherwise. That boglings don't eat large animals."

Fredderick rubbed his chin. "Well, my knowledge is purely anecdotal, but that seems to align with what I've heard. Still, they are also known to be territorial and sometimes violent. Nasty creatures by all accounts."

Amandine turned and continued walking again. There must be some link to make the boglings take the blame. "Lord Miller said boglings have been raiding his grain stores too."

"Yeah, I heard the same," Fredderick agreed. "And that's probably true. His people followed the trails of spilled wheat and barley. Found footprints. Claim to have even seen a couple of the fae, closer to darkfall. Why they are taking wheat is a mystery, though."

They passed through the gates and onto the road that led down the embankment towards the Wolfshenta River. They only had to step aside a few times for wagons coming from the docks and when they arrived at the edge of the huge pilings, Amandine could only see one barge moored. The huge, flat deck of the river craft was covered in crates and barrels that had been fitted with netting and lashed to the hull. Large runes were painted in yellow near the prow of the ship.

"Going to ask the crew of that ship? Not a bad idea. I'll bet they have been about and might know something," Fredderick said.

Amandine stared forlornly at the empty docks. "That was the idea, but I was hoping there would be more boats."

"Most of the independent traders try to stay aligned with the barges run by Irongate or Anvilroot," Fredderick said as he stroked Dumpling's head. "Easier to swap cargoes and make trades if you aren't stuck waiting at every single dock or port. This crew is probably doing a dry run down to Irongate."

"How can you tell that?"

"Well, the yellow lettering means it's independent, and the name of the ship is in Dwarven runes. The Gloryhammer."

"Oh. I see."

Fredderick eyed her shrewdly for a moment. "Wait. You can't read, can you?"

Amandine frowned and looked away. "I can read some!" she said.

Fredderick pointed at a small wooden signpost hammered to the first mooring. "Then what does that notice right there say?"

"Fredderick is a rude person," Amandine said while squinting and pretending to read the sign.

"I'll take that, I guess, but no more bird comments until you can read a book, miss."

Amandine stuck her tongue out at him and walked with a purpose onto the docks. The crew of the ship was mostly dwarves, with beards of various lengths and colors. Many of them wore a strip of thin cloth over their faces to shield their eyes from the bright Low Summer sun, but a few still removed their blindfolds briefly to examine the mushroom when Amandine produced it.

"Augh, looks like something elves use for medicine, but I dunna know the name, girl," one said in a gruff, gravelly voice. "Maybe you should ask a healer. Or an elf, if any of the leaf-lovers are runnin' about here."

They returned to town. Amandine scuffed the dirt along the way, dejected. "How about that herbalist near the Golem?" Fredderick asked.

"No, he sometimes does business with Chef. Herbs. For all I know that's where he gets them."

"I could have a look," Fredderick said as he vanished.

"No! No more sneakiness. You are going to get into trouble!" Amandine said in exasperation.

Fredderick reappeared again and shrugged. "Fine. Someone in town is bound to know."

"Maybe, but it's getting late. I don't have a light, and if the roads aren't safe, I want to be back at the manor before dark."

"And you want to avoid the Ravenex Sister, yeah? Who was she anyway?"

"Sister Corbin. I was a ward of hers back in Artemis. She was training me as a Bone Gaurdian and wants me to go back there with her, but I hated it there. I don't know if she has talked to Lord Estevan or Lady Gia yet, but they might have come back to the manor today and I don't want to go anywhere with her."

Fredderick frowned and stroked Dumpling's head. "Bone Guardian, huh? I never would have marked you for that. You'll be at your majority in about three years though, right?"

"Two. Year after next is a shiv," Amandine said.

"Well after that, she doesn't get a say anymore."

"That's a long time to hide from her, Fredderick. I want her to just go away."

"Would she would have a claim if you were someone else's legal ward? Like an apprentice?"

"I don't know, but Chef hasn't taken an apprentice in years, not even the cooks he works with," Amandine said with a sigh. "If I can figure out what this thing is and replicate one of his dishes with it, maybe Chef would see my worth and take me on? I don't know what else to do."

"Does it have to be Chef Brutsche?"

"Yes."

"Well, ok," Fredderick said, sounding disappointed. "I'll keep asking about the mushroom, I guess. If I find out anything, I'll come and see you."

"Fine."

"Hey, you could maybe learn to read too? A book might have the answer."

"Go away before I throw something at you."

"Say goodbye, Dumpy," Fredderick said. Dumpling barked and Fredderick made one of his tiny paws wave at Amandine before they both vanished again.

Goats

"Tuskers, sometimes also referred to as beast-men, or pigmen, have a sanguine history in Beregoth. It's not known whether they were native and the Giants were the interlopers or the other way around, but the fact stands that all of the major Tusker warbands were thralls to the Giants during the Time of Sorrow. After the fall of the Giants, their magic was broken, and so was their control over the shreds of the Tusker people. They mostly resumed an agrarian hunter-gatherer style of livelihood, but their fearsome appearance and size would sometimes put them at odds with Dwarves and Elves alike. The Arrival further decimated their numbers as Tusker bands found themselves in competition with humans for land and resources. They are a scattered and dwindling people now. Prized as slaves by Olgothian lords, resented by the Courts, who have long memories of the pain they once inflicted, and simply feared by everyone else."
  - Lecture notes, Third Fireday, High Summer, 1201

THE WHEAT AND barley were chest high to Amandine as she walked along the verge back towards Manor L'Eau. Soon, they would be taller than her and the harvest would come. She eyed the tall green and golden shafts warily. Anything could be hiding in the fields, but it was still daylight, so it was unlikely to be boglings. At least, that's what she told herself.

She passed a flock of spearbills foraging in the stalks. With their pearlescent plumage, red crests, and beaks as long as she was tall, the giant birds could be fearsome at first glance, but were actually quite docile. The one closest to the road dipped its head in a rapid thrusting motion and came back up with a writhing rot-slime pierced on the end of its beak. It eyed her as if wondering whether she might want to contest it for the morsel.

"No, sah, that's for you," Amandine called out. "Make sure you and your family get all of them so that the wheat grows up healthy!"

The spearbill cocked its head to look at her with its other eye and then in a swift, practiced motion flipped the hapless slime down its gullet and began scanning the field for more.

Something strange caught her ears. It was a creaking and swaying noise, mixed with what sounded like crying children. The spearbills simultaneously gave off eerie trilling cries and launched into the air in a flurry of shimmering wings. Amandine's heart skipped a beat as she tried to look over the tall grasses, and then she turned around.

There was a wagon coming up the road behind her. The creaking was from the axles. The rest, she realized, were goats. A wagon full of goats.

The driver of the wagon wore a strangely shaped orange-brown hat and had dark skin. As it drew closer the driver called out to her.

"Miss Amandine, is that you?"

Amandine stopped walking. With a hand over her eyes to block the sun, she peered up at the person on the front bench. "Madam Sheeria?" she asked.

"Ah, it is you then. Hello!" Sheeria said as she brought the wagon to a stop.

It was drawn by two shaggy prongs: furry antlered beasts that lived in the mountains and were often domesticated by dwarves for pulling loads. They were notoriously lazy, though, and the pair were more than glad to stop moving when the reins were pulled. A row of spotted goat heads popped out to peer at her through the slats of the high-sided cart. They seemed curious as to why their trip had halted. Amandine realized that Sheeria was wearing her long, reddish hair up in a top knot that caused it to bulge out and shade her eyes like a small-brimmed hat.

"Are these all yours?" Amandine asked while looking at the goats. "Where are you taking them? Why do you have prongs? How did you do that with your hair?"

Sheeria laughed and peered down at her with a broad, indulgent smile. "All of 'em, and more. This is my second cartload of the little girls today. The sheep hate the cart, but the goats seem to like the ride. I am taking them to our 'stead, out past Gold Hills. The prongs are great! Cheaper to feed than horses and easier to clean up after. I bought them in Anvilroot years ago. As for the hair? My mother taught me this trick when it was first long enough to pull up. Haven't needed to wear a hat in the fields since. Hop on, I'll give you a ride if you are going to Manor L'Eau."

Amandine climbed into the seat next to Sheeria. A pair of goat heads poked out between them and one nibbled at her shirt.

"Hey, stop that!" Amandine said.

Sheeria let loose a loud whistle. There was a deep bark from the rear of the wagon and the goat heads hurriedly retreated. A moment later a larger, shaggier head replaced them. The dog's long tongue lolled from its mouth as it looked back and forth from Amandine to Sheeria.

"And this is Hamood. He keeps the rabble in line," Sheeria said as she ruffled the fur on the dog's head. "Let him sniff you and he'll leave us alone. He just wants to inspect the new passenger."

Amandine did as instructed. Hamood sniffed her hand, gave it a single lick and then disappeared back between the slats. There was a second bark and some plaintive bleating and then it grew quiet again. Sheeria snapped the reins gently and the prongs, who had sat down on their forelocks, made grumbling noises and stood back up.

"Why are you moving your goats, sah?" Amandine asked as the wagon began rolling again.

"Boglings. I've lost too many already. The grazing is not as good near our 'stead, the ground is too rocky. Lady Ophelia and Lord Kalvin like the goats and sheep in the pastures because they eat weeds and shrubs that'll make the cows ill, so it's a boon for everyone. But I can't absorb the losses anymore. I need to move the flocks somewhere safe until this is all sorted."

Sheeria looked at Amandine with a frown. "And you probably shouldn't be on the roads alone."

"But boglings live in the swamps, right? The fork to Manor L'Eau doesn't go near the fens," Amandine said.

"Still, you should be more careful."

"You and the Sheriff live out past the Gold Hills? That's a long way from Stoneman."

"Kimber only comes home maybe twice in a tenday, unfortunately. She has to travel the entire area, and oversee all sorts of nonsense for Lady Everdawn."

"That must be lonely."

"Oh, it's not so bad. She *does* come home. Her work keeps everyone safe. And in the betweens, I have Hamood and my plinth-hounds."

"Plinth-hounds? What are those?" Amandine asked.

"Blink dogs, fae hounds, ghost dogs. They have many different names depending on where you are from. They are really smart. One of them, Okistre, can even speak in simple sentences, in Elvish and Olgath. They are loyal, fierce, and see through magic that clouds the mind, but for all that, they can't roam far from their runestones, or plinths."

"They sound amazing," Amandine said.

"They cost a fortune. We were gifted ours as a wedding present by some Elven fellow who knew Kimber from a long time ago. Between them and Hamood, the 'stead is well protected."

The sound of hoofbeats came from up ahead. With the cart's higher vantage, Amandine could see riders barreling down the road at a fast clip. Four horses sped by the cart in rapid succession. Their riders leaned over in their saddles and snapped their reins to keep the horses running. Once they were well behind the wagon, Amandine turned to Sheeria.

"Who were they?" she asked.

"I am not sure, Amandine," Sheeria said, looking worried. "They were armed, moving fast, and wearing heraldry, but I didn't catch the pattern. My guess would be messengers. Maybe from the East Bends, or even Artemis."

"Do you think it's bad news?"

"I think they want to be inside the walls before dark. And since this is a glowstone lit, well traveled road, that means word of the boglings might be spreading," Sheeria said as she glanced back over her shoulder. "The world is a dangerous place outside of civilized areas like this. If people think that fae or other threats are encroaching, it could lead to violence. Like with the Tuskers a few years back."

"The beast people with the huge teeth like boars? What happened with them?" Amandine asked.

"Oh, a splinter band of them took up residence in the hills north of Waterbeetle. They started thieving, mainly from travelers, but never hurt anyone. The braver ones would sneak into town with hoods on and steal things. Food mostly. They were primarily a nuisance, and there was a standing bounty for their capture, but then a few of them got into it with a Lord's hunting party. Killed his hounds... and his son."

"That's awful!" Amandine gasped.

"Yes well, I knew them both, and I'm inclined to believe it wasn't the tuskers that started the fight, large and fearsome though they are. Lord Kalvin is a proper floppy duck," Sheeria said with a shake of her head.

Amandine laughed at her commoners' phrase for an uppity, rude noble. It seemed out of place coming from Sheeria. "What happened then?"

"A party of Seekers, in concert with soldiers from Artemis, tracked their band down and murdered all of them. Even the young ones."

Amandine's mirth was squelched. "Oh," she said quietly. "Oh, that's awful too."

The wagon continued to roll on with its bed full of bleating goats, but Amandine didn't feel like talking anymore. Sheeria likewise seemed pensive as she looked out over the rippling fields. Amandine thought of the news from Fredderick, and wondered if history was about to repeat itself.

Fennel and Silver

"Coins made from precious metals have been a medium of trade since the Arrival. The Great Courts still rely on fair exchange and barter internally, but have grown accustomed to using coin as a means of dealing with Humans and Dwarves. Since the Olgothian Empire, the Gold Crown, also known simply as the 'Crown' or 'Sunburst', has remained a stable and uniform measure of value between all nations. Lesser coins made from silver, copper, bronze, and iron are minted by every nation and clan according to their preferences. For this reason, gold is the accepted standard of trade between nations, but most common folk deal day to day in whatever currency is local to them."
    - Lecture notes, Third Fireday, Low Autumn, 1201

"IN. VEN. TORY," Amandine said while squinting at the chalk slate hanging in the back of Miss Jacinda's soup kitchen.

"Exactly!" Miss Jacinda said, her face beaming. "I see your lessons with Mister Green have been fruitful."

Amandine nodded. "It's still hard, but I am getting better. Dwarven runes are confusing."

Jacinda reached past Amandine and added three pips to one of the number symbols beneath a column labeled *Rice*.

"What number does that make it now?" Miss Jacinda asked.

"Fifteen," Amandine said instantly. She already knew numbers. On the whole, she found them easier than reading.

"Correct, and since we need twenty sacks for a cycle, we're five short. So our job today will be to make sure we order enough from the merchants, or take in enough from donations that everyone will get a bowl during the next cycle's services."

Miss Jacinda pointed to the other columns. "What I want you and Gil to do is go and fetch donations that have already been committed to. I will buy the rice and oats, they rarely get donated and I can negotiate a better price, I think."

"Oh, so what else is needed?" Gil asked as he studied the chalk lines and their numbers. "I see peppercorns, goldleaf, potatoes, greenstalk, carrots, and fennel."

"Yes, the peppercorns, goldleaf, and fennel you can get from Master Telvor. The rest is from Miss Daisy, the Halifax wholesaler near the East Gates. They are far apart, and the roots will be heavy, so I suggest you do one and then the other," Miss Jacinda said as she tied her hair back.

"Will we need coin?" Amandine asked.

"No, these are all donations, like I said," Miss Jacinda replied. "Watch Daisy, though, she might try to wheedle a service fee out of you. It's nonsense. Just ask her if she still has that problem with mice in her pantries if she does."

"Mice. Got it," Gil said.

"I'm off then," Miss Jacinda said. "I'll meet you back here in the afternoon."

Amandine and Gil departed the soup kitchen. The Low Summer sunshine was muted somewhat by a layer of fog that had rolled in off the river. Beads of dew formed instantly on Amandine's coat.

"Where shall we go first, Amy?" Gil asked.

"I don't know," Amandine said.

It was Third, but there was no service today at the soup kitchen. Once a cycle, Miss Jacinda closed the doors so she could clean and restock. Amandine had intended to use the rest of her day trying to find more information on the strange mushroom Fredderick had taken. It had been nearly two tendays since her fruitless trip to Stoneman and Chef had been keeping her very busy. She was beginning to think he burned things in that awful cauldron on purpose.

On the bright side, her chores at the manor had concealed her from Sister Corbin, who had begun stalking the manor again in hopes of pleading her case before Lord Estevan. Lady Gia had returned a tenday ago, but Lord Estevan had been moving from holding to holding, conferring with the various other noble families, for nearly a cycle.

The two halves of mushroom were wrapped in cheesecloth in her coat pocket. She touched them to reassure herself they were still there. They had become slightly desiccated, but she hoped someone might still recognize them.

"I mean, I don't really like Telvor either, but it's not like we're going there for treatment," Gil said.

"Yes, but I also brought this to town with me today," Amandine opened her pocket and showed him the mushroom halves.

"Oh! Well that's perfect. If anyone would know what they are—" Gil began.

"Absolutely not!" Amandine interrupted. "We can't just ask him. He does business with Chef. He might even be where Chef gets them, and if I am caught with something from the pantry..."

"Ah, hmmm," Gil said as he considered her words. "Well, we still aren't there for anything unexpected. Just, I don't know, look around? See if he has some in a jar or something? Might have a label?"

"That's... not a bad idea, Gilly. Our task for Miss Jacinda is the perfect excuse. That's brilliant, actually."

"I am the smartest one in my family," Gil said a bit smugly.

"Your cousin fell from a hen house while trying to use it to step up into an oak to steal eggs."

"Yeah, so?' Gil asked.

"He owned a hen house. With hens. And a ladder," Amandine replied.

Gil shrugged. "Like I said, smartest of mine."

Amandine laughed. "Ok, fine then. Let's go see Master Telvor."

They made their way towards the North Central portion of Stoneman where the square surrounded by the Stomping Golem, Wizzlecog's Emporium, and Telvor's shop resided. Amandine stopped briefly to watch the brass animals and monsters make a circuit of the clockwork fountain and then she and Gil entered the open front door of Telvor's Apothecary and Herbary.

The first thing Amandine noted was that the light didn't change. Normally, going inside meant that sunlight diminished. Rays snuck in through windows and door gaps. Light could filter down through loose thatch or bad shingles. But in the Apothecary, it was as if you stepped from outside into—outside; only slightly warmer.

The entirety of the building was one enormous space. There were shelves along the walls but the middle was filled with rows of plants. Low benches held pots and planters, urns and soilboxes. The entire space felt like a forest of herbs and grasses and green growing things.

Amandine and Gil moved along the rows slowly, examining every plant they passed. Amandine checked every sign she could read, bulbs or flowers or shrubs. Nothing seemed to match the mushroom.

At the back of the space was a small counter that was set in front of a door leading to an outbuilding where Telvor dried and stored the things he sold long term. Amandine heard voices as she approached. One had the staccato rhythms of Zulathia, and the other had a townie cadence. She waved back at Gil to tell him to stay quiet.

As they crept closer, Amandine saw who was speaking. The first voice, as she suspected, was Telvor Aran himself. He was Zulathan, but unlike the sergeant of the Stoneman Guards, Xia, Telvor had wavy hair that fell to his shoulders. He kept it tied back in a Zulath fashion, but unbraided. He wore a loose tunic and baggy pants that he belted with silk rope. The sleeves of his tunic were rolled to the elbows and one forearm was festooned with a series of three braided bracelets that seemed to be made from wheatgrass.

The most notable thing about Telvor, however, was his tattoos. Sailors often had skin art. So did many of the street folk in Artemis that Amandine had known. Sometimes even a noble would get inked, if only for a whim. Telvor's tattoos were not the same. They covered him, from where his ankles were visible beneath the cuffs of his pants, to just under where his cheeks met his eyebrows. They were intricate and mazelike, and Amandine sometimes felt as if they themselves might be some kind of magic.

Amandine was surprised at the owner of the second voice. Tilly, the server from the Stomping Golem, was sitting on a stool next to Telvor's counter. She had her shirt pulled up to reveal her back as Telvor daubed salve with his fingers.

"Bertrand will fire you if this keeps up, Tillandra," Telvor said as he applied medicine to her skin.

"It weren't my fault!" Tilly grumbled.

"You tried to kiss a Zulathan porter," Telvor said placidly.

"He wanted a kiss!" Tilly protested.

"The chair he broke over your shoulders would say otherwise," Telvor said in the same level tone. "I know you have never lived in the Sunlands, but the people from there, our people, don't take kindly to such invasions of personal space."

The look on Tilly's face could only be described as 'sulky'. She hissed as if something Telvor applied had stung her.

"And then you knocked him out," Telvor added.

"I only did what ya taught me to do, Uncle Aran," she muttered.

"That was not a criticism," Telvor amended. "But perhaps it's better not to instigate the beatings."

"So I should only accept a kiss if it's na' asked for?"

"Absolutely not. Please knock out those ones as well."

"Augh!" Tilly said as she pulled at her hair. "Yer impossible, ye old…"

"Yes, children, what is it you need?" Telvor called out.

Tilly blushed and pulled her shirt down as Amandine and Gil revealed themselves.

"This is not a play area. Do you have business?" Telvor asked.

Amandine spoke first. "Miss Jacinda sent us! We're here for the donation for the soup kitchen, sah," she said while managing not to stammer.

"Ah, yes. Please allow me to finish with this patient, and then I can assist you," Telvor said before yanking Tilly's shirt up a hitch to apply more salve.

Tilly yelped and stood up. "I'm lumi, Uncle. Thank ya. Master Kale will be lookin' for me soon. Best be off. See you on Starday for practice."

"As you wish," Telvor said. "Be well, Tillandra."

She hurried past Gil and Amandine and walked quickly out the door, but not before shooting Gil a sidelong glance. Gil appeared not to notice even after Amandine grinned and elbowed him in the ribs.

"What?" he complained, rubbing his side.

"Nothing," Amandine said in a sing-song voice.

"Feel free to look about, but unless you know what it is, please don't touch. You may get a rash," Telvor said as he placed the salve on the counter. "I will gather the things promised to Jacinda."

Amandine and Gil looked at each other. Gil grinned.

"Have a look, with permission, I'll keep him busy if you need," he said softly.

With a nod, Amandine went to examine the shelves near the back that had jarred, dried herbs in them. Gil began to walk the rows, occasionally asking questions while Telvor fetched things and put them into a basket.

"Woah, what is this weird thing?" Gil asked.

"Spineleaf, from the Wastes. Do not touch," Telvor said with barely a glance.

"What does it do?"

"It hurts if you touch it."

"Then why have it?"

"So I can tell people who ask annoying questions to touch it."

"And this one! It smells. What does it do?"

"Ah, hmm... it makes you feel good."

"Can I buy some?"

"No."

Amandine suppressed a laugh as Gil continued to issue questions about every plant in the row. She wasn't having much luck, however. All of the jars were labeled, but she could only read a few of them. A couple even had mushrooms, but they were fairly common shelf mushrooms and small white-capped forest buttons. Nothing in the jars looked like the things in her pocket.

The floorboards creaked as someone entered the shop. Amandine looked up to see Heather Mince, the matron of the Stoneman stockyard, striding up to Telvor's counter.

Heather was half-Tusker. She stood as tall as a large human man, with black, braided hair and dark tanned skin that was slightly leathery. Two huge, pronounced canine teeth jutted from her lower lip. They were smaller and less sharp than a full-blooded Tusker's were, or so Amandine had been told, but they still lent her a frightening appearance.

She was dressed in leather buckskins and a rough woolen shirt with the sleeves rolled past her elbows. Only a glance was spared for Gil as she reached the counter and waited for Telvor to acknowledge her.

When he continued to sort herbs without speaking she tapped the counter. "Master Aran, we need to talk, sah." Her voice was deep and had a scratchiness to it.

"About?" Telvor asked.

"You know what. Have you gotten the delivery yet?" Heather growled.

"I haven't. The contact hasn't shown himself at all this cycle, and will not likely come into town given the mood."

"Can't you talk to him?"

"No. I do not communicate with him, I only pick up the bundles. We need Serand for that."

"Well then, get him to do it!"

"Heather, please understand. My business has taken as much of a downturn as yours with the supply issues we're facing, but we cannot pull too hard on this weave. This isn't like dealing with the nobles, or Halifax, or even the Olgath Cartels. We must be delicate."

Telvor finally stopped what he was doing to give his full attention to the large woman. He didn't appear fazed by her physical size or fearsome teeth at all. Amandine noted that Gil, however, had moved two rows away and was watching her warily.

"Children," Telvor called while still looking at the fuming half-tusker. "Please come collect your basket. The pouch on top is to be given directly to Jacinda and not left sitting around the soup kitchen. Please inform her that I will have less than usual next cycle."

Gil hurried forward and lifted the basket. He jerked his head at Amandine.

"We still have to get to Halifax. Let's go, Amy," he said.

Amandine felt both Heather's and Telvor's eyes on her and Gil all the way out the door.

"What were they talking about?" Amandine asked once they were clear of the shop.

"I don't know," Gil said with a shrug. "It didn't feel like something they wanted us listening to, though. Telvor only gets that look when he's about to dose you."

"I didn't know Tilly was getting into fights at the inn, either," Amandine said.

"Oh, that's old news. You don't get into town as much as I do, I guess. Every tenday or so, especially if the barges are in, some sailor or merchant gets their lip adjusted by her. The locals all know better than to mess with her at this point."

"It sounded like she started it," Amandine said.

"And finished it," Gil added with another shrug. "She flipped Bertrand on his arse once. I swear by Leonid it's true! It was an accident though, I think he just startled her. Miss Jacinda laughed until her sides ached."

"Oh, wow," Amandine said. She looked down into the basket. "What's in the pouch?"

"No idea."

Amandine picked it up as they walked and peeked inside. It was filled with silver coins. Most were Irongate minted with the fortress bridge stamped on one side, but a few were the thicker Anvilroot doubles, with the mountain and axe impressed on their faces.

"That's a lot of silver," Amandine said.

"Coins? Huh, I wonder what they are for?"

They arrived back at the soup kitchen with the basket as Miss Jacinda was also returning. She was pushing a small wheelbarrow filled with sacks of oats.

"Excellent timing, loves," she said as she dropped the handles and relieved Gil of his burden. "Oh? What is this?" She settled the basket on one hip and took out the pouch.

"Master Aran said we should give that directly to you, and that he would have less next cycle," Amandine related.

Jacinda's eyebrow rose. "I wonder what he means by that? I shall have to ask him," she said. With a flick, she folded the top of the pouch down and tucked it away into a pocket on her dress.

"What is the silver for?" Gil asked.

"Perhaps he has a tab with Bertrand? It's no matter to you two. Have you been to Halifax yet?"

"No, sah," they both answered.

"Get on with it then. I'll get this all inside and sorted and then I am off again," Jacinda said as she hefted the barrow's handles again. "Apparently Old Gert is working on a new way to farm bees for honey. It's a box he coaxes them to live in, like a hive. Parts of it slide out to access the combs. It's rather ingenious. I think it might be worth investing some coin into."

Amandine made a face. "Farming bees? That sounds painful."

"It seems to be working. If you're quick about it, I may also have some honey and oat muffins from Master Fern, who has been buying Gert's new stock."

"All right!" Gil said enthusiastically. "Come on, Amandine!"

Amandine smiled and waved to Miss Jacinda as she hurried after Gil.

Honest Business

"The Stone Folk have a curious culinary tradition that favors strong fermented and preserved foods. Pickled fish, mushrooms, and root vegetables are the time honored staples, but in recent decades they have turned their craft to preserving sunlit crops and meats in a similar fashion. Stone-pickled cow tongue is a delicacy worth paying the extra silver for."

> *- Seeker's Kitchen, Chapter 8, Cuisine from the Deeps - Dwarven and Stone Folk Fare*

AMANDINE SAT AGAINST the town wall and watched the river as she ate the last crumbs of her muffin. Stoneman was built inside an ancient fortification. The wall was twenty feet high and the massive stone blocks were chiseled so finely and set so carefully that it didn't even need mortar to hold it together.

And so, when she had big things to think about, Amandine would come sit against the giant stone wall and watch the even more massive Wolfshenta River drift lazily by. Below, near the water, people scurried about like ants carrying crates and barrels on the docks pushed out into the shallows.

With a crunching of boots, Boomer McKragen rounded the corner. His beard swayed as walked briskly along the wall and glanced up towards the battlements at intervals. He paused his inspection as he passed Amandine.

"Yer not part of the stonework, kid goat," he said while staring at her through his odd green eye lenses. His nose twitched at the air. "I smell honey…"

"I like the view, and the wall, sah," Amandine said after licking her fingers. She reached out and ran a hand along one of the thin seams. "It's like a quilt of stone. I wonder if the Giants made it."

Boomer grimaced and spat in the dirt. "Nay. Na' Giants. Olgothians, long ago, when they still ruled all you *gyre*. Not sa fine as my kin's craft, but serviceable."

"How did they move them? How did they cut them?" Amandine asked.

"Magic, fer some. Numbers and sand and water fer the rest. Their technique were solid, if lackin' imagination."

"Numbers and sand to cut rock? That still sounds like magic," Amandine said.

Boomer laughed. It was an odd guttural sound, and at first she thought he might be choking.

"Aye. It is a bit magical to the untrained eye, I'll grant ya. I must be on. Stoneman will be comin' round soon. I hope the wall suits ya."

Boomer continued his circuit, muttering under his breath in a language that sounded like Dwarven. Amandine thought it might be counting numbers from the cadence of it.

She pulled the strange pieces of the lump Fredderick had stolen out of her pocket and examined them again. Were they something from Chef's homeland on the other side of the world? Trenash spicers had all sorts of rare herbs, many of which only grew on the other side of the Wastes, so that's who she needed to ask.

There were no spicers this tenday, though. She had already looked. At risk of being found out, she even showed it to a few of the locals, but no one seemed to know what it was.

The ground shuddered beneath her as if from a small earthquake. Amandine looked up as the namesake of the town rounded the tower that marked the Northwest corner and slowly passed her.

The Stoneman was almost fifteen feet tall and roughly humanoid-shaped. That is to say it had two arms, two legs, a torso, and a head. The legs were thick and ended in flat round pads like tree trunks. The arms had enormous hands with three massive fingers and a thumb that could open and close, but mostly remained curled into giant fists. The features of the head, which may at one time have had some sort of helmet or face design carved into it, was worn smooth by wind and rain and snow.

A bird nest was located in the small hollow on top of it where a family of jays chirped noisily. The body was likewise worn smooth, but small imprints and divots made Amandine think it might have been carved to look like armor at some point.

Unlike the wall, the Stoneman was definitely magic. Very old magic. It was one solid chunk of volcanic rock, but moved fluidly, as if alive and made of flesh instead. No one living remembered who had carved it, enchanted it, or why it continued to slowly patrol the outer wall of the town. It never ceased, rain or shine, unless something (or someone) foolishly got in its way, which had not happened in a very long time.

Its movement was so regular that Wizzlecog set the town's clock based on the position of the Stoneman in relation to where the sun was. That it was passing her now meant that it was mid-afternoon, and she should be getting ready to return to the Manor.

Thinking of Wizzlecog reminded her. She still hadn't asked him about the mushroom! Surely whatever Fredderick had done to anger him had cooled by now. Carefully, she tucked the halves back into her pouch, stood, and walked quickly along the wall in the wake of the Stoneman until she came to the Western gates that the river workers used to move goods to and from the docks. The town militia guarding the portal didn't even glance at her as they stopped others coming in and out to inspect cargo and collect taxes.

The city was busy today, as it was when the barges were in. Merchants haggled and bartered over goods that had been brought upriver from Irongate, or downriver from Anvilroot the previous day. The roundabout that led towards the gate was jammed with carts waiting to go one direction or the other, as well as pack animals and groups of sailors. She ducked and wove her way through the stalls and wagons and took the most direct path possible to Wizzlecog's Emporium, which led her through the back alley behind the smithies and cartwrights and into the stable yard of the Stomping Golem.

The horses in the stables neighed as she strode past. Amandine flinched as the back door to the inn's kitchen opened with a bang. Bertrand strode out into the yard wielding a frying pan like a club.

"Get on out of—oh, Amandine, lass. It's you. I thought it might be one of those scoundrels from the scrapper again. Caught a little beetle trying to make off with spare horseshoes and the manure shovel. Of all things! Where are you off to, lass?"

"I am going to Wizzlecog's," she replied as she continued across the yard. "I'm sorry I bothered the horses!"

"You're no bother, Amandine," Bertrand said with a friendly wave. "I need to pick up some plates from him, actually, but I am worried about leaving the yard unwatched while my stable boy is off duty. Colorless scrappers."

"I'll get them for you!"

"You're a peach, Amandine," Bertrand said with a huge smile. "They're already paid for, just tell him I sent you."

Amandine smiled back and nodded. She hurried out of the yard and into the square, passed by the central fountain with its inlaid clock face and moving brass sculptures, and entered Wizzlecog's shop.

A tiny bell announced her arrival as she entered through the lower level's doors.

"I'll be with you shortly!" Wizzlecog's high-pitched voice called from somewhere in the stacks of shelves. "Please feel free to look about and if you have any questions, just shout them out!"

"Mister Wizzlecog," Amandine called back. "It's Amandine, from Manor L'Eau. I work with Miss Jacinda sometimes at the soup kitchen. I'm here on an errand for Master Kale, and may I ask you a question, sah?"

"Certainly, certainly, come to the counter at the rear, child!" the voice echoed.

She made her way through the untidy and sometimes precariously stuffed shelves of the shop, careful not to bump or jostle anything. Large bags of sugar held up piles of wagon spokes. Small kegs of oil and grease were mixed with glass jars of all sorts of pickled vegetables and mushrooms. In at least one place, rope was being employed to keep overfull shelves from tipping under the weight of their contents. Amandine felt that even the slightest displacement would send some of the ungainly piles crashing down in a cascade of dry goods, and so she hurried past as quickly as she could.

The back counter was set at a human height, which meant she could barely see over it, but the opposite side featured an elevated floor so that Wizzlecog could always look his customers in the face. A rolling ladder came sliding along the back wall with the small man attached to it by one arm and leg while his free hand held a large jar that appeared to be packed with pickled fish. He nimbly stepped off the ladder as it passed the counter and set the jar down as the ladder itself kept on moving in its never ending, clockwork-propelled, circuit of the store.

Wizzlecog was bald, with ruddy pink skin and a monocle over his left eye that was connected by a silver chain to his fine coat. His ears were slightly pointed, and his eyes were steel gray. Like all Stone Folk he had an extra pair of pointed teeth, which made him seem somewhat savage, despite the fancy clothing. Sunflower had once told her that although they were kin, Stone Folk and Hill Folk were very different. Amandine got the impression she wasn't just talking about the odd teeth, either.

"Oh yes, I remember you now. You were sleeping in the barn with the creamery's milk cows for a spell, yes? That horrible old Trenash man took you on as a... what? Floor sweeper?" he asked.

"Scullery, sah," Amandine replied. "Although the cooks there have been teaching me a little."

"Oh, lumi, luminous indeed," Wizzlecog said with a satisfied nod. "Young people should all learn a proper trade. Too many layabouts and daydreamers. And don't get me started on those Seekers Guild types. Always off looking for Mage War relics or old Oglothian ruins. Good way to end up dead. Indeed. No doubt. You are a smart child, I can see it in your hair."

He spoke so quickly that Amandine had a bit of trouble keeping up. "Don't you mean eyes, sah?"

"Why would I mean that? Eyes take information in, they don't display it outwardly. Well cared-for hair, however, is a sign of culture and education, and yours is quite tidy. Yes, very nice. I remember hair. It was fun while it lasted," he commented in a near continuous stream. Wizzlecog rubbed his bald pate absently. A faint smile crossed his face as he adjusted locks that were no longer present.

"Yes, well, as you are also a man of education, I thought you might be able to help me solve a bit of a mystery," Amandine said, hoping a touch of flattery might get him to cooperate, or at least stay on topic.

"I do not typically like mysteries. Things unknown and forgotten are often that way for a reason. Proper scientific study is the way to Truth, not random rainbow chasing and dungeon delving. Dear gods, that time the Korvass Krew came back with the cockatrice egg. What a mess. I still have the statue it made of my cat. Poor little Dandelion. He was a good cat, but not too bright. Cockatrices look a bit like chickens you see and—"

"No, sah, nothing like that," Amandine said, hurriedly cutting him off. "I mean, I only hope it's a mystery to me and something known to you? Here let me show you."

She pulled the lump-halves out of her pocket and set them on the counter. Wizzlecog peered at them curiously. He picked one up, smelled it and then poked it with a finger. "It's some sort of fungi, young one, but I am not familiar with it. The apothecary would be a better source of information I think. Where did you find it? Unknown mushrooms can be quite dangerous."

"It's from Chef Brutsche's pantry, sah. He cooks with them, I believe, so I don't think it's dangerous," she said.

"Ah, why don't you ask the Chef what it is then?" he asked, setting the piece back down.

"I... erm... someone I am acquainted with took it without asking, sah," she said. When Wizzlecog narrowed his eyes she quickly added, "It wasn't me, sah, I swear it. By Kayla, I do!"

"I see," Wizzlecog said, tapping his fingers on the counter and staring beadily at her.

Amandine felt a stab of panic. This had been a mistake. Her stupid mouth! If Wizzlecog told Chef that she had taken it, she would be released from service at the Manor for certain.

"A young man came into my shop almost two tenday ago asking about ways to open locks. Specifically the triple tumbler Dwarven kind. The only such lock I know of, that is not installed in Lady Everdawn's Manor or in The Stomping Golem, is the one your employer uses to secure his pantry. I thought it an outrageous expense for guarding spices at the time. Quite excessive. I told the lad, for starters, that 'Dwarven' locks are actually designed by Stone Folk like myself. And since I did not create or install that particular mechanism, I would not know how to disable it without study. Furthermore, even if I had such access and inclination, I too am an engineer of the Third Circle Within and such vandalism would be unthinkable. Imagine you are an artist, miss, and someone comes to you and says, 'Will you destroy that statue over there if I pay you?' Would you do it?"

His litany paused as if he were actually waiting for an answer.

"No?" Amandine ventured.

"No! Of course you wouldn't. Artists secure in their own genius do not vandalize or defame the work of their fellows! They celebrate it! They encourage it! I asked that scoundrel to leave, forthwith and not to darken my counter with his knavery again!"

The volume of Wizzlecog's voice had raised half an octave and his already ruddy face began to purple slightly as he recited to Amandine. He paused and took a deep breath as if to calm himself and then adjusted his monocle.

"So, no, child, I do not think you are the thief, but if I may offer some advice. Free of charge?"

Amandine felt a small measure of relief, but was holding her breath anyway. "Yes, sah?"

"A secret, freely shared, is more valuable than one that has been stolen. Beware of those that offer knowledge through theft. Their motives are seldom pure and the benefit of such knowledge is lessened by the manner of its procurement. Ask to be taught, child, and if that old grump won't do it, then seek Truth on your own terms, but not through lies and deception."

Amandine nodded mutely.

Wizzlecog ducked behind the counter and hefted a wrapped parcel onto the surface that clinked with the sound of clay dishware. "I am guessing the errand Master Kale asked you on was for these, correct? Luminous day to you."

Without another word he grasped the moving ladder as it passed by again and vanished into the stacks.

With a heavy sigh, Amandine gathered up the strange halves of mushroom and the parcel. As she passed the Apothecary, she thought about the conversation she had overheard earlier. Telvor was definitely the person to ask, but nothing she had seen in his shop matched. What if he thought she was wasting his time with the query? An image of needleleaf tea filled her mind and the phantom smell of it, remembered in gruesome detail, filled her nose.

Amandine shuddered, hurried instead to the Stomping Golem, delivered the parcel to Bertrand, and began the long walk home.

Pyrestone

"No one knows the true method of creating or harvesting pyrestone, save the Dwarves, and thus far they have managed to retain the secret. Every clan has a slightly different version of the substance, hence the postulation that it is manufactured rather than harvested, although these differences in color and consistency could also be from varying methods of refinement. Needless to say, there would be many more cold toes during High Winter if not for these amazing stones and their seemingly endless outflow of warmth."
- *Lecture notes, Third Mistday, Low Autumn 1201*

IT WAS QUIET and dark in the warm cellar. Amandine lay on her cot, belly down, facing towards the furnace. The massive iron bulb radiated heat from the endlessly burning slab of pyrestone within. They were incredibly expensive. The glowing red hot stones emitted warmth that never faded and had to be transported in sand from the Dwarven nations. Brass piping fed heated air throughout the house, and a set of knobs allowed the staff to lower or increase the amount of air flowing to the various rooms. The cellar where it was housed, however, was always toasty. Amandine liked the warmth. It was comforting in a way that tickled at her memories.

She stared at the half of the weird mushroom in her hand and sighed.

"What do you think, Grendel? Should I leave it out for Chef to find again? It's not mine, after all."

The fat, striped cat didn't reply, but sat and stared at her from the floor next to the cot. His tail swished against the packed earth in a way that Amandine felt was rather accusatory.

"Don't look at me like that! I didn't take it!" she said.

Amandine rolled over to stare at the ceiling. Dark patches marked where the heat had dried out the plaster. Cracks, like tiny spiderwebs, radiated from the dark areas. Sometimes small flakes would drift down onto the floor.

"What if I did that and Chef blamed Kivel, or Sunflower, or one of the house staff? I don't want to get anyone in trouble, Gren."

Grendel leapt up on her chest with a small sound halfway between a purr and a meow and began kneading his claws.

"Ow!" She gently swatted one of his forepaws. "Don't do that now. Have a nap if you must, but I'm not a fence post!"

The portly cat blinked slowly at her and stopped his kneading, then spun twice and curled up on her chest to sleep. His deep rumbling purrs vibrated through her as he dozed off.

Amandine tucked the mushroom away into the pouch that held her savings. It sat inside a small satchel full of her "treasures" she kept under the cot. She didn't own much: an old prayer book a visiting Delinkhal Sister had gifted to her while she was still at the orphanage that she couldn't read, a seashell she had been given by a traveler who claimed it was from the Azuredark Sea, and three smooth stones of different colors she had kept after a day playing in one of the streams that fed the Wolfshenta. They seemed to change colors when soaked and she would sometimes rub them between her fingers when she wanted to think.

There was also a plain white cloth handkerchief, with no embroidery or decoration, which had been tucked into the basket she had been found in as a baby. She had no proof whatsoever of what it was, but she liked to think it belonged to her parents, whoever they were.

Finally there was a small ledger with a handful of string-bound pages that she kept her "notes" in. She didn't know enough writing to make proper cooking instructions, but it included doodles and her own pidgin cipher that helped her to remember techniques and recipes she had learned by watching Chef Brutsche and the other cooks. She would need to buy more pages for it soon, but paper was outrageously expensive in Stoneman.

Amandine stroked Grendel as she thought about her conversation with Wizzlecog.

"Seek Truth on my own terms?" Amandine asked the sleeping cat. "What are my own terms? It sounds a lot like the religious sermons the Night Sisters liked to give, you know?"

Grendel yawned for an answer and began to purr louder.

"Do you think Chef Brutsche would actually agree to teach me if I asked? Kivel and Sunflower have been working with him for years and he doesn't show them his secrets, why would I be different?"

The warmth of the cellar covered her like a blanket and Amandine drifted off to sleep herself, where she dreamt of a kitchen all her own.

First Mate

"The spice cartels of the Trenash peoples are the sole source of many of the most sought after seasonings in Beregoth. It's always a good idea to visit any Trenash spicer you happen across while out at the market. If possible, try to catch them when they are outbound, back to their homeland. The selection may not be as good, but many of their spices are perishable, and a shrewd spicer will sell you their wares at a discount rather than let it go to waste!"
  - Seeker's Kitchen, Chapter 4, Salts, Oils, and Spices

IT WAS SUNDAY and Amandine was busy stirring a pot of oats and honey for the house breakfast. The smell of sizzling bacon on the heated slate filled the kitchen and Kivel, in an exceptional mood, was singing softly to himself as he fried eggs in a pan. Chef was not there. He often went into Stoneman on Sunday mornings to procure ingredients and usually dragged Kivel along with him. Kivel hated going to town and so his good mood was probably due to his escape from the dreaded chore this tenday.

Amandine carefully sniffed the steam from the oats as she had been taught, and then used a long round wand to drizzle more honey from a pot next to the stove. She traced the thin golden line and drew a picture of a cat and then a flower until the honey that was stuck to the wand ran out.

"No ta much now, foal," Sunflower chided her. "Lord Estevan don' like it so sweet, and the honey is dear." The small woman was stacking up logs for the hearth in the woodbox. Any one of them would have taken Amandine both hands, but she arranged them with just one; all the while watching Amandine and continuing to talk.

"Yes, sah," Amandine said as she put the wand back in the pot. "I heard that Old Gert is trying to raise bees. Like cattle."

"Oh, an' who told ya such a daft thing?" Sunflower asked.

"Miss Jacinda," Amandine said, a touch annoyed at the idea of anyone calling Jacinda 'daft.' "She said he's building a box they would live in like a hive, but with parts you can slide in and out to collect the honey."

"That old fool better have fur like a wumpus if he don' wan' ta be covered in welts!" Sunflower said with a tsking sound. "I had a cousin that died after he upset a hive in a log. Bees are fierce when protectin' their homes! Like cattle, indeed!"

"That would be a trick, though," Kivel opined as he began filling a plate with fried eggs. "Think of how much more often we could indulge in fritters and cakes!"

"Sometimes, I think yer brain is made of cake," Sunflower muttered, but Kivel apparently didn't hear her and began singing again.

The back door to the kitchen opened and Chef strode in. A small person trailed in his wake. At first Amandine thought it was a child and then she realized it was a Stone Folk woman. She had long silver-white hair done in intricate braids and a pair of thick lenses that were mounted in frames to rest on her nose. One of the lenses had multiple smaller lenses on a swivel so they could be stacked in front of each other.

"Luminous day to ya, Chef," Sunflower said with a bow. "Back from Stoneman already, sah?"

"No," Chef Brutsche said grumpily. "I haven't left yet. I was waitin' fer Master Hingewheedle ta arrive so she could have her look at my pantry."

"Is something broken, Chef?" Kivel asked.

"I'm not sure yet," Chef said as he frowned at the pantry door. "It's all yours, Master Locksmith. Here's the key."

Master Hingewheedle waved his hand away. "No need for the key, dear. I built it. I can do what's needful without unlocking it, and whatever you have inside shall remain secure."

Chef Brutsche nodded. "I have nary a doubt of yer craftsmanship, sah. But someone did burgle me, and so I must be sure it were no fault of the lock."

Amandine stiffened and cocked her head. He had noticed something was missing. She still had the mushroom stashed with her secret belongings in the warm cellar, but she wondered again if it had been wise to keep it.

"Indeed," the locksmith said in an absent-minded fashion as she lowered two of her movable lenses and inspected the mechanism. She pulled a small thin tool off of her belt, which was festooned with a dizzying array of arcane-looking apparatus. "I may be a tok or five."

Chef Brutsche folded his arms and sighed. "I'll leave ya to it then, sah. I have business I am late to attend. Amandine!"

Amandine was so startled to hear her name that she dropped the spoon into the oats. "Shadowed hells!" she cursed.

Kivel and Sunflower both raised an eyebrow at her, more for the swearing than for dropping the spoon, she was sure. Chef stomped across the kitchen and glared at her before looking into the pot.

"It seems I would be doin' the crew a favor by removing you from the galley," he growled.

This was it, Amandine thought. He knew she had the mushroom and was going to release her. She would have to go back to living in the barn, if Berty would let her. Sister Corbin would drag her back to Artemis for certain. She felt her eyes start to tear up.

"Oh, stop yer sniveling girl. Jus' get the ladle and fish the colorless thing out and then meet me by the wagon. Yer gonna be my first mate on the trip ta Stoneman today."

"I, uh, why—um, yes, Chef," Amandine said as she wiped her eyes and hurried off the stool to go fetch the ladle.

"Why do ya need her in town, Chef," Sunflower asked. "She can na' lift any of the heavy sacks Kivel hauls for ya."

Kivel made a shushing motion at Sunflower from behind Chef's back.

"I'll haul the grain t'day. Gonna visit Heather as well. I want the girl ta go buy from the creamery. She gets on well with that half-fae lass that married old Bertrand."

"Her name is Miss Jacinda," Amandine said a bit peevishly as she fished out the sticky wooden spoon from the pot of oats.

"Aye, and she's a beautiful shark, but still a shark," Chef said with a frown. "It's the Olgothian half of her to be sure. Shrewd merchants, the lot of 'em. You get me a good price on the butter and cheese on my list and I'll add a bonus to yer pay this cycle."

Amandine handed Kivel the spoon and ran downstairs to fetch her coat from her sleeping place in the warm cellar. Grendel, who had taken over her cot, stretched and yawned an enormous cat yawn and then blinked at her as she tugged her arms through the sleeves of her coat.

"I get to help Chef in town today!" she said to the cat. Grendel seemed bored at the pronouncement and leapt down from the cot to begin cleaning his paws. "Fine, be that way," Amandine said, sticking out her tongue. "You're just jealous!"

She rumpled Grendel's head and then ran back upstairs to meet Chef in the wagon yard of the estate. He was already in the driver's seat and holding the reins on the wagon's horse, Juniper. He made an impatient wave with his hand and pointed at the seat next to him.

"Come along now, girl, the tide ain't waitn' fer us!" he said. Amandine swung herself up onto the bench next to Chef and they departed.

As they trundled down the road away from the estate, they were passed by a group of people on horseback. The lead rider was dressed in chainmail armor that gleamed in the sunlight. He had a large sword buckled to the side of his steed and a round shield tied to the other side. The group trailing behind him was a motley assortment of humans and Hill Folk, some in boiled leather armor, some in mail. One human woman wore red robes with intricately sewn symbols all along the hem and cuffs. The two Hill Folk at the back of the train, a man and a woman, appeared to be speaking to each other with only their hands. She didn't understand a bit of what they were talking about but their facial expressions made it seem like an argument.

"Who are they?" Amandine asked once they had passed and were out of earshot.

"Seekers Guild folk," Chef said with a shrug. "Lord Estevan paid a bunch of them looking fer an easy coin to patrol the fields after word of them dark fae got 'round. Least the ones he hired seem more competent than the usual lot."

Amandine knew about Seekers. Like a lot of orphans she lived with while growing up in the Ravenex convent of Artemis, she had dreamed of joining the Guild one day and finding some ancient treasure. It sounded grand compared to cleaning gravestones or dressing corpses. But then fate landed her in Stoneman, hundreds of yarns to the South, and she hadn't thought twice about the Seekers until now.

"Is there a Guild in Stoneman?"

Chef snorted. "Don't be daft. A backwater like this is mostly jus' a place for those types to resupply and catch a nap before they get on wit' the business of killin' themselves."

"Is it really that dangerous to be a Seeker?"

He was quiet for a moment and Amandine thought he might not answer her question, but then he spit over the side of the wagon and spoke: "Aye, it be perilous, but lots of things are. When I were still afloat, I ran amok of many wearisome things. I sailed all the Great Rivers and all four seas. I escaped bandits, fought river beasts, and a storm once shipwrecked me. Nothin' is truly safe in this world, but ye knew that already, didn't ye?"

Amandine nodded as he eyed her sideways from his seat.

"The difference between bein' afloat, or bein' a soldier or even just gettin' up in the mornin', is that regular folk, no matter their profession or tribe, don't seek danger. They live behind walls, take safe routes, travel 'n groups, avoid being out at night, and follow orders. Seekers... yah, they don' do none o' that. They hunt the danger out with a purpose. Some do it because they feel a need. Others just want riches. Fool way ta get rich. Better way ta get dead."

"Wizzlecog said the same thing."

Chef nodded. "Yeah, that ol' stone has some wisdom, if ye can tolerate his jabberjawin'."

"Did you know many Seekers?"

"Yup," Chef said, but did not elaborate.

Amandine burned to ask another question, but the dark pensive expression on Chef's face meant the subject was at an end. She painfully swallowed her curiosity and instead watched the countryside pass them. In the distance, a pod of leviathans floated near the clouds. Their oblong, striped bodies drifted on the air currents like fish in a stream. A smaller one darted around the larger ones, in and out of the clouds, leaving trails of puffy white mist.

"I wonder what they eat?" Amandine asked herself aloud as she watched the creatures play.

"Eh?" Chef asked, seeming to awaken from whatever dark reflection had taken him. He looked up. "Oh, levis? I've no idea. I heard of a wizard once that tried ta use magic to fly up and study 'em, but the air was so cold she passed out and fell into the Azure-dark Sea."

"She flew? With magic?" Amandine asked.

"Yeah, wizards do all manner of strange things, fer strange reasons most of the time," Chef said. He spit over the side of the wagon. "She was rescued by the fae what live in the ocean. Wrote a book about the experience. Been years since I last read it."

"That sounds interesting," Amandine said. What she found more interesting was that Chef read books. There was not a single cookbook in the kitchen and she had never seen him so much as pick up a written list. He seemed to do everything from memory.

"I heard Mister Green is teaching you letters. That's good. He's an odd twig, even fer an elf. Them Sisters at the convent never taught you readin'?

Amandine shook her head. "The Sisters would tell us that people speak truth only with their voices, and that written words were full of falsehood. Only the holy scriptures are truth, and only the most dedicated of the Order learn to read them."

"That's the most foolish thing I have ever heard," Chef grumbled. "Full of falsehood, bah. It ain't wrong that sometimes people will put false things ta paper, but that doesn't mean it's all lies. Ye have to learn how ta look at what's written, compare it with what ye see and hear, and then make up yer own mind."

"So do you think the book you read about the wizard that tried to fly was true or false?" Amandine asked.

Chef watched the leviathans and seemed to think about the question for a moment. "I don't reckon it matters much," he said at last. "It weren't trying to convince me of nothin'. It didn't make any claims other than her own experiences. It jus' told a story. I liked the story. Whether it were true or not didn't mean anything. She might have made up the whole thing, but I still liked readin' it."

"I think it might have been true."

"Oh, why is that?"

"I mean, when I have heard people lie, it's usually to make themselves look better, look bigger, look smarter. If she was lying, why would she say that she failed and had to be rescued?"

Chef nodded. "True, true. But sometimes even the worst lies have a grain of truth to 'em. In this case, yer probably right. Mages don't much like ta be wrong, in my experience."

"I wish she hadn't fallen. I still really want to know what they eat."

"Me too, fingerling. Me too."

Good Deals

"Trade between nations is regulated by their respective governments, but the actual work is done by large trade consortiums that manage the day-to-day logistics. The largest of these in Serentia is the Halifax Trade Consortium, notable not only for its size and reach, but also because it is managed almost entirely by Hill Folk."

- Lecture notes, First Sunday, Low Winter 1201

"THREE GOLD MARKS and five silvers," Miss Jacinda said. The estate's order of cheese and cream was laid out on the counter in jugs and wrapped in cloth. A small cask filled with soft butter sat on the floor nearby. The sharp smell of the aged sheep cheese made Amandine's nose tickle.

"If we agree to buy more of the greenwax wheels, will you discount the total order?" Amandine asked.

Jacinda rested her elbows on the counter with her chin in her palms and peered down at Amandine through narrowed, brown eyes. "That's the third time you've tried to wheedle a discount out of me. Did Chef Brutsche put you up to that?"

There was no accusation, or even annoyance in her tone, but the question made Amandine feel like she had been caught doing something wrong anyway. "I am to get a bonus if I get a good price, sah."

"Ah, you see, that's why you are doing so badly," Miss Jacinda said. Her tone was slightly disappointed, which made Amandine squirm.

"Why?" Amandine asked.

"You are negotiating with no leverage, child. I have everything you want," Miss Jacinda explained while motioning to the cheese. "But you are not offering me anything I want in exchange. In fact, you are asking me to take *less* of what I want, which is your silver. This is not how good negotiations happen. To make it worse, you revealed to me your own stake in the bargain, so now I have more information than you. I can broker a better deal for me, easily."

"Then how do I do it right?"

Miss Jacinda's stern facade broke and she laughed. "I like you, Amandine. You are always so refreshingly direct. It's not in my interest to teach you how to have any sort of leverage over me in making a bargain, but I will give you some advice and if you can figure it out on your own, I'll give you the discount."

Amandine nodded.

"In a fair trade both sides have something the other wants. The key to good negotiation is to figure out what *else* the other side wants and to leverage that to get a better deal on what *you* want. For instance, I know that Madam Raven at the bathhouse loves stickle-berries. So I have a fresh basket of them when she comes for her order. We have a bramble of them out back that the goats keep in check. It takes almost no extra effort on my part to gather some berries for her, but she gives me an extra two silver for the treat. I get more of what I want, at little cost to myself, and she is also happy with the bargain. *That* is the trick, Amandine. Now what is it that you think I might want?"

Miss Jacinda smiled and folded her arms while Amandine thought furiously. "I... I will come and help on Third and on my other off-day on second Fireday."

"Oh, that's better!" Miss Jacinda said with a smile. "Much improved, but here's the thing. I know you are getting a bonus for the discount and I have a shrewd idea of what Chef Brutsche will pay out to you. I also know how much you get paid in a tenday.

Therefore, I can deduce that the extra day of work at the soup kitchen is far less of a cost to you than to me with the discount you are asking for. So I know to hold out for more, because?"

"Because I told you about the bonus," Amandine said, unhappily.

"Don't frown, this is a lesson, not a punishment," Miss Jacinda said in a soothing tone. "What can you do to sweeten the deal?"

Amandine thought about it a bit more. What did she have that she could offer, that cost her nothing, that might be valuable to one of the wealthiest women in Stoneman? Suddenly, an idea occurred to her.

"I will give you my recipe for the mash. And show you how I make it."

Miss Jacinda's expression shifted. She raised an eyebrow and put her hands on her hips. "Well, you *do* learn fast, don't you?"

"Is that enough?"

"I will discount the order," Miss Jacinda said as she drummed her fingers on the countertop thoughtfully. "And give you an extra wheel of sharp-orange as well."

"That's very kind," Amandine said, her face flushed.

"No, that's still a very good deal in my favor," Miss Jacinda said with a nod. "You best follow through with your promise then on next Third."

"I will!" Amandine promised as she counted out the coins she had been given to pay for the food. "Thank you, sah!"

"Knock on wood to make it good," Miss Jacinda said, rapping her knuckles on the counter. It was a very old Olgothian custom Amandine had seen repeated at the markets when a deal had been struck between merchants.

"A promise has been made," Amandine replied as she also tapped the counter.

"Perfect," Miss Jacinda said with a wide smile. "I'll call Herbert to help you load everything into your wagon."

Amandine carried the smaller wheels and the butter keg while Herbert helped her with the larger items. They loaded the back of Chef's wagon, which was already partly full with sacks of grain, a barrel of ale, and three huge cloth wrapped parcels that she knew were Dwarven icehouse salt beef from the market.

Chef Brutsche was not waiting in the wagon, however. Amandine didn't think he would be out of sight, especially with goods sitting openly in the back, and sure enough spied him a moment later in the doorway to the apothecary. He had one eye on the wagon while having a conversation with someone inside. A moment later, Telvor stepped outside, exchanged a pouch to Chef for some coins and then waved him off with a shake of his head.

Amandine waited patiently on the runner as Chef ambled back across the square past the clockwork fountain.

"How'd ya do, fingerling?" he asked as he approached the wagon. She answered him by handing over the pouch with the remaining coins. He peered inside. "Adequate," he rumbled. With a gnarled finger he fished out three coins and handed them back to her. "Yer bonus."

With wide eyes, Amandine examined the three silvers in her palm. It was more than an extra tenday's pay. "Thank you, Chef!"

"Thank yerself, ya spared me a portion o' my allotment. I can get extra spices and sundries now. Let's go see Heather."

Amandine pocketed her new wealth and nodded. Heather Mince was the matron of the Stoneman Stockyard, as well as the local butcher and an expert in the cleaning of game.

"You there! Brutsche!"

Amandine winced at the sound of Sister Corbin's voice. Why wouldn't she just go away?

Chef put down his reins and turned in his seat to look down at the old woman. She had her hood up to block the sun, but Amandine thought it made her look like she was hiding.

"Yes, sah?" Chef asked in a surprisingly mild voice.

"Don't think you've gotten away with this theft!" she hissed. "She was already apprenticed to me and my order. She cannot be made a ward of House L'Eau without our consent, which we have not given!"

"We've been over this," Chef said in the same calm voice. "Lord Estevan and Lady Gia took her under their roof and vouch for her care. I was there, as you were."

"You met with Lord Estevan?" Amandine said in alarm.

"Yesterday, while you were in Stoneman," Chef explained before turning his attention back to Sister Corbin.

"They can vouch all they want, but it's not the same as adoption. There are rules. There are traditions. You cannot take another master's apprentice without leave!"

"She's not my apprentice, sah."

Amandine wilted a bit at the pronouncement, but Chef Brutsche didn't notice.

"Correct, she is mine."

"I am not your property!" Amandine said, raising her voice. "I am not going back to Artemis!"

"You are an apprentice! You swore an oath! You are not of majority age! You were not given leave to travel here, and if you do not come with me right now, I will take my complaints to the Sheriff and the Magistrate!"

Amandine drew in a breath to yell at Sister Corbin again, but Chef reached out and laid a hand on her shoulder. His eyes glittered dangerously as he spoke.

"Yer welcome to take yer complaints to the Magistrate. Maybe she'll even grant ye a hearing. But I have no proof of yer claim or good will other than yer word, which if truth be told, I don't much care for. Be about your business, Sister, or I will call for the Sheriff on account of you blocking my cart."

Brutsche and Sister Corbin locked stares again, much as they had done before in the kitchen.

"You have striking eyes, master cook. They are out of step with the rest of you. You asked me once what my real purpose was, but I think that question is better posed to you," Sister Corbin said. Chef didn't reply and she smiled at him. "I see. Well then, you shall be hearing from me again soon. With a Magisterial writ in hand."

Sister Corbin turned and strode away. People in the square moved aside for her when they saw her cloak and pin. A few glanced over at Chef and Amandine in the cart.

"Bah, let's go," Chef said, flicking his reins.

"What did she mean about your eyes, Chef?" Amandine asked.

Chef Brutsche shook his head. "Old superstitious nonsense. Can't expect much else from illiterate windbags like her. Remember our talk about what's true?"

"Yes, Chef."

"Well, she is an expert at bending that truth. Folk only speak true with their voices? Bah, people can lie with 'em too. Hopefully Lady Everdawn sees her for the eel that she is and sends her packing back to Artemis."

"Could she really force me to leave with her? Since I'm not of age?"

"Maybe. Did ye really swear an oath of apprenticeship?"

"Yes," Amandine admitted, "Years ago after the last shiv. But I didn't understand what it meant then. At the time it felt like those of us that were picked to take it were being rewarded. We got extra food, and more free time."

"I see, so ye were even younger than now. And did they have you sign to it?"

"On paper? No, sah, we spoke the words in the Temple of Ravenex, before the Stone."

Chef frowned. "So they get a bunch of kids, and make 'em 'prentices before majority, with nothin' but some words spoken before a rock? I'd say it's nonsense and you have nothin' to worry about, but the godsworn have a lot of pull on the oars of this land. Hopefully Everdawn's sense is greater than her piety."

"What can I do if it isn't, Chef?"

Chef Brutsche frowned. "Focus on the bends ahead of ye, watch fer rapids, and do what ye can. Fer now, we have a job to be about, so let's be about it."

When they rolled up to the stock yards, Chef Brutsche did not turn into the wagon yard where others had tied off their teams and rigs. Instead he turned down a side lane parallel to the yards and continued past a crowd of merchants bidding on mutton-stock sheep as a Hill Folk auctioneer rattled off numbers and names in a rapid cadence.

"Are we to buy a lamb or fresh butcher, Chef?" Amandine asked.

"Not today, fingerling. I jus' want ye to watch Juniper while I conduct business with the matron."

"What sort of business if not meat, sah?"

"My business," Chef replied with a growl and Amandine did not press further.

He pulled the wagon up next to a pair of double doors that fronted a large, flat roofed shed. Amandine immediately smelled the nauseating mixture of blood and feces that emanated from the structure, then as if to confirm her suspicions, the harrowing death squeal of a hog filled her ears and was abruptly cut short.

Chef handed the reins to Amandine and climbed off the bench. He walked to the doors and pounded on them hard enough to rattle them on their hinges. After a moment, Heather opened the doors and stepped into the sunlight wearing a waxed leather apron that glistened with blood.

Her braided hair was wrapped up tight under a large bandana and she was wiping her hands on a towel. She nodded as Chef made a thumb jerking gesture at the cart. Heather pulled the apron over her head, hung it on the doors and then walked around the corner of the building and out of sight.

When she returned she had a heavy-looking bundle slung over one shoulder. Chef approached her and folded the canvas back from one end, nodded and then walked with her back to the wagon.

Heather dropped the heavy bundle into the wagon and then, as if they weighed nothing, took two of the three wrapped halves of salt beef out of the back, put one over each shoulder, and walked away.

Chef climbed back onto the bench and took the reins again.

"She took the beef, Chef," Amandine said.

"She took her payment," Chef replied.

"Payment for what?"

"Barracuda will get yer nose with such questions, fingerling," Chef said. He snapped the reins and began driving them towards the northern gate.

Amandine was burning with curiosity, however. She continued to sneak glances back at the bundle. It was larger than one of the salted beef halves, and the canvas it was wrapped in looked like rough muslin rather than the tightly woven sailcloth the drygoods merchant used for covering salt meat. A large hoof peeked out of the end that was tied with hemp rope. It looked like a steer's hoof but was larger than any Amandine had ever seen. It was easily as big as her head.

"That's a big cow," she said to herself.

"Aurochs. Not a cow."

"Ah!" Amandine exclaimed in recognition. She had seen a herd of the large, shaggy animals when she had traveled from Artemis. They had been roaming the wild plains and the caravan she had been with took care to avoid them. The bull of the herd had been more massive than the covered wagon the wealthy grain merchant had driven, and probably weighed twice as much.

"I thought aurochs were totally feral," Amandine said as she examined the hoof. "Heather knows someone who farms them?"

"Aye. That she does."

Chef's wagon slowed as they approached the gate and joined the queue of other wagons and horses leaving the city. The guards at the gate, accompanied by a man dressed in Lady Everdawn's livery, inspected cargoes and collected tolls from those that were required to pay for access to the road. When their turn was about to come up, Chef leaned over and spoke to Amandine in a loud whisper.

"Ye keep yer hatch secured. I'll be the only one talkin' or ye will be walkin' back to the manse."

Amandine nodded that she understood.

"Destination?" The guard asked as the liveried servant read a ledger behind her.

"Manor L'Eau," Chef said.

"Cargo?" she asked.

"Just things for the larder, no trade."

"What is that?" she asked, pointing to the wrapped bundle.

"What it usually be, Dena," Chef said with a conspiratorial wink. "Ye want a taste?"

The guard, Dena, glanced back at the tax collector, who was still absorbed in his ledger.

"I'll need to inspect that bundle, driver," she said aloud with a wink back at Chef.

Chef jerked his head towards the bundle and Dena folded back a flap of cloth to reveal the red and brown, dry-salted haunch beneath. She produced a long knife from her belt and carved off a chunk from the thigh, sniffed it and took a bite.

"Is there a problem?" the liveried man called from the side of the gate.

"No, sah, all is in order. It's just dry goods for Manor L'Eau," Dena said over her shoulder. "Move along, Master Chef."

He waved at her as their wagon rolled past and she saluted them with her hunk of salted meat before taking another bite.

"Are we not supposed to have that?" Amandine asked once they were well out of earshot.

"Eh, maybe it's no thing ta be worried o'er. But havin' it would start a chain o' questions that would make things hard fer Heather. I don' want ta cause her no trouble."

Amandine wondered at that. What kind of trouble could the matron of the stockyards be in for having haunches of meat?

"Where does Heather get the aurochs?" Amandine asked.

Again, Chef was silent and she thought he might not answer her. Then he spit over the side of the wagon and said: "Folk large enough to tame and handle aurochs."

"Oh," Amandine said, slightly confused. Then it dawned on her. "Oh! Oh my!"

She looked out towards the hills in the distance and imagined the enormous men and women dressed in furs and stone that were rumored to live there. Giants. The Old Peoples of Beregoth, used as stories to frighten children and whose tempers were said to cause destruction that only fierce High Winter storms could match.

"Not a word," Chef Brutsche said in a warning tone.

"Yes, Chef," Amandine replied.

Floppy Duck

"Magic is the enforcement of one's will over reality. Some spells will create things that endure. They will have a lasting structure and energy of their own once manifested. Some spell effects will dissipate when the attention or concentration of the Practitioner is diverted. Only those properly attuned to the rekh, or spirit of, well, everything, can harness the energy needed to outwardly create spells. Human practitioners usually choose a specific field of magic to specialize in, while longer lived peoples often take a more holistic approach to the Art. Others can be assisted by the use of Arcanum. And many more have small, innate connections to the universe that give them magical-seeming abilities without any conscious thought at all. It's theorized that every living thing has a connection to the universe that is the conduit for magic, and that the spark of life itself may indeed be an aspect of this phenomenon."

- Lecture notes, Second Ironday, Low Winter 1201

"I TOLD YOU it was good, Berty," Miss Jacinda said.

Bertrand Kale, the innkeeper, scooped another enormous spoonful of mashed potatoes and parsnips into his mouth. The satisfied sound he made was his only response.

"Amandine's cooking is lumi," Gil said in agreement as he scraped the dregs of his own bowl with a spoon.

Amandine bumped his shoulder. "You helped, Gil."

They were all standing in the kitchen of the Stomping Golem. It was a busy Thirdday evening. Amandine's work at the soup kitchen was done and she had fulfilled her debt to Miss Jacinda by showing her and Bertrand how to make the mash. The common room outside buzzed with activity, occasionally punctuated by laughter and drunken singing. The barges were leaving tomorrow, and the sailors—Dwarves, Human and Hill Folk alike—were making a time of it before returning to the river.

Tilly poked her head inside the swinging shingle that separated the kitchen from the commons. "I could use an extra pair o' hands ou' here!" she said with a desperate note to her voice.

"I'm coming, Tillandra, keep your boots on, lass," Bertrand rumbled. "And tell the drunks we have a new special tonight: Mashed taters ala Amandine!"

With a sniff and a nod, Tilly vanished again, but not before smiling and waving at Gil.

Amandine grinned and poked Gil, who had waved back.

"What?" Gil asked with a frown.

"Gods, you're dense," Amandine said. She turned to Bertrand instead.

"Are you sure you want it on the menu, Master Kale? You think it's good enough?"

"Of course! It tastes amazing and it's easy enough to make that even a plow-handed oaf like me can do it. I'd be a fool not to. Whole reason I gave all those roots to the soup kitchen is that I couldn't do a colorless thing with them, and here you have gone and made magic, Amandine. If Brutsche knew what was good for him, he'd apprentice you and get that old harpy from Artemis to stop bothering everyone."

"She's been here?" Amandine asked as she wilted a bit.

"Nearly every tenday, the old raisin," Miss Jacinda said as she set her empty bowl down. "Don't you worry about her. It really is very good, Amandine, you should be proud. Consider our debt settled." She stood on her toes to kiss Bertrand on the cheek and turned to leave. "I'll go assist Tilly, dear Berty. You might want to make an extra pot of the new mash, I expect it will be popular."

"I'll help!" Amandine said.

"Me too!" Gil added.

"If you ever open an inn, I might go out of business," Bertrand said with a chuckle as he fetched a large copper pot down off a shelf. "Maybe I can hire you out from under Brutsche, eh? Think he would be mad at me?"

"I don't know..." Amandine said. She felt awkward at the praise.

"Definitely," Gil said with a nod. "That crusty old badger would have a fit, I think. Sunflower can't reach half the kitchen and Kivel is lazy and cleans things wrong. They need her there."

"Don't be mean to Kivel!" Amandine scolded.

"I like Kivel! He taught me a really funny song last tenday. But he *is* lazy, Amy. That's truth," Gil said.

Amandine frowned at him anyway, but then Gil began to sing:
"Oh, the wheat is tall,
Jus' before the fall,
And the walls are green with ivy.
But the wind won't blow,
Les' the rooster crows,
From my pants it flows behind me!"
Bertrand laughed and wiped a tear from his eye. "Gods, I haven't heard that one in *years*."

"Kivel taught you a song about flatulence? Really?" Amandine said as she rolled her eyes.

Gil smirked at her and launched into the second verse as he began stripping herbs. Bertrand joined in. Amandine sighed.

"Boys," she muttered.

Still, it *was* a funny song she decided. They were into the fourth verse and Amandine was considering joining them, when suddenly, Bertrand grew very quiet. Gil noticed and halted mid-word. Amandine realized why he had stopped. The common room had gone silent.

"You two stay here," Bertrand said. He stepped around them and through the shingle-door.

Amandine quickly followed and peeked under the flap into the common room. Gil appeared over her shoulder a moment later. "Oh," he said. "It's Hemm."

An old man wearing a sloping black felt hat and shimmering green robes with intricate gold-thread embroidery stood at the counter. He held a gnarled walking stick in one hand and gripped an ornate clay mug in the other that was full of ale, judging from the foam.

The room was silent. All eyes were on the old wizard. It reminded Amandine of a bunch of rabbits watching a circling hawk.

"'Eve, Barnabilius," Bertrand said with a smile as he approached the counter. "You're in late today, sah. We have a new special if you need a meal."

"No, Master Kale, and thank you," Hemm said. He extended a hand and a mug that had been filling itself at the taps drifted over to him. "I am here to relay some news, and then I shall depart. Although I do love your inn, sah. It's always so very nice and quiet."

The wizard took a long pull from his mug as people shifted uneasily in their seats throughout the room. "There has been another attack. Closer to town this time. Horses were taken, but no people. The survivors claim it was not boglings, but some sort of animal. None of them got a good look, however, despite their mounts being dragged into the fens."

"The Sheriff know?" Bertrand asked.

"Of course."

"And Everdawn?"

"Likely."

"Do you think Irongate will get off its arse and come help us?"

"Not for wild animal attacks, no, I don't think so."

"Perhaps we should speak with Telvor and—"

"Horse apples!" a voice said.

Amandine turned to look. A human male dressed in a finely made, unlaced white shirt and black silk pants had approached the counter. It was obvious from his swaying walk and wild hair that he had imbibed far too much ale or spirits. Or both. He slapped his lace ruffed arm on the counter next to the old wizard and leaned in close.

"Do you have something to say?" Wizard Hemm asked.

The words were polite, and the old man seemed completely nonplussed by the proximity of the disgustingly drunk nobleman, but it felt to Amandine like the warmth had been sucked out of the room. The lights from the oil lanterns even seemed to dim a little. She heard Gil's breath catch behind her. The drunk continued on as if unaware.

"Yer in league with 'em. The dark fae! Makin' excuses for your vile friends, right? Everyone knows what yer up to, sorcerer! We ain't fooled!" The man's words were so slurred, Amandine could barely make out what he was saying.

"You've had too much," Bertrand growled. "Take a seat or I'll show you one in the dirt outside, lord's son or not." The threat was delivered calmly, but Amandine could see Bertrand's arms tense as he prepared to grab the man if needed.

"You say you are not fooled," Hemm said after taking another sip. "But if it quacks like a duck…"

He set down his mug and tapped the man's wrist with a gnarled finger. There was a grotesque slurping and squelching noise as the man's features distorted and compressed. The air seemed to ripple visibly. Someone screamed.

And then there was a black and white feathered duck on the counter. It looked stunned for a moment and then began quacking noisily and flapping its wings. Hemm waved a hand as if dismissing it and returned his attention to Bertrand.

"I should be going. Let us see what the Sheriff and Lady Everdawn decide," Hemm said as he drained his mug.

"Aye. I suppose that's wise," Bertrand said as he eyed the angry duck on his countertop.

"Safe evening," Wizard Hemm said. He tapped his mug politely on the counter to indicate that he enjoyed the drink and tucked it inside his robes before turning to leave.

"And what am I supposed to do with this now?" Bertrand asked as he gestured to the duck.

"Cook it?" Hemm suggested without looking back.

The duck grew suddenly silent and seemed to stare warily at the innkeeper. As soon as the wizard left the building, however, there was a second dizzying pulse of air and noise and the duck was a man again, who promptly fell off the counter and onto his rump.

"Idiot," Bertrand seethed while looking over the edge at him. "You are lucky you're still breathin' you colorless, wumpus-brained, carp-fish. Get out of my inn!"

"My mother shall hear of this!" the man wailed as he stumbled from the room, rubbing his backside.

"More like the entire town will hear of it by tomorrow," Gil said softly to Amandine. "That was one of Lord Miller's children. He's known as a sloppy drunk. No one will take him seriously."

"Have you ever seen magic like that, Gilly?" Amandine asked.

"No, not ever. That was really... something," Gil said.

Miss Jacinda, who had been also watching from across the room, walked quickly back to the kitchen door and ushered them both inside. "You both will stay here tonight. I insist!"

"But I have a huge bake to help with in the 'morn!" Gil complained.

"Master Hawthorne will be sympathetic, I think. I'm sure he'd rather you were there to help him after sunrise, than be eaten in the dark by some animal. There is a room vacant now. I'll make sure Berty doesn't fill it and you can both sleep here tonight."

"Thank you, Miss Jacinda," Amandine said. "Come on, Gilly, we have mash to finish."

Miss Jacinda smiled and gave them both an encouraging pat before returning to the commons. The volume had slowly begun to rise after the wizard left, but it no longer had a cheerful air to it.

"What do you think the Sheriff will do, Amy?" Gil asked as he resumed preparing herbs.

"I have no idea, Gilly," Amandine said softly. "But I imagine we'll find out soon."

A Sharp Knife

"A sharp knife is a Chef's best friend."
   - Serand Brutsche

AMANDINE WAS FEEDING the chickens and frelkin while daydreaming. She imagined running her own inn, and populated the fantasy with elaborate dishes and a full kitchen complete with an iron stove, double ovens, and an indoor herb garden like Telvor's.

If she continued to learn from Chef and Kivel and Sunflower, then she might even return to Artemis one day, but as a chef herself and not just an orphaned street urchin. She wondered if her parents might be proud of her. Thinking about her missing parents ruined the fantasy somewhat.

It wasn't that she often dwelled on them. How could she miss something she had never known? Still, the mystery of who they were, and the square of white cloth she had been found with as an infant, sometimes gave her a headache.

Grendel sat nearby and watched her spread the dried corn. His head followed the arc of the grain and then reset back to her hand in the pail with each toss, while his tail swished on the ground behind him in time with her work.

The chickens, with their fluffy white and brown feathers huddled around the grain, while the scaly, long-necked frelkin darted their heads in between them. Beaks and lizard-like snouts competed for the kernels, but the larger chickens bullied the smaller reptiles around. Occasionally one of the frelkin would flap its large membranous wings and scatter the nearby chickens so she and her brood-mates could get in a few extra bites.

Amandine wondered again what it might be like to be a Seeker. To travel the world on her own, have adventures, and see all of the strange sights she was sure waited beyond the great river and the mountains it flowed from.

"The great underground waterfalls of Ur-Ferro. That would be an amazing thing to see, right Grendel? I was told that they were hundreds of spans high, but deep beneath the earth. Or maybe the ancient trees of Southern Serentia. Past the Emerald River. Hundreds of spans in the opposite direction. So high they touch the sky. I want to see that. How about you?"

Meow.

"You say that, but I'll bet they have lots of tasty birds there," she said as she tossed the kernels about.

Grendel flicked his tail and continued to watch the corn.

A sharp yipping and barking sound crashed through her daydream as a small roly-poly ball of fur launched itself through the pecking chickens, sending them clucking and flapping in all directions. The frelkin cried out in a ululating trill and flew up onto the fence, away from the disturbance. Grendel hissed and bolted off into the garden, leaving a trail of dusty puffs in his wake.

Amandine shrieked and dropped her pail of dried corn. The tiny whirlwind of fur resolved into the strange little dog that belonged to Fredderick. Dumpling chased the remaining few chickens who were brave enough to remain near the spilled corn to eke out another peck. They went flapping and squawking across the yard as she turned to face the laughing young man behind her.

"That was mean!" she scolded Fredderick, who was wiping a tear of laughter from one eye.

"It was hilarious," he said with a wide grin. "Hey, Dumpling, you missed one, buddy!"

The small dog came charging back to chase off a hen that had tentatively returned to the upended bucket.

"You stop that!" Amandine said. She stomped her foot down to block the funny little dog, but he merely yipped louder and began running circles between her legs. His tail wagged so furiously that his entire backside quivered.

"Ok, that's enough, Dumpy," Fredderick said. The dog instantly complied and ran back to sit by his feet and stared up at him with adoration. "Let me help you with that," he continued, and with a wave of his hand, the bucket righted itself and the spilled corn flowed back into it like water. The one remaining brave chicken squawked and fled again. Amandine made a similar noise before catching herself and pursing her lips at Fredderick.

"I wish you wouldn't do that!" she said.

"Clean up the mess? Alright."

He wiggled his fingers and the bucket began to tip again.

"I mean the sneakiness!" Amandine exclaimed, snatching the pail's handle before it could fall. "And the magic," she amended.

"I won't apologize for either," Fredderick said with a shrug. "Take it or leave it."

"Good day, sah," Amandine said with a sniff as she stalked past him towards the shed.

"Brr!" Fredderick replied as he followed in her wake. "You are feisty, you know that?"

"At least I am not a thief!" Amandine shot back. "You don't even work for any of the nobles do you? You are a grifter and I don't care if you're a mage. Go away!"

"You wound me," Fredderick said in a mock hurt voice. "And I thought we were friends."

Amandine rounded on him. "You stole from my employer, lied about who you work for, insulted the Hill Folk Gilly and I work with, upset Master Wizzlecog, embarrassed me in public, and, and..." she flailed about mentally for another stone to throw, "and you scared Grendel and all these poor frelkin and chickens! Shame on you!"

Dumpling wilted and lowered himself into the dirt and stared up at her mournfully. Fredderick, faced with the litany, at least had the grace to stop smirking at her.

"I think I know what that mushroom is and where it comes from," Fredderick said, putting his hands in his coat pockets. "I told you I'd come and see you if I found out anything else."

"I don't care," Amandine replied.

"Not even a little?" Fredderick asked.

"No," Amandine said as she folded her arms and glared at him.

"Well, alright, but if you change your mind about it, maybe ask your Chef about the Sheriff's bounty on boglings and see what he thinks. Come on, Dumpling."

"Wait! The Sheriff is going to pay a bounty on the boglings? Do they have proof that the boglings have been behind all the attacks? I overheard Old Wizard Hemm say that it was a beast, not boglings. And lots of people have mentioned that boglings don't usually hunt anything that large. Why would she do that?"

Fredderick paused at the torrent of questions and shrugged.

"Well she's under a lot of pressure to do *something*, and the boglings have definitely been stealing Lord Miller's grain. I guess it's a matter of appeasing the nobles. Bounties like that usually get taken up by Seekers Guild members or monster hunters. Mercenary companies might also hunt beasts or chase bandits as a side job between contracts. It's a fair sum. Three hundred gold crowns for proof that the fens are clear of boglings."

Amandine's jaw dropped. Three hundred crowns? A person could buy multiple horse teams with that much, or even build a house in town. It was a fortune.

"If you change your mind, I'll be staying in Stoneman for a while yet. See you later, Amandine," he said.

Fredderick sauntered off and Dumpling trailed behind him barking happily.

"Why in the world did he care so much?" Amandine thought to herself as she watched him go. She had known her fair share of con men and grifters during her time on the streets of Artemis, and had learned to avoid them. Most of the orphans the Sisters looked after quickly figured out who was trustworthy and who was not. The thing was, Fredderick did not seem to fit the familiar mold. There was no apparent gain for him to be so keen on where Chef procured his ingredients, and what did the bogling attacks have to do with anything?

She scattered a bit more corn for the frightened chickens and returned to the manse. When she entered the kitchen she was surprised to see Sunflower talking with a stranger.

He was a Hill Folk man with braided hair and a half-vest made partly from boiled leather. The hardened hide plates were sewn to his clothing as a sort of light-weight armor. He casually twirled a long handled dagger in one hand while using his other hand to accent the story he was relating in a bombastic tone:

"...and then, moving as silently as a hawk on the wing, I crept up behind the Tusker and," he dramatically thrust his dagger forward.

"Oh my!" Sunflower said, her face flushed. "That's quite the excitin' story, Master Birch!"

"Did ye stab him in the kneecap?" Amandine asked, feeling surly. "I'll bet that made him mad."

Both Hill Folk gave her such a baleful look that she instantly felt ashamed at the barb, but it was obvious that the fellow in the armor was a blowhard. Was he a Seeker? He might have been one of the group she had seen pass a few days ago on the way to Stoneman with Chef.

"Who is this, then?" Birch asked in a grumpy tone.

"She's just the scull, sah, don't pay her rude mouth no mind," Sunflower said with a disapproving glower.

"Chickens are fed," Amandine said with a shrug. She hadn't meant the jibe to offend Sunflower, but she wasn't going to apologize for calling out a liar on a lie either. "Shall I set the tray for tea?"

"I'll do it," Sunflower snapped. "Ye get along to yer other chores now!"

Amandine made a polite bow to Sunflower and went to fetch the bucket she used to fill the wash station.

"You've got a smart mouth, child," Birch growled as he hopped off his stool and crossed the kitchen.

Amandine stiffened. She knew what the look on Birch's face meant. Old habits immediately made her begin searching for an exit.

The windows were latched. The path to the back door and garden door were blocked by the Hill Folk Seeker and Taster Nous' door was on the other side of the kitchen past the fry slate and prep tables. While keeping an eye on the dagger he held, she attempted to sidle along the wall and gain an opening to run for it, but he easily side stepped to block her.

"No you don't!" he said with a sneer. "Tall folk love to have a go, don't they? Think we're all just a joke. Maybe you'll have a new per-spec'ive if I reduce ya by hand or so?"

"That's 'nough, Master Birch!" Sunflower shouted. "She' jus' a child, sah! Put 'way yer blade now!"

Chef's voice suddenly boomed across the kitchen: "What salt-blasted mutiny is afoot here!"

The gnarled form of Chef Brutsche filled the back door frame. An iron pan he had taken to the hamlet to be mended was in one hand and a sack of onions was in the other. His face was a picture of rage that Amandine had never before seen on the man.

He shouted and swore often, and said mean things as a matter of course, but the look on his face at that moment frightened Amandine more than the dagger Birch was still menacing her with. She realized then that she had never truly seen Chef angry before, not properly, and instantly decided she would never do anything to make him so.

"And who is this then?" Birch asked, as he rounded on Chef and twirled his dagger.

"Did ye let this raccoon pretendin' ta be a Seeker into my kitchen, Sunflower?" Chef growled. "Go fetch the broom, lass!"

"Right, you first then, ya shriveled arse!" Birch roared as he launched himself across the room.

What happened next was so fast that Amandine wasn't sure if her eyes were fooling her. There was a spark as the blade struck the pan and something whistled through the air past her. Sunflower screamed. Onions went flying everywhere. There was a grunt, a sound like celery stalks snapping and then Chef Brutsche had Birch, hoisted by his trousers and the back collar of his leathers, and was carrying him to the door like a stray cat.

Birch's face was bloody, and he mumbled something incoherent as Chef tossed him bodily from the house.

"And stay gone, ye thievin' bluefish!" he called out the door before slamming it shut.

Taster Nous appeared in his doorway a moment later.

"*What* is going *on* in here!" he demanded.

Amandine and Sunflower both started to speak but Chef held up a finger and Sunflower remained silent. Amandine quickly followed suit.

"One of them scabby Seekers jus' assaulted my crew!" Chef snarled. "And he were stealin' from the house ta boot, ya blind suckerfish!"

Chef upended a pouch over the table next to him. A smattering of coins fell out as well as a silver necklace, half a set of silver spoons, a Stone Folk crafted folding knife that Amandine knew Lord Estevan kept on display in the Upper Parlor, and no less than five other household items, all made from silver, electrum or precious stone.

Nous' face blanched and he quickly moved to retrieve the pilfered objects. "I will inform the Lord and Lady at once, of course."

"And apologize to Hedgehog you lout!" Sunflower declared. "Ye practically accused 'im of takin' that knife yesterday in front of Lady Gia. Shame on you, sah!"

Nous looked like he was about to argue but shut his mouth at the coupled glares of Sunflower and Chef Brutsche. He scurried from the kitchen without another word.

Chef turned and seemed like he was about to say something to Sunflower, then stopped and looked directly at Amandine. She flinched under his gaze, but what he said next surprised her.

"That were a bit o' violence you should have been spared, fingerling. And he nearly got ya anyway. Are ye hurt?"

"Hurt, sah? I didn't—" Amandine began, but she saw Sunflower pointing to her own arm and wincing.

Amandine looked down. Her right sleeve was torn next to the shoulder. A thin red line of blood seeped from a cut on her upper arm. She poked it gingerly and it stung. She hadn't even felt the blade touch her. A glint of metal made her turn around further. The dagger was halfway embedded in the plaster wall behind her. The underlayment was mortared brick. She wondered what in the world that blade could possibly be made from.

Chef approached and very carefully examined her arm. "Just a graze," he pronounced. "I am sorry he hurt ye, Amandine. Let's get ye ta Nanny and have that sewn and bandaged."

"I'll get the onions then, Chef?" Sunflower asked. Chef merely nodded as he led Amandine from the Kitchen.

"I've had an eyeball on that scoundrel since we took our trip ta Stoneman," Chef said softly as they took the servant's hall to Nanny's chambers. "Remember the pair talkin' with their hands?"

Amandine nodded, she remembered.

"That's *Livete*, a type o' speakin' used by elven scouts from the Great Courts. Let's 'em have private conversation with no one nearby the wiser unless they also be knowin' *Livete*. Thing is, I know it. A bit anyhow. Enough ta realize that fangfish was up ta scavenge whate'er he could afore they left Lord Estevan's pay. This is my fault, Amandine. I should o' told the Lord days ago that he were up ta mischief, but I had no proof until he jumped ye and I got a hand on his purse."

"Lady Gia uses it too. The hand signs."

"Yup, but her version is modified, more intricate. Made for folk lackin' hearin' to speak with others. These two were jus' usin' it to aid in their thievin'. I have no doubt they can hear jus' fine."

Chef was unusually pensive. Amandine had never seen him look ashamed of anything and his tone suggested that he was truly sorry she had been injured.

"It's not your fault, Chef. I tossed a jape about a story he was tellin' Sunflower and made him cross at me."

"So cross he'd cut a child with an Olgath steel dagger? Nah, he were justified not a wit. But perhaps ye should leave off tauntin' armed Seekers in the future," Chef said. They stopped at the door to Nanny's room. "Here's Nanny. Get yer cut seen ta and meet me in the kitchen. I'll have some things for ye ta do that won't be strainin' a hurt arm."

"Say, Chef," Amandine said before he could trun around. "Did you know that Sheriff Stolm has put a bounty on the boglings? It's big too. Three hundred crowns. Do you think the Seekers will go hunt them?"

"Who told ye that? That scab with the dagger?" Chef asked.

"No, sah, I heard it from another. I don't think it was a lie, sah."

Chef stood for a moment with his lips pursed. "They'd be huntin' the wrong thing. Goblins don't kill livestock. Nothin' as big as cattle anyhow."

"How do you know?" Amandine asked.

"Bah! Get yer arm sewn and come back to work. No sense worrying about goblins," Chef said with a scowl. He turned and walked away muttering to himself, his usual grumpy persona back from wherever it had retreated.

Chef's Pantry

"Stone Folk clockwork is a marvellous example of the practical application of underlying thaumaturgical principles. By utilizing the circumstances inherent to base materials and combining this knowledge with keen insight into how the interactions of moving objects coincide, they can create devices that replicate, in many ways, the effects of simple magical applications."
  - Lecture notes, Third Riverday, Low Autumn 1201

AMANDINE RETURNED TO the kitchen. Her torn sleeve had been removed and a bandage was tied across her stitched cut. Sunflower was on the step stool frying eggs over the wood stove. Chef was nowhere to be seen.

"Where's Chef?" she asked. "He said he had a task for me."

"Don't ya fret about chores a mo'," Sunflower said as she slid two bright green frelkin eggs from her pan onto a plate next to some fried onions. "You sit an' have a nosh."

Amandine sat down as Sunflower pushed the plate in front of her and added a fork.

"I'm sorry I barked at ya, foal," she said.

"I'm sorry I made that stupid jape," Amandine said before taking a bite. It tasted wonderful.

"It weren't great, true. But it likely had a truth to it, seein' as he lost his co'orless mind about it. Don't you stop calling out untrue things for one rascal's bad turn."

"I'll try to be more careful 'bout how I do it," Amandine said around a mouthful of egg.

Sunflower patted her leg and smiled. "That sounds like a bit o' wisdom sprouted, yah? You have pretty eyes, foal, ye know it? Liken ta jade they are, deepest green. If'n ye'd let me put ya in a dress for Godhome…"

"Dresses are stupid," Amandine said, still talking with her mouth full. "They flap around your legs and leave you cold and get in the way in the kitchen. The nobles can keep 'em."

"Have you ever worn one then?" Sunflower said with her hands on her hips.

"No."

"Then ya don't really know then. Meself, I think ye'd look a right proper butterfly, miss, Delinkhal as my witness!"

It was true that she'd never worn one, but it didn't change Amandine's feelings about them one bit. She shrugged and speared another bit of egg with her fork. "These are really lumi, Sunflower!"

Sunflower rolled her eyes, but let the topic drop. She patted Amandine on the leg again and went to clean her station at the block.

Amandine finished her plate and took it to the wash basin. She noticed that the dagger was still embedded in the wall. With a firm grip on the handle she gave it a yank and it slid smoothly out of the bricks. Thin wisps of red clay dust swirled off its blade.

"That's a wicked thing," Sunflower said disapprovingly as she wiped her egg pan.

Amandine turned it slowly in front of her. It was surprisingly light, despite its length. The curved steel of the blade had patterns in it that reflected the sunlight like ripples in water. The edge was ground so fine that she was amazed there were no chips in it after being shoved through brick.

"It's beautiful," Amandine said. She carefully tested the edge with her thumb and discovered it was still razor sharp.

"No good in a kitchen," Sunflower said with a sour note in her voice. "Only one thing such a blade is good for."

Amandine took an apple from a nearby basket and placed it on the chop block. Carefully she tried slicing it with the dagger. It passed through the fruit like paper and only a few drops of juice trickled down the sides of the blade in clear beads. Sunflower was right, however, the handle was too long and the blade's shape was wrong for most tasks. Maybe if she found someone who could put a cleaver's grip on it…

"I guess the Seekers are leavin'," Kivel said as he entered the kitchen and doffed his favorite wide-brimmed straw hat. "I also saw Chef actually riding Juniper towards Stoneman as if his apron were on fire."

He noticed the dagger in Amandine's hand and pulled up short. His eyes drifted from the blade, to her missing sleeve and bandage, to the hole in the wall over the wash station.

Sunflower answered his unasked question. "It's been a wee bit o' a raucous mornin', Kivel."

"It seems I missed the excitement," Kivel agreed. "Any idea why Chef would be going to Stoneman in a hurry without his wagon?"

"When he left he said some words 'bout bein' off to see th' apothecary. Perhaps he has an ailment?"

Chef? Sick? Amandine doubted the leathery old codger was capable of being ill.

Taster Nous appeared in his doorway and cleared his throat. All eyes turned to him. "I am to inform you that the Lord and Lady have decided to dine with Lady Jadet and her noble husband this evening. Once you are done with your daily tasks you may have the rest of the day to yourselves. Carry on."

He disappeared again without waiting for acknowledgement, although Amandine was certain she had seen him eye the dagger askance before he left.

"Well that's a treat!" Sunflower said. "I'll finish the morning prep for tomorrow then, if you will sweep the pantries, foal. Kivel can ya rotate the herbs please?"

Amandine found a leather blade wrap that wasn't in use and put away the dagger. As she began sweeping she heard Kivel: "Oi, it looks like Chef forgot to lock up his stash."

She poked her head out of the grain pantry and saw Kivel with his head inside the bug-curtain of Chef's pantry.

"You two ought to come see this!" he exclaimed.

"I don' know as if'n we should..." Sunflower said, but Amandine was already halfway across the kitchen. "You scamp!" Sunflower scolded, but Amandine didn't care. She was finally going to get a look inside!

She slid under Kivel's arm and past the curtain. The cabinet was lit inside, but not by a lantern or candle. Instead a strange glowing crystal was set into the ceiling of the small chamber. It gently pulsed with soft blue-tinged light.

The two longer walls were lined with shelves filled to bursting with jars and tins, but unlike the root cellar and its store of pickles and jams, whose jars were all identical cylinders of foggy glass, every container in Chef's pantry was different. The tins were made of copper and brass, steel and ceramic. Some had lids tied with twine, while others had small latches. A few were open on top and covered with a fine wire mesh.

The jars were equally varied. Some were tinted green or blue. Some were stoppered with wooden plugs and others with metal lids.

Most of the visible contents were strange. One jar had some kind of creature with tentacles and a parrot-like beak. Another contained what appeared to be carrots, except they were vividly blue. A third jar was filled with sand and Amandine swore she saw something moving in the silt.

The back wall housed a huge rack from which dangled a variety of strange cured meats and sausages. She recognized the aurochs haunch immediately, but there was also something that appeared to be an enormous dried bat wing, a leg that looked like it belonged to a giant grasshopper with a hard green glistening exoskeleton, a string of wrinkled meats that turned out to be various tongues in all sorts of lengths and shapes, and a taloned foot that looked like it belonged to a raptor—if the bird were as large as a horse.

Sunflower's head popped in under Kivel's. "Well ain't today a day fer strange sights," she said as she took in the contents.

"I wonder what it's all for?" Kivel asked.

"Or even what it is," Sunflower added.

"That's cured aurochs," Amandine said, pointing to the haunch. "I was there when he got it from Heather. And those herbs there. I know that smell. He puts that in the corn soup."

"Good nose," Kivel said. "And that there looks like the strange brown salt he rubs on his boar roasts."

"And that pickled fish, th' one with th' single huge tooth in front? I am certain he uses those skins when he boils clams," Sunflower added.

Amandine looked about for the tray Fredderick had described. Finally she found it. A small clay dish covered with a white linen cloth. Gently she removed the cloth and revealed three ugly black lumps resting in a bed of coarse salt crystals.

"Ew, what are those?" Sunflower asked, wrinkling her nose.

"Some kind of mushroom, I think," Amandine said. She picked one up. Part of one end had been sheared off, revealing the veiny inside she had seen in the one Fredderick had taken. Behind the tray was a metal sheet punched with small holes.

"He grates them with this, right?" she said, pointing to the tool.

"Yes!" Kivel exclaimed. "He keeps it covered with that cloth, but I have seen him shaving something into the batter for the egg puffs. I'll bet it's those. No wonder he keeps them covered. Otherwise it would look like he was grating a turd into the dish."

"The famous Serand Brutsche, caught servin' his guests shite poofs. I can hear the scandalous gossip now," Sunflower said with a tsking sound. "I don' blame 'im for keepin' it out o' sight!"

Amandine's breath caught.

"What?" she demanded, spinning to Sunflower. "What was that you said?"

Sunflower seemed taken aback by her sudden flare of emotion. "I weren't havin' a go at him, foal. I jus' —"

"No, no! I know, it's fine, turd puffs, I get that. The other thing you said. His name!" Amandine said rapidly.

"Serand Brutsche?" Sunflower ventured as she eyed Amandine sideways. "Are you feelin' alrigh'?"

"I didn't know that was his name!" Amandine exclaimed.

Sunflower seemed to consider this a moment. "No, ye haven't been here but half a year, righ'? I suppose it don't come up much. His proper name, I mean. He do prefer the title for certain."

"Hells, I didn't know his given name until I worked here a year, Amandine," Kivel said with a laugh.

Of course! Amandine's mind spun as something clicked in her memory, something she had overheard at Telvor's Apothecary. Chef's name was Serand. The person that could speak to Telvor's and Heather's mysterious contact was named Serand. Chef knew about the bounty on the boglings and immediately rode off to see Telvor. He spoke elven. He knew *Livete*. Could he speak to other fae as well? It stood to reason, that like Heather with the aurochs, Chef was aiding Telvor to get rare ingredients from the boglings—who wouldn't show themselves because everyone was up in arms against them.

"I think I know why Chef is going to Stoneman!"

Riding Crust

"Horses are not native to Beregoth. They came with humans during the Arrival, along with many varieties of domesticated dogs, cats, and livestock. Like humans, they have thrived here, and share a special bond with humankind. It's said that the greatest riders of the Zulath peoples can perform feats from horseback that defy the laws of nature and border on the magical."
- Lecture notes, Second Fireday, High Winter 1201

AMANDINE HURRIEDLY PACKED for a trip to Stoneman. She put on her coat and pocketed both withered halves of the pilfered mushroom. She also secured her small pouch of coins into an inside pocket and slung the dagger over her shoulder by the tie strings of its leather wrap. Grendel was nowhere to be found. She imagined he might still be hiding in the garden after being chased by Dumpling. On her way through the kitchen, Sunflower stopped her.

"I don't know what all the fuss is over, but take some lunch with you, foal," she said while pressing a neatly tied bundle into her hands. "An' please don't be tellin' Chef we was inside 'is pantry, yah? I like workin' 'ere."

"I am not going to get you in trouble, Sunflower, I promise," Amandine said as she took the bundle. "I think Chef might be trying to halt the bounty on the boglings."

"An if'n he were, what would a wee thing like you be doin' about it?" Sunflower said with a frown.

"I want to help!" Amandine insisted. "It's my fault the Seekers got released. If they decide to go hunt the boglings now instead... I think Chef gets his mushrooms from the boglings, with Telvor's help, and if they all get killed then I'll *never* learn how to make the egg puffs!"

Sunflower raised an eyebrow at her and shook her head. "I know you think them boggers have something' ta do with those strange... things Chef keeps in the pantry, but you don't know for sure, foal. I have no doubt that ol' buzzard has been in more scraps than you or I e'er have been. Perhaps you should—"

Amandine hurriedly gave Sunflower a kiss on the forehead and walked away. "Thank you for lunch, Sunflower!" she called over her shoulder as she left the kitchen.

"Foolish, squirrel-headed, rambunc—" Sunflower's litany of scolding was cut off as Amandine shut the door behind her.

"Where are you off to?" a familiar voice asked.

Amandine tried to suppress her impatience as Gil approached carrying a sackcloth-covered board that smelled of freshly baked bread. He was still wearing his flour dusted apron, something Master Hawthorne would likely scold him for when he returned to the bakery.

"We were given a holiday. I am going to Stoneman."

"Lucky! Hey, is that a knife?"

Amandine ignored him and hurried across the yard. She couldn't afford to lose time being bothered with Gil's nonsense, as friendly and endearing as it was. It would be a bell at least to travel to Stoneman, and that was if she moved with purpose.

After walking for a while, doubt began to creep into her mind. She passed the wheat and barley fields without even a glance at the rippling waves as she thought furiously.

Sunflower had a good point. She was not prepared to fight anyone, especially a bunch of armored Seekers when one of them was likely to be quite cross with her, if that was even what Chef had in mind. He was tough, but she doubted he would pick a fight with an entire group of well equipped Seekers. Perhaps she could find another way to help.

If the boglings were not to blame for the livestock deaths, then what was? Grimalks? Poachers? Wizard Hemm seemed to think it was a beast.

The sound of clopping of hooves on the hard-packed earth snapped Amandine out of her thoughts and made her check over her shoulder before giving way. To her surprise, Gil was rapidly catching up to her on the small chestnut gelding named Crust that he rode sometimes when making deliveries. He pulled rein alongside her.

"Sunflower told me what you are up to and what happened with the Seeker," he said with a frown.

"I am not going to argue with you about it too, Gilly. I am going to find some way to help Chef Brutsche and that's that!"

"I wasn't going to argue," Gil said as he reached down a hand. "I was going to give you a ride."

She paused for only a moment before allowing Gil to hoist her into the saddle behind him. He didn't ask what they were doing, or about the knife, nor did he comment further on the incident in the kitchen. They rode silently on the trade road to Stoneman at a slow canter so she wouldn't be jostled in the saddle behind him. Even at their pace, she would be in town twice as quickly than if she had refused the ride and walked alone.

"Thanks, Gilly," she said.

He nodded, but continued to say nothing. She wondered if he was upset. "What are you thinking about?" she asked.

"That we should go talk to Sheriff Stolm or her brother. Tell them what that Seeker did."

"But Lord Estevan already released him and his party. If they aren't hunting the boglings like I fear, then they probably rode North or East towards the fording towns. Do you think the Sheriff would really send people after them? Over a kitchen scull? I don't think Captain Rivaldo is allowed to do anything outside of Stoneman anyway. That was what she told the nobles when they gathered at the manor."

"Hrmph," Gil grumbled. "We need to do something. It isn't right! He could have killed you, Amy!"

"He didn't, though."

"He tried!"

"I'm fine."

"You're my only friend, Amy," Gil said with an uncharacteristic quaver in his voice. He swiped his nose with a hand and stared out into the fields.

"That's not true!" Amandine protested. "What about Tilly? Lots of folk like you, Gil."

"Only one my age. Tilly is pretty, and nice, but sort of intense. I sort of like her, but she is older than me and lives in town. Our hamlet is so small, it doesn't even have a proper name on the maps. You're the only one!"

"But Master Hawthorn's children—"

"Are a quarter my height and only ever want me to pretend to be a tusker to toss stones at," Gil snapped, cutting her off. "I love Master Hawthorn and his family, but it's not the same, Amandine."

Amandine considered that. She thought she understood how he felt. Gil was the first person here to talk to her like a friend and not just a noble's servant. He never told her she was small or stupid. He never even teased her about her dark skin and hair or how different her eyes were, the way the other orphans back in Artemis sometimes did. She hugged him from behind as the horse clopped along towards Stoneman.

"I'd miss you if you were gone too, Gilly," she said.

Lessons With Green

"Elves of the Court of Starlight are a rare sight outside of their ancestral lands North of the Kalebites. Serentia has more than the usual share, due their proximity to that frigid island nation, but mostly they tend to be less travelled than their southern peers, more insular, and less prone to fraternization with other races."

- Observations of the Fae, Third Volume, The Elven Courts

IT WAS FIREDAY, which meant the streets of Stoneman were packed with wagons and teams transferring cargo to and from the docks in the shallows of the Wolfshenta River in anticipation of the next raft of barges. Many merchants, some of whom had travelled over a tenday out of their way to get here by the Eastern route and avoid the fens, had set up small roadside stalls with blankets and folding tables, to sell a bit of their wares to locals while they waited their turn in the long queue. Many of these hawkers called out to Amandine and Gil as they slowly clopped by, but it wasn't until they passed a Trenash spicer that Amandine paid any notice.

"Hey, Gilly, stop a moment. I want to see what he has for sale."

Gil stopped Crust and allowed her to climb down in front of the man's cloth-covered folding table.

"Welcome, ripple, welcome wave!" the red-haired man intoned in a jolly voice. "A baker, young wave? I have what you need for the most delectable baked treats, oh yes! And you, ripple, have ye seen what a pinch of mandoragan powder will do for a soup or stew? I have all of the finest dried herbs and salts from the sea and the stone!"

His accent was lighter and his diction cleaner, but the way he spoke was exactly like Chef Brutsche. The Trenash people were a sea and river loving folk from the West, and while this fellow lacked Chef's dark skin, he was very similar in many other ways.

"Do you trade in mushrooms, sah?" Amandine asked.

His eyes lit up at her question and with a flurry, he deftly rotated tins and bottles around on the tables and indicated the ones now at the front. "Of course, ripple, of course! Please examine my fine selection. I know the flavors and medicinal quality of each of my wares, so please ask me anything!"

Amandine carefully considered each bottle and opened a few of the tins gently and sniffed at the contents. None of them were like what she had in her pocket.

"Is there something I can help you find?" the merchant asked cautiously. Her dilly-dallying probably had him expecting some sort of swindle by this point. At the very least she was delaying other customers. Amandine reached into her pocket and removed half of the mushroom that Fredderick had stolen.

"I was looking for more like this," she said. She held out the half for him to see, but when he reached for it, she withdrew slightly.

"Well, that's a rarity," he said as his grin widened. "Where did you find that now?"

Amandine thought quickly. She didn't want to lie to anyone, but it *was* stolen, and she really just wanted to know what it was. He was the first Trenash spicer she had seen in Stoneman in three tendays. "They grow here. It was found in the fens. Do you know what it is?"

"The elves call it 'bogwort'," the merchant said. "The people of Zulath call it 'black apple'. It used to grow in all the wetlands of Olgath before the great Mage War, but alas, it is a rare thing to see these days. You say it grows near here? Are you sure?"

"The one who gave me this says so, but he's a notorious liar. Will you trade for it, then, if it's rare?"

The merchant frowned at her and chewed his lip. "Aye, I'll trade for that nugget. But it's no good fer season, only elven medicine. Six silver would set us right."

Amandine heard Gil's intake of breath behind her. Six silver was a cycle's pay for either of them. But she had also caught the merchant in a fib.

It *was* good for seasoning. She knew that first hand. It was one of the best seasonings she had ever experienced. Still, merchants would be merchants, and she didn't have a lot of time to haggle. She only needed half of it to confirm her theory with Telvor, and they might need the coin to help Chef.

"One crown, four silver," she replied.

The red-haired man sucked at his teeth at the counter-offer, but didn't immediately call her down. That was good. It was just like Miss Jacinda had told her. If you have something the other side wants…

"One and two," he said with a frown.

"One and two, and three pouches. Of that, that and that," Amandine said as she pointed to tins of salts and mixed dried herbs.

The Trenash man paused for a breath longer and then nodded. "Fair deal," he said in the manner of his people.

"Knock on wood to make it good," Amandine replied.

"Aye, a deal has been struck, you little viperfish," he grumbled.

He counted out her coin and measured the pouches of spices for her and then she handed him the half of bogwort.

As she and Gil rode away, he turned in his saddle to look over his shoulder at her. "That was a lot of money, Amy! Are those ugly things really worth that much?"

"To him they are, obviously. It wasn't really mine to sell, but we might need the coin."

"For what?"

"I am not totally sure yet," Amandine replied. She was telling the truth, but now that she knew what it was, it was clear that

Telvor was the next person to talk to. "Turn here. Take us to the apothecary."

As the glass roof of Telvor's Apothecary came into view, Amandine began to have doubts. Telvor's talent as a doctor and herbalist was well known, but he was given to lecturing his patients as much as helping them. He had treated her a handful of times before she had been taken in by Lord Estevan and Lady Gia. His cures and tonics always worked, and he had never charged her on account of her being a child, but she had found the experiences unpleasant. The thought of his narrowed coal-black Zulath eyes and silent displeasure at her "childish carelessness" made her cringe at the memories.

"Do we have to go inside?" Gil asked in a voice just shy of a whine. "The last time I was here for twists, he made me drink a tonic that forced me to throw up everything I had eaten into a bucket. We don't have an excuse to be bothering him this time, Amy."

"We're not here for treatment, Gilly, just information," Amandine said, but she eyed the door to the building with equal trepidation. "Just a few questions and we'll leave."

The truth was, Wizzlecog had also recommended that she talk to Telvor. He really was the most qualified person to answer her questions, so Amandine steeled herself and tried to put on a brave face. He wasn't going to make her drink anything. She hoped.

Gil tied off his horse's reins to the hitching post outside and they went together to the front entrance. The sun glinting off the glass roof was practically blinding and Amandine held up a hand to shield her eyes.

When they were under the eaves and she lowered it again, she noticed a sign hanging from a peg on the door with carved Olgothian script (with subscripts in Serent and Zulath) that read "Closed for the day. Please do not die on my stoop."

"Oh well, some other time then," Gil said with cheer in his voice as he turned about and began walking back to the horse.

Amandine felt ashamed of her own relief at reading the message, but then felt a bit of frustration as well. To whom would she ask her questions now? Where had Chef gotten to?

"I thought it was you two," a familiar voice called out.

Fredderick waved to them as he crossed the square past the clockwork fountain. Dumpling charged forward, his tiny paws kicking up small puffs of dust from the cobble as he barked happily. He put his forepaws on Amandine's leg and whined at her.

"Hello, Dumpling," Amandine said with a laugh as she scratched the little dog's head. "Hello, Fredderick," she said, a bit more cooly.

"Go away," Gil said, dispensing with any pretense of friendliness.

"Ouch," Fredderick said in mock indignation. "Is that any way to greet a comrade?"

"We're not comrades," Amandine said, without any malice. It was simply a fact to her mind. "You're a thief, and very rude."

"Former, guilty," Fredderick said with a shrug. "Latter, by what account? Have I not helped you? You are here to confirm the tip I gave you, yes?"

"We don't want your help," Gil insisted. "If you don't scram, I'm going to punch you in the nose!"

"I'd like to see you try," Fredderick said, his eyes narrowed. Dumpling lowered himself and growled at Gil.

"Stop it! All of you!" Amandine shouted. "This is really stupid! Gil, you don't need to punch anyone. Fredderick, I agree with Gil, we don't need your help."

"Now, now, what is all of this?" said a new voice.

The trio turned to see Mister Green rounding the corner. Behind him trailed the L'Eau children, Marlette and Fiona.

He was dressed in a light green cloak and a set of well-tailored clothes dyed in a tan color like baked clay. It made his pale fae skin seem to glow in the bright sunlight, while his long ears were shaded by a wide-brimmed, similarly colored hat that was clearly Serent in fashion. Marlette and Fiona were both in their cloaks as well, and dressed in long-sleeved riding dresses whose colors matched the family crest of Manor L'Eau: silver and green and blue.

"*Soeje*!" Amandine exclaimed in surprise as she gave a polite bow. "We were just here to speak to the apothecary, sah." The bright sunlight seemed to counter the eerie effect of his shadowed eyes, but in truth, they didn't bother Amandine as much as they once had.

"Are you ill, child?" Mister Green asked with concern in his tone. "You could have come to me or to Nanny. She is quite skilled."

"We are having an outing!" Fiona burst in, apparently unable to contain her enthusiasm. Her blonde curls bounced as she bobbed on her toes and began speaking rapidly. "Mother and Father are visiting Lady Jadet, but she's terribly boring and so Mister Green offered to take us to town for lessons! We saw the aqueduct! And we are going to also visit Master Boomer and learn about geography!"

"Geology," Marlette corrected gently. "Do not speak ill of Lady Jadet, she is an ally of our house!"

Mister Green indulged the outburst, but softly waved his hands and Fiona obediently tucked away her retort to her older sister and bowed. "Sorry, *soeje*."

"Enthusiasm for knowledge is not a sin, dear girl," Mister Green replied. "But still, you have not answered my question, Miss Amandine. Do you need a doctor?"

"No, sah," Amandine said. She noted that Fredderick had gone rigid. It reminded her of someone unsure whether they should run away or stand up to something frightening. Did Mister Green also make him uncomfortable? She wondered if he could also see through the glamour that hid his eyes.

"We... I just had some questions for him, sah," she continued while trying not to be distracted by Fredderick's behavior.

Mister Green raised an eyebrow. "About what, if I may ask?"

Amandine paused. She felt Gil nudge her in the ribs. "Show him," he half-whispered. "The elves have a name for it, right?"

With a nod, Amandine reached into her pocket and revealed the other half of the strange mushroom. "I wanted to know where these grow, sah, and if the boglings might be the ones that grow them."

"Ah, bogwort," Mister Green said as his solid black eyes fell on the lumpy fungus. "May I?"

Amandine handed the half to him. He examined it closely and sniffed it, then handed it back.

"What is it?" Marlette asked as she wrinkled her nose.

"A rare mushroom. Once found all over, now quite exotic," Mister Green said as his voice slipped instantly into the tone he used when lecturing. "My people have used them medicinally for ages, but their flavor is awful."

"That's not true!" Amandine exclaimed. "Chef uses them! They're wonderful!"

Mister Green raised his eyebrow again and she immediately felt ashamed at interrupting him. You simply did not interrupt your *soeje* when being lectured. His expression held no anger, however.

"Well then, is this from Chef's odd pantry? I know that non-fae have a taste for them, but my people find them incredibly repulsive. If not for their uses in treating maladies of the head and spine, I doubt we would care much for them at all. How interesting. What does he cook with them?"

"Um, the egg puffs, I think," Amandine said. "Maybe some other things?"

"Well that explains why I am the sole dissenter on the flavor of that particular dish," Mister Green said with a chuckle. "Perhaps he made the shortbreads as an apology."

Fredderick had begun to slowly back away while Mister Green spoke. Without looking, the elf pointed a finger at the young man and said in an unusually firm voice: "Stay."

Dumpling immediately sat on his haunches and licked his nose with a wide pink tongue. Fredderick also stopped moving but continued to look incredibly uncomfortable. Gil finally took notice of the other boy's discomfort and shot a confused look at Amandine. She ignored them.

"Is it true the boglings grow them, sah?" she asked.

"Grow them? Unlikely. They cannot be farmed. The method of their proliferation is largely unknown, save that they seem to grow exclusively in brackish, swampy soil. Hence their name."

"Are you helping Chef with procurement?" Marlette asked. "I heard you were with him on his last trip to town."

"Um…" Amandine said. She was unsure of how to answer without lying. She was certain that Mister Green would know instantly if she was untruthful.

Gil spoke instead. "Sheriff Stolm put a bounty on the boglings. Amandine thinks they are where Chef has been getting his bogwort and that maybe he came to town to try and stop the collection on them. We wanted to help. If we can prove it's not the boglings, the bounty can be changed, right?"

Mister Green's face grew dark. The patient and pedantic expression she had come to associate with his features was replaced by a furrowed brow and a grimace that made him almost seem feral. Even Marlette and Fiona took a step back at the sudden shift.

"I do not abide bounty on any fae, but it is not within my power to rescind such an action," he said, a sharp edge to his voice. "They are unruly and often horrible, sometimes even enemies, but they *are* kin. I have already expressed my views to the Sheriff, as have others. She is a stubborn woman with deep prejudices."

"So you agree it's not them killing the cattle, then?" Amandine asked.

"Of course not!" Mister Green snapped. "Children, what do boglings eat?"

"Water plants and fungus," Marlette said quickly. "Also small swamp animals, insects and sometimes small birds."

"Indeed. Anyone with a scrap of knowledge agrees that boglings will not attack cattle outside of their natural habitat, and probably not even if they were encroached upon. They are small and cowardly creatures," Mister Green said. "This bounty is a farce to appease angry, racist, human nobility."

Amandine was surprised and unsettled by the emotion in Mister Green's voice. She had never seen him display anything but absolute calm. His anger was subdued, but frightening, like lighting crackling in high clouds, looking for a place to strike. He found it as his shadowed eyes turned to Fredderick.

"You! Walk with me a moment. Children, please remain here."

Mister Green strode towards the fountain and Fredderick stiffly followed him, trailed by a sulking Dumpling.

"Have you ever seen him angry?" Amandine asked softly as she watched Mister Green gesturing as he spoke in hushed tones to a pensive-looking Fredderick.

"No, never," Marlette confided with a touch of awe in her voice. "Who is that young man he's upbraiding?"

"A troublemaker," Amandine said with a scowl.

"He's sort of handsome," Marlette said appraisingly.

"He's a thief and a scoundrel," Gil put in.

"Is he now?" Marlette said with a smirk.

Amandine rolled her eyes. "Ask him to tea if you like. But something tells me he won't come within fifty spans of Manor L'Eau after this."

"What happened to your arm?" Fiona asked, pointing to Amandine's missing sleeve and bandage.

"Uh, an accident in the kitchen," Amandine lied. Gil began to open his mouth but she silenced him with a look. Marlette also gave her a raised eyebrow.

"That seems to happen a lot in Chef Brutsche's kitchen," she commented dryly.

Amandine opened her mouth to retort, but just then Mister Green stalked back their direction with a sullen-looking Fredderick in tow. The elf looked over his shoulder at him as they approached and spoke.

"You have been told. You refuse instruction, and so now you shall receive warnings. Wizard Hemm has cautioned you. I have cautioned you. Continue to cross us at your peril, *baikai*."

Mister Green's gaze shifted back to them. The transformation of his features was nearly instant. The dark storm of anger was replaced by the calm, placid expression Amandine was more familiar with. Only the edges of his solid-black eyes held any hint of his previous emotion.

"We have lessons to conclude. I think you and young Gil Crouste should accompany us. Master McKragen's knowledge of the earth and its makeup is quite extensive."

The very last thing Amandine wanted to do was go listen to Boomer talk about rocks. She didn't see a way to refuse, however, without further offending Mister Green or the children of her patrons. Before she could agree, however, Gil spoke up.

"If it's all the same, sah, I have been away from the bakery too long this morning and Master Hawthorne will be worried. I brought her to town, so if she likes, I can take her back with me to the hamlet and Manor L'Eau."

Mister Green sighed. "She is not officially my charge, so I leave it to her, then. You will be at regular lessons next Starday, yes?"

"I'll be there, *soeje*, and thank you for your instruction, sah," Amandine said quickly.

Mister Green nodded and walked away. "I'll expect you to keep working on your reading in the meantime, Amandine," he said without looking back.

They watched as he led the L'Eau girls past the fountain and out of the square. Gil turned to Amandine.

"So then, what are we really going to do?" he asked.

The Price of Bogwort

"Hedge wizardry, that is the practice of magic without collaboration or formal instruction, is highly frowned upon amongst practitioners. Subjecting one's will over the firmament of reality is a risky proposition even with such assistance, and so those that lack such guidance, by fate or by choice, can be a danger both to themselves and others. Not all Hedges are incompetent, however, and some have risen to greatness in spite of their handicap. Still, it cannot be denied that at least one catastrophe has been laid at the feet of such a mage (appendix 2.3, Calamity, The), and so the practice of magic in solitude is in large part, discouraged."

- Thaumaturgical Primer, Volume 1, Chapter 2, The Unbroken Circle

"WHY IS HE still hanging around?" Gil asked as he jerked a thumb towards Fredderick in the seat next to him.

They were seated at the end of the long bench table in the common room of the Stomping Golem. Amandine had decided to splurge and buy lunch from the inn since the bundle Sunflower had given her was not enough to share. A bowl of steamed rice covered in vegetables and thick brown sauce sat in front of each of them.

"Because I'm hungry," Fredderick said as he fed Dumpling a stewed carrot. The small dog barked as if in agree-ment.

"Quiet, both of you," Amandine snapped as she took another bite of rice and tried to think.

"So what was Mister Green so mad at you about anyway?" Gil asked. "Did you steal from him too?"

"That's not your business," Fredderick said with a frown. He had barely touched his food, despite his previous comment.

Gil pointed his spoon at him. "It is if you're going to keep hanging around. You're a lot of trouble, and I'd rather know what kind of trouble."

"Augh, will you both give it a rest? I am trying to think!" Amandine growled at both of them.

No matter how hard she thought, Amandine was at a loss. It seemed everyone knew the boglings had nothing to do with the cattle deaths, but only Chef and Mister Green seemed to care. If Seekers or bounty hunters killed them or drove them away, it wouldn't stop the cattle losses, but the secret ingredient to Chef's famous egg puffs would likely be lost. What could she do? What was really killing the cattle?

The only way to know would be to try and hunt down whatever was eating them, but Amandine didn't know the first thing about tracking wild animals, and the only things she had ever killed were chickens for dinner. Even then, she hated it so much that she often bribed Kivel into doing it for her by taking on his clean-up chores.

A chime above the door rang. Gil hissed softly into his mug of cider and nudged Amandine. She looked up and saw Mando Fame, the head of the dockman's union, enter the inn. He was dressed in a similar outfit to what she had seen him wearing on the evening he had stopped Miss Jacinda to talk, and his orange and red flame tattoos were even more vivid against his dark skin in the daylight. He walked with a cocky swagger as he crossed the common room, forcing patrons to step aside for him as if he owned the place.

He was trailed by two women: one was wrapped in a Zulath-style robe embroidered with strange symbols and exotic-looking flowers, the other clad in supple leathers that had hardened plates sewn on to protect vital parts of her body. A coiled whip hung from her belt. Both of them were incredibly fair with raven black hair and the slightly pointed ears that hinted at partial fae ancestry. They would be beautiful, Amandine thought, if they didn't both look as if they had just eaten something sour.

"What's Mando doing here?" Gil whispered. "I thought Berty banned him from the Golem?"

"Who are they?" Fredderick asked. He kept his voice low as well.

"I've seen him before. That's Mando Fame and his, uh…" Amandine searched for the right words. She had no idea who the two women were.

"Thugs," Gil said. "Gabriella and Yasmina. Yas is the one in the fancy Western robes. Mando is the head of the dockman's union. But Master Hawthorn says it's just a front for a bunch of crooks. All the other trade guilds hate him and his people, but Lady Everdawn never does anything about him. Master Bertrand, the innkeeper, forbade him from coming here in Low Autumn, last season, after he picked a fight with some Seekers passing through. Half the tables needed to be turned into firewood and replaced."

"I see," Fredderick said as he watched the trio take a table in the corner that was already occupied by a lone patron. "And who is the halfling?"

"I told you not to—" Gil began, his voice rising in anger.

"Oh hells, Gilly, shut up!" Amandine hissed as she pulled her hood up.

"But he—" Gil protested.

"Look! It's the Hill Folk Seeker that Chef Brutsche threw out of the kitchen!" Amandine pleaded, trying to keep her voice low.

The Hill Folk man wore the same armor that Amandine had seen him in earlier that day, but sported a black eye and a swollen jaw from his confrontation with Chef. His eyes scanned the room but passed over Amandine and the others without pause as he shifted his tall chair aside to make room for Mando and his bodyguards.

Gil craned his neck to have a look and then ducked back down over his bowl. "That's really him? The one who tried to stab you?"

"He what?" Fredderick growled as his eyes narrowed towards the seeker. Dumpling bared his teeth as well.

"Yes!" Amandine said through gritted teeth. She pointed at her bandaged arm for Fredderick's benefit. "Please be quiet!"

"But I thought you said they went East?" Gil whispered as he turned again to look.

"I thought they might... obviously he didn't. Stop looking at him! Fredderick, sit down!"

Fredderick took his seat again with a disgruntled expression.

"Amandine!"

She cringed at the sound of her name, but looked up and saw Miss Jacinda beaming down at her.

"It's not a soup kitchen day, and Gil is with you, I see. Having a holiday?"

"Sort of," Amandine said.

"Why is your hood up? And what happened to your arm?" Jacinda asked with a frown. "Is there trouble?"

"I thought Mando was banned? Where's Tilly?" Gil interjected quietly.

Miss Jacinda folded her arms and gave them all a stern look. "Berty banned him, but my husband is out and Tillandra has the day off. I told Mando he could have his table back on probation. Now answer *my* question please."

"No trouble!" Amandine said in a rush to keep Gil from interrupting again. "I had an accident in the kitchen and the Lord and Lady are traveling today, so we got time off."

Jacinda continued to frown, but nodded in acceptance of Amandine's explanation. She turned to Fredderick. "And you, these kids are some of my favorite people. If you are running a game, I will not be pleased."

"No games!" Fredderick said defensively. He held up his hands in a pacifying gesture and Dumpling yipped.

"You know Fredderick?" Amandine asked.

"We're acquainted," Jacinda said coolly. "Still grifting for sport? I went easy on you when you tried to trick me. Chef

Brutsche or my husband will leave you looking like that poor fellow."

Amandine didn't have to turn to know Miss Jacinda was pointing at the Hill Folk Seeker.

"Actually, Chef is the one who pummeled him," Amandine said.

Miss Jacinda's eyebrows rose. "Is that so? Well, that might explain a few things."

"Like what?" Gil asked.

"Never you mind. You lot stay out of mischief. I'll have some bread and a wedge of greenwax brought for you to go with your meals. My treat."

Miss Jacinda stepped away from their table and towards Mando's. Amandine chanced peeking around to see. Whatever the Seeker had been saying to Mando was paused as Jacinda approached. Birch looked put out at the interruption, but Mando and his bodyguards were strangely deferential to Jacinda and so he folded his arms and waited while they spoke.

Amandine strained to hear what they were discussing, but couldn't make out a single word. At one point the woman in the Zulath robes, Yasmina, laughed, as if at a joke Miss Jacinda had made, and with that, the cheesemaker walked away.

Mando returned his attention to the Seeker, who resumed talking, but in a voice that carried between the tables that separated them.

"So you see, I had the money, Mando," Birch whined. "But after that old bastard robbed me, I don't even have my blade no more. My crew decided to go East, but Thornberry and I don't want no trouble with the Union. Didn't want you thinking we ran out on you! Just give me a few more days and I can make good!"

Mando chuckled. "Master Birch, I don't care that you got caught. You didn't decide to stay, your fellow Seekers dumped you. I don't care about your knife, either. You picked a fight with the wrong old bird if you tangled with Brutsche, and you still owe me. I suggest you find some way before tomorrow, or one of my associates will come to collect."

"Just three more days!" Birch pleaded.

"Tomorrow," Mando countered. "I hear the Sheriff posted a bounty on some boglings. That should cover what I am owed with some to spare for you."

"And what would I do with no blade? Talk 'em to death?" Birch asked with a sour look.

"Not my problem," Mando said with a shrug. "If you try to skip town, I will know. Now go away, you're ruining my lunch."

Birch turned and slunk away, muttering to himself. Amandine faced away from him as he passed their table and made his way to the common room's taps.

"Serves him right!" Gil said fiercely under his breath. "I hope Mando collects his ears!"

"That's... gruesome," Fredderick commented.

"I've heard that's what he does!" Gil said. "Fingers too!"

The boys began arguing about the merits of Gil's claim and whether it was wise to dismember someone whom you wanted money from, but Amandine wasn't listening. An idea had occurred to her. It was crazy, but...

"Hey, where are you going?" Gil asked as Amandine stood up and began walking away from the table.

"To hire a scout," she replied.

Gil realized where she was headed and began to stand and follow her, but Fredderick firmly pushed down on his shoulder and re-seated him.

Amandine was grateful for the silent vote of confidence, because if she was being honest with herself, what she was about to do terrified her. Swallowing her fear, she strode to where Birch was filling a mug with ale and tapped him on the shoulder.

He turned and when he recognized her, rolled his eyes. "You again? Come to have another go? Sic your grandpa on me perhaps?" he snarled.

"Neither." Amandine said, forcing her voice to be calm. "I came to apologize. And to offer you a job."

Birch paused mid sip and looked up from his mug. "You... what?"

"What I said was unkind. I'm sorry. I'm *not* sorry that Chef hit you, though. You were being scary."

Birch eyed her critically and took another sip of his mug. Amandine tried not to fidget while she waited for him to respond. Finally he spoke:

"You have some stone in yer spine to be certain. I can respect that. What's the job?"

Amandine took a breath and delivered her pitch: "It's about the boglings. The Sheriff has a bounty on them because cattle are dying and people have gone missing, but my friends and other people I trust think she's put the bounty on the wrong creatures. You are a scout, right? I saw you using *livete*."

"Yeah, I am. You know Elven hand sign, kid?" Birch asked.

"Not really, someone told me what it was. But if you trained with elves, maybe you could help us track down what is really killing the noble's cattle. I think the Sheriff would pay out the bounty if the killings stop."

Birch chuckled. "That's not really how bounty contracts work, kid. You *think* doesn't guarantee me a green copper. Besides which, yer gramps didn't return my blade when he tossed me, so hunting anything is going to be a wee bit hard. No thanks to ya. Now get lost and let me drink."

Amandine unslung the wrapped blade from her shoulder and handed it to Birch. He set his mug aside and unfolded the leather cover.

"I... I never thought I'd see this again," he said. His eyes seemed to caress the blade as he tested the edge with his thumb.

"Yes, well, it's yours so have it back. Now that you have a weapon again, will you reconsider?"

"It still don't solve the problem of no coin. Giving me my own property back is well, but I don't work for free, kid."

Amandine untied her coin purse and dropped it on the table next to the mug of ale. "That's a little over two gold, mostly in silver. Is that enough? It's all I have."

Birch chuckled as he slid the long-handled dagger into a sheath tied to his belt. It looked like a full-length sword on the small man.

"Not nearly. That bounty is worth three *hundred* crown. I think it's a safer bet to hunt the boggers than some other critter, that may or may not even exist, on a whiff of a promise from a child."

"But the boglings haven't done anything!" Amandine protested.

"Says you. Lady with the gold says they are worth three hundred dead. If you can't beat that, then we don't have an accord. Sorry, miss."

Birch picked up his mug and slid the small pouch of coins back to Amandine. "Thanks for returning my blade."

Another Hill Folk, a woman, approached and slipped past Amandine. She was raven-haired and wore it in coiled braids. Her attire was similar to Birch's and when she saw Amandine, her brow knitted. She tapped Birch on the shoulder and when he turned around, she made several *livete* hand gestures while glaring at Amandine.

Birch rolled his eyes, but responded out loud. "Nothin'. She was just leavin', Thornberry."

"Good," Thornberry said in a high-pitched voice as she continued to stare daggers at Amandine. "We have work to do, B. Let's go while there is still daylight."

"After my mug," Birch said as he shrugged her off.

"One mug. If yer drunk goin' into the fens, I ain't gonna carry you out again," Thornberry said with a sniff. She sneered at Amandine. "Disappear, scullery girl. Ye have done enough for a day, aye?"

Amandine snatched up her money pouch and stalked back to her table.

"You're mad, Amy!" Gil said, his eyes wide. "You gave that lout his weapon back? What were you even trying to do? That other woman looked ready to finish what he started!"

"Hire him," Amandine said as she sat back down and stirred her bowl of rice, dejected.

"Whatever for?" Gil said, aghast. "He tried to stab you!"

"Only after I insulted him. We need a guide if we're going to find out what is really terrorizing everyone and keep the boglings from being hunted. He's a Seeker, and an Elven trained scout. But he won't do it. I don't have enough money."

Amandine laid her head down and stared at the side of her bowl. It was looking more and more like the boglings were doomed and she had just given a dangerous Seeker the thing he needed to go hunt them. Her day couldn't get much worse.

"How much does he want?" Fredderick asked.

"More than the bounty on the boglings, and that's three hundred crown."

"Three hundred!" Gil said in shock. "That's a fortune!"

"It's a fair sum," Fredderick agreed. "But I know how you might be able to raise at least part of the money."

"How?" Amandine asked.

"Without stealing," Gil added.

"The bogwort is incredibly valuable," Fredderick said as he fed Dumpling another carrot. "Small ones can sell for five or six crowns, large ones like the one I gave to you could be worth three times that amount if you found the right buyer."

"That ugly thing was worth fifteen crowns?" Gil asked in disbelief.

Amandine moaned and banged her forehead on the table. Her day just got worse.

"You still have it, right?" Fredderick asked.

Amandine slumped the rest of the way onto the table.

"She sold half of it to a Trenash spicer on our way into town," Gil explained.

"How much?" Fredderick asked.

Amandine felt like she might die from shame. "One and two, and some spices. Gods, I'm an idiot. He's probably having a great laugh."

Fredderick winced as if the recited amount had slapped him in the face. "Yeah, he got the better of you for certain."

"Stupid, stupid, stupid," Amandine chanted softly as she threw her arms over her head.

"If you show him to me I could—" Fredderick began.

"No more stealing!" Amandine and Gil said at the same time. Amandine gave her friend a weak smile. "You already stole it once, Fredderick. This is Kayla scolding me for keeping it to begin with."

Fredderick pursed his lips. "Fine, you still have the other half, yes?"

Amandine nodded and sat back up.

"Well that's something," Fredderick said. He rubbed his chin in thought while Dumpling plunged his head into the cold bowl of food. Gil made a disgusted noise as rice flew across the table.

"What do you think we can do?" Amandine asked.

"Us? Nothing, we're pretty useless," Fredderick said with a sigh. "But I think I might know someone who can help. Is that good, Dumpy?"

Dumpling licked his nose with his wide pink tongue and belched.

A Prayer to Kayla

"Kayla is the daughter of the Lord of Light, Akradath, and the Lady of Mercy, Milintanth. She is radiant, intelligent, and beautiful, both inside and out. All things feminine and graceful fall into her domain. She is the patroness of song, music, and competitions of the mind. Followers of Kayla administer wedding rites, compose and play music, adjudicate disputes of love and intellectual property, and in general, try to spread joy as far and wide as possible. Kayla is female over male, mind over body, love over hate, and above all, joy in living."
- *Lecture notes, Second Thirdday, Low Autumn 1201*

"WE'RE GOING TO see Old Wizard Hemm? Really?" Gil asked.

"You don't have to come with us," Fredderick said with a shrug.

They were walking down the Godsway Road towards the East gate of Stoneman. Most of the traffic was going the opposite direction they were traveling and so they often had to step aside for peddlers and wagons making their way towards the market circle. As they passed the huge stone-wrought temple dedicated to Akradath, a bell tolled and worshippers began to exit through the giant oak doors and down the marble steps into the road. They paused for a moment to let the throng pass.

Amandine looked over her shoulder at Gil and handed him another slice of the bread Miss Jacinda had given them.

"It makes me nervous too, Gilly. He is a bit mad, but I have to see this through! Shouldn't you go back to the bakery? Master Hawthorne is going to be incredibly cross with you."

Gil gnawed on his bread and eyed the back of Fredderick's head balefully. "No, I'm coming with. If I am going to be scolded, then I may as well fully earn it. Crust is all the way back at the Stomping Golem, anyhow."

They continued past the temple as the crowd thinned. Fredderick stroked Dumpling's head and glanced up at the carved stone facade as they walked by.

"You said you used to live in Artemis, right?" he asked.

"Yes. I was born there. I think. I never knew my parents." Amandine replied.

"You said before you lived in a convent. Was it Ravenex, then? That old woman had her symbol on."

"Don't be rude!" Gil snapped.

"It's fine, Gilly. That part of my life really doesn't bother me. Yes, Ravenex. Sister Corbin was my teacher." Amandine said.

"So why aren't you still there? With the Night Sisters, I mean. Training to be a Bone Guardian or Soul Keeper or whatever it is they call the folks that dress up dead people," Fredderick asked.

"Bone Guardian. Soul Keepers work with the army. The orphanage and the school burned," Amandine said as she kicked a rock out of her path. "We were all outside at the time doing cemetery work, so only one of the sisters was killed. She was really old. I think she died while praying and her candle set the place aflame. No one knows for sure though."

"And they just let you leave?"

"Not really."

"So you ran away?"

"Not really."

"Which is it?"

Amandine thought for a moment and took a bite of bread. It was a nutty dark-bake from Master Hawthorne's. Bertrand and Jacinda bought the good loaves for their inn. She savored the crunchy seeds on the crust and thought about her old life in Artemis.

"This is why I left," she said finally and held up the bunt-end of the bread.

"Bread?" Fredderick asked, confused. "I mean it's lumi, don't get me wrong, but that's quite a trip for a five-copper loaf."

"No, I mean food. The Sisters had a strict, bland diet and we ate well enough, but when we went on calls to homes that had lost someone, there was always food. When we would show up to take custody of a body, the families would often feed us. The Night Sisters do not take payment for their services, but the people were usually quite kind. Even to the trainees like me. I got to try all sorts of interesting foods, from people all over Beregoth. I wanted to see it for myself, and so in the confusion after the fire, I took my satchel and what coin I had and joined a trade caravan heading South and West. My goal was Anvilroot, but I only made it as far as Stoneman."

"I've never been to Anvilroot. The dwarves are famous for their smoked meats. The beer is quite good too. Why did you stay here then?"

"My money ran out. The caravan didn't need me for the return trip, and I didn't want to go back anyway. I tried to get passage on a barge going up river, but..."

"You're a kid," Fredderick said, finishing her thought. "No one would hire you."

"You're not that much older than us," Gil said with a frown. "Don't act so puffed up."

Amandine made a shushing motion at Gil and then shrugged. "Yes, that was basically what I was told. I was helping Master Bertrand with some kitchen chores to earn my dinner and Chef Brutsche came to see him and noticed me. The next day he offered me a job. I didn't want to take it at first, Chef was sort of scary, but then Master Bertrand gave me a meat pie, and I changed my mind."

"Did he drug it?" Fredderick said with a chuckle.

"You're a scab," Gil snapped. "The pie was one of Chef's. I've had them too. They are probably the best meat savories this side of the Wolfshenta."

Amandine nodded. "I knew then that Chef had the knowledge I needed. If I could learn to cook, then I could travel wherever I wanted. People would take me on if I could feed them, right? But when I saw what a true genius he was..."

"He's still a troll in an apron," Gil said around his final mouthful of bread.

Amandine laughed. "For certain, he's a sour apple, but I like him. And I like the other cooks, and I am learning *so much*. I am going to be the greatest chef in Beregoth someday, you watch!"

"That is a tall mountain you're looking to climb," Fredderick said with a thoughtful nod. "Perhaps I can help you get over a boulder or two."

Dumpling yipped.

"Why are you helping me?" Amandine asked.

"I like good food," Fredderick said with a grin. "Anything that allows me to sample the finest foods is worth my time. And your parsnip mash was incredibly good."

"Also, the turd-mushrooms are worth a fortune," Gil said sarcastically.

Fredderick glanced back at him and frowned. "Don't be crass. If all I cared about was the gold, I would have taken all of them, sold them, and left town."

"If *all* he cared about was the gold, he says," Gil said, mimicking him. "I still don't trust you."

Fredderick looked away. "Good thing your opinion does not matter then."

Gil opened his mouth to retort, but Amandine made a pacifying gesture at him and he silenced.

"Your opinion matters to me, Gil, please don't argue anymore," she pleaded. "I would rather, however, that you didn't steal anything else from my friends, Fredderick. If you like my mash that much, you can sample my cooking any time, without the thievery."

Fredderick shrugged.

They cut across the gardens that held the Shrine of the Revered. Every town had one and Stoneman's was fancier than most. It was a small, circular, stone-pillared structure that housed an altar and statues dedicated to all of the gods of Beregoth that did not have full temples in their honor.

"Can we stop here for a moment?" Amandine asked.

Fredderick nodded. "If you're going in there, though, I think I'll just wait outside."

"Guilty conscience?" Gil asked over his shoulder as he followed Amandine into the shrine.

"Oh, Gil, stop," Amandine said with a sigh. "Are you going to leave an offering to Leonid?"

"I didn't bring anything," Gil replied as he glanced around.

They weren't the only ones in the shrine. Several townsfolk were scattered among the statues, either kneeling in prayer or speaking quietly with each other.

Amandine made her way to the alcove that contained the statue of Kayla. The artist had depicted her as a beautiful woman with long, flowing hair and a playful smile. As the goddess of love and womanhood, she had also been carved without her clothes, but some other worshiper had draped the figure with a simple cloth scarf that provided the goddess a semblance of modesty. Amandine still thought she looked rather chilly. She reached into her purse and withdrew a single silver. She dropped it into the offering box next to the statue and then bowed her head.

"I thought you were dedicated to Ravenex?" Gil whispered.

"Kayla is also the goddess of competitive spirit and strength of mind. I can use a little of that right now," Amandine whispered back. "Besides, Ravenex has had enough of my life. She'll get the rest when I am done with it myself."

Gil scratched his head and wandered off to view the statues of Leonid and Old Jack, leaving Amandine to her thoughts. She didn't feel especially pious, kneeling in front of the statue. In fact, she felt rather silly. The silver coin she had just donated represented a lot of money to her and it gnawed at her pragmatic nature, but the bogwort *had* been stolen. Giving a little back might help level her scales, if nothing else.

"Kayla, if you are listening, help me choose my path wisely," she whispered. "Help me to be the best I can be, for myself and my friends. For we all close the circle."

It was mostly a rote prayer she had learned as a child with the Night Sisters, but it felt important to say it out loud this time. Amandine reached out to touch the foot of the statue, then her lips, then stood and motioned for Gil as she walked back to the entry.

"What did Kayla have to say?" Gil asked jovially.

"That you have dough for brains, but she likes you anyway," Amandine said with a smirk.

They found Fredderick where they had left him. He had somehow acquired what looked like a tree-sugar cake and was tossing small bites of it to Dumpling while a group of onlookers laughed and pointed. The tiny dog would do some sort of trick, a roll or a spin, even a backflip, before catching each bite.

The children in the crowd cheered at the antics, and even the adults were laughing. Fredderick caught the last bite in his own mouth before Dumpling could and the tiny dog flew into a frenzied dash around his ankles while barking. The crowd erupted in laughter again. Dumpling sat down in a disgruntled fashion until Fredderick picked him up. His wide, pink tongue began to lick sugar from his face and Fredderick joined in the laughter.

As the onlookers began to disperse, a few handed Fredderick some coins. Amandine and Gil approached and Dumpling stopped licking him to greet them with a small yip.

Fredderick bounced the copper coins on his palm. "Have a good time talking to the god rocks?"

"Yes, thank you," Amandine said quickly before Gil could retort. "It's not much further to Old Wizard Hemm's home, right?"

"Nope, he lives right over there, actually," Fredderick said, waving a hand in the direction of the town walls.

"Near the wall?" Gil asked, "In the shanties?"

"No, in that tower there," Fredderick said. He pointed to the massive crenelated watch tower that formed the Southeastern corner of the town's defenses.

"Wait, Lady Everdawn allows that? He actually lives *in* the guard tower?" Gil asked.

"He's a wizard. A proper one. Member of the Ancient Order of Highrobes and everything. I'm sure he has all the permissions he needs. And even if he didn't, who would stop him?"

"Fair point," Gil conceded, scratching his chin.

Amandine wondered if Gil was also remembering the duck on Berty's counter.

"Will we need to pay him for his services?" Amandine asked. "Chef told me that the best way to get a wizard to do you a trick is to pay them in advance."

"Well, maybe," Fredderick said as he scratched Dumpling behind the ears. "He and I had a disagreement a little while back, but I don't think he harbors any ill will towards me. When we get there, I'm going to let you do the talking, Amandine."

"A disagreement about what?" Amandine asked.

"Homework," Fredderick replied. "Come on, daylight is burning."

Tea, Dumplings, and Lizard Tails

"The Ancient Order of Highrobes is actually a coalition of several specialized orders of human and half-fae wizards who have been practicing magic for hundreds of years. They were instrumental both in great tragedies, like the War of the Magi, and in more heroic endeavors, such as helping create the Conflux after the Calamity that ruined the Bolath nation. Its membership is exclusive — not just any hedge mage or street performer can gain admittance, and the power they wield, both literally and politically, is not something to be taken lightly."
  - Lecture notes, Third Ironday, Low Summer 1201

THE ENTRY TO the tower reminded Amandine of an oven hatch. The heavy door was rimmed in iron and constructed to be so flush with the surrounding stones, she wasn't sure she could fit a knife blade into the gap. A horizontal slot pierced the center of the portal and was covered from the inside by a sheet of steel. A heavy ring that bore a knocker in the shape of a dragon's head had been affixed to the door. At least she thought it was a dragon. The scaly visage matched the descriptions she had heard about in stories.

Fredderick grasped the dragon by the snout and swung the knocker down twice. The boom it created against the seared oak planks reverberated through the air around them and the shutters on nearby shanties rattled with the force of it. The locals, who lived in the hovels near the town wall, shied away at the noise.

Amandine saw a few of them dash inside their makeshift abodes and slam their doors.

The narrow street between the shanties seemed to be holding its breath as they waited for a response. Gil shifted uncomfortably and licked his lips. He looked around them as if seeking an escape route.

"Are we sure this is a lumi idea?" he asked. "Mister Green is one thing, but this fellow is mad. He wanders about talking to himself and some people claim he's spelled them by accident while muttering. I mean, we saw him turn Lord Miller's son into a duck, Amy!"

Fredderick blew out an exasperated breath. "That's nonsense. He's perfectly lucid and aware of everything he does. If people think he's mad, it's because he wants people to think he's mad."

"Why would he do that?" Amandine asked.

"If you wanted to be left alone, what better way? Anyhow, he's only dangerous if you seem a threat, and well..."

He looked up and down at Amandine and Gil and shrugged.

Amandine swallowed and nodded. She wanted to trust Fredderick, but braced herself to run if anything seemed out of place. There was a loud scraping from inside the door, as if something large and metal were being dragged across the wood, and then the door slowly opened. The hinges were whisper silent despite its huge size.

Daylight flooded into the lower chamber of the tower, which was appointed with only a simple rug and five folding chairs of a kind sometimes used in Miss Jacinda's soup kitchen. A tiny table sat between the chairs and held three steaming clay mugs. The stone staircase that led to the next floor of the tower curved along the back wall and up through the ceiling into pitch darkness.

Fredderick gestured to the open door. "Well, that's our invitation. Let's have a seat. I hope it's not the mulberry tea again."

He entered the room and set Dumpling on the floor before taking one of the chairs and sliding it closer to the table with the mugs. Amandine followed him in and Gil trailed behind her. The moment Gil crossed into the room, the massive door swung shut behind them with a crash, plunging them all into darkness.

Amandine flinched at the sound and began to panic. She wasn't scared of the dark precisely, and tight spaces didn't worry her, but the room was utterly silent. It was so dark she couldn't even see her hands in front of her face and when she heard Gil yelp, the sound seemed to be muffled somehow, as if they were underwater.

A soft glow appeared and the table and chairs were dimly illuminated. Fredderick held his mug in two hands. It glowed like a lantern, but the light it shed was soft and blue tinged. It didn't flicker like an oil flame or a candle.

"Come on, you two, sit. It's not the mulberry. It's quite good actually."

"That's a handy trick," Gil commented as he took a seat next to Amandine and picked up a mug.

Amandine glanced into her own mug. It appeared to be filled with a dark tea that was steaming hot, but the clay of the mug was only barely warm. She blew on it and tentatively took a sip. A spicy melange of flavors greeted her tongue. It was bitter black-leaf tea, but seasoned with spices she couldn't quite identify. It was delicious. She really wanted to know what was in it.

"Why is it so dark in here? And why is everything muffled?" Amandine asked. Her own voice seemed strange to her ears, as if she were talking through a blanket.

"Defensive wards," Fredderick said, his voice also distorted. "If an enemy who knew magic tried to enter through here, their ability to create spells would be hampered by impediments to their senses. It's not that difficult, actually. I could probably do most of this if I had the right arcanum. It also deters supplicants who come to him with trivial matters. People who actually have something important to discuss will wait it out. Those that do not, well, they usually panic and try to escape, and he opens the door to see them on their way."

"You really seem to know a lot about this fellow," Gil said. "Mister Green too. Is it because you also know magic?"

Fredderick eyed Gil sideways. "Um, yes, you could say that."

Amandine caught his hesitation. His relationship with the other mages seemed contentious at best. She began to wonder again if this really was a luminous idea.

They sat in the light of the glowing mug and sipped their tea. Gil was unusually quiet, Amandine thought. He watched the stairs intently over the top of his mug, and occasionally glanced at the shadowed outline of the door. Fredderick was also silent, and barely drank, apparently lost in his own thoughts. The blue glow lit his face from underneath and gave him a rather sinister air, Amandine decided. Dumpling ruined the effect, however, asleep at his feet and snoring loudly. A small snotty bubble formed in his nostril on each rumbling exhale.

"Wizard Hemm will see you now," a gravelly voice pronounced.

Gil yelped and Amandine shrieked at the appearance of a small creature near the table. It stood about the same height as one of the Stone Folk, and was dressed in a vest and trousers, but its skin was coal black. It had no hair on its body. Eyes that glowed with a faint orange light shifted quickly between them and a wide mouth full of small, needle-like teeth spread in a feral grin.

Fredderick held up a hand. "Relax, it's just Kibble. Good to see you again, sah."

Kibble nodded at Fredderick. Dumpling awoke and wagged his tail while looking up at the strange creature.

"What is it?" Gil gasped, clutching his chest as he caught his breath.

"So rude," Kibble said, although the wicked smile never faltered. "I am of the *Iskrix*, the masters of the Dark Realms and the Lords of All. Kneel before my glory!"

"Don't," Fredderick said, holding up a warning finger. "They all talk like that, but only have power over you that you allow. This one serves Wizard Hemm."

"What's in the tea?" Amandine asked.

Everyone in the room, including Kibble, cocked their heads and looked at her.

"What? If Kibble is the servant, then they made the tea, right? I really want to know!" Amandine insisted.

"Black leaf mixed with keeshu nut powder, spice bark, lemon rind, and anise," Kibble muttered. "I am pleased you like it."

"It's really delicious," Amandine said, before draining her mug.

Fredderick raised an eyebrow at her but turned back to Kibble. "Well, lead on, sah. We shouldn't keep the old man waiting."

Kibble snapped its fingers and the darkness vanished. Amandine was not sure from where the light emanated, but it was a warm yellow that somehow made the bare stone seem more inviting. Kibble vanished and reappeared halfway up the stairs.

"Come," they intoned.

Amandine and Gil started to move but Fredderick stopped them. He looked up at Kibble and frowned. "What was that?"

Kibble sighed and their feral grin finally vanished. "Come. Please."

Fredderick nodded and began to walk up the stairs. "When one of them issues anything resembling a command, it's wise not to obey it. It gives them power over you."

"So if we had followed it could have eaten our souls or something?" Gil asked. He fidgeted as he eyed the back of Kibble's head.

"Uh, no, they don't do that sort of thing, and for a command so trivial, the most they would likely have been able to do is make you trip or something. Still, be cautious."

Amandine and Gil nodded. Kibble muttered and looked over a shoulder at Fredderick.

"I never get to have any fun," they whined at him.

Fredderick made a 'get on with it' motion. Dumpling ran up the stairs ahead of them, barking happily.

They climbed and climbed. Every floor they passed was slightly different. The first appeared to be some sort of sitting room with padded lounges and a fireplace. The next two were crammed with bookshelves and more books and scrolls than Amandine had ever seen in her life. The next was a storage room packed with boxes and crates. Next, a bedroom appointed with a four poster bed and elegant furniture made of a dark wood she didn't recognize. After the sixth floor something occurred to her.

"How many floors does this tower have?" Amandine asked. It only had four windows from the outside.

"As many as the Wizard needs," Kibble answered. "He added a new one for his bath last Starday."

"That's... impossible," Gil said. He stopped to look out a window next to the staircase. "It looks like we are still on the third floor from here."

Amandine felt a chill run up her spine. Magic. She had seen more of it in the last few tendays than the rest of her life combined and it only got weirder, the more she saw. She didn't think she would ever get used to it.

They ascended three more floors before coming to a stop at what appeared to be the top level. The ceiling was higher than the other floors and consisted of thick wooden beams and planks. A ladder, leading to a trap door, was attached to the wall next to where the stairs ended. A wide window was set on one side of the circular chamber, allowing sunlight into the space. Beneath it was a basin with a pump, a long butcher-block counter filled with strange glass apparatus, and a wood-fired stove with a smoke pipe sticking up through the roof. The rest of the room was dominated by an enormous hearth surrounded by squashy-looking stuffed chairs. Thick woolen rugs covered the floor in dizzying swirls of color, and the wall opposite the ladder had a bookshelf that was curved to fit the shape of the room.

Wizard Hemm reclined in one of the chairs near the unlit hearth. Without his robes on and dressed in a simple linen shirt, he looked incredibly ancient to Amandine's eyes. He slowly turned the pages of an enormous book that was lying open across a quilted blanket that covered his legs. His feet were propped up on a padded stool whose wooden frame was carved to resemble a dragon, much like the knocker on the door below.

He had no beard, but his hair was solid gray and long enough that it sometimes fell across his eyes, forcing him to blow it away with an annoyed mutter. Amandine noted that his feet were covered in thick socks, but each one was missing fabric near the toes.

"You still haven't replaced your socks, old man," Fredderick said as they all entered the room.

"You still haven't learned any manners, boy," Hemm replied without looking up from his book. "Who have you brought with you then? You know I don't have time for your silly obsessions."

"This is Amandine, who is apprenticed to Chef Brutsche, and Gil, who likes to complain a lot," Fredderick said by way of introduction.

"I'm not—" Amandine began, but Fredderick trod on her foot, causing her to yelp. She glowered angrily at him, but he merely raised an eyebrow at her and shook his head. Gil seemed upset as well, but she noted that he also kept his mouth shut, so she did the same.

Wizard Hemm finally glanced up from his book and peered at them. It wasn't the rheumy gaze of an aged bookworm, but the piercing look of a man who saw everything and missed nothing. His hard eyes looked from Fredderick, to Amandine, to Gil, down to Dumpling, lingered there a bit, and then back up to Fredderick.

"Still haven't got rid of it?" he asked.

"I'm not here to talk about that," Fredderick said with a dismissive wave. "Amandine had something to ask you about, and I couldn't think of anyone more qualified to help her with her problem."

"I am not in the business of helping children find lost toys or play—" Hemm began.

"I want to save the boglings!" Amandine blurted.

Wizard Hemm looked at her curiously and slowly closed his book. "Continue."

Amandine stepped forward. The wizard didn't seem very imposing. He was just an old man in a comfy chair. With holes in his socks. But the way he stared at her made her hair stand on end. It was as if the air in the room suddenly became like thick cream. At first she thought it might be a spell, but then she realized that she was simply afraid. He scared her. Just by looking at her.

Amandine swallowed and spoke.

"The boglings, sah, the Sheriff put a bounty on them."

"I am aware," Hemm said as he drummed his fingers on the cover of the book.

"Well, I think she made a mistake, sah. I don't think killing them will stop the cattle from dying."

"Of course it won't," Hemm said with a touch of impatience. "Even the Sheriff knows this in her heart. Boglings don't usually hunt animals that large."

"Then why?" Amandine asked.

"Because Kimber Stolm hates goblins. The cattle deaths are an excuse for her to rid the area of them," Hemm said. He raised a finger as if for emphasis. "The real question is why do *you* care what happens to a bunch of dark fae?"

Amandine reached into her pocket and pulled out the other half of the bogwort. "These, sah. I think Chef Brutsche gets them from the boglings. If they die, his most famous recipe will lose its key ingredient and I'll never learn how they are made."

"So you want to save them just because you will lose something you want? How disappointing. Kibble, please see them out."

Kibble bowed to Hemm and turned to face Amandine and the others. Before they could speak, however, Amandine stepped past them and spoke again.

"And it's wrong! Mister Green is mad about it too! It's wrong to hurt them just because they took some grain! There is no proof that they have been terrorizing anyone at all, in fact. Chef is trying to help them, I think. Maybe he went to see the Sheriff. I want to get proof to help him convince her, but I don't know how!"

"Impertinent!" Kibble said in a gravelly voice. "I will—"

Whatever he was going to do was cut short as Hemm raised a hand and made a shushing motion. "I think it's unlikely she will be convinced even with proof, child. But I admire your earnest soul. Humility is a rare quality in young people these days." His eyes drifted to Fredderick who grimaced and looked away.

"I will provide counsel, then," Hemm said. "But first, I will want some proof of your credentials. You are a student of Brutsche, yes?"

"Um, I study his techniques very closely, sah," Amandine said.

Wizard Hemm tapped the cover of his book emphatically. "Excellent, I'm famished."

He waved his hand and the blanket over his legs whirled into the air and folded itself into a neat square. Then it, and the book, floated to empty spaces on a bookshelf.

Hemm sat up and motioned to Kibble. "My staff, if you please."

Kibble bowed again and hurried across the room to grasp a long twisted branch that was propped up near the hearth. They brought the staff to Hemm and the old man hauled himself out of the chair with a grunt while leaning on it.

"Wow, is that magic too?" Gil asked.

"Don't be ridiculous," Hemm said with a snort. "It helps me to walk. See if your legs work properly after two centuries!"

Gil mouthed the words "two centuries" with wide eyes. Fredderick rolled his own.

"Well, get on with it, Amandine, make the old man some supper. Kibble, care for a game of stones?" Fredderick asked.

Amandine followed the hobbling wizard to his small kitchen across the room. She turned and motioned for Gil. "Help me out, Gilly!"

Wizard Hemm's kitchen was tiny compared to the one at Manor L'Eau, or even the one in Miss Jacinda's soup kitchen, but all of the basics were at Amandine's disposal. The wood stove had two openings for heat, and a split burn chamber. There was a thick oak cutting board that had been sanded to a perfectly smooth texture. A soft leather wrap contained a set of knives, and a small rack hanging from a beam held long-handled spoons, a ladle, and an assortment of pans of different sizes. A cabinet next to the basin contained bowls and plates.

"What sort of food do you prefer, sah?" Amandine asked as she rolled up her one sleeve.

Outwardly she sounded confident, but inside, her heart thundered in her chest as if it was about to burst. She wished that Fredderick hadn't lied about her being Chef's student. She washed dishes, hauled ashes, and stirred pots. She knew how to cook, but she wasn't even as good as Sunflower or Kivel, and Chef actually *did* teach them things. She prayed that the old magician picked something simple.

Hemm leaned against his staff and peered down at her. One hand absently scratched his chin. "It has been a long time since I have had black spice dumplings. As I recall, Chef Brutsche would prepare them as part of a stew with tubers and assorted vegetables. Sometimes thinly sliced meat as well? That would be splendid."

Amandine's heart sank. She had only seen Chef make that dish once, shortly after she had joined the staff, and only because Lord Estevan's older brother had requested it. Brutsche had often griped about that dish being one of his worst failures and that only someone with the palate of an oxen would actually enjoy it. It wasn't a hard dish to make, but Amandine was certain it would be bad. Incredibly bad. Just the memory of the smell made her stomach flip.

"V—very well, sah. Please tell me where you keep your larder. I will need flour, eggs, butter, milk or cream and whatever spices, roots and vegetables you have to hand. Oh, and if you want added meat, I will need that too, whatever kind you prefer."

Hemm casually waved a hand and then rapped on the countertop next to the stove. The cabinet below the counter popped open and revealed all of the ingredients she had listed, and nothing more. For vegetables there were several large carrots, two rikol roots, and a few bunches of greenstalk. A water filled vase held fresh herbs and there was even a small brass tin marked in Olgath script that read "blackspice".

"Woah," Gil said. "You can just make food appear too? You could feed everyone in town!"

"Fool, boy," Hemm said with a snort. "Magic does not work that way. Everything is a trade: life for death, death for life, water for sand for air for fire. You cannot summon a potato from nothing. If I conjure one here, it means there is one less somewhere else. All of this is from stores I keep preserved within the tower. I pay for my bread like any other person." He looked over his shoulder at Fredderick who was seated across from Kibble at a stones board. "Like most other people, anyhow. Now let's see what you have learned, student of Brutsche."

Amandine gathered the supplies from the cupboard and organized them carefully in the small space she had. She used the time to think frantically about what to do. She knew the basic recipe, but not Chef's ratio of spice. And even if she did, it was awful, even by Chef's own admission. What could she do?

The blackspice overpowered the entire dish and scorched the tongue to the point of numbness. It had no subtlety, no grace. You may as well pour blackspice into water and drink it. That was the problem with the spice. Kivel had said it was Olgath in origin and the dark black seeds were just fine when ground up and applied to roasted meats where most of the dark shells would bake away and the oils of the roast would soften their pungency, but in soups and stews it was a disaster. It just made everything in the pot unpalatable. Sunflower once quipped it was as if peppercorns were cursed by the heat of the sun and then breathed on by Seteg. She needed more time to think.

"Gil, please begin making a batter for the dumplings. I need it to be sticky and firm, not runny. Can you do that?" Amandine asked.

"Of course, that sounds like breakfast drop biscuits," Gil said.

"I want to see your skill, not his," Hemm said, shaking his head. "It doesn't count if others do the work for you."

"Chefs have assistants. I know how to make the batter, but Gil is Master Hawthorne's apprentice and will do an excellent job. I am still going to do the rest. If you want to eat before sundown, please allow him to help."

Wizard Hemm stared at her for a moment and then his mouth turned up in a small crooked smile. "Very well, Chef Amandine. Please proceed."

Amandine blushed at the title. Was he making fun of her? With a grimace, she washed her hands in the basin with the pump and then began preparing vegetables.

This was a task she was very familiar with, from working in the soup kitchen and watching Sunflower. Using a large straight knife she carefully sliced and chopped, not being slow exactly, but not working too quickly either as she pondered the problem of the blackspice.

To her left, Gil was mixing flour and water with clumps of soft butter and eggs into a large mixing bowl. The expression on his face was intent and focused. Amandine rarely got to see him working, even on the occasions she visited the bakery. He moved with confidence from task to task—measuring, mixing, stirring. She looked back to her own work and tried to harness that energy for herself. She *was* good at this. Everyone said so. She could find a solution.

"I find it interesting that you harbor no ill will towards dark fae," Wizard Hemm said in a conversational tone as she worked. "Most folk would not go to any length to save boglings."

Amandine shrugged. "I've never met one, so I suppose I don't have an opinion on them."

"Almost no one has met one of the dark fae, they are very insular and reclusive. Yet people still hate them. Do you know why they are called 'dark fae', young lady?"

"No, why?" she asked.

"Because they are evil?" Gil suggested.

"They abhor the sun. They are nocturnal or subterranean. Not all dark fae are inherently evil, although I will admit, goblins have many, how might one say it? *Personality flaws*, especially by human standards."

"Mister Green said almost the same thing," Gil said as he flipped the lump of batter he was mixing with a large spoon. "I suppose not only humans have a dislike of them."

"True enough," Hemm said with a nod. "The divisions between the tribes and courts of the fae are numerous and ancient. Humans are generally very proud of how clever they are, but the vast majority have little notion of what exists beyond their walls and gardens."

"I want to know more," Amandine said. She paused her work and looked up at the old man. "I really do! I want to see Anvilroot, and taste snowberries, and travel across the Wastes to Zulathia and Tren! I want to see it all!"

Wizard Hemm was silent and simply continued to look at her. Was he making fun of her again? Amandine felt her cheeks heat and looked back to her vegetables. She began chopping them again, perhaps a bit more firmly than was necessary.

"It's almost ready, Amy," Gil said as he wiped his forehead with his sleeve. "What's next?"

"Fill a pot halfway with water, and then make fires on both sides of the stove." She swept her chopped vegetables from the board into a bowl and pulled a small cloth covered plate out of the cupboard. She removed the thin cloth to reveal a scaly lizard tail, as thick as her arm.

"I hope you don't mind," Hemm said as he pointed to the tail. "Olgothian Sun Lizard has a most delicate flavor. You do know how to prepare it, yes?"

Amandine had no idea. The meat was dark and had a texture similar to chicken when she poked it with a finger. The hide was scaly on top, but leathery underneath, so a fish knife was not the answer. It also still had the bones in.

"I... will figure it out," Amandine said while trying to keep her voice calm. First blackspice and now a lizard tail? She wanted to pull at her hair, it was a nightmare. If it was truly as delicate as he claimed, the blackspice would ruin it too.

Taking a deep breath, Amandine selected a boning knife from the roll of cutlery and decided to start with what she could control. The bones had to come out.

She disliked butchery. Kivel did most of it, and she hated the way it made her hands stink and the slimy bits under her nails. It was part of cooking though and so she had watched anyway, and even tried it from time to time; with split chicken or legs of lamb, never on something that had the skin still on.

With great care, she sliced the tail open from the bottom and then cut through the flesh as well until she felt bone. Sawing the knife slowly, she split the tail down to the tip and then used the blade to peel some of the skin back and reveal the meat. There was a thin layer of fat under the skin, like with chicken. She started to remove it, but then something else Kivel had taught her came to mind.

"Fat is flavor," he had said, while turning a boar roast over the spit. "You can use seasonings, true, and you must rub them into the meat and the fat. Some will drip off into the pan below and you can then make a sauce from that, but the rest will melt into the meat itself and transport your spices directly into the heart of the dish. Never remove all of the fat!"

"Fat is flavor," Amandine muttered while looking at the tail.

"What did you say?" Hemm asked.

"I think I know how I want to prepare this. I've never tried it, but I'll do my best."

"I look forward to it," Hemm replied. He gestured with two fingers. A stool slid away from a wall across the smooth floors and stopped behind his knees. With a sigh, he sat down on it and leaned his staff against the counter.

Amandine set to work on the tail. Very carefully, she tried to cut around the bones in the middle with the tip of the knife. It was difficult work and more than once she shattered a sliver of bone and had to dig it out of the soft meat.

As she removed the bones, she opened the tail up and rolled it flat, in a manner similar to the boar thigh that Chef and Kivel had prepared for the unexpected dinner with the Magistrate. When the last bit of bone had finally been extracted, she flipped the kite-shaped flap of meat over and exchanged the knife for one used to fillet fish. Working steadily, she peeled off the leathery skin, but left as much of the thin layer of fat as possible.

She wiped the sweat off on her sleeve again and examined her work. The fires Gil had been making were burning low now and would be ready for pans soon. The meat was a bit tattered. She had bruised part of it as well, and a piece near the tail had been sheared off with the skin, but all in all, she felt as if she had managed what she wanted. Mostly.

Her hands were gross. She paused to wash them again and then opened the spices she had traded for with the other half of the bogwort. In a small bowl she combined some of each with flour and milk until she had a paste-like rub that smelled of herbs and salt. She spread it across the fatty side of the meat and rolled it up, just like the boar thigh, until it sort of resembled a tail again.

"Gil, please take some of the blackspice and crush it in the mortar until it's mostly in pieces. I am going to prepare the pans."

Gil nodded and set to work with the small stone mortar and pestle on the hard, black seeds. Amandine placed the water-filled soup pot over one of the smoldering holes in the stove and then found a high-sided pan made of brass and placed it over the other. Once she felt it was hot, she dropped a scoop of butter into it like Sunflower did for fried eggs.

"Ok, Gilly, give me what you have," she said.

Gil handed her the mortar and she dumped the crushed spice into the bubbling butter. A pungent smell like pepper and wood smoke filled the room. Amandine's eyes watered at its intensity. Gil began to cough.

"What in the gods... that's vile, Amy!" he exclaimed.

Amandine waved a hand in front of her face and used a wooden spoon to stir the seeds. Gil retreated to the space by the basin and covered his nose with his apron. Wizard Hemm seemed completely unaffected by the odor and began humming to himself as she continued to mix the pungent spice with the butter.

Finally it stopped smoking, but the smell lingered. Amandine used the spoon to carefully swipe the biggest bits of seeds out of the pan, leaving only the browned butter within. She placed it back on the fire and gently lifted the rolled tail and placed it in the pan. As it began to sizzle, she turned back to Gil.

"Stop being a wimp and put the vegetables in the boil, please," she said with a frown. "Add some cream and flour too."

Gil swallowed and nodded and took the cut vegetables and dumped them into the pot. He pulled a wooden stirring rod off the rack of pots and pans and gently spun the contents of the pot to keep it from boiling over as he added the rest.

"What are you doing, then?" he asked her.

"Well, Kivel told me about how roasts can gain extra flavor when you cook in the fat after adding spices, and Sunflower sometimes adds spices like greensprig and garlic to her butter before making eggs or sauté, so I thought... well, I *hope* it will help to make a stew that doesn't taste entirely like blackspice."

"Whatever you say," Gil said as he covered his nose again. "That's nasty."

Amandine ignored him and focused on the tail. She let it brown on the pan and then gently turned it, and turned it again, until it had seared on all sides. The spice rub was starting to seep out of it into the pan now, but that didn't matter. She let it mix with the butter and kept turning the meat until all of the red spiral inside had changed to a dark tan color. She removed it from the heat and onto the cutting board then took the larger knife and thinly sliced it, then left it to cool.

"Time for dumplings, Gilly! Bring me your batter," she said.

Gil stopped stirring and brought her the bowl of sticky dumpling batter. Using the same spoon she had used for the butter, Amandine added more of her overpriced spices and mixed them into the dough. Then she portioned out clumps of it onto the cutting board and sprinkled each with flour. One by one, she took the clumps of batter, and using the spoon again, floated them into the soup pot, which was close to a full boil now.

After the last one was in, Amandine unceremoniously dumped the pile of sliced meat into the pot and lidded it. "Now we wait."

Gil helped her clean up the scraps and then fetched bowls. Wizard Hemm had stopped humming and acquired a book from somewhere. It lay open on the counter and the only sounds were the bubbling pot, the rustle of pages, and the soft clack of stones on the game board where Kibble and Fredderick were dueling.

"Tell me," Wizard Hemm said, breaking the silence, but without looking up from his book, "Where are you from, young lady? Your hair is too dark for Serentia, but your skin is too fair to be Bolath or Olgoth. Your eyes are the right shape but the wrong color to be Zulath. Who are your parents?"

"I don't know, sah," she replied. "I was raised by the Night Sisters in Artemis."

"An orphan then? Not surprising, really. Children of mixed heritage are sometimes abandoned by those who wish to avoid the social stigmas such offspring entail," Wizard Hemm said absently as he turned a page.

"That's so rude!" Gil said, almost sputtering in his indignation. "Apologize!"

Wizard Hemm looked up. The motion was rapid and precise and his eyes locked onto Gil's like a wolf that had just sighted a hart. Amandine saw Gil wilt under that steely gaze, but he stuck out his lip anyway, despite his obvious fear of the old wizard.

"I will not apologize for pointing out the logical or obvious," Hemm said coolly. "The girl doesn't know who her parents are and is not outwardly of any of the Six Tribes, nor is she fae. Your heart is in the right place, but your mouth is out of line, boy. Learn some caution."

"It doesn't bother me, really," Amandine said in an attempt to handle the situation. "Really, sah, it doesn't. I don't know why everyone makes such a great deal about it."

"You are not even a bit curious, then?" Hemm asked.

"Well, I was, a long time ago, but then it just sort of occurred to me that it didn't really matter. Either they died, and I'll never know, or they ditched me and to the hells with them."

She hadn't meant the last part to sound as fierce as it had and covered her mouth in embarrassment. "Forgive me, sah, I didn't mean to use such rude language."

To her surprise, Wizard Hemm chuckled, and then laughed out loud, throwing his head back in mirth. "I see why you like her, Fredderick. You two have similarly shaped rocks in your skulls."

"Yeah, yeah," Fredderick said as he leaned over the stones board intently. "Gods, Kibble, how do you do this to me every time?"

"Kibble cheats, you dolt," Wizard Hemm said. "You should know that by now."

"Then how do I win sometimes?" Fredderick said defensively.

"Sometimes you cheat better than Kibble does." Hemm swirled his hand and the book before him closed with a snap. "That smells like it's nearly ready, don't you think?"

Amandine realized that the odor of burnt blackspice had faded and the room had taken on a savory smell that reminded her of Chef's kitchen at Manor L'Eau. Gil began sniffing the air like a hound on the scent.

An idea occurred to Amandine and she quickly produced the other half of bogwort and very carefully sliced several thin shavings off the cut side of it. Gil ladled soup into bowls and then before she handed the first one across the counter to Wizard Hemm, she shredded some of the slices and sprinkled them across the top of the stew.

As Hemm began to eat, Fredderick, Dumpling and Kibble wandered over from the stones board and Amandine served them as well. Finally she prepared bowls for her and for Gil.

"Oh, gods, this is lumi, Amy!" Gil exclaimed after a few bites. "It's... it's..."

"Delicious," Fredderick said as he slurped broth. He tossed a slice of meat in the air for Dumpling who jumped to catch it with a happy bark.

"It's revolting!" Kibble said, pushing the bowl away. "Humans are mad!"

Amandine wilted a bit inside at the critique as her spoon hung from her mouth in a dejected fashion. She thought she had done a good job, too. Gil might just be saying it to be a friend and Fredderick...

"Don't mind the grumbling," Wizard Hemm said before blowing on a spoonful. "I saw you add the bogwort at the end. Fae do not like the flavor of it as much as we do. I think your stew is more than palatable, even if the meat is a tad overdone."

"Does this mean you'll help me?" Amandine asked.

"No, it means I'll advise you," Wizard Hemm replied as he finished his bowl. "There is a difference. I do not think there is a safe path for you in any of this. As intelligent as you seem, anything that hunts and kills full grown cattle is nothing you could hope to stop. Not alone. There are many things it could be and most of them would be a deadly threat to you."

"Then what do I do?" Amandine asked.

"Use your head and use your skills, and most of all, seek out allies. Perhaps a few that are more competent than these two," Hemm said, indicating the boys with his spoon. "Then, I would start looking in the south fens, near where the Silverwood borders the Bluesands. Take a cat with you. A tame one."

"A cat?" Amandine asked.

"Indeed."

"Why?" Gil asked.

Wizard Hemm tapped his spoon on the counter. "Thank you very much for the meal, Chef Amandine. Luminous day!"

There was a sound like rushing wind and hot air stung Amandine's eyes. She lifted her hands to block it and when she lowered them, she was standing on the street outside the tower again. Gil, Fredderick and Dumpling were also there.

"Aw, no fair," Gil said as he looked at his empty hands. "I hadn't finished mine yet!"

Seeking Allies

"The Seekers formed as an offshoot of the Fearless after the revolution and subsequent war against Olgothia. The motivations of the Fearless rebels were primarily political in nature, while the Seekers mission is not tied to any one nation or philosophy. Rather, they challenge the darkness in all of its literal and metaphorical forms; sometimes in the pursuit of riches, but just as often for the sake of bringing light to shadowed places."
  - Lecture notes, First Fithday, Low Autumn 1201

AS THEY WALKED back to the Stomping Golem to retrieve Gil's horse, Amandine thought about Wizard Hemm's advice. She wasn't sure who she could find that would be a suitable ally.

Birch wanted to be paid, and she didn't have the money. She had no idea where Chef had gotten to. Miss Jacinda would probably scold her for being foolish. The kitchen and house staff of Manor L'Eau were not going to assist her with this either, she was certain. Mister Green might simply magic her into a chair for a lecture if she suggested such an adventure to him. Gil and Fredderick were all she had.

"I don't know if this is going to work," Amandine said finally. "Wizard Hemm said we aren't strong enough, and I have no idea who to ask besides you two. Unless Chef is doing better than we are, I think the boglings are done for."

"It is sort of mad," Gil agreed. He quickly waved his hands at Amandine right after he spoke. "I'm not saying you're mad, Amy, I am talking about this whole mess! I mean we're just kids, right? Apprentices. This is something for soldiers and hunters and maybe Seekers."

"I'm sixteen and four. I'm at majority, not a child," Fredderick said. Dumpling, trotting by his feet, barked as if in agreement. "Kimber Stolm became a Seeker when she was fourteen and three. If you're old enough to be a journeyman, or accompany your seniors, then you're old enough. But Hemm was right about us not being strong enough. I don't fancy getting eaten on account of a bunch of boglings."

"Wait, the Sheriff used to be a Seeker? How do you know?" Amandine asked.

"She's my cousin."

Amandine just stared at him for a moment as it sunk in. His fancy clothes, his excuse for being at the manor the evening of the dinner party; it all began to add up in her mind.

"You really were there with a noble family. With Sheriff Kimber and her wife," she said.

Fredderick nodded.

"I... I'm sorry I called you a liar," Amandine said.

"Oh, I was totally using it as an excuse to snoop about. Like I told you, I love good food and Chef Brutsche is a legend. That scary elf mage caught me though," Fredderick said.

Gil bounced on his toes. "This is perfect! I mean, she was a Seeker right? And you are family. We could ask her to help us and..." His enthusiasm trailed off as the problem with his suggestion dawned on him.

"Except?" Amandine prompted.

"The Sheriff posted the bounty and hates boglings," Gil said with a frown.

Amandine patted him on the shoulder. "I'm glad that you are helping me, Gilly."

"And she doesn't really like me," Fredderick admitted. He rubbed his nose in an embarrassed sort of way. "When that fellow, Green, hauled me in front of her, she cuffed me good and threatened to tie me to the back of her horse for the ride home if I got caught again. She and I don't really get along. My father sent me to Stoneman to be her page as a 'way to instill some discipline.'" He spoke the last line in an imitation of an older man's voice and snorted at the end.

"You know, that's the same thing my da' told me when he sent me to be Master Hawthorne's apprentice," Gil said.

Fredderick smiled weakly at him. "At least in your case it worked out. You have some skill with dough."

Amandine hated the sad look on Fredderick's face. "But you can use magic! Surely that's valuable enough to gain an apprenticeship with the Highrobes, or a house mage like Mister Green? You don't have to be your cousin's servant, Fredderick!"

"It's sort of complicated," Fredderick muttered. Dumpling whined at him and he bent down to pick up the small dog who began licking his face. "My ability is... unconventional."

"How so?" Amandine asked.

"I don't really want to talk about it," Fredderick said.

Gil pointed to the fountain square down the street. "Well, we're almost back to the inn. Are we just going home then, Amy?"

"I don't really see another option," Amandine said unhappily.

They passed the clockwork fountain in the town square. The shadow of Wizzlecog's Emporium lined up with it to make the mechanical animals and people rotating around it appear to be riding a giant black boat. Amandine paused to watch the fountain for a moment. The arcs of water shooting from the mouths of the brass seals made tiny rainbows in the late afternoon sunlight.

It was like magic, in its own way, even though she knew under the surface there were an array of thin pipes and gears. She had seen a glimpse once when Wizzlecog had one of the hatches open to make repairs.

Her situation felt similar. It seemed like a simple problem on the surface, but the layers of conflict and issues beneath it were a tangle. She didn't understand politics or bounties or mages or even Seekers. All she knew is that she wanted Chef's magic to keep working and she needed to help fix it.

Fredderick stepped up next to Amandine and stroked Dumpling's head as he held him cradled in one arm.

"There's a good reason Kimber hates boglings, you know."

"Why is that?"

"Back when she was a Seeker, maybe only a little older than myself, she and her crew did something to make a bunch of them really angry. They were harried through the swamps in the South of Bolathvia for nearly a tenday. The boglings killed a third of her crew. Her friends. People she cared about." Fredderick blew out a breath and ran a hand through his hair. "I've only heard the stories second hand from Sheeria. They weren't kind about it, Amandine. Those Seekers died awful, gruesome deaths. Boglings are not safe creatures to deal with. Are you sure you want to help them?"

Amandine considered this. The story did explain a lot about Sheeria's reaction the night of the dinner when she herself had first heard the rumors. It also put Mister Green's reaction in a different light for her. But if Chef Brutsche and Telvor were trading with them, they couldn't be wholly evil, right? Wizard Hemm had said it. Being dark fae was not the same as being a villain.

"Yes. I do. I think she's wrong about this bunch. Even the grain thefts must have a purpose. If Chef has been trading with them, why would they steal? But I am out of ideas. We don't have the help we need to do anything."

They both watched the fountain a moment longer and then Fredderick nodded as if he had decided something.

"Actually my cousin might help," he said.

"The Sheriff hates boglings and doesn't like you. How do you think she will help?"

"Not her, my other cousin. Her brother. The Captain of the town guards, Rivaldo," Fredderick explained. "Do you know where to get a cat?"

"How will a cat help convince your cousin to help?" Gil asked.

"It won't, but Wizard Hemm said we'd need one, so it's important. If you can handle that part, I might be able to get us the help we need. Can you, Amandine?"

"Yes. Yes, I think I can," Amandine said.

"Superb. Meet me outside the North gate before sundown. We might need some other supplies as well. A light besides my magic at the very least."

"I can handle that," Gil said.

"Then I suggest we all hurry," Fredderick said, and with that, he vanished.

"I hate it when he does that," Gil said.

Amandine smirked. "I don't know, I think it's sort of neat. Go get Crust, Gilly, we have chores to do!"

Gil jogged off across the square, dodging between late afternoon patrons of the Stomping Golem, towards the stable yard behind the inn.

Amandine turned back to the fountain and thought about Wizard Hemm's last words. How exactly was having a cat along supposed to help? They had keen eyes and noses, so perhaps it was a way to track down what they sought? And what would they do if they discovered a Grimalk den or some other large beast? Hopefully the help that Fredderick had in mind could deal with a wild animal if they encountered one.

"It is rather fascinating, even if it can't compare to the water gardens of the Promenade."

Amandine stiffened and turned. Sister Corbin stood behind her. She reached up and pulled down her hood.

"What do you want?" Amandine said as she slowly backed away.

"The same thing I've wanted since you vanished after the fire, child. Your safe return to the convent."

"I hate it there! I don't want to go back!"

"So you have intimated. Why?"

Amandine stood gaping for a moment. Sister Corbin had not advanced, tried to grab her or do anything, really. She looked stern, but then she always looked stern. Sort of like Chef.

That was why the simple question stumped her. She had explained her reasons to Gil and Fredderick, but those were the reasons of a child seeking an adventure. There was more to it. That Sister Corbin reminded her of Chef suddenly made the real reason apparent.

"I'm tired of death. I want to live," Amandine said.

"Death is a natural part of all life," Sister Corbin replied placidly.

"I... I know that," Amandine said, seeking her footing. "But the Night Sisters make it the most important part. There's more! I've seen it and tasted it and I want to experience it all."

"There are dangerous things in that 'all.' That cursed fae wizard for one. I imagined a thousand ghastly things that could have befallen you when you disappeared, Amandine, but finding you in the tutelage of a Breaker made my heart clench."

A Breaker? Amandine had never heard that term. "*Soeje* Green has been teaching me letters and nature, not magic."

"That is well. He and mages like him are responsible for horrific tragedies. You can see through his glamours, yes? You have seen the darkness within him?"

"How?" Amandine asked, taken aback.

"Yes, I know about that, and more. Like the identity of your parents."

"You know who they were? Tell me!"

Sister Corbin held up a gnarled finger. "If you want the knowledge I have, you will return with me to Artemis. You will resume your apprenticeship, and you will agree not to contact Serand Brutsche again."

Amandine was speechless. She tried to think of a response, but her brain refused to connect to her mouth. She knew her parents? She knew about her ability to see Mister Green's eyes? So many questions she had could be answered. But leave Stoneman? Leave her friends? Never see Kivel or Sunflower or Chef again?

Chef. Why did the thought of leaving him hurt the most? He was grouchy and loud and foul mouthed.

Amandine wiped her eyes with a sleeve. She realized she was crying.

Chef was also smart and talented and... he cared. About his job, about his crew, about her.

"I see this is hard for you. I am not a monster, Amandine, but I will not back down from this. You have until daybreak and then I will come to Manor L'Eau to collect you. I have a writ, signed by the Magistrate that enforces this. Here."

She reached into her cloak and handed Amandine a rolled parchment sealed with wax.

"A copy to show your employers," Sister Corbin explained. "Safe evening, apprentice."

Amandine crammed the parchment into her pocket and turned back to the fountain. She dried her eyes as Sister Corbin's footsteps retreated across the square.

"Gods, what am I going to do?"

Maps and Onion Sacks

"Night Trains are a fairly recent innovation in trade that owes its existence to the discovery and refinement of glowstone. Before the Arrival, in the Era of Giants, the elder races used magic to overcome the dark of night. Elves, Dwarves and many other fae can see well at night with only faint starlight or phosphorescent plants underground, but on a cloudy night even that can be tested. Glowstone and greenflame lanterns have revolutionized trade, insomuch that trains no longer need to stop right at dusk and some even travel in total darkness on glowstone-marked roads."

- Lecture notes, Third Riverday, Low Autumn 1201

THE SUN WAS hanging low in the sky when Gil dropped Amandine off at the garden gate to Manor L'Eau. He lent her a hand down and then gave the reins a light flick.

"I'll be back in half a bell!" he called over his shoulder as Crust began to pick up speed.

"I'll be waiting!" Amandine called back. She hadn't told Gil about her encounter with Sister Corbin. It wasn't his problem to solve. She had decided to follow Chef's advice: watch ahead of her and focus on what she could control. Chef still needed help and if she was going back to Artemis, the least she could do is finish what she had started.

The house was quiet. Chef and the cooks had homes in the nearby hamlet. So did Lily, Hedgehog and the other staff. Only

Mister Green and Nanny had rooms in the manor. And herself, she supposed, if one counted the pallet in the warm cellar. Before she went inside, Amandine stood on the steps and watched the growing shadows over the wheat fields. Small twirls of smoke from the hearths of the hamlet-folk made streamers in the darkening sky.

"They should just call it the Golden Hills and add it to the map," a voice said.

Amandine squeaked in surprise and turned to see Nanny sitting on a small folding stool near the corner of the kitchen's chimney. Her red patterned dress and the shadows had made her seem part of the stonework and Amandine hadn't noticed her until she spoke. She held a long-stemmed pipe in one hand and a clay mug in the other. Something hot steamed within it.

"The hamlet you mean, sah?" Amandine asked.

The old woman nodded and drew a puff on her pipe. "It's been there since I was a babe," she said as she exhaled. "I was born there. I'll probably die there. But in all this time, the folks that do draw the maps can't be bothered to give it a name. It's always been Golden Hills, though."

"If the people who live there know what it's called, that's enough, right?"

Nanny chuckled and shook her head. "You're a sweet child, Amandine. With no official recognition, it can't have no mayor, nor temple. With no god-folk and no mayor's medallion, the nearest noble is in charge. Collects the tithes. Decides how they get spent. It's not about what people know or don't know, it's about who gets to make the rules."

Amandine thought about that for a moment. "That doesn't seem fair."

"No, it's not much for being fair, but it could be worse. Lord Estevan and Lady Gia are about as good as noble folk get. Patient, wise with money, pious. Lady Ophelia works her hamlet-folk like Olgothian slaves."

"But they aren't slaves, they could leave," Amandine said.

"True, and the ones that can afford to, often do," Nanny said with a nod. "But then the Lady just puts up some coin as a lure, and a fool even more desperate takes up the work instead. She steps a narrow jig, but does it well."

Amandine considered this as Nanny puffed on her pipe. She had never given much thought to the actual purpose all of the unnamed hamlets served. It had always been her assumption that they were places people lived because they wanted to. She wondered how many of the people in Gil's hamlet didn't really like it there.

"Has Mister Green returned with the girls?" Amandine asked.

Nanny grinned. "Nah, they will probably take rooms at the Golem. Mistress Fiona has been begging to do it since the start of Low Summer. It's just me, tonight. Blessed quiet."

Amandine frowned. Nanny was being awfully chatty and free with her words. "Did you put gold mash in your tea again, Nanny?"

Nanny made a shushing noise at her and grinned even wider. "Not so loud. That Tusker, Nous, hasn't gone back to his lair yet. Let an old woman have her fun, yes?"

"Was it his?" Amandine asked.

"Of course it was. Girls like us have to break the rules now and then, right?"

She winked at Amandine and laughed. Her cackle was infectious and Amandine found herself laughing too. Taster Nous would be very cross if he discovered that Nanny had been nipping his personal stash, but she definitely wasn't going to tell on her.

"Enjoy it, Nanny. I need to go find Grendel," Amandine said.

"Oh he'll find you, I'm sure. That naughty cat has been in a snit since you left. He never took to anyone but Mistress Fiona until you came along. Probably knocking the crystal off the shelves in the sun rooms…"

Nanny trailed off into a mutter as she turned her attention back to the setting sun.

Amandine entered through the kitchen and went down into the warm cellar. She crouched and collected her satchel from under her pallet. There was nothing in it that would be useful in the fens, so she removed all of her belongings and slung the empty bag over her shoulder.

On the way back through the kitchen, she took a dried fish from the pantry stores and began searching all of Grendel's favorite hiding spots. She looked under the washtub, in the cupboards, behind the hutch that held the crockery and plates; but Grendel was nowhere to be found.

"Grendel," she called softly. "Come here, Gren, I have a fish for you!"

The dried sardine in her hand was one of his favorite treats, and so when he failed to reveal himself, she began to wonder if he was really inside the house like Nanny thought.

"Of all the nights for him to be off wandering the hills," she grumbled. "Silly cat!"

Just then, somewhere on an upper floor, she heard a crash and thump, as if something heavy had fallen over. A muffled voice swore an oath. Although distorted by rugs and thick floors, she recognized Nous.

Not wishing to have an encounter with the Taster, even when off duty, she began to step more quietly as she continued to check each of the lower chambers for a sign of Grendel.

She was crossing the entry hall and trying to decide if it was worth attempting to sneak upstairs when her luck ran out. Henri Nous rounded the corner at the top of the carpeted stairway; a sack over one shoulder and the other holding a thick candle in a drip tray. The light from the tiny flame gave his face a ghoulish appearance.

"Amandine," Nous said. His tone suggested it was neither a greeting or a scolding, but rather just an acknowledgement that she was there.

"Taster," she replied with a polite bow. "Nanny said you stayed late today, sah."

"Yes," he replied, his eyes narrowed. "I am taking care of some laundry the 'butler' and his people neglected. Why are you sneaking about in the dark, girl?" The way he invoked Hedgehog's title spoke volumes as to how he viewed both him and his position in the household.

Amandine bit her tongue. Hedgehog neglected no detail when he cared for the house and its inhabitants.

"I was just looking for the mouser, sah. Have you seen him?"

"That pestilential cat hasn't ever caught a mouse that wasn't already half dead," Nous said with a sniff as he began to make his way down the steps. "It might do better if you and the Mistress were not always feeding it."

"He does catch them!" Amandine said in defense of her friend. "He left the heads of three on the back stoop not even two days ago!"

"It breaks valuable glassware, leaves its disgusting matted fur on every cloth surface, makes a yowling racket at ungodly times of night, and more than once has been caught stealing food from tea trays! It's a menace!" Nous grumbled as he stomped down the steps with each accusation.

Something about the sack caught Amandine's attention; she could have sworn she saw it move. "That's not a bag from the laundress. That has the Bilgwin Farm crest on it. It's an onion sack. Hedgehog would never pack linens in an onion sack, they would reek, even after being washed!"

"It just goes to show how incomp—" Nous began.

"Grendel!" Amandine called, interrupting him. "Grendel, come out!"

A mournful meow issued from the sack.

"You let him go!" Amandine yelled. "What are you doing?"

"Ridding the house of a pest!" Nous growled at her. "Mind your tongue or it will be rid of two before next Godhome!"

"You have no right!" Amandine cried. "He belongs here! Mistress Fiona will be heartbroken!"

"I have every right! I run the house at the Lord's behest! Me! I allot the funds dictated by our patrons. That fat halfling isn't in charge here, neither is the broken old scamp who plays at being a chef! Raise your voice to me again, child, and I'll see your pay cut! Persist and I'll see you to the road you were found on!"

Nous' moustaches flared as he caught his breath. His cheeks were red with anger as he marched straight towards the foyer and the front entrance to the manor.

Amandine quivered with helpless fury. What could she do? She had never in her life wished ill to anyone, but at that moment she did. She wished it so badly that she began to cry.

"What is all this ruckus?" Nanny said as she entered the hall from the sunrooms. She held a small oil lamp in a glass box for light. The tiny panes of glass threw motes across the dark walls like sun reflections on water.

Nous hefted the sack and began undoing the latches on the front door. "None of your concern, Ursula. I am just reminding our scull of her place here."

"My concern is with all of the children of this house, Henri. And I see one now that's a cryin' because yer such a toad. Amandine, what nasty thing did he say?"

"Mind your business, Nanny," Nous said as he tried to open the door. Something was stuck however and he returned to twisting the latches.

"Oh, I am," Nanny said with a dismissive gesture. "Come now, child, why the tears?"

"She is not a ward of this House!" Nous yelled as he finally wrenched the door open.

"She is," Nanny snapped back, "You jus' don't have the eyes, or the heart, to see it!"

"Grendel!" Amandine wailed.

There was a tearing sound and a surprised yowl. The sack over Nous' shoulder split and out tumbled a rumpled-looking Grendel to the floor of the foyer.

Nous swore as he tripped and hot wax spilled from the candle tray he had set aside to open the door. It spattered him on his free hand and he hissed in pain. Grendel echoed the sound from beneath his feet and bolted out the open door into the twilight.

Amandine didn't hesitate. Tears still streaming from her eyes, she dashed away from Nanny, past Nous, and followed Grendel into the dark.

"You have no more place here, girl!" she heard Henri Nous roar from the open doorway behind her. The sound of the door slamming echoed in her ears all the way back to the road.

The Dark of Night

"Of the bare handful of surviving human writings that predate the Arrival, one in particular makes mention of a 'light high in the sky at night', an apparent counterpart to the sun. No such thing has ever existed in Beregoth, and even the pre-Arrival writings of the Giants and Elves make no mention of such a phenomenon. It is more likely that this light is a religious metaphor, referring to Akradath, the Lord of Light, and how he is said to have guided the human vessels across the Seas to this land in ancient days."
- Lecture notes, Third Starday, High Winter 1201

"HE REALLY SAID that?" Gil asked as they made their way slowly down the road back towards Stoneman's North gate.

Amandine nodded as she hugged Gil from the back of his horse. She had managed to coax Grendel into her satchel and his striped head poked out from under the flap to peek up at her. He meowed. Amandine thought it sounded apologetic.

"It's not your fault, Gren," she said. She reached a hand down to rub Grendel's head. He began to purr.

"Can he really just release you like that, though? Doesn't Chef Brutsche get a say?"

"The Taster runs the house. He could even kick out Chef if he wanted, but releasing someone so important without asking would probably make Lord Estevan angry. Me though? I doubt there will be any fuss over me."

"I'd make a fuss!" Gil said stoutly.

"Don't you dare get in any more trouble with Master Hawthorne than you already are. Did he scold you?"

"I dodged him," Gil said with a shrug. "I'm sure I'll get it in the morning. Master Leon said that he was searching the hamlet for me with his rolling pin."

Gil slowed Crust as the gloom deepened. The sky was partly cloudy and the dim light of the stars was reduced to a mere glimmer. They followed the trail of glowstone set into the edges of the road to make their way, but Gil had to be cautious so that Crust didn't lame himself in a rut or ditch.

"You brought light, right, Gilly?" Amandine asked.

He nodded and reached down to turn a small knob on a lantern hanging from Crust's saddle. There was a hiss and a click and a small green flame appeared inside the glass casing. It shed a tepid light along the road, flickering and wavering with the movements of the horse.

After a few moments he turned the knob again and the flame went out. The clear sides of the lantern began to glow with a soft yellow light. The glowstone-infused glass absorbed, and then changed the intense heat of the green-flame and radiated it back out as bright light. The stones in the road absorbed the sun throughout the day, which gave them their faint glow, but the intense, hot flame of Gilly's lantern caused the light it emitted to shine brighter than the flecked rocks.

"I only have enough gas for about three bells. But glowglass is not hot once the flame is off so it won't distress Crust. We'll have to use some oil torches once we dismount, I think, to conserve the gas."

Ahead of them, a train of lights appeared in the gloom, coming towards them down the road. Amandine could hear wagon wheels and creaking axles and the clop of hooves.

"Riders ahead!" a man's voice called in the shadows.

"Safe evening!" Gil called back. "Akradath's light be upon you!"

In the persistent gloom of night, such exchanges were common to assess the distance and intent of people passing on the roads after nightfall. In some parts of Beregoth, no one would dare venture out of their homes after sunset, especially on a starless evening. The Gold Hills were reasonably safe, however, and night travelers were not unheard of.

The scout for the wagon train that had spotted them eyed them cautiously as they passed one another, but said nothing. A loaded crossbow was laid across his lap and his horse was barded in boiled leather. The driver of the first wagon looked surprised when he finally saw them, however. He called out as they passed by: "Children? Young masters, you should be safe in your beds! Stoneman is still half a yarn South if you follow the stones! It's going to rain most like. Go as fast as your horse can dare!"

Gil waved to him in friendly acknowledgement, but did not reply. Amandine watched the wagons proceed slowly past them, each filled with an assortment of barrels, or crates, or small cages filled with squawking fowl and squealing piglets.

"Where are they going, do you think?" she asked Gil softly.

"They're Halifax Guild—see the emblems on their cloaks? So probably anywhere. They are the only trains well protected enough to run long distances after nightfall. Didn't you travel with one?"

"No, the train I came here with stopped at night, and only had a few guards. We circled the wagons and made a watch fire every night."

"That's what smart people do when it's too dark to see. This is mad, you realize, what we are doing? If that con man hasn't found the help we need, I am taking us to the Golem and to the Pit with the boglings, Amy."

Gil's head swiveled as if he were trying to see through the inky blackness, but even with the fancy glowglass lantern they could not see more than twenty spans ahead of Crust's muzzle.

Amandine nodded in silent agreement. It *was* mad. Being out after dark was dangerous for anyone, and not just because of wild animals or fae—the darkness itself was a threat. All enveloping, impenetrable. There were many, often shared, anecdotes of people who braved the night without light and were found dead from falling, drowning, or simply walking into something sharp and impaling themselves.

As they approached Stoneman, the form of the enormous wall became a hazy yellow line in the distance, lit by the torches and glowglass lanterns of the town's watch. The trail of stones marking the road was supplemented by posts with regular oil lanterns set to a low flame, and Gil was able to speed up Crust a bit with the path being more clear.

At the final turn into town, where the gates became visible, Amandine caught sight of Fredderick standing under one of the posts. He was wearing a cloak and holding Dumpling in his arms. The small dog began to bark excitedly as they came into view and he waved to them.

Standing next to him was a tall woman. It was hard to tell at a distance, but she seemed pretty, with her long, hazel hair tied back in a ponytail over her shoulder. She was wrapped in a thick green cloak with a hood. In one hand she held an unlit lantern, and gripped a long boar spear in the other.

Once they were close enough for a better look, Amandine came to a different conclusion. She wasn't just pretty, she was gorgeous. Easily taller than even Lord Estevan, she was nearly as broad as a man in the shoulders and had a bearing that radiated confidence. Her features were like a statue of Kayla that had been given life and breath. When she smiled at them, it had the warmth of an old friend, not someone she had never met.

"Everyone, this is Dena. She works for my cousin in the town guards," Fredderick said as he jerked a thumb towards the tall woman.

"*With* your cousin, kiddo," she said with a smirk. "I recognize you! You're the one that came through Stoneman with Chef Brutsche on his last provisions run."

Amandine was faintly embarrassed that anyone would remember her at all and nodded mutely.

"I'm Gil," Gil said, his voice faltering a bit. "The baker's apprentice from Gold Hills. M— Master Hawthorne's. Pleased to meet you!"

"I live there too. I probably had some of your handiwork at breakfast then. Well met, young master," she replied.

Gil blushed. Amandine glanced at him incredulously. The woman was easily twice his age or more, but she sort of understood the reaction.

Dena handed Fredderick her lantern, propped her spear against the lamp post and then reached up and lifted Amandine down from the saddle as if she weighed nothing. Amandine caught a glimpse of leather and mail armor beneath her cloak when she did; her hands were gauntleted in thick hide gloves with the fingers cut out.

Dena pointed to the town gates. "Master Gil, please go tie your horse inside the wall at the guard's picket. The fens are no place for a heavy animal like him, he'll get hurt. Then hurry back. Guards Oliver and Primrose have been told to expect you, so don't worry about him."

Gil nodded, still blushing, and trotted Crust towards the wall.

Amandine tried not to stare at Dena, but it was difficult. Her presence was so commanding, yet comforting. It made her heart begin to fill with optimism about their task again.

"You look different without your helmet on," she said. A sheepish feeling crept over her when Dena only replied by grinning at her. "I mean, I didn't recognize you at all, and…"

Fredderick rolled his eyes. "She's beautiful, everyone gets it. Dena can also lift one hundred and fifty stone without a sweat and regularly pummels my cousin in sparring. So say thank you, Amandine. She is really going out on a limb for us."

"Yes, thank you!" Amandine said quickly, regaining her composure. She felt incredibly silly. "Did Fredderick tell you why we needed a guide at night?"

"Oh, I know all about your little 'duck hunt,'" Dena said. The way she emphasized the words made Amandine think that she was being coy about their true purpose, but she played along.

"You hunt ducks at night?" Amandine asked.

"If you want to catch a lot of them. My brothers and I did it often. A glowglass lantern, when turned on suddenly, dazzles them and they just sit there looking stupid as you harpoon them."

"That doesn't seem very sporting," Amandine said.

"It wasn't for sport. It was efficient. We were trying to feed a family of twelve after all," Dena said with a shrug. "And I know you aren't really hunting ducks. The fens are familiar to me at night, so I will try and help you find what you need to exonerate the boglings. I'm betting it's just a snapjaw that wandered up from the delta, or wolves, or maybe even a grimalk. If we keep our flames burning and travel together, they will not bother us. The scent of humans frightens them nearly as much as the fire."

Amandine thought of the huge swamp cats and their storied fierceness. "Why are grimalks afraid of people?"

Dena held up a gloved hand, the leather was supple and had an odd sheen to it. "These gloves are made from grimalk hide. Animals avoid things that smell like death, unless they are scavengers. If we do find a den, we will *not* try to take it. I'll mark the trail and a proper hunt can be staged in daylight to clear out the beast or beasts. Nothing fights more savagely than an animal cornered in its lair. Sound fair?"

Amandine nodded. It was more than fair. She felt like they had an actual chance to help now. "Maybe Chef Brutsche can still sway the opinion of the Sheriff. At least I think that's what he's trying to do. I haven't seen him since early this morning."

"Is that what he's been about today?" Dena said thoughtfully. "I spied him galloping around town on that poor old nag of his. To the inn and apothecary, and to go see Master McKragen, and others. It wasn't a provisions day for him, so I wondered what he was doing."

Gil jogged up the path from the gates a few moments later. He had a knapsack over his shoulder and his glowglass lantern in his hand. "Under Sergeant Primrose says if we catch a brownback, that she wants a roast from your Grams. What did she mean?"

"Didn't you know? We are duck hunting," Amandine said with a grin. She laughed when Gil looked confused.

"I guess I'll have to be on the lookout for an actual duck then," Dena said with a chuckle. "Come on then, you three. Stay close, and everyone holds a light. It's about two yarns to the south fens, that way." She pointed off into the darkness in the general direction of the Wolfshenta river.

They made their way across a field and then onto a foot trail that Dena knew of. Amandine and the boys allowed her to lead as they followed, single file. Gil took up the rear with his glowglass lantern. Fredderick held a stick aloft that glowed with his blue magical light, and Amandine gripped a long oilcloth torch. She made sure her satchel was on the opposite side so that the occasional hot oil drip would not land on Grendel. The cat peered out from the bag with wide eyes. His ears twitched left and right at the sounds of the night around them. Amandine was sure that if his tail was visible it would also be twitching.

Dena used her small oil lantern, but had lowered the hood a bit so that its mirror reflected the light into a beam that shone deep into the inky darkness and allowed her to follow the trail. Before long the rushing sound of the river became louder, and even though Amandine couldn't see it, she knew it was somewhere to their left. Swamp wisps, small elemental creatures that appeared to be made of blue fire, darted above the water, then dipped and vanished beneath the surface when they came into sight, making the surrounding marsh glow in rippling blue patches. A chorus of frogs silenced as they walked by and resumed croaking once they passed. Their footsteps and their light created a bubble of quiet in the night time activity as the nocturnal denizens evaluated the interlopers and their strange illumination.

"The trail ends at Little Ferry and then we go into the muck," Dena instructed. "We'll all have wet socks before this is through, but if you want to keep the rest of you dry, I recommend stepping where I step and avoiding anything with paddle-leaf growing on it, even if it looks solid."

They all nodded in agreement, even Fredderick. For all his usual outward confidence, Amandine noted that he was more than willing to follow Dena's instructions to the letter. At the turn in the trail that led to the small ferry dock, Dena stepped off into the reeds. She used her spear to part them ahead of her and stomped them flat with her boots before moving forward.

Amandine heard it before she saw it. Dena's boots squelched into soft mud and the butt of her spear splashed as she tested the ground ahead. They had entered the fens.

"So you told us about the animals," Amandine said. "But what about the boglings? Do you think they will be mad that we are in their home?"

Dena shook her head. "In all my life living here, playing in the river and the woods and hunting the fens, I have never seen one. My oldest brother saw one once and it gave him a fright, but he said when he cried out it dashed off into the reeds and he never saw one again. I'm not sure they deserve the sinister reputation they have been given, and if Serand thinks well of them, then that settles it for me."

"Serand?" Gil asked.

Dena gave him a quizzical look over her shoulder and Fredderick whispered back to him, "Serand Brutsche, your Chef."

Gil looked surprised. "Oh! Everyone calls him by his title. I had no idea."

"I didn't know that was his name until earlier today either, Gilly," Amandine whispered in his ear.

"It's just... I am good with names. Almost no one calls him that. I'd have remembered!"

"Serand does seem attached to his fancy title, doesn't he?" Dena said with a grin. "I think it suits him, though."

They were perhaps half a bell into their trek through the fens when Dena paused. She slowly scanned the ground with her lamp and then used it to sweep the reeds around them.

"What is it?" Amandine asked.

"I found our grimalk," Dena said.

Amandine looked to where the beam from Dena's lantern pointed. Partially concealed in the weeds was a large, furry body. It lay unmoving. The fur of the pelt shimmered, rainbow-like, in the flickering light. Grimalks were fae creatures and their fur could make them nearly invisible, even in daylight. Amandine had never seen one before in her life.

"It has no head," Gil said softly. He coughed to suppress a gag.

"What could do that to a grim?" Fredderick wondered aloud.

Amandine wondered the same thing. The headless body was the size of a horse, with paws as large as dinner plates and claws like small knives.

"Well, I would say this rules out a grimalk," Dena muttered. "It hasn't been here long enough to rot. Something is not right, we should head back to town."

Amandine smelled it then. The same odor she had detected on the dead horse, days ago.

"I think whatever killed it, also kills the cattle. It smells the same."

"Oh, wow, it does. Like that dead horse," Gil agreed.

"What dead horse?" Fredderick asked. Before Gil could answer, he turned to Dena, who had moved the beam of her lantern. "Dena, what are you looking at?"

"Look at the reeds, and the water," Dena said.

Amandine glanced down. The water surrounding their small hillock of earth was rippling. It was different than when you dropped a pebble in a bucket, though. It was more like something was shaking the bucket, very fast. The nearby reeds were also vibrating. The rustling sound created a buzz in her ears.

"Have you ever seen this happen before?" Gil asked, an edge of fear creeping into his voice.

"No, never," Dena said. She lifted her lantern a bit higher.

A low growl emanated from Amandine's satchel. She looked down at Grendel. The fur on his neck was standing on end, his head turned to look out into the night as if fixated on something, both ears forward. He growled again and hissed. Dumpling began to whine.

"All of you, stand back, I am—" Dena began, but she never finished.

A black, roiling shape exploded from the swampy earth and swallowed the light from Dena's lamp. A wave of brackish water and mud crashed over Amandine and the boys, dousing her torch.

Grendel yowled. Gil and Fredderick were both yelling, but it was muffled. Amandine realized that was because she was underwater. She panicked and pumped her arms to try and reach the surface, but couldn't move. She felt her legs pinned by a heavy mass. In a panic she tried to breathe and swallowed murky water. A second wave washed over her and the mass lifted away.

Frantically she pushed herself to the surface and pulled her body across the churned mud of the mound they had all been standing on. She thought she saw the ball of blue light from Fredderick's magic through the reeds, thought she heard his voice, but mud was in her eyes, in her nose, in her ears. She coughed and spat up water and bile.

"Wait!" she tried to call out, but her voice cracked and her stomach heaved.

She vomited swamp water and mud and what was left of her meal from the wizard's tower. When she finally stopped and managed to push herself up to her knees, she thought perhaps she had gone blind. Then she realized that there was simply no light left to see by.

"Gilly! Fredderick! Dena!" she called, but even the frogs refused to answer her.

Amandine was alone in the dark.

A Cat's Eyes

"Finally, every good kitchen needs a cat. The obvious advantage of reducing vermin aside, a cat is quiet, is quick to get out of the way, and keeps itself clean. One must be sure that containers are kept sealed and away from ledges. Otherwise cats are the perfect kitchen companion."
- Seeker's Kitchen, Chapter 2, Tools of the Trade

AMANDINE GRASPED AROUND in the darkness, trying to make sense of her surroundings with numb fingers. Rocks. Mud. Reeds. A branch. Another rock. She felt rain begin to fall on her head.

Her hands touched cloth. She clutched at it desperately. Who was it? It wasn't what she feared. Not a cloak, or a scrap of clothing. It was her bag. Between her fingers, she felt the cold metal of the buckle for the flap. It was empty. Grendel was no longer inside.

"Gren? Grendel?" she called tentatively. Had he drowned? Could cats swim? Her heart ached at the thought that her foolish adventure might have killed him. The rest of them knew it was dangerous, but Grendel trusted her. She was his friend. And she… she…

Amandine began to cry. The cold and wet seeped into her skin from her sodden clothes. She hugged the bag to her and wept as the rain made duplicates of her tears down her face.

"I'm sorry, Gren," she sobbed through chattering teeth.

Meow.

Her breath caught. A cold, wet nose touched her hand, followed by a paw. Amandine gently reached out with her fingers and with a trilling noise the familiar weight of Grendel rubbed against her palm.

"Thank Kayla," Amandine whispered. "Oh, Grendel, you are soaked too. Come here."

She slung the bag across her shoulder again and lifted up the heavy cat in her arms. His whiskers tickled her face. She almost started to cry again, but held back. Crying wasn't going to help her. She needed to find the others. Whatever had taken Dena was still out there and they needed to get away.

With a bit of fumbling, she pulled the sodden hood of her cloak over her head to block the rain. It wasn't much better at keeping her dry, but the drops ceased striking her face, and it sheltered Grendel as well. She breathed deeply, and tried to think. She closed her eyes.

The river was audible behind her.

"That meant Stoneman would be..." she said to herself as she mentally pointed in her head.

"But the light from Fredderick's spell had been..." she mentally pointed in roughly the opposite direction.

"They are going the wrong way, Grendel! We have to find them!"

Amandine opened her eyes. Grendel's face was still close to hers. She imagined she could see his rumpled, soggy face and twitching whiskers and the black diamond shape that sat in between his eyes. She stroked his head and saw the outline of her fingers running through his damp fur.

When she looked up, instead of a black void, she saw... shapes. Reeds. The ground. Rippling water. The outline of a scrub oak. Amandine squinted. Was she hallucinating? She even felt that she could see the rain, like a pattern moving across her vision. Gently, she set Grendel down and stood. The images and lines were swallowed by blackness again. She gasped. What was happening?

A questioning meow drifted up from her ankles. Grendel rubbed up against her shins. Amandine reached down, picked him up again, and held him to her.

Her eyes watered as she strained to see in the void, and then, ever so faintly, the outlines and ghostly images of her surroundings began to emerge again. Had the old wizard spelled her? Was this the reason he had told her to go fetch a cat? She set Grendel down again as an experiment. His annoyed meow made her feel guilty, but she needed to check. The images all vanished again in an instant.

"Sorry, Gren. Here, kitty, I won't drop you again," she said as she picked him up once more.

Her strange vision began to return, and Amandine tried to get her bearings.

"If we survive this, Gren, we need to thank Wizard Hemm properly. Maybe with a meal that I am actually good at making, yes?"

Meow.

"Right, and we'll also have a chat with Fredderick about his poor explanations for magical things. If he knew this was Hemm's plan, he should have said something!"

Tentatively, she began to make her way in the direction she thought the others had fled. The rain felt loud in her ears. The night creatures began to call again and the heavy drops played counterpoint to the croaking frogs and small skittering animals. Water splashed and she even heard a night bird singing. She turned her head towards the sound and so did Grendel. He was hungry. She didn't know how she could tell, she just knew.

"I can't let you hunt, Gren. Please, stay with me a bit longer? Gilly has food, if we can find them," Amandine said softly to the cat. Grendel's attention drifted away from the bird. He seemed sulky, but content.

They made their way towards a small stand of the stunted oaks that grew in the stinking mud. It was a bit more sheltered from the rain. Amandine paused to take stock. She couldn't see any lights, but the outlines and shapes seemed to be growing stronger and more defined. There was no color. Distances were hard to judge, as if she had only one eye open, but she could definitely make out where some of the reeds had been trampled.

"That way, then."

It wasn't long before she lost the trail again, at a sort of natural crossroads where a pair of fallen trees formed a bridge across the fen in two different directions.

"Which way do you think they went?" Amandine asked Grendel.

She had intended the question to be self-reflective. It was basically a coin toss as to which way they might have gone, and so she was surprised when she felt a strong urge to follow the left path. Grendel's head and ears were both focused in that direction and his tail swished as if he were hunting.

"Can you sense them, then? Are you helping me?"

Grendel didn't answer her. He was just a cat after all, but the urge to go left remained and his head continued to focus on the path as if something that greatly interested him lay in that direction.

If it was a spell, Amandine decided to trust it. What did she have to lose? She stepped carefully across the log-bridge and continued on her way. The cold in her boots was beginning to seep into her legs. Hugging Grendel helped a little, and she felt better without the rain on her head, but she was still soaked to the bone. Her teeth chattered from the chill.

She and Grendel passed through another bank of reeds and came into a small, mostly dry, clearing. A larger tree lay near the center of it. Its gnarled branches reached out over the surrounding swamp like crooked fingers. Moss draped from them like old cobwebs.

Something else also dangled from one of the larger branches. The lumpy form swung slowly in the night over the twisted roots and churned mud beneath the tree. Whatever it was seemed to be tied to the branch by a long rope or vine. A glint in the mud below it caught her eye, like a coin at the bottom of the clockwork fountain.

There was a moaning sound and Amandine ducked into the reeds. At first she thought it might have been wind, but the tepid breeze that swirled the rain wasn't strong enough for such a sound. Then, she heard coughing. It was coming from whatever was dangling beneath the tree.

"Who is there?" she called from the reeds. "Can you hear me?"

"Help…" a weak voice gasped.

Amandine was torn. It didn't sound like Gil or Fredderick, and every fiber of her body screamed at her that something was wrong with this. It was dangerous. It was—

Lightning flashed, and for an instant the scene was lit as bright as day. A small person was dangling there. He was tied in vines that restrained his arms. Beneath him, sticking out of the mud was a long-handled knife. She recognized it immediately.

"Birch? Birch the Seeker? Is that you, sah?" Amandine called out.

"Who—" the weak voice started to ask and then coughed again. "So many. Teeth, all teeth," he wheezed.

Amandine made her decision. She wasn't going to let Birch dangle there, helpless. With Dena gone, he might be able to help her find the others and escape. He was a scout, right? She hoped he wasn't too badly hurt to be useful. Her heart ached at the thought of Dena. She was going to cry again, later, she knew it, but for now she needed to focus. Fix what she could fix.

"Stay close, Gren, in the bag, if you please," Amandine said as she lifted the flap of her satchel. To her surprise, Grendel climbed in without complaint and stuck his head out of the flap.

Amandine approached the dangling Hill Folk Seeker with one hand resting on Grendel's head so that she could continue to see. She knelt and drew the dagger out of the mud. It was as light as she remembered, and the water-like patterns in the metal seemed to shift in her eerie magical vision.

"Be still, Master Birch. I need to cut the vines one-handed, and I don't want to hurt you."

Ever so carefully, Amandine began to cut the vines. Birch moaned again as the first one snapped. "They gabble like madness. Am I mad or are they?"

Amandine frowned. He sounded delirious. The instinct to run away from this place hit her hard again. He would obviously be useless in his state, and now she had a weapon, at least. She stopped cutting. Should she leave him?

"No," Amandine said aloud. She began cutting the vines again. "I don't know what happened to you, sah, but I will get you down. I hope to the gods that you can walk."

Lightning flashed again. Amandine's breath caught. Eyes reflected in the brief light. She could see them now, all around. The entire clearing was encircled.

Eyes, wide like saucers, peered lidless at her from squashed, misshapen faces. Mouths opened below the eyes that split the bizarre heads of the creatures in two. Double rows of triangular teeth, like those of a pike, filled them. Spindly bodies were draped by arms that looked much too long, and ended with hands that seemed outsized for the rest of their forms. Wide, flapping, webbed feet supported stumpy legs. A chorus of hissing filled the air.

She had never seen one before, but had heard the stories— traveler's tales and campfire yarns. They were boglings. Goblins. The dark fae.

The circle of fae began to close on her and she sawed at the vines more frantically. "Stop!" she cried. "I am here to help you!"

If they understood, they showed no sign. Long, frog-like tongues licked their hideous faces while semi-translucent membranes slid upwards over the black orbs of their eyes, like upside-down eyelids. A second chorus of hisses circled her.

Amandine's heart raced as she tried to get the last few vines off of Birch, one eye on her work, the other on the slowly closing circle of hostile fae creatures. Grendel hissed back.

The fae stopped. A few stepped away.

Grendel hissed again and let out a low, angry sound.

The inward movement completely ceased. The creatures seemed confused. Amandine finally cut the last of the vines and Birch tumbled into the mud, moaning.

She dropped the knife and raised her free hand. "Please, you must believe me! Brutsche! I know Brutsche!"

A gabbling sound began to circle through the group of fae. Their wide mouths flapped and contorted with the weird syllables of their speech. The cacophony of it was unnerving, like fingernails on slate. Amandine covered one ear and winced.

She noticed that several of the fae had long sharpened reeds; makeshift spears. Her fingers itched for the knife she had dropped, but then she wondered: what good would it do her? She didn't know how to fight. Knives were for cooking in her world, for trimming fat and chopping vegetables. If she picked it back up, made them afraid of her, she was certain that she would die.

Grendel stopped growling at the fae and his head snapped to look off into the darkness. All of the mad chatter between the fae ceased as their heads whipped around to look in the same direction.

"A worm! I am a worm!" Birch cried as he curled into a ball in the mud and gripped his head. "A wriggling worm on a hook!"

Amandine felt it. The earth shook beneath her feet. The reeds rattled in the damp soil. The ancient, gnarled tree quivered. Just like it had before it took Dena. It was coming.

The Creature of the Fens

"Boglings, also known as Goblins in the West, are cowardly creatures, but are not completely without spines. When threatened by an encroaching presence, they will often retaliate as a group, ensnaring their tormentors and using greater numbers to wear down and fell large opponents. Many a careless warrior has underestimated these small fae, to their doom."
- Lecture notes, Third Fithday, High Summer 1201

THE BOGLINGS SLOWLY backed away into the surround-ing reeds. Their strange forms seemed to vanish into the lumpy earth and meld with the shadows of the fens. Amandine wasted no more time.

"Master Birch, get up!" she yelled. "We need to get away. Up the tree, perhaps. Hurry!"

Birch began to rock on the ground, moaning. He didn't move.

The tremors grew stronger and Amandine did something she had never before done in her life. She kicked Birch, hard, in the shins.

"Ow!"

"Pull yourself together, you fool, and climb the colorless tree!" Amandine screamed at him.

Birch seemed to come to his senses and scrambled on all fours for the gnarly oak. Amandine boosted him up to the lowest branch and he clung to it, upside-down, like a possum. Bracing herself, Amandine pulled her other hand out of her satchel where it had been touching Grendel and also leapt for the branch. She felt her arms wrap around it just before her strange night vision failed again.

She pushed Birch up to a higher limb so she could get her footing and haul her feet away from the earth below. The tree rocked as something collided with it and the bottom of her boots slid along something hard and smooth that dragged at her soles before she lifted her legs up and also wrapped them around the branch.

With a heave, she pulled herself into a sitting position and put her back against the trunk. Lightning flashed again, and she saw it.

The beast was huge. Hard chiton glistened with rain and slick mud. Its segmented body vanished into the swampy earth while long, pointed legs, like those of a centipede, carried what was above the ground in a wide circle as it searched for its prey. The head was eyeless, but the gaping maw had rows upon rows of sharp, backward-pointing teeth. Its mouth opened and closed as if tasting the air.

Amandine had never seen anything so grotesque. She had heard stories of monsters her entire life, many from drunk caravan guards, or chatty merchants, or other children. The kind of stories one tended to dismiss as exaggerations or outright lies meant to entertain. She was not entertained.

She tried to make not a single noise, to become one with the tree. Amandine closed her eyes and prayed to Kayla for a miracle. Her hand reached inside her satchel to hug Grendel close to her.

Her night-vision returned. The creature still searched for prey. More of its hideous body had emerged from its tunnel. The visible part of it was longer than two wagons, easily. Suddenly its head twisted and looked towards the reeds. Amandine heard something.

Barking.

She saw the light then, Fredderick's blue mage-light, bobbed through the reeds towards the clearing. A stab of fear coursed through her. They were going to run right into it. They couldn't see it!

"Fredderick! Gilly! Run away, don't come any closer!" she screamed.

The beast swivelled back to the tree and raised itself up. Its head was at a level with her now, its mouth opened wide and sucked at the air. A smell like rotting meat and dead plants, overlayed with something sharp and bile-like, filled her nose and mouth and made her gag.

Gil crashed through the reeds into the clearing. With a wordless cry, he hurled his lantern at the monster.

Amandine saw the flickering green flame within just before it shattered against the shell of the beast and exploded. A rush of warm air swirled around her as the clearing lit up again with the fireball caused by the greenflame gas igniting all at once.

A keening cry emanated from the monster as it reeled from the impact. Fredderick followed Gil into the clearing with Dumpling running ahead of him. The blue glow was attached to a branch held in the small dog's mouth.

Fredderick clapped his hands together and Amandine could see the air ripple before him. A boom like thunder exploded in her ears. Earth and reeds flew into the tree from the shockwave created by his magic and the giant creature reeled again.

It recovered and struck like a snake. Gil barely avoided the sucking maw of the beast as it slammed into the ground next to him, knocking him over. He kicked at it and tried to scoot away backwards on his hands, but it was already upright again, poised for another strike.

The ground around it churned and its submerged half tore through mud and reeds, striking Fredderick like a whip and sending him flying into the water. It slashed the other way and struck the tree.

Amandine slipped as the trunk split and was pushed over at an angle. She tumbled into the soft mud beneath. As she pressed herself up out of the sticky mess, she realized her night vision was gone again. Grendel was no longer in her satchel, but the remnants of burning liquid on the beast's shell, where the lantern had struck it, bathed the area in an eerie green glow.

Gil rolled and picked up something from the ground. A battered old shield was in his hands, buried and lost in the muck from some long forgotten battle.

He thrust it up as the maw of the beast fell upon him. When it rose up again, Gil dangled from the shield's arm bars. The round disk of rusty metal was firmly wedged in the monster's mouth. It whipped around, thrashing, and Gil screamed as he went sailing through the air, crashed into the reeds, and fell out of sight.

Amandine ducked as the tail end of the monster whipped past her head and crashed into the tree again, splintering the trunk further. The shield bent in the middle and fell from the creature's maw.

She tried to find Gil or Fredderick in the flickering green glow. She looked frantically for Grendel. None of them could be seen.

An oil torch sailed through the air and landed in the middle of the clearing. The huge head of the beast turned to face the hot, burning brand, and when it did, another person burst from the reeds into the light.

Amandine's breath caught as Dena appeared from the darkness, holding her spear.

Dena ran silently forward, and issued no cry. She was missing her cloak and her face was covered in mud and blood and rain, but the fire from the torch seemed to reflect in her eyes like coals. Her boar spear pierced the side of the beast, shattering its hard chitinous armor, and emerged out the other side. The monster screamed and writhed. Its head struck at Dena, but she twisted the long spear and its rows of serrated teeth found only air.

"Run!" Dena cried out! "I can't hold it for long!"

The monster struck again and this time found Dena's arm. She screamed and released the spear. Her other arm swung hard at the beast. When her clenched fist struck the thing's head, it sounded like a meat mallet striking a chop. There was a crack and the beast released her.

Dena fell to the ground and grasped her bloodied arm. The monster seemed dazed from the blow and twisted its head about in the rain as if trying to shake something off.

A glint of metal caught Amandine's eye. The handle of Birch's knife stuck out of the mud a few feet from her. As the monster reared up again, she scrambled through the muck and pulled it free.

The thing reared back and struck at Dena again, but she kicked out at it and her boot collided hard near the jaw of the monster, knocking it wide.

Amandine yelled and hurled herself at the head of the monster, holding the knife with both hands. It spun to face her, colliding with her legs and throwing her to the ground.

It struck again. Amandine felt the weight of it crashing down upon her, and then the darkness returned and she felt nothing.

Familiar Faces

"Not many Seekers retire. Most meet grim fates well before their dotage, but the handful that do leave the wandering life behind often continue to take on roles as protectors and leaders within the communities they settle in."
- Lecture notes, Second Starday, Low Autumn 1201

WHEN SHE OPENED her eyes, Amandine felt warm. The rain had stopped. Small stars twinkled in the night sky above her. A furry face filled her vision and whiskers tickled her nose.

"Hello, Gren," she whispered. And then she remembered where she was. A shock of terror ran through her and she sat up straight, gasping for breath. There was a painful throbbing in her head and her vision blurred momentarily.

The blur resolved into a tiny campfire that sat in a muddy hollow in the earth. The shadow of the broken tree loomed behind her. Around the fire, wrapped in their cloaks and shivering, were Gil, Fredderick, and Dumpling.

"Thank the gods, Amy!" Gil said. His left arm was in a makeshift sling under his cloak. "You took a fierce blow. You wouldn't wake up. I thought—"

"Where is Dena?" Amandine asked, cutting him off. She held a hand over one eye as the pounding in her head spiked.

"I'm right here."

Dena walked around her and knelt down to look into her eyes. Deep worry etched her face as the bare fingers of one gloved hand gently stroked her hair and traced her temple.

"You'll have quite the bruise. Blows to the head are dangerous. You are very lucky."

Amandine noticed that Dena's other arm, the one that had been bitten, was bound to her side, tight, with a long belt. Blood caked the chainmail links near her shoulder. Several looked like they had been crushed inwards. If Dena was in pain, however, she showed no sign of it.

"The monster? What—" Amandine began, but Dena merely nodded over her shoulder towards a coiled mass lying in the darkness beyond the light of their tiny fire.

"I grabbed the spear again with my good arm; managed to pull it wide so it didn't bite you. That *Olatharr* you had went right through its lower maw, probably hit whatever passes for a brain in its head. It coiled up like a dead centipede and has been still ever since."

"*Olatharr*?" Amandine asked.

"Olgothian war-knife. Made from water-steel. Quite a rare and expensive weapon for you to have tucked away. Where did you come across such a thing?"

"It wasn't mine. Is Master Birch alive?" Amandine asked. "It was his."

"You mean that one?" Dena said, pointing to the shadowed tree. Amandine could make out a small form huddled against the bent and shattered trunk, slowly rocking. "He hasn't said a word other than 'worm' since I found him there. Won't come to the fire, either. Whatever happened to him, he's not in a good way."

"He's a Seeker. An elven trained scout. He was here to collect the bounty on the boglings."

Dena eyed birch and frowned. "I see. Well I haven't seen any boglings yet, but that thing was horrible enough. Rest. As soon as we have dawn-gloom, enough light to avoid any pitfalls, we are going back to town. You need to see Telvor."

"You need him too!" Amandine protested. But even as she said it, she winced in pain as the mallet striking her temple resumed.

"You and your friends first. I've had worse, actually, if you can believe it."

Amandine looked up at the large woman, who was smeared in blood and muck and who knew what else, and yet still looked regal somehow. In control. Amandine could believe it, she definitely could.

Dena rooted around in a small bag and pulled out dried meat wrapped in oilcloth. She had Gil tear it into strips for her and then handed some to Amandine. Amandine split hers to share with Grendel who curled up with his treat in her lap and began to purr loudly.

"I'm not hungry," Fredderick said when Dena offered him some. "Please, give it to Dumpling."

Dena shrugged and tossed the meat to the tiny dog, who ran an excited circle around the food before settling in to gnaw on it. Amandine thought Fredderick was being oddly quiet.

"What's wrong, Fredderick?" she asked.

He shook his head and looked down at his hands. "That conjure was the most powerful thing I know. It didn't even faze it. I... failed to..." his voice trailed off.

Amandine considered him for a moment. He was a mage, a good one, she knew it in her heart. But just as she was not as good a cook as Chef Brutsche yet, Fredderick wasn't going to create spells as powerful and subtle as Wizard Hemm, or Mister Green. He was just being hard on himself. Amandine could relate.

"I thought it was amazing. You both were amazing. And brave. I would be dead right now, if you hadn't at least tried. Master Birch too, and probably Grendel. Please don't be sad."

Fredderick smiled at her. He didn't answer, but to Amandine's eyes at least, it looked like he was sitting up a bit straighter.

A sound in the brush made Dena leap to her feet. She turned towards the darkness and pulled a small knife from her belt with her unbound arm.

"Dena?" a familiar voice said.

Chef Brutsche entered the ring of firelight. His graying hair was tied back under a bandana. He wore heavy boots and a thick padded vest and leggings made of the same batted material. A bandolier was slung across his chest, festooned with an array of small knives. A pair of wickedly curved hatchets hung from loops on his belt.

"Kurloon's beard, it *is* you, Dena! And the children!" he exclaimed. "Hoi! Bert! Tel! I found them! Signal Heather and the others!"

Dena dropped her knife as Brutsche strode forward and to Amandine's surprise, the pair embraced. Hugs for friends, old and otherwise, were a fine thing in Amandine's mind, but this was obviously more than that. When they parted briefly, she was sure they were about to kiss, despite how dirty Dena was. Chef spied her watching and gently pushed himself away to come and kneel down next to her.

"Oh, fingerling, that's a bad one," he said as his gnarled fingers brushed her bruised face. "Might give ya a scar, despite Telvor's ointments. But I am frightfully glad yer still breathin'."

Amandine felt like her heart was about to burst. She threw her arms around Chef Brutsche and cried. All of the fear, and hurt, and worry came bubbling up all at once and she simply couldn't contain it any longer.

He held onto her until the tears subsided, and when she finally let him go, she found that others had joined them in the clearing.

Ruddy-faced Bertrand, the owner of the Stomping Golem, was wearing a steel breastplate and had a heavy mace hefted over one shoulder.

Telvor, the apothecary, was there as well, dressed as he usually was in his light linen shirt and trousers, but with a hexagonal staff, carved with writing she didn't recognize, held in his hand.

Miss Jacinda stood to one side, equipped in boiled leather armor that had been dyed black. Her hair had been tied back in a tight braid over one shoulder. The two other half-fae women that had been with Mando Fame, Gabriella and Yasmina, were with her. They looked just as haughty and dangerous as they had earlier.

Heather from the stockyard loomed over all of them. Her braided hair was tied back and the sleeveless shirt she wore under her thick apron revealed the massive muscles of her arms. She carried a long-handled cleaver with a blade half as long as she was tall, the kind used for slicing sides of beef. Heather smiled at her. Despite the tusks, it had a friendly look to it that made Amandine smile back.

Mister Green stepped out of the gloom, attired in a set of clothes that seemed to blend in with the reeds and the mud. He knelt down next to her and Chef Brutsche.

"And what have we learned from this?" he asked gently, his eerie black eyes searching hers.

"Always bring a cat when hunting monsters at night," Amandine answered instantly.

Grendel meowed as if in agreement, and Chef Butsche threw back his head and laughed. It had a raucous quality to it, like a gull screeching. It was a sound Amandine had never heard from the old grump, and she decided she rather liked it.

"This is a skellix," Telvor said as he poked the carcass of the giant worm-like creature with his staff. "The Seekers in the Wall are doing a poor job if one made it this far South and East."

"Bah, a pox on the Wall," Brutsche said. He stood and turned to face him. "Self righteous navel-gazers. We can handle our own out here."

"I don't really disagree," Telvor replied in his thick Zulathan accent. "But it is still worrisome. Beasts from the Conflux so incredibly far outside their range means something is out of balance."

Mister Green lifted a hand in a fist and the others fell silent. "We are being observed," he said in a low, cold voice.

Amandine looked around and her heart began to race. The boglings had returned. The ring of them had grown. There were dozens and dozens of them, all just beyond the light of the fire, watching with their strange, upside-down eyes, softly gibbering their madness-inducing babble.

"Easy, Bert," Brutsche said as he waved a hand at the innkeeper. "Put that down, old friend."

Bertrand, who had unlimbered his massive mace, slowly let the head fall and grounded it in the mud. He kept his hands on the handle, but seemed to be relaxed instead of ready to swing.

"I don't know why you abide them, Serand," he muttered. "But so be it."

"Aye," Heather growled in her rough, sandpapery voice. "Boglings are nothing but trouble." She likewise lowered her giant cleaver, however, and let it rest by her side.

"I agree with the Chef," Mister Green snapped. "Violence would be disadvantageous. We have brought much iron and steel into their domain. They are very agitated."

Chef nodded and unslung his bandolier and let it drop. He also removed the hatchets and dropped them as well. He walked slowly towards the ring with his hands outstretched. One of the larger boglings stepped forward to meet him.

It had a string of teeth, all of different sizes and shapes, strung around its thick neck. It also wore a pair of ragged wool socks, complete with patched heels, on its spindly arms. The long clawed fingers of its hands poked through the fabric like gloves and gripped a reed spear topped with a jagged point of glossy black stone.

It seemed almost comical to Amandine how tiny the bogling looked compared to Chef, but they stood, facing each other as equals, muttering softly, seemingly over the top of one another. Finally, the bogling abruptly spun about and returned to the line-up. Chef turned back to the group.

"Well, I don't understand all o' the nonsense, but it seems our young friends interrupted their sacred hunt. They have been baitin' it with goats an' sheep lured with stolen grain fer a while now. But then the small livestock vanished and so they found new bait."

Chef cleared his throat and looked sideways to where Birch sat rocking against the shattered tree.

"Their quarry is now contaminated with iron and must be purified 'fore they can feast."

"What? What hunt?" Gil asked.

"I think he means the skeli-whatsis," Fredderick said.

"Ayup," Chef agreed.

"They are going to eat *that*?" Miss Jacinda asked, clearly revolted.

"Cow's milk is deadly poison to 'em, so I am sure they feel the same way about yer Greenwax, sah," Chef said as he stuck his thumbs through the empty loops on his belt. "Old tales abound about leavin' milk out ta bribe fae. Nah, weren't for bribin' em, was for poisonin' the little guys. Creates some trust issues, ya see."

"What do we do then, Serand?" Telvor asked.

"Pull the knife out of the colorless thing's head fer a start."

"I'll do it," Dena said. She stepped over to the corpse of the skellix and reached for the knife handle jutting from its jaw.

A chorus of hisses rose up from the ring of dark fae. Dena paused with her arm outstretched and looked to Chef. He waved her back. She inched away and the hissing subsided.

"They are sayin' the one that killed the beast needs ta do the cleansin'," Chef said. He looked over at Birch, huddled against the shattered oak. "Knife is his, right?"

"Actually, sah," Amandine said, raising her hand. "I had the knife when it happened. I did it."

Brutsche looked stunned, as did the others. He looked to Dena and she nodded in agreement. "I saw it, Serand. The boys distracted it, I wounded it, but Amandine's blow killed it."

Chef sucked at his teeth the way he did when he was considering something.

"Ever shelled a crawfish?" he asked Amandine.

"Yes, sah," Amandine replied nervously.

"Same thing, but bigger. I can talk you through it."

"I can do it, sah," Amandine said, feeling more confident.

"One wrinkle, though."

"Yes, Chef?"

"Their digestive acid can melt stone, so the guts will be a bit o' a trick."

Amandine felt her stomach drop into her boots.

A Feast for Boglings

"Cleaning shellfish is, admittedly, one of my least favorite kitchen tasks. The sharp edges and tedious labor of it can make even an experienced Chef feel tired and sore after preparing a large batch. So in this section I will outline several techniques that will simplify and speed up the process. I will cover everything from river clams, to crawfish, to sea-spines and fae limpets. Troublesome as it is, the produce of the rivers and seas can make for some of the most delectable meals imaginable, and so these are skills all good cooks must hone."
    - Seeker's Kitchen, Chapter 3, Essential Ingredients

AMANDINE TRIED TO hold the knife steady and licked her lips nervously. Heather and Bertrand had uncoiled the huge creature from its death rictus and held opposite ends of it to keep it from balling back up. It stretched the entire length of the clearing. Occasionally a leg would twitch, but Chef had assured her that it really was dead.

"Start at the head and go slow, fingerling," Chef said, indicating where Amandine should start cutting. "Jus' the tip o' the knife 'ill do with a blade that sharp. See the groove there in the center?"

She nodded. There was a deep cleft in the chiton of the belly of the monster that stretched its length.

"That's where it's thin. Jus' a stretch o' tissue there. Slice careful now."

Amandine took a deep breath and began to cut. The thin membrane where the outer chiton connected sliced easily, like paper, beneath the blade. The smell was nauseating. It was the same embalming odor she had detected around the corpse of the dead horse she and Gil had seen so long ago. She covered her nose with her shirt as she continued, but that only helped a little.

The others stood nearby, watching silently. Beyond them, the ring of dark fae had also silenced their chatter and watched her, in seeming anticipation. Amandine's knife caught on something tough, and after she sawed through it, a puff of guts and orange-hued meat, like raw crab, swelled out of the slit. She jumped away in fright and checked herself for any bile spatter, as Chef had warned her.

"Every few segments you'll hit a knot like that one. Nothing to be worried over. Jus' cut it careful," Chef said with an encouraging gesture.

As Amandine resumed cutting the membrane, Dena walked up next to Chef. "How do you know the method of butchering one of these... things?" she asked, wrinkling her nose.

"Oh, had a bit o' trouble with 'em along the borders with Bolath land. Years ago."

"And you cut it up?" Dena asked, incredulously.

"When yer crew is stuck in the North Marches, with no rations and surrounded by Grey Court fae that want ta skin ya and put yer head on a stick, ye don't turn down a meal. Any meal."

"It was foul," Bertrand agreed. "But Serand can cook just about anything."

"You were there?" Dena asked.

Bertrand nodded.

"Yer doin' fine, Amandine. Steady now," Chef said.

Amandine nodded and resumed cutting while the others continued to talk. She listened as she worked, using their voices to distract her from the awful odor of the skellix.

"To be entirely fair to my cousins in the Marches," Mister Green said. "They have valid complaints against humans. The Conflux affects them more than others."

"Tell that to the next Bolath person ya meet," Chef said with a sharp edge to his voice.

Mister Green seemed nonplussed by Chef's ire. "I didn't say I approve of their hatreds, just that I understand them."

Amandine didn't really understand what they were discussing. Most of her focus was on not nicking the guts of the horrible stinking thing in front of her and being melted down to her bones by its acid. Her head hurt. Her back hurt. Hells, nearly everything hurt. She just wanted to be done. Finally, she reached the tail of the beast and wiped her blade off on a cloth that Bertrand handed her.

"Well done," the innkeeper said as he patted her shoulder.

"Aye, that's adequate," Chef agreed as he sucked on his teeth a bit. "Now comes the fun part. We need ta separate both ends of its gut an' pull the whole mess out o' the cavity."

"Are you sure we can't help somehow, Serand?" Dena asked.

"You want ta fight a melee with fifty angry goblins, with one arm, while protectin' the little ones? No, Dena, this is the right way ta do things. I know she has the skill ta do it."

Amandine held her head up. "I can do this, sah. Please let me help fix this!"

Dena still looked worried but nodded. Amandine turned back to the carcass and, following Chef's instructions to the letter, reached inside the cavity of the beast near the head and found where the gut connected. She had to put her arm inside up to her shoulder. Silently, she thanked Kayla that all she had in her stomach was a bit of dried meat, or she was sure she would have vomited again.

With her other arm, she reached in and sliced through the gut-lining with the knife and then pulled the end of the pale, orange-colored gut out into the air.

Chef reached into a pocket and brought out a coil of twine, and then tossed it to her. "Tie it with that. Good an' tight now, like a sausage casing. Don't want nothin' leaking out do we?"

Amandine did as she was instructed and then repeated the disgusting process with the other end of the beast.

"Right. Now fer this part, Heather should probably lend a hand. If they get rowdy, I'll try an' talk to 'em, but they seem ta be pleased with us so far."

"How can you tell?" Gil asked.

Chef shrugged. "They ain't tryin' to eat us, boy. Heather, lass, get a firm grip on the twine and help her pull it all out and away from the body. Gentle as ya go with it."

Heather stepped away from the front of the monster. It was no longer trying to coil in on itself with all of the chiton cut. She took a hold of one end of the tied gut. "On three, and then three again until it's out," she growled at Amandine.

Amandine gulped and nodded and grabbed her end with both hands.

"Once, twice, three!" Heather called, and they pulled. The gut of the creature began to come out into a large horseshoe-shaped mass.

They repeated the call and the pull twice more before it all came free. Amandine set her end down and Heather did the same. Part of the gut near Heather was bulged in an odd way. Suddenly a bone split through the orange tube of flesh, with a hoof still attached to the end of it. Orange bile sprayed. Amandine dove away, and Heather tried to dodge as well, but some of it spattered her.

Amandine had never seen Chef move so fast. In an instant a blade appeared in each of his hands as he dashed towards Heather. The blades sliced through the air and the heavy leather apron fell to the ground, smoking as if on fire. Chef dropped the knives and grabbed Heather by the arm and then twisted, ducked, and threw the enormous woman into the nearby swampy water.

Heather came up sputtering and roared at Brutsche, "What was that for!"

Chef simply gestured to the still hissing remnant of her apron. "Get any on ya?"

At the sight of the leather rag that used to be her work apron, Heather's demeanor became subdued. "Nah. Maybe a bit on my hands, they feel like I touched a hot pan," she grumbled.

"Glad to hear it," Chef said as he turned away. "Now that the exciting part is finished, one last thing ta do, Amandine."

"Yes, Chef?" Amandine asked as she regained her feet.

"Slice off the head, then cut out the segment that Dena speared. They won't want the parts that had iron embedded in them for any length o' time. We'll take the head ta Sheriff Stolm. The other, just chuck in ta the swamp."

Amandine gathered up the knife and did both tasks. The blade was too short to do it in single cuts and she had to slowly saw through the grotesque meat of the dead monster to finally remove the head and then the broken segment.

After the bits that had been embedded with iron were removed, the fae let out a chorus of babbling and swarmed the body of the skellix. Amandine quickly stepped away, as did the others. She watched in horrid fascination as the boglings covered the carcass like ants, and bit by bit, broke it apart and carried it off into the reeds.

As the last of them vanished, one lone bogling approached them and dropped a sack at Amandine's feet. It gabbled at her and then dashed on all fours off into the swamp. She bent down, picked it up, and peeked inside. It was filled with bogwort. There were twenty, maybe thirty in the bag, all of them large.

"Kayla's heart," Amandine whispered in reverence. "So many!"

Chef Brutsche leaned over to peek into the bag and nodded.

"Not everyone can truthfully say they prepared a feast for the dark fae," Chef said. The look on his face spoke volumes. "You did well, Amandine."

Gabriella stepped away from Jacinda, uncoiled her whip and spoke, "This has been... interesting, but if the festival is at an end, we will be taking that one back with us and be on our way." She pointed to Birch who was still cowering beneath the tree.

"Leave him alone!" Amandine protested. "Master Birch has been through enough!"

"He owes us a great deal of money," Yasmina countered. "You have fire, though. I can see why our half-sister adores you."

Miss Jacinda said nothing but raised an eyebrow at Amandine.

"Wait," Amandine said. She reached into the sack and picked out five of the largest bogwort. "Take these. They are worth a lot of money. Please sell them and cancel his debt?"

Yasmina wrinkled her nose at the lumpy mushrooms. "I'm afraid–"

Miss Jacinda spoke over her, "I'll take them, and then you shall have your debt money." She took the offered bogwort from Amandine and deftly made the mushrooms vanish into a hidden pocket in her armor. "Come along, sisters. Master Fame will not complain so long as he has his gold."

Before she and the other women left, however, she looked back at Amandine and gave her a wink and a nod. "Don't stay out with the boys too late now, dear Berty!" Jacinda called to her husband as the trio vanished into the night.

"Aye, and you tell that bald scoundrel he's still banned!" Bertrand called back.

Amandine passed the sack to Chef and approached Birch. He was still sitting beneath the tree, rocking, but as she neared he seemed to grow a bit more lucid. He blinked at her in the dim light of the campfire and torches.

"This is yours," Amandine said. She handed the knife, handle-first, back to Birch.

He shook his head and gently pushed the handle away. "No... no, I don't think it is. I've been parted with it twice in two days now, and it didn't help me a lick. Or Thornberry. The skellix, it ate her. Knife's yours now. And I hope it brings you better than the evil it's brought to me."

Amandine remembered the Hill Folk woman she had met at the Stomping Golem. She covered her mouth in horror as Birch looked away. "She was your friend, right?"

"Yes. We were cousins. Grew up together, joined the Seekers together. Spent time locked up now and again for our mischief. Together. We should still be together..."

"I'm so sorry, Master Birch. Don't stay here, though. Come back with us. I'm sure there is something you can still do. Something different."

Birch nodded and slowly stood. He tried to brush the mud from his pants, but only succeeded in smearing it about. "Mayhaps," he said softly. "Mayhaps…"

"I'll see to this one," Heather growled from over Amandine's shoulder. "You did a good turn by him. I'll make sure he doesn't waste it. Go see your friends, girl."

Amandine nodded and went to join Gil and Fredderick by the fire. Dumpling yipped excitedly and ran around her ankles. Grendel poked his head out of the satchel and blinked at her as she sat down.

"You need a bath," Fredderick said with a smirk.

"That's not very nice," Gil said.

Amandine laughed. "No, he's right, Gil. I think we all do. I… wanted to thank you both for coming with me. I had no idea it would be this dangerous, and… thank you."

"I don't really regret it," Gil said as he stretched his uninjured arm, "But the next time you want to go save boglings, I think you should hire this lot." He gestured to Bertrand with his enormous mace and Heather with her cleaver.

"Or just let them fend for themselves. They seemed to have it under control before we barged in," Fredderick said.

Gil rolled his eyes. "Oh, you just get to know her a bit better like I have. That won't happen."

Fredderick grinned at her. His long hair was in a wild tangle and the fancy shirt and pants he liked to wear were torn and stained from shoulder to ankle, but maybe Marlette had a point, Amandine thought to herself. He was a *little* handsome.

Dawn-gloom began to peek through the trees and the darkness of night retreated into a gray haze around them.

"Gather up your critters, kiddos," Dena said. "Let's go home."

They made their way out of the fens. Bertrand carried the head of the skellix tied to the haft of his mace. Fredderick helped light the way with his small blue light and Mister Green added his own, a larger red orb.

"Chef," Amandine said as they slogged through the muck. "Can you take me back to the Golem, please? Taster Nous released me, so I can't go back to the manor."

"He what?" Brutsche said angrily. "No, you ain't leavin' my kitchen unless ye want to, I'll sort out that rat with mustaches!"

"It won't matter, Chef. Sister Corbin got a writ from the Magistrate. She is coming to get me this morning. I will still need my things from the house, though."

Chef Brutsche eyed Amandine sideways. "Mariana Everdawn signed a writ to turn you over to the Night Sisters?" His tone suggested surprise at the idea. One of his shaggy eyebrows was cocked up in an arch.

Amandine nodded.

"That seems out of character," Bertrand said thoughtfully. "Given her past and all."

"What do you mean?" Amandine asked.

"B'fore she became mayor an' then Magistrate, Lady Everdawn was an adherent of Milintanth. She an' the Bright Light of the temple in Stoneman were friends as girls even. Were Dedicated together on the same day, as I heard it," Chef said, rubbing his chin.

"So why would she do that, do you think, Serand?" Dena asked.

"Not a notion at all, ta be honest," Chef said as his brow furrowed.

"Well, first thing to do is obvious," Bertrand said.

Amandine looked up at him. "What's that, sah?"

"We *all* need to go to the Golem, sit down and have something hot to drink to take this colorless chill off. Then we need to summon the Sheriff and sort this colorless thing out," he said as he jerked a thumb over his shoulder at the head of the skellix. "While we await her, we can discuss what this might mean."

"Gods, I could use some tea," Gil said. He yawned. "And a nap."

Grendel meowed from Amandine's satchel. She stroked his head. "I think he agrees with you, Gilly."

"Smart cat."

Amandine bumped shoulders with him and grinned. Gil laughed.

"Hey, take it easy, I'm injured here!"

Mister Green and Fredderick appeared to be deep in a quiet conversation. Amandine wondered what they were talking about. He seemed to be fidgeting, moving his ball of blue light from hand to hand. At least this time, Mister Green didn't appear to be cross with him.

"Caught you staring," Dena whispered to her.

With a bit of jump, Amandine realized she had been smiling as she watched Fredderick and felt her face heat up. "It's nothing like that!" she hissed.

Dena patted her shoulder. Her lips were tilted into an amused smirk. "Of course not. My mistake."

The gray light of dawn continued to creep through the trees as they made their way out of the fens and back to the ferry path. Amandine could see the walls of Stoneman rising along the banks. As they drew nearer, the hollow thud of the Stoneman's footsteps made the ground beneath her tremble slightly. The giant golem slowly plodded along the walls by the North gate, its smooth stone body glistened with morning dew.

Amandine gazed up at the steady yellow lights shed by the Watch's glowglass lanterns and wondered if this was the last time she would see this place.

Bounties

"Bounty hunting varies from region to region. Serentia and Tren often work closely with the Seekers to handle such work, while people in Zulathia find the practice to be a barbaric form of blood money. In that nation, rewards for self-policing are less formal, and often involve the consensus of tribal elders and local warlords. Olgothian bounties are posted and paid for by the noble caste themselves and not subsidized by the King, although royal requests are not unheard of, and often pay quite lucratively."

- from Cities to Wilds, A Seeker's Account of Beregoth

GUARD PRIMROSE SAW them first. The Hill Folk woman called out to Dena from the wall. "Is that you, Under-Sergeant? I was just 'bout ta summon Master Iblid and a squad to go lookin' for ya!"

Dena waved back at the red-haired head peeking over the wall. "All is well, Prim! Run and fetch the Sheriff if she's in town! Wake up Toplin and make him open the colorless gate, I know he's snoozing!"

Primrose grinned, saluted and vanished from the wall.

Amandine poked Gil. "You should go fetch Crust."

Gil nodded with half-lidded eyes. He stumbled a bit and Master Bertrand steadied him with a hand.

"Thanks, sah," Gil said, stifling a yawn.

"Just bring him to the stable at the Golem, lad," Bertrand rumbled. "No sense trying to ride until you've had a rest and warmed yer bones. 'Specially with that arm."

The heavy iron portcullis rose, opening the North gate for them. Gil shuffled towards the picket to retrieve his horse. The guardsman turning the winch, Toplin, blinked sleepily at them, but offered Dena a salute, which she returned with her uninjured arm.

"Are ye hurt U-sarge? Shall I fetch Master Aran?" he asked.

"He's right here you colorless fool! I'll be fine. Stop sleeping on duty or I'll have you scrubbing mail for the rest of the cycle." Dena sounded stern, but Amandine caught the amused glint in her eye. Toplin seemed to take her warning at value and saluted again, with more vigor this time.

An early morning caravan was forming in the yard beyond the gate. The wagon drivers and porters turned to watch as they passed. Amandine heard nervous muttering and saw pointed fingers as the folk realized what was tied to Bertrand's mace.

"They sound afraid," Amandine said softly.

"Aye," Chef agreed. "Most o' these folk have perhaps only heard 'bout a skellix before now. Maybe even thought they were just the tall tales of caravaners an' sell-swords. This'll cause a stir to be certain."

Bertrand mumbled his agreement and Dena also nodded her head. Telvor tapped his ornate staff against his shoulder and sighed. "I'm more concerned with why it was here to begin with. Away from the locus of the Conflux these creatures should not be able to thrive." His normally placid voice was tinged with an echo of concern that made Amandine feel uneasy.

"A puzzle for another day, friend," Bertrand said. Telvor frowned, but nodded.

Word traveled quickly. A crowd of gawkers had formed around them. A few who knew Bertrand or Telvor shouted questions to the group, but were waved off. Amandine noted the increasingly fearful glances and anxious expressions. She could almost feel their unease, like a fog in her mind. More than once a child began to cry as the hideous remains of the skellix were paraded past them.

The crowd parted as they approached the fountain square and Primrose appeared again as the onlookers parted for her. She had her helmet under one arm and a huge maul resting on her shoulder. It always amazed Amadine how strong Hill Folk were, and Primrose, with her spiked red hair and dense freckles, was even stronger than most.

"Sheriff and Capt'n Rivaldo are coming!" she said in a cheerful voice. "Gods, that thing is ugly!"

"Should have seen it when it was alive," Dena replied. "Thanks for running the message, Prim. This crowd is getting bigger, round up a few of the recruits and help Rivaldo keep order, yeah?"

Primrose grinned, saluted, and dashed back into the crowd.

"Do you think there will be trouble?" Amandine asked.

Dena shrugged. "A fearful crowd is like a wild animal. You need to treat it firmly, but gently. These folk are going to be frightened spitless and have too many questions for us to answer. Better to keep eyes down and lips sealed until we can sort it out ourselves."

"Aye, that's wise," Chef said. "Ain't nothin' like a mob fer random violence. Better not to stoke the fire."

A murmur of assent rippled through the group.

The crowd grew even larger as they made their way past the clockwork fountain towards the Stomping Golem. Amandine spied Wizzlecog standing on the edge of the basin, his mouth agape as Bertrand passed with the skellix head. His eyebrows rose so high that his monocle popped free and swung on its chain.

"Oi, Bertrand!" he called. "Will you be needing something to cover that with, sah?"

"That would be helpful, Brinkenbrak, thank ye! Meet Telvor and I 'round back of the Golem."

The small Stone Folk man nodded vigorously and leapt down from the fountain. "Be back in a tok!"

There was a call to make way and the crowd parted again just before the doors to the inn. Sheriff Stolm and Guard Captain Rivaldo Stolm strode through the gap. Amandine thought that the

Sheriff seemed especially cross as her hard eyes scanned the bedraggled group of people before her. Despite the early hour, she was fully dressed and armored with a light mail shirt. Her raven-handled dagger, the mark of her office, hung on her belt. All talking ceased.

"Where is Fredderick?" she asked sharply.

Amandine heard the snap in her tone, but also saw the creases around her eyes. The stony expression on the Sheriff's face seemed to crack as Fredderick shuffled forward. Dumpling slunk along behind him, his belly low to the ground, whimpering.

Sheriff Stolm turned to Fredderick and folded her arms. He lowered his head in shame. "Kimber, I..." he began.

Her arms unfolded and she wrapped Fredderick in them. Fredderick's arms haltingly rose to return the hug. "Colorless Night," she said as they embraced. "You are a pain in my arse, cousin!" They parted and she put her hands on her hips. "Uncle Gregor would flay me if you were killed doing some reckless thing under my watch!" She took a deep breath and seemed to compose herself. The hard mask returned to her features. "I am very glad you're safe."

Fredderick nodded. He looked at her and sighed. "It was foolish, I'm sorry."

"Apologize to Sheeria, not me. When she finds out what you were up to..."

"I will, I swear it. And...thank you."

"My thanks to you as well, Under-Sergeant," Sheriff Stolm said, nodding to Dena. Dena stood straight and saluted.

The Sheriff waved her down. "As you were. My brother explained how you decided to keep a lookout on this one. I owe you a debt."

Captain Rivaldo winced and rubbed his head in an embarrassed fashion. Amandine felt that his expression seemed rather guilty. The look the Sheriff gave the Captain as she spoke was definitely frosty.

"You did well, Under Sergeant. I thank you also," he said.

"I'd do it again in an instant, sahs. They are good kids," Dena replied.

"Not kids for much longer are they? Especially after this. Master Kale, let's get that thing out of sight, yes?" Sheriff Stolm suggested as she removed her gloves and tucked them into her belt.

"I'll take this 'round back, Sheriff," Bertrand said. "Telvor, can ye keep an eye on the foul thing while I wash up and make everyone some tea?"

"Yes, that would be prudent," Telvor agreed as he and Bertrand broke away for the side gate. The crowd parted for them like a cloud of buzzers withdrawing from a flame.

"Right. Skellix," Sheriff Stolm said, returning her attention to Chef and Dena. "I will have questions, you realize."

"Naturally, sah," Chef agreed.

"Who killed it?"

Chef hooked a thumb at Amandine. "She did."

Sheriff Stolm did a double take. Nearby members of the crowd began to murmur. Amandine cringed at what she heard. Many of the whispers were audible to her as she stroked Grendel, fear was replaced by awe and disbelief.

"I would ask if you are japing–" the Sheriff began.

"I saw her do it, I will formally attest to it," Dena said immediately.

"I saw it too!" Gil said as he finally caught up with his horse. The crowd grumbled as he led the large animal through the mass, but stepped aside for him anyway. "And Fredderick!"

The Sheriff looked to her cousin. Fredderick nodded firmly. "It's truth, Kimber. I swear it."

"I… I was also there," Birch said, speaking up for the first time since the swamp. Everyone turned to look at him. "It was my old knife she used to end it. She saved my life, for what little it's worth."

His voice trailed off at the end and his eyes were downcast. Amandine felt bad for him. Despite her injuries, and Dena's, he had suffered the worst. "None of this was your fault," she said softly to him.

Birch smiled weakly. Heather reached down and firmly clamped his shoulder in solidarity. "Aye, you'll be well," she rumbled. "Seekers are stout folk."

With a frown, Sheriff Stolm looked between Birch, Amandine, Dena and Chef. She took a deep breath. "And the boglings?" she asked.

"Not at fault fer the murders," Chef said, folding his arms. "As I am sure many have already told ya, sah. They did admit ta stealin' goats and grain, but offered repayment of sorts, so those that were robbed can have some justice."

"And you are sure of this? If they—"

"If I am wrong and they take a life, you can lock me up fer it!" Chef snapped. "I know you hate 'em, but is every flower a weed? Every fish, a shark? How about Olgothians, sah? They *all* be slavers an' villains?"

The face Kimber Stolm made reminded Amandine of someone who had just bitten into an unripe gojo fruit. It was equal parts anger, distaste, and embarrassment. The last part about Olgothians, given who her wife was, must have hit a nerve. After taking another deep breath, the Sheriff threw up her hands.

"Your point is made, Serand. But do not lecture me or make such comparisons again. I know you can speak their vile language, so you will see to it that they are warned off the pastures and warehouses and mind their business! If I hear so much as a murmur of missing livestock, food, or mayhem from them again, I will reinstate their bounty and double it! Am I clear?"

Chef nodded. "I will see to it, sah."

"Grand. Next, we have to deal with you."

Sheriff Stolm looked to Amandine. She shrank back at her gaze. It wasn't angry, or accusatory, but she was so intense that Amandine felt guilty anyway.

"All agree you killed it. What do you say?"

"I did, but I didn't mean to. It just sort of—"

"One hundred and ten," Sheriff Stolm said, interrupting her.

"What?" Amandine asked, confused.

"I can't pay the bogling bounty. I have no proof of dead boglings. But you located and eliminated a dire threat to the town and the region, and so, as bylaws for Seekers, mercenaries, and vigilant citizens dictate, I am authorized to pay you the deputized rate for uncovering and eliminating the skellix. One hundred and ten crowns."

Amandine was lost for words. Gasps rippled through the watching crowd. She looked over at Gil and saw him mouthing the number silently in disbelief.

Chef rescued her. "Aye, that be a fair judgment. Thank ye, sah."

Sheriff Stolm nodded and when she looked at Amandine again, there was a ghost of a smile on her lips. "Well done, Miss Amandine. Please come to my offices in Stoneman to collect your payment next tenday."

Amandine nodded wordlessly. Sheriff Stolm nodded back as if that settled it and turned towards the stable gate of the inn. "Captain, I leave you in charge of the crowd."

Rivaldo saluted. Primrose had joined him, as well as half a dozen other town guards. They fanned out and began trying to push the crowd back. A few slipped past and ducked into the inn.

"We'd best get inside too, 'fore all the seats get nabbed," Chef murmured. He held the door for them and blocked some townsfolk so that Amandine and the others could get inside.

"I'll join you after I stable Crust!" Gil called.

Amandine caught a glimpse of a harried-looking Captain Rivaldo trying to corral the curious onlookers. Dena clasped her shoulder with her free hand.

"Don't fret, Amandine. I'm sure Primrose can handle it."

She saw the diminutive woman barking orders to the guards as Rivaldo ineffectually waved at people still trying to get into the inn. The door shut, cutting off an oath by the Captain.

Apprentice

"Apprenticeship is the backbone of society. In such traditions, the knowledge of the elders is passed to the next generation, and in the best partnerships, the master learns as much as the student."

- Lecture notes, Second Sunday, Low Winter 1201

JACINDA WAS WAITING for them at the service counter. She had changed out of the leather armor and back into a flowing dress made of soft green fabric, but her hair was still tightly braided. "I heard," she said as she guided Amandine onto a seat. "I already made tea, and Berty is getting some food for everyone."

She chased a few gawkers away from the common table. "You lot find other seats!" she scolded. "And either buy something or get out! This is a business, not a sideshow!"

The curious townies muttered irritably, but moved to other tables. Amandine sat at the long common table next to Chef and Dena. Heather escorted Birch upstairs to a room to see him settled, and Mister Green sat with Fredderick across from her.

Tillandra approached carrying a tray filled with steaming mugs and began handing them out. Gil arrived from the stable through the back door, and Tilly gasped when she saw him.

"Oh gods, were you hurt?"

Gil seemed to wake up a bit as he grinned and swung his makeshift sling as if flexing. "Nothing I couldn't handle!" he said.

Fredderick rolled his eyes. "A skellix tried to eat him, but choked."

Tilly gasped again. Amandine and Dena laughed. Gil looked sort of embarrassed as he took a seat near the end of the table. "That's sort of truth," he admitted sheepishly.

Amandine sipped her tea. As the warm liquid melted the ice coating her bones, a deep weariness settled over her. She wasn't sleepy, though. In fact, she didn't think she'd be able to sleep for days after this.

Heather came back down the stairs and took a seat. Tilly had sidled in next to Gil on the bench and leaned close, her eyes wide as he softly recounted the battle with the skellix. Mister Green and Fredderick were speaking quietly. With Grendel's odd enchantment in effect, Amandine's ears seemed to become as sharp as her eyes, and while she heard everything else around her clearly, all she could make out of Fredderick's and Green's conversation was an indistinct buzzing. Mister Green looked up at her as she stared and a knowing smile crossed his face. Amandine quickly looked away. Did he realize she was trying to listen in?

Serand interrupted her thoughts. "Alright, fingerling. Now let's get to the bottom of this mess with Sister Corbin. What exactly did she say?"

Amandine related her conversation with Corbin at the clockwork fountain. Chef looked stern, as usual, but nodded thoughtfully while she spoke. Dena gasped towards the end.

"She knows who your parents are, but is trying to blackmail you with that?" she said, aghast. "I really don't like this woman."

Chef grunted his agreement.

"I'll miss my cot in the warm cellar," Amandine mused. "This tea is good, but that would take the chill away for certain."

Dena blinked and looked back and forth from her to Serand. "Wait, you sleep in the cellar?" She turned to Brutsche without waiting for an answer. "She sleeps in the *cellar*, Serand?"

"Hard living builds character." He folded his arms defensively. "She ain't never once complained about it!"

"*Honestly*, Serand," Dena seethed.

As Chef opened his mouth to retort, the front door to the inn opened again.

"Sorry, no more custom at the moment! We–" Miss Jacinda began.

"I have business here that is no concern of yours."

Amandine's head snapped up at the sound of Sister Corbin's voice. She spied Captain Rivaldo closing the door behind the godsworn, an exasperated expression on his face. "She gets in on Church business!" he shouted at the grumbling crowd outside. "Back off now!"

The door shut. The murmuring of the people who had taken seats inside ceased. All eyes turned to Sister Corbin.

"And what business would that be then?" Miss Jacinda asked cooly.

Sister Corbin drew back her cowl. Hard eyes took in the group of disheveled, tired people at the common room table and then scanned the rest of the occupants. Her lips drew into a thin line.

"I am here to collect my apprentice. Am I interrupting?" she asked with a hint of frost in her tone.

"No, sah," Heather said quickly, rising to her feet at the same time Chef said "Aye, go back to Artemis."

Heather's eyes widened as Chef looked away from Sister Corbin and sipped his tea.

"I will gladly be gone from this place, as soon as I have collected Amandine. You're a mess, child, what *have* you been up to?"

"Saving the town, I dare say," Mister Green interjected.

"Silence, creature, you were not addressed!" Corbin snapped without looking at him. "Amandine, are you injured?"

Amandine saw Mister Green smirk as if the insult had amused him. Miss Jacinda hissed in anger at the remark, however.

"No, sah, I am not hurt. Um, not badly, anyway. I think." She had to look away from Sister Corbin as her scowl grew.

"Excellent, then you shall come with me now. The sun has risen and it's time to depart. We have a long way to–"

"Over my dead body!" Miss Jacinda said.

"She's not leaving," Dena said at the same time, standing up.

"Excuse me?" Sister Corbin asked, blinking in surprise. "And who are you?"

"Dena Stonebrook. Under-Sergeant of the Stoneman Militia. I would say I am pleased to meet you, but I'm really not," Dena's tone was calm, but there was an undercurrent that made Amandine wince.

"Then it's your job to enforce the writs of the Magistrate, yes? I have one that says she is coming with me. So neither you or the half-breed have any say in what I do here."

"Now see here!" Bertrand shouted angrily from the kitchen doorway. "You take that back, you–"

"Oh no, Berty, she has to deal with me, love," Miss Jacinda snarled. Amandine had never, ever seen Miss Jacinda angry. Her fae features became even sharper as her eyes seemed to cloud over. A feral look overtook her.

"Oh my," Mister Green chortled. He seemed to be enjoying the row.

"Stop!" Chef bellowed. Everything paused. Amandine was certain that even the dust had ceased drifting. Miss Jacinda had halted mid-stride towards Sister Corbin. A blade was in her hand, but Amandine had no idea where she had produced it from. It was not a kitchen knife, either.

"Colorless Night," Chef swore. "Don't let her bait ye like that, lass." He looked at Sister Corbin and set his mug down. "You have a writ? Can you produce it?"

"It is filed with the Magistrate. You may petition her. I am going to take Amandine and leave. If any of you try to stop me, or threaten violence..." her eyes turned to Miss Jacinda. "...I will summon the Captain and have you held for assault on the body of the Church."

Amandine looked frantically between Chef, Miss Jacinda, and Dena. "Please, no violence! There's been enough death! I will go with her! Just... please..."

"Not so fast, fingerling. You said she gave ya a copy of the writ, yes?" Chef asked.

"Oh! Yes, hang on..." Amandine fished in her coat pocket.

"We don't have time for–"

"A moment to read the decision of the Magistrate is not amiss, I think," Mister Green said smoothly. "Unless you feel it will not hold up to scrutiny."

Sister Corbin seethed and folded her arms. "Be quick. This is foolishness."

Amandine found the rolled parchment where she had crammed it. It was soaked, rumpled and torn from her adventures in the fens. When she handed it to Chef, part of a corner fell off onto the table.

"Err," Chef said, looking at the sodden mass. "Ain't no good to no one like this."

A weight like an iron cauldron seemed to sink into Amandine's chest. "I'm sorry," she said.

"Um, if you will allow me?" Mister Green asked. He extended a hand across the table to Chef. Grendel laid back his ears and hissed at the elf. Chef glanced at the cat, but handed over the lump of sodden parchment.

Mister Green spoke words in the same odd language he had used when helping with the oven. The air around the hand not holding the parchment began to ripple as if from something hot, like an oiled skillet. He slowly passed it over the damp lump. There was a hissing and crackling sound. Amandine smelled something that reminded her of burnt toast. After the second pass of his hand, Mister Green gently picked up the writ and gave it a flick. The parchment unfolded with a rustle and a snap. It was whole again. Black inked words covered it from top to bottom. He handed it back to Chef Brutsche.

"Small fires. Useful."

Sister Corbin's face had paled. Amandine overheard her muttering a prayer to herself as she warily eyed Mister Green. The elf merely nodded to her and smiled, which caused Corbin to shiver visibly.

Chef eyed the mage sideways as he began to read. His mouth moved slowly as he silently scanned the document. Occasionally a muttered curse escaped his lips.

Amandine felt Sister Corbin's eyes on her. She had recovered her composure after Mister Green's display of magic, but she tapped her foot impatiently. After a few moments that felt like bells, Chef lowered the parchment and handed it to Dena.

"And this is why the Night Sisters are a pack of fools," he said.

"Don't speak ill of the godsworn," Heather gasped. "You'll be cursed."

"Your insolence is expected," Sister Corbin said, ignoring Heather. "I will not forget how you have obstructed me in my duty. Nor will the Order."

"Carp shite," Chef snapped. "Anyone who don't learn ta read is a fool. I'll stand on that gallows 'til they hang me for it!"

"Given what trouble you have made for us, that may be arranged," Sister Corbin snapped back.

"Now who is making threats?" Bertrand growled.

"Peace, Berty," Miss Jacinda said as she laid a hand on her fuming husband. The knife she had been holding was gone again. Amandine had no idea where she had stashed it, given what she was wearing. "Is there something in what's written there, Serand?"

Dena gasped as she read the parchment. "Serand, do you mean this part? It says that Amandine can only be remanded into the custody of the Night Sisters if her current Apprentice Master is willing to release her, since no documentation was provided that she was ever lawfully apprenticed to the Bone Guardians."

"The Order has–" Sister Corbin began.

"No contract," Serand finished, cutting her off. "Pack of fish-brained fools. Yer not high enough in their ranks to know how to read, I'll bet. Probably had this document summarized for ya. Ya also don't know that Mariana is an adherent and Dedicated of Milintanth. She likely put the clause in there ta give Amandine an escape hatch. Ain't no love lost between the clergy of the Lady of Light and the Night Sisters."

Dena laughed and Bertrand joined her. The others all looked to Amandine and Chef, but something still wasn't right.

"But Chef, Dena, I am not an apprentice to anyone in Stoneman," Amandine said.

"That can be remedied. Dena's been on my keel ta train someone. I'd sign the contract ta make you my apprentice right now if'n I had one."

"It can *not* be remedied," Sister Corbin snarled. "She is *my* apprentice and has been for years," Sister Corbin said. She took a step forward. "I've had enough of this. Amandine, you–"

Mister Green cleared his throat and stood. Sister Corbin looked wary and halted.

"I think I have the necessary document here, actually," He unrolled a parchment and placed it on the table.

"What? How?" Chef asked.

"Well, if you were not going to make the offer, I was. Amandine has a deep well of latent talent, I think," Mister Green explained. Amandine couldn't be sure, but something about the way he looked at Chef seemed rather accusatory.

Corbin's eyes widened. "I will die before I let a Breaker corrupt her! This is madness!"

"The only madness I see is a bunch o' crazy godsworn that'll swear small children to apprenticeships 'fore they can understand what that means," Chef said. "But the lass is sittin' right here and the choice should be hers. If you were to be an apprentice, Amandine, who would you want as your master, if any of us?"

Amandine's mind raced with what was happening. She could stay? And be an apprentice like Gil? It only took her a moment to decide.

"I want to learn to cook, sah. I want to learn from Chef Brutsche. I mean no offense, Mister Green. I am enjoying learning to read, sah, and I want to learn more, but…"

Mister Green shook his head and smiled. "No need to apologize, child. It is quite obvious where your passion lies."

"But you are already an apprentice!" Sister Corbin shouted, her patience breaking. "How would you even sign it! You don't know how to…"

Bertrand thumped past Sister Corbin and slapped a pen and inkwell down on the table, then turned and folded his arms as if daring Sister Corbin to try and bully past him.

"About colorless time," Miss Jacinda muttered. Amandine stroked Grendel. He meowed as if in agreement.

Chef frowned at Jacinda as he picked up the pen and wrote his name in a precise hand at the bottom of the contract. When he had finished signing he slid the paper to Amandine.

"Want me ta read it to ya, Amandine?" he asked.

"Um, no, sah. I think I understand," Amandine said. She didn't. Most of the contract was written in words she didn't fully comprehend yet, but she didn't want to admit it. Still, she trusted Chef. She trusted Mister Green, even though he still made her uneasy. Most of the people in the room had helped her, they were her friends. She took the pen and after glaring at Sister Corbin defiantly, slowly scrawled her name under Serand's. The letters were messy and crooked, but she felt pride all the same. Only a few cycles ago, she wouldn't have been able to even do this much.

"You were going to ask how she would sign if she can't read or write. I have been teaching her," Mister Green said placidly. "She is a good student." The grin he showed to Sister Corbin had far too many teeth to be friendly, even if she only saw his glamoured eyes.

"You'll need witnesses," Bertrand said. He bent down and signed the contract as well, followed by Miss Jacinda.

"You are all making an enormous mistake," Sister Corbin said.

"The only one making mistakes here is you," Dena said firmly. "She's Serand's apprentice now. Furthermore, we'll be adopting her."

The color drained from Corbin's face. Chef seemed startled and turned to look at Dena. "What in the colorless…"

"You didn't put her in that cellar, Serand, but you can take her out!" Dena seethed. "Amandine, you are coming home with us."

"Now just–" Chef began.

"I… I couldn't–" Amandine stammered.

"And if Serand has a problem with that, he can sleep on the hearth and you can share the bed with me!" Dena continued as she glared daggers at Brutsche.

"It's *my* colorless house!" Chef yelled at her.

Dena ignored him and returned her attention to Sister Corbin. Their eyes locked and Amandine held her breath waiting for the explosion.

"It's the duty of the Convent Orphanages to see unloved children find homes, yes?" Miss Jacinda said softly into the tense silence. "I'd say she's found one and you can tell your superiors that you've done good work here… Sister."

Corbin's eyes shifted away from Dena to Jacinda, then Serand, and finally Amandine. She held Amandine's gaze as she spoke. "This is not over. I have been misled and the Order will be making a formal complaint, through me, to the Magistrate."

"Sounds grand," Chef drawled as he picked his cup back up. "Don' let the hatch swat ya on yer way out." He slurped his tea noisily.

Her cloak whirled as Sister Corbin spun and left the room. She slammed the door as she exited.

"Old bat," Jacinda muttered.

"Hag," Dena agreed.

"You lot are all going to be cursed! Treating godsworn that way!" Heather exclaimed in her bass, rumbling voice. "Honestly, you are all madder than those colorless boglings!"

Fredderick barked a laugh. Amandine's shock faded and she grinned too. "I…I don't know what to say, Dena, Chef…"

"I did that without your consent," Dena said, folding her good arm across her chest and looking pensive, "I'm sorry, Amandine. If you don't want to…"

"I do!" Amandine said instantly. "I just…"

"Think about it, kiddo. You don't have to decide right this moment, but I meant what I said." Dena smiled at her and stretched. "I am going to go clean up. And maybe pour myself something stronger than this tea."

"I'll join you. I have the perfect bottle," Miss Jacinda said. "Come with us, Heather. But shouldn't you go see Telvor first, Dena?"

"That's what the drink is for. I think I dislocated it," Dena said.

"Oi, that's rough Den," Heather said with a wince. "Angry mama cow did that to me once. You might need two drinks."

Chef watched the three women depart thoughtfully.

"You're married to Dena?" Amandine asked.

"Not properly, no," Chef said, returning his attention to her. He seemed embarrassed. It was an emotion Amandine had never associated with him. "But I do love her, and for what I'm worth she seems ta love me. We share a croft in the Gold Hills hamlet."

"I had no idea," Amandine said.

"Not many do."

"I don't want to be a bother."

"Fingerling, you aren't a bother. It makes good sense, her decision. Especially if I am to properly apprentice you."

Amandine held the apprenticeship contract in front of her as if in a dream. She was going to stay! Chef was going to teach her! The thought of it made her feel like she was going to float out of her seat. She prayed that she didn't wake up, that this wasn't just some fever dream as she lay in the rain somewhere in the fens. Gil and Tilly came to her and hugged her in turn. Betrand ruffled her hair. Mister Green nodded to her and lifted his mug of tea in a sort of salute. She looked across the table and spied Fredderick blowing on his fingers as if he had burned them, while Dumpling ran circles around his feet barking. He glanced up at her and grinned.

"Tried to do that drying spell," he said.

"Stealing other's magic is a grave offense," Mister Green said as he sipped his mug.

Fredderick looked mortified, but Amandine recognized the smug look on Mister Green's face. It was the same expression he wore when she finally grasped something difficult in her own lessons. She laughed. Fredderick seemed confused, then smiled at her and bit his lip. She thought he might be blushing too.

Chef's voice pulled her attention back.

"Ye sure you want ta do this? You know I run a tight kitchen and ye are going ta work hard, despite yer newfound wealth from the skellix bounty."

"Why me, though? What about Kivel and Sunflower–" Amandine began, but Chef overrode her.

"What you did tonight? Kivel would have pissed himself an' gotten eaten. He's got skill, but he's lazy, and a coward. No adventure in his soul and it shows in his cookin'. And Sunflower, well she may have fared better, but she has no imagination. Does everything by rote. Her food is fine, but it never changes. A little bird told me that ya actually improved my recipe fer black spice dumplings."

"Wizard Hemm told you about that?" Amandine asked, surprised.

"No, I mean a small bird lit on my shoulder an' actually told me. Wizards are strange folk. It's also how I knew ye'd probably jump off ahead o' me and get in deep. Daft old green-robe sending you lot haring off into the swamps! Maybe he hoped I would catch up, but I ended up being too late ta stop ya. I was down South of Stoneman trying ta sniff out an old member of my crew."

"Someone you sailed with?" Amandine asked.

Chef nodded. "Amongst other things."

"So the Sheriff didn't listen to you?"

"Hells, I didn't even *try* to convince Kimber. She's smart an' stout hearted, but hates boglings with a vengeance. I just needed to figure out what it really were that was doin' the killin'. I had a notion that the cattle might have been taken by poachers, or maybe a pair o' mated Grims. That would have explained the rumors of wild beasts an' the larger livestock an' horses bein' stalked. Human thieves might have explained the grain thefts. Grimalks will sometimes stalk humans an' fae too, when they get a notion.

"But ta handle either, I had a need fer some stout allies at my back afore I went lookin' fer trouble. Took me a bit ta find ones willin' ta ride with me. The three of ya just charged off into it, at night no less! Fortunately that lad, Fred, had the good sense ta speak with Rivaldo, and Dena had jus' come off o' duty an' caught wind, so she decided ta tag along with you lot."

Chef gestured to the back door of the inn. "She didn't know about the skellix, though. None o' us did."

There was a murmur of agreement from those in the room. Mister Green cleared his throat. "I feel somewhat to blame. I should have sensed the skellix, but did not. Wizard Hemm might have had a notion, but… I agree with Master Aran. Something is wrong to the North."

"Leave it, Green. Ye did nothin' wrong, and I thank ya fer comin' with me," Chef said. His gnarled hand reached out to ruffle Amandine's mud-caked hair.

"You'll make a good apprentice, I think," he said.

"Well, alright, but I want to keep Grendel too, and Nous hates him," Amandine said.

Meow.

"Aye, and the cat. He's a good one, despite his mischief. Does his job well like you do."

Amandine blushed. Chef never paid anyone a compliment, and here she had gotten two in one evening. "I'll do my best, sah!"

"Don't 'sah' me. If we're cookin' or discussin' cookin', 'Chef' is jus' fine. Any other time, well, ye can call me Serand. That seems proper."

He rubbed at his nose and looked away, but Amandine thought, just for a moment, that he was smiling again.

"Very well, Chef," she said, trying her very best to imitate Dena's tone. "When will we discuss my pay increase, then?"

"Hey, now!" Chef said.

Bertrand roared with laughter.

ABOUT THE AUTHOR

Jason grew up (mostly) in central California, surrounded by rolling hills, wheat fields and grapevines. He has been creating worlds for himself and his friends for decades, and is a gigantic nerd for everything sci-fi and fantasy related. Role-playing games, board games, video games and cooking are just a few of his many hobbies. He currently lives near Portland, OR, in a muli-generational home with his wife, two kids, two inlaws, and a neurotic bernadoodle.